# The Eagle's Shadow

# Keith Nixon

THE EAGLE'S SHADOW

Published by Gladius Press

Copyright © Keith Nixon 2014

Keith Nixon has asserted his right under the Copyright, Designs and Patents Act 1998 to be identified as the author of this work.

CONDITIONS OF SALE

All rights reserved. No part of this publication may be reproduced, stored in a retrieval system, or transmitted in any form by any means, electronic, mechanical, photocopying, scanning, recording or otherwise, without the prior permission of the publisher.

This book has been sold subject to the condition that it shall not, by way of trade or otherwise, be lent, resold, hired out, or otherwise circulated without the publisher's prior consent in any form of binding or cover other than that in which it is published and without a similar condition including this condition being imposed on the subsequent purchaser.

All characters in this publication are fictitious and any resemblance to real persons, living or dead is purely coincidental.

For my children
William, Florence & Tabitha

And my wife, always
Nina

# British Tribal Territories AD 43

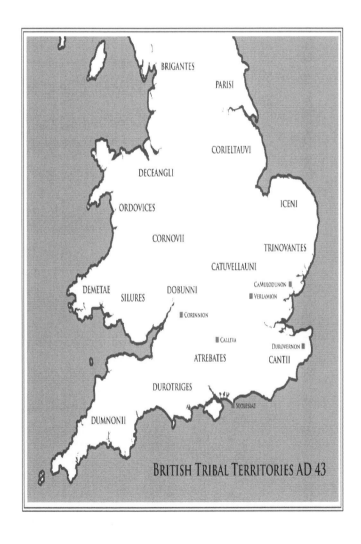

## Place Names

The Iron Age Britons, like their Celtic neighbours, did not commit their histories and records for communication to future generations in writing. Instead they passed them on using the power of speech, in lore and song. Although much more romantic than today's electronic world, this nevertheless makes assigning the correct name for a location in use almost two thousand years ago all the more difficult. Additionally, the Romans, when ascribing place names, did so in a Latinised form of the original.

That being said, some of the place names from the period covered in this book have survived to the present day. For example, Julius Caesar's account of his invasion of Britain in 55BC and 54BC, although scant, nevertheless provides some information. The Ravenna Cosmography, compiled by a monk in a monastery located in the town of the same name in Italy during the 7th Century, lists the known roads and road stations in the Roman Empire, including those in Britain. In between these periods the Greek mathematician Ptolemy published a work on British geography. The Antonine Itinerary is another useful work.

Rivet and Smith carried out an exhaustive assessment of these works in their publication, The Place-Names of Roman Britain. Finally, Richard Coates, Professor of Linguistics at the University of Western England, gave the benefit of his knowledge and support where the text was lacking.

| | |
|---|---|
| Abona | River Avon, Somerset |
| Bicanbyrig | Bigbury, Kent |
| Blahwōn | The Forest of Blean |
| Bredegare | Bredgar, Kent |
| Calleva | Silchester, Hampshire |
| Camulodunon | Colchester, Essex |
| Coed Andred | Andredsweald Forest |
| Corinnion | Bagendon, Gloucestershire |
| Derventio | River Darent |
| Dubras | Dover, Kent |
| Durobrivis | Rochester, Kent |
| Dūn | The Downs |
| Durovernon | Canterbury, Kent |
| Ealdanbyri | Oldbury, Kent |
| Fordeuuicum | Fordwich, Kent |
| Gallic Straits | The English Channel |
| Gesoriacum | Boulogne, France |
| Hoe | Hoo, Kent |
| Ligan | River Lea |

| | |
|---|---|
| Limana | River Rother |
| Meduuuæian | River Medway |
| Mona | Anglesey, Wales |
| Rogulbio | Reculver, Kent |
| Rhenus | River Rhine, Germany |
| Rutupia | Richborough, Kent |
| Scepeig | Isle of Sheppey, Kent |
| Seolesiae | Selsey, Sussex |
| Stanora | Stonar, Kent |
| Stur | River Stour |
| Sualua | River Swale |
| Tamessa | River Thames |
| Tanneton | Isle of Thanet, Kent |
| Uantsumu | Wantsum Channel |
| Verlamion | St. Albans, Hertfordshire |

# Prologue

Kynthelig dreamt again of the marauders who came in their thousands from over the water to conquer. They slithered across the land in a snaking column, miles long and six men abreast, faces twisted with hate and rage, their advance relentless and crushing.

Brave warriors tried to halt the onslaught but died under a hail of spears that plummeted from the sky like a hawk mercilessly attacking its prey. Still the warriors did not give up. Time and again they threw themselves against their enemy's lines but broke apart like the sea against a cliff — stern, cold and immovable.

The invaders filled the rivers with blood, razed villages and towns, turned the sky black with a pall of smoke and choked the land with slaughtered carcasses that were picked over by Babdah, who haunts the battlefield and feeds on the flesh and blood of the dead.

Women were raped and cast aside, the dead were looted. Whatever was left was turned to ash by purifying flames, the smoke blocking out the sunlight. Crops failed, people starved and chaos reigned as the multitude of gods that normally inhabited every facet of British life deserted their subjects.

Still the marauders were not satisfied. They cut their way across the country, from east to west and north to south, the pounding of their feet terrifying in its rhythmic monotony as they drew ever closer to the sanctuary. The very ground shuddered as they marched...

The shaking invaded Kynthelig's dreams and jolted him awake. He shouted and sprang upright expecting to see the enemy, such was the strength of his lurid vision.

"I'm sorry, Lord," the slave said. He had retreated a few feet, taken aback by Kynthelig's violent arousal. "I was sent to fetch you as the hour is late."

"Tell them I will be there as soon as I can." Kynthelig waved the young man away.

"I was told..."

"I don't care what they said! Leave me!"

The slave bowed and reluctantly left the room, hoping he wouldn't be punished for Kynthelig's resistance.

The old man flung back the animal hides covering him in an attempt to chill his naked, wrinkled skin, which was flushed and prickled with sweat. His bones creaked and his backside was still sore from the long journey on horseback across the width of the country. It had taken weeks to travel from Camulodunon through the land of the Ordovices to the extremities of the western coast and he had loathed every moment of it. He hated horses and avoided them whenever possible, but the journey would have taken far longer any other way so he stoically bore the discomfort.

By comparison the trip across the narrow ribbon of water that separated Mona, holy sanctuary of the Druids, from the mainland was brief and without event. The waters that could be so treacherous this time of the year proved mercifully kind.

When he was sufficiently cooled and his heartbeat had slowed to a more normal pace he rose and dressed as quickly as his withered body would allow. His actions were purely automatic as, on another level, his mind mulled over his recurring dreams — no, *nightmares*. They were becoming alarmingly vivid and were always of the same thing — the terror of his youth poisoning his adopted land.

Years before, Kynthelig had escaped persecution as his kind were hunted to near extinction one by one. The Druids were perceived as a malevolent force that was to be eradicated and the Romans largely succeeded in the task they so energetically pursued. Those unfortunate enough to be captured were guaranteed a slow and painful death via a long, drawn-out ritual of torture and eventual execution.

Kynthelig had travelled across most of Gaul with one nervous eye permanently cast over his shoulder. The Romans were everywhere and arrest was a constant, nagging prospect. He had finally escaped by making the short journey across the Gallic Straits and into Britain on a scruffy fishing boat. It took him weeks to rid himself of the smell, but he didn't care.

Britain, the spiritual home of the Druids, had been where the young were taught their craft before issuing forth back into the world to spread the cult, but it was so no longer. Its shores now delineated the confines of the Druids.

Kynthelig paused in his dressing and eyed his bed. It was a sight he dreaded. He had recently developed the habit of staying up as late into the night as possible, until he was so tired he could barely keep his eyes open. Several times a slave had had to carry him to his furs from where he had fallen asleep. But after some initial success the ruse then failed — the invaders returned to punch their way into his dreams just the same.

Perhaps there was another way to deal with this, he thought, tying his long, grey hair and letting it fall over his back. Running away from his apparitions had not worked so far — if anything, the visions grew in strength as they clamoured for his attention.

Maybe I should run towards the problem, he thought. Maybe I should deal with it actively rather than allowing myself to be controlled by the wraiths of the future.

The idea sent a shiver of fear coursing down his bent spine. But he sat down for a moment and forced himself to consider it. A revelation struck him. There was one who was exposed, one who could be used to bring about action on what was being avoided. But it would need stealth and guile. Kynthelig smiled — these were skills he possessed in abundance.

The old Druid stepped out into the sunlight, ignoring the impatient but fearful look from the slave who ushered him through the huddle of huts and across the open land they sat within. Although Kynthelig knew the route well he was happy to trail behind the slave as he thought furiously.

After a few minutes walking they came to a heavily-wooded hill that rose curiously untouched from the surrounding landscape of tilled fields. His already punished muscles screamed as he climbed, aiming for the peak itself, and his breath tore out of his lungs, but at last Kynthelig emerged from the darkness of the trees into a natural clearing through which sunlight poured onto a rounded rock. On its worn surface stretched out a naked man. He was unrestrained, surrounded by people from the very young to the very old, all clothed in a similar fashion. All were waiting for Kynthelig.

He took his place and then chanted a short prayer to the Goddess Nemetona, who watched over the sacred groves, the gathering of boys and men intoning with him. Kynthelig accepted a knife, its blade honed until it was razor sharp. He offered another, much longer prayer to she to whom sacrifices were made, the Goddess Taranis. Then Kynthelig raised the knife into the air and after a pause plunged it into the chest of the naked man, who willingly accepted its slicing kiss. He lurched as the dagger pierced his heart and then lay still, mouth and glazed eyes open to the heavens. Bright red blood spread across his pale skin as it seeped out of the rent Kynthelig had torn.

Kynthelig — druid, seer, historian, magistrate and poet — stepped back from the body. The tale, invented as he walked towards the gathering and refined during the sacrifice, writhed through his mind, bursting to escape from his lips. It would be the greatest story he had ever told. It would have to be, because their very way of existence, probably even their lives, depended upon it.

# I

**November AD 39**

Fionn paused, about to leap into the saddle, and watched with idle curiosity as the unconscious man was dragged effortlessly past by two warriors who gripped one skinny arm each. The man's head lolled backwards, revealing a livid bruise on his thin face that would soon darken and swell into a nasty black eye. His heels dragged along the ground, scoring a line in the snow.

Fionn's interest peaked when he saw Caradoc following in their wake, a troubled look stitched on his normally good-humoured face. From the way he held his hand Fionn guessed it was his cousin who had inflicted the knockout blow.

Caradoc glanced up and spotted Fionn. "Come with me," he ordered.

"I was about to go hunting," Fionn replied, gesturing at his horse. He and Brennon, who for some unfathomable reason always chose to hunt with his axe strapped to his back, had been stalking a stag for the last two days. However, much to his chagrin it continued to elude Fionn's bow.

"Not any more," Caradoc said over his shoulder, following the drag mark.

Fionn sighed in frustration. His cousin would regularly haul him into political or family situations that Fionn had absolutely no interest in. This looked like another one.

"We'll go later," he said in reply to Brennon's questioning look, shrugging in apology. "That stag is ours later. I promise!"

Brennon scratched his beard, shook his head irritably and then led the horses back to the stables, sure in his bones that fate would dictate their quarry would remain out of their reach.

The warriors lugged the still-unconscious man into a hut then reappeared a few moments later, standing either side of the door. Both were big men, and Fionn doubted the prisoner would be capable of escaping when he awoke.

"What's going on?" Fionn asked, still mournful at missing out on some sport but starting to think there was perhaps better to be had here, although the prey would be different.

"Trouble," Caradoc hissed, his blue eyes narrowed. He pulled Fionn to one side, away from the guards.

"This man came to us with something of incredible significance, finally some hard evidence of what I have suspected for so long. This could be the opportunity we've been looking for, but we have to be sure of ourselves. So far only a few know of what he says and I need to keep it that way until I am sure of him. I need your help."

"There's a stag in the forest that Brennon and I are hunting,"

"Life isn't just about enjoying yourself, Fionn," Caradoc spat. "Sometimes the drink, the women and the fun have to be paid for. Now get inside!"

The man slowly came around. For a few moments he felt light-headed and struggled to focus as his vision swam. Briefly he wondered if he was suffering the ill effects from drinking an amphora or two of Roman wine the night before. Unfortunately his brain quickly told him this was not the case and the brutal reality of his situation started to seep through the wool fogging his thoughts.

He could only blearily see out of his left eye and the right hand side of his face felt like he'd been kicked by a horse or punched by his wife. Both were strong possibilities and equally feasible. He lifted his hands and probed gingerly at the rising bruise. They were heavy with metal shackles that bound them at the wrist and he found it hard to control his movements, pressing too hard at the bruise and swearing at the red hot poker of pain that sliced across his face. His tongue felt like a piece of worn sandal in his parched mouth.

"Water. Please, water!" he croaked but no one heard him, or if they did no one cared.

He tried to swallow to relieve the feeling but only succeeded in generating a dry retch. His mouth now felt like the sandal that formed his tongue had stepped in something particularly nasty left behind by an animal several days ago.

He had scorned the gods years before, blaming each and every one of them for his woes. Perhaps this was their revenge, their way of showing he couldn't do without their blessing, that he needed them.

He pushed the thought to one side and wondered how he was going to find a way out of the stupid mess he had got himself into. As always, his predicament had started with a small regret, an unsubstantiated assumption, a weak resolve. His situation had then degenerated in a steady downward spiral, and before he realised it the problem had swollen to unrecognisable proportions. Then each time he made a move to correct the setback it simply made the spiral twist narrower, faster and steeper.

But then, mercy upon mercies, along came the golden opportunity to solve all his difficulties! He hadn't dared tell his wife, she would have screamed at him for being a fool. Anyway, he consoled himself, she was largely unaware of the extent of his 'complications'. So he'd closed his eyes and leapt into the decision, believing it couldn't place him in a worse situation than where he found himself at the time.

How catastrophically *wrong* he had been...

His dark thoughts were shattered by two men entering his cell. Both were finely dressed, marked out as noblemen by the torcs at their necks — like golden snakes that threatened to strangle them, they were such a good fit. They wore chain mail armour, partially hidden by rich cloaks swept over the shoulder and held in place by gold brooches the price of which would have solved the prisoner's problems in an instant. Each possessed a long sword that was strapped to the waist and hung almost to the floor. The younger-looking of the two, blonde-haired and clean-shaven, strained to hold back a large dog that seemed to be all tooth and claw. It slavered and snapped at the end of a short leash.

He thought both men looked hard and cruel. The slavering dog would probably show more mercy than these two. They stared at him for what seemed like an age, neither speaking, neither blinking. He couldn't meet their eyes and instead looked down at the dirt floor. The dog quickly got bored and flopped down, dripping saliva in great white foamy globules which splattered on the ground.

The older-looking of the pair squatted on his haunches, bringing himself to the same level as the prisoner, who could no longer resist his stare. Their eyes locked. The nobleman's long hair hung past his shoulders, framing a tense face that seemed to drink in every detail of the prisoner. His lips, outlined by a trimmed beard, were pressed into a thin, bloodless line. The prisoner became aware of his own stench of stale sweat and urine and his spirits slipped even further with shame.

"Who are you?" Caradoc asked gently.

The prisoner did not immediately reply, remembering the sucker punch, and merely stared back mutely. Caradoc stood and waved for Fionn to rouse the dog.

"My name is Barick!" he shouted with the hound's dripping teeth just inches away from hands raised to protect his throat.

Caradoc squatted again, satisfied that he had the prisoner's full attention. He appeared not to notice the reek of fear that filled the air around Barick. "Do you have family, Barick?"

He nodded, glad to be on some familiar ground. "Yes, a wife and four children, with another on the way."

"So many mouths to feed. Yet you do not look very successful," Caradoc mocked, looking Barick over and taking in the patchy clothes and single boot with a hole in the sole.

"Things will improve," Barick shrugged.

Caradoc looked at Fionn, "An optimist!" he laughed. Fionn stayed stony-faced.

Caradoc looked back at Barick and produced a small, sharp dagger from the folds of his cloak. He spoke in a harsh whisper.

"Do you realise the implications of the fiction you dare to bring before me? I could have you executed for it! I could torture you for days until you screamed for death and then throw your body to the dogs. No one would know, and no one would care."

Barick quivered. "I am a Gaul. I do not know of your laws."

"This is not about law, this is about honour!"

The dog sprang into life, incensed by Caradoc's shout. Its breath washed over the Gaul and he almost gagged. With a supreme effort Fionn dragged the beast away. Barick tried to press himself further into the wall, hoping he could melt into it, wishing he could be anywhere but here.

When the commotion had died down Caradoc smiled at Barick. "Tell me about yourself," he said.

Barick, his eyes on the dirt floor, quietly explained that he had been a market trader in Gaul but had found it hard to make ends meet. Over several months of watching others around him he'd concluded there was more money to be made as one of the middlemen buying and selling rather than as the idiot at the end of the chain, making the smallest profits selling poor wares in flea-bitten bazaars.

So, much to the chagrin of his wife, he had borrowed money, bought a beaten-up old boat that leaked in too many places, hired a crew who seemed to spend more time drunk than sober, and begun to weave across the dangerous seas between Gaul and Britain. But Barick had misjudged his market and the goods he initially bought were discarded at a heavy loss. So he'd taken out more loans to purchase finer products such as wine and metalwork to sell in exchange for raw materials, slaves and the renowned British hunting dogs the Romans prized so much.

But precious few people were prepared to finance Barick's operation and so he had been forced to take a second loan from the hardest backer of them all, a man who would break legs in a heartbeat to extract payment. And that was just for starters. Chopping sensitive things off in an effort to be more persuasive very quickly followed.

"That would have solved the problem of your growing family!"

Caradoc cut in and the two men laughed. Barick didn't participate and continued with his story when the laughing stopped.

Barick believed in his own skills, so he swallowed any fears of retribution from his new backer, convinced coins would soon be rolling in uncontrollably. He assumed there was a powerful connection between high costs and high profit.

Unfortunately, this had turned out not to be true and so very soon he was forced to flit from one shadow to the next to avoid his persistent financier and his gnarled, heavily-armed employees. To the grumbles of his crew, they spent a lot of time at sea, returning to port rarely and only at unsocial hours. On the other hand, he saw little of his family and despite his fear of soon being limbless, or worse, he was able to sleep a little more than he could at home, thanks to the absence of screaming children and a vocal wife. But none of this evasion solved his predicament, just delayed it.

Then, a few days ago, a British nobleman, dressed much like his interrogators, had come to him as his saviour. To the sound of water lapping against the mooring the nobleman told

Barick what should be said and to whom. Barick drove what he felt was a hard bargain and walked away from the meeting a very happy man. In his pocket jingled the first payment, a handful of silver coins, with much more promised on completion of the deal. Perhaps he would even make a profit out of the venture after paying off his debtors.

But now here he found himself, chained in the iron shackles he used to bind the slaves he had infrequently traded. He was only inches away from the snarling, slavering bunch of tensed muscle and sinew of one of these selfsame hunting dogs as it pulled at its distinctly weak-looking leash, desperate to provide Barick with a sharp and nasty death by tearing his throat into a bloody mess. The opportunity didn't sound such a good idea any more.

"And you weren't suspicious at all?" Caradoc sounded very dubious.

"I was desperate! Now it sounds like a stupid story but I was offered a way out of the mire I had got myself into." Barick was frantic to persuade the pair of Britons that his tale was true. Somehow he knew his survival depended upon it.

"Enlighten me again with what you were told."

Caradoc listened intently to the jumble of words that fell from Barick's mouth.

## II

An hour later Caradoc and Fionn were chewing over Barick's confession, turning the account over and over, trying to pick holes in its fabric. Barick lay in the next room, exhausted and suffering.

"I think he's telling the truth," Caradoc said.

"I agree," Fionn said. "We scared him half to death and he stuck exactly to what he first told us. We have to take this to the King."

"Togodumnus also needs to know about this."

"Why? He will do nothing with it!" Fionn challenged.

"He is my older brother and second in line to the throne. Because of what we have heard he could be the next King when the time comes. You know he cannot be ignored, whatever you think of him."

"You should be King, not he."

"That is not my decision and you know that!" Caradoc raised a hand as Fionn opened his mouth to protest further. "We will speak no more of this. Togodumnus first, then Cunobelin."

Fionn grudgingly agreed. Not that he had any choice.

"We are both old men, you and I," Cunobelin said.

"You do not look it, Lord," Kynthelig replied.

Cunobelin gave a short, barking laugh. "I am well aware of your aptitude as a wordsmith, Druid."

Kynthelig remained impassive at the mocking rebuke.

Cunobelin moved closer to the charcoal fire burning in the centre of the roundhouse. As a child he had been fascinated by the ever-changing flicker of the magnificently-coloured tongues of flame, and even as he neared the remarkably old age of sixty-five the allure remained as strong as ever. Smoke curled lazily upwards from the blaze to poke its way through the loosely-packed thatch of the steeply-pitched roof above. Despite the surprising warmth it produced Cunobelin felt the cold deep in his bones. With a shiver he pulled his furs tighter around him.

"The future worries me," he said, his eyes still on the flames.

"Ah, you think too much," Epaticcus replied, tossing a chicken bone he had been gnawing on into the fire, then laughing as a shower of sparks sprayed out at Kynthelig, who skipped out of the way with surprisingly agility. Epaticcus was disappointed. He hoped to see at least one ember land in the Druid's beard. Perhaps some small flames would have ignited in the tinder dry hair and licked up to his face.

*That would have been hilarious*, Epaticcus thought, and laughed again.

Kynthelig glared at Cunobelin's younger brother, once a powerful warrior, now run to seed. His grey hair was dirty and his beard was shaggy and unkempt, below ruddy cheeks and a puffy nose. But his eyes were still bright, albeit somewhat yellow and bloodshot. Epaticcus toasted Kynthelig, some of the wine spilling down his clothes as he drank.

Cunobelin still stared into the fire, unaware of the exchange between Epaticcus and the Druid, as if mesmerised. He sounded uneasy as he spoke.

"For nearly thirty years I have reigned over my empire, the most expansive this country and its people have ever witnessed. It would take a man a week without sleep to ride its breadth. We are rich and privileged. The Romans continue to provide us with gold but still I am troubled — and I do not know why."

"We can live without Roman gold," Epaticcus said breezily. "We have trade enough with the continent to keep our grandchildren wealthy until they are infirm."

"But that can change," Cunobelin replied, thinking of the Durotriges. They were once an affluent tribe thanks to significant trade with the Gauls, until Cunobelin's grandfather, Cassivellaunus, wrestled it away from them after Julius Caesar brought Rome to Britain.

"Maybe the eye of Rome will fall once again on Britain," he said.

"Then we will fight them and we will win," Epaticcus said in a matter-of-fact tone. "That lunatic Emperor of theirs is nothing to worry about. I doubt he even knows which day of the week it is, never mind being capable of giving any thought to us."

Cunobelin shrugged, uncertain. He saw Rome as a necessary evil, a vast and powerful force with which one had to co-exist, not fight against as many others had, failing utterly.

His younger brother had spent his whole life enjoying himself with women, drinking and fighting. He cared little for himself and even less for the Romans. But Epaticcus's instability was straightforward in its notion, and Cunobelin had successfully neutralised his volatility over many years. It was simple: if you gave Epaticcus an enticing enough bone to play with he would run away with it, to the expense of all else. Periodically, new bones would have to be unearthed and tossed to Epaticcus, but in general he was manageable.

What worried Cunobelin more were his three sons, his own flesh and blood, imbued with his strength and his wife's stubbornness. The old chief knew there was only a little time left to him in this life. Already once this year he had woken to a sharp pain in his chest, and his arm stayed stiff and difficult to move for some time afterwards — a fact he kept hidden from those around him. How long his empire carried on after his death was a constant concern.

Cunobelin finally looked away from the fire, to the walls where rounded, swirling patterns were painted and war shields hung. Battle trophies jostled for space. Brightly-coloured rugs adorned the floor in many places, making the place look far more cheerful than the King felt.

"Your sons agree with me," Epaticcus said, banging his empty goblet down on a table.

"Not all of them."

Epaticcus opened his mouth to reply but was interrupted by a commotion outside. Frigid air suddenly gusted in, making the fire gutter, as the rug covering the entrance to the roundhouse was lifted momentarily to allow Caradoc and Fionn to cross the threshold. Between them they dragged a dirty man dressed in rags, unceremoniously pitching him to the beaten dirt floor. He lay there, face down and unmoving as if dead.

Another blast of cold air erupted into the room as Togodumnus entered.

"Oh, it's you," Epaticcus said, reaching for his goblet again.

A tall man with an unremarkable and perpetually straight face, Togodumnus paused at the sight of Epaticcus, his aversion to his uncle momentarily overcoming his desire to be present during the inquisition.

Caradoc had always been Epaticcus's favourite nephew and he made no secret of his views. Ever keen to court controversy, Epaticcus had bluntly and loudly told Cunobelin on numerous occasions that Caradoc should rule whenever the time came — despite being the youngest of Cunobelin's three surviving sons. But Cunobelin had enough problems to contend with so, to Togodumnus's exasperation, he would just grin, offer Epaticcus a drink and steadfastly ignore the advice. Although many others agreed with Epaticcus, Cunobelin was simply too loyal to his lineage and so the strained status quo remained in a teetering balance.

"What is he doing here?" Togodumnus pointed at Fionn, ignoring Epaticcus, who snorted in derision.

Caradoc sighed. "Because I asked him to be. We questioned the prisoner together."

Togodumnus shook his head. "You trust him too much."

Caradoc was as close to Fionn as Epaticcus had been with Caradoc years before. Togodumnus believed it was because the pair shared many traits. Both had the same easy attitude and made friends with no apparent effort, while Togodumnus always struggled with small talk. The pair could laugh at nothing but be chillingly brutal when needed. Whenever there was the opportunity to carouse they would take it, and to Togodumnus's disgust Fionn could usually be found drinking with the lower classes and servants. Even shoddier, Fionn seemed not to care what others thought of him. The one major difference between the pair was Fionn's utter disinterest in power; he made no effort to take the responsibility that he was due from his birthright. He was his father's son and Togodumnus despised Fionn for it.

"What is this?" Cunobelin demanded.

"I have uncovered a plot, father," Togodumnus said. "This man, a Gaulish trader, brought us information that a faction in our tribe is working with Rome to aid an invasion."

Fionn stared at Caradoc, open-mouthed. Togodumnus had made no such discovery and he fumed that it was allowed to appear so. But Caradoc ignored his silent protest.

Cunobelin flushed with anger. "Do you believe him?"

"Yes."

At a signal from Caradoc, Fionn dragged Barick to his feet and lifted the prisoner's shackled arms up. The heavy chain running from his wrists to the iron ring around his neck rattled as he did so. One of the prisoner's hands was mangled by torture, dripping blood from where the fingernails should have been. There was a crimson stain on the floor where Barick had lain. Kynthelig blanched and turned away.

"Satisfied?" Togodumnus asked. He waved at Fionn who let go of Barick. He slumped back down into the dirt like a discarded sack of vegetables.

"This is treason. Find them and bring them to me for execution!"

"Whoever they are?" Caradoc asked.

"Of course! No one is above my law."

"You're fully prepared to publicly execute your own son?"

"I always knew that boy was trouble," Epaticcus rumbled, receiving a look shot through with anger and shock from Cunobelin. "Well, it's true," Epaticcus shrugged matter of factly.

A tense silence fell on the room. The only intrusion was the intermittent pop and crackle of the fire. Barick stayed as still as he could, hoping he had been forgotten. He didn't have the nerve or energy to attempt an escape and just hoped his part in this dreadful game would soon be over, no matter how it finished for him.

"Adminius is to blame for this?" Cunobelin finally replied. He struggled to take it all in. He knew his son was pro-Roman but found it hard to comprehend that even Adminius could turn on his own flesh and blood.

Caradoc left little room for suspicion. "There is no doubt, father. Adminius has been communicating directly with the Roman Emperor for months, maybe even longer. We have heard there is a lot of unrest in Rome, and Caligula's own position is at best tenuous. It is said he needs some positive news to divert the attention of his people away from their internal troubles and the best way of doing that is a victory in some far-flung country like ours. Adminius is guaranteeing to open the door to the Romans and provide them with safe passage right up to the Tamessa."

"Which as good as means to Camulodunon," said Togodumnus.

"Even though he is your heir, you cannot let this go unpunished, Lord," Kynthelig quietly advised. Epaticcus nodded his head in agreement.

The accusers had spoken. It was now up to Cunobelin to make a judgement. He sat down heavily, all thought of his aches and the cold banished. His mind felt oddly separated from his body, floating somewhere over his own shoulder as if listening to someone else's problems, someone else's discussion.

"I do not understand this. Why would Adminius betray us?" he asked.

No one replied, but he already knew the answer. A half-formed suspicion, which he had banished to the depths of his soul long ago and steadfastly ignored ever since, despite the warning signs, broke free of its bonds and ascended to curl and twist around his heart. He breathed in sharply. Beneath his cloak he clutched at his left forearm as it stiffened and pain coursed across his chest. His heart thumped loud enough for all to hear and blood sang in his ears.

"We'll find out for sure when we have him," Caradoc said, oblivious to Cunobelin's suffering.

"Bring him to me, alive," Cunobelin croaked through gritted teeth, waiting for the pain to subside.

"It will be done." Caradoc turned to Epaticcus. "Will you lend me some of your men? My numbers are too few."

Epaticcus glanced at Cunobelin, who sat stiff and unmoving on his throne. "They are yours. Take Fionn and my best men."

"Then let us finish this business."

Caradoc strode out of the hut shouting orders, his face contorted with the distaste he felt about the task ahead.

Togodumnus hauled Barick to his feet and thrust him towards a slave. "Take those irons off then clean him up," he ordered.

"Are you hungry?" he said to Barick who nodded mutely, staring at his benefactor, taking in the pallid, washed-out face and eyes. "Feed him too."

Barick almost collapsed with relief and had to be supported by the slave as he was taken away. He swore he would never scorn the gods again.

"You did the right thing, Lord," Kynthelig said, the impassive look on his face masking the exultant singing in his heart. Cunobelin said nothing and stared at nothing.

Epaticcus shook his head and spat into the fire, which hissed in response. He'd be the first to admit he had little time for the pompous Adminius, but nothing good would come of this, he knew.

# III

"There is no time!" Ahearn urged. "They could be here at any moment, we must leave now!"

Adminius stopped piling his riches into the sack and turned to the massive warrior. Over the years many had underestimated the small, weak-looking man but he possessed the volcanic temper of his father, even if he lacked his capacity to inspire his followers.

"We will leave when I am *ready*!" he exploded.

Ahearn had the ability to snap Adminius in two, as effortlessly as he would a dry twig, but neither the bulging muscles, or the livid birth mark splashed across his face, had any effect on Adminius.

"Then we will die."

"If that is my desire, it will be so!"

Adminius stood up and began pacing the roundhouse, displaying a distinct limp. It was an old wound that had a tendency to seize up if he stood or sat in the same position for too long.

Ahearn ground his teeth at the circular, self-pitying argument and he allowed it to bubble up to the surface.

"After four years stuck in this godforsaken place I would have thought you would be desperate to leave!"

"I wanted this on *my* terms, not theirs!"

Ahearn spun on his heel and went out into the icy, sheeting rain before he physically vented his fury on Adminius. In seconds he was soaked to the skin and his jet-black hair, deliberately tied back to accentuate the scar, hung in wet strands, but he welcomed the quenching shock of the downpour. He ignored Adminius's shouts for him to return. Within moments the rattling sounds of more objects being added to the sack began again as Adminius returned to his trinkets.

It was no time to cross the Straits but Ahearn felt they had little choice — Adminius had been treading a dangerous path for quite some time. The slightest error at any point in the game he was playing was always certain to have brought fatal consequences. Now it looked like a slip had finally occurred somewhere and the hounds of hell were set on them.

In truth Ahearn was surprised Adminius had got away with his plotting for as long as he had. He half believed Adminius wanted to be caught, his attitude towards Rome becoming more open and brazen the longer he was frozen out from Cunobelin's court. Ahearn thought back over the sequence of events that had led to this sudden flight...

It was this outward support for Rome and all it offered that had ultimately brought about Adminius's banishment to Cantium. At first Adminius's pro-Roman tendencies were an effective counter to his brothers' negativity, Cunobelin being the fulcrum that balanced them. But over time Adminius's views grew too extreme even for Cunobelin's tastes. He had to go.

But Epaticcus steadfastly refused to accept the tainted Adminius in Verlamion and the Catuvellaunian neighbours jostled with each other to avoid the responsibility of taking such a difficult and dangerous charge. So Cunobelin gave his son a choice — exile, or rule over the south-eastern depths of his kingdom.

As Adminius bitterly relocated his throne, Togodumnus and Caradoc seized both their brother's vacated lands and the initiative. As Cunobelin's health failed the pair became bolder and the empire's attitude towards

Rome subtly changed. Open aggression was surely just a question of time.

And so Ahearn journeyed with Adminius to the backwater of boredom that was Cantium, to its flea ridden 'capital' Durovernon. He thought it an odd place to send someone in punishment for being a Roman supporter. The province was the closest point in the whole country to Gaul, only 20 miles across the Straits at its narrowest point. On a clear day the coast of Gaul itself could quite easily be seen.

Although the vast majority of the trade from the continent landed at Camulodunon, the small port of Fordeuuicum, just a few miles up the river from Durovernon, handled the export of oysters harvested from the Cantium coast to Gaul and even Rome itself. This easy access to shipping regularly crossing the Straits gave Adminius his communication channel with Rome. More than once he made the perilous trip himself across the dangerous and testy waters.

Ahearn knew he should have tried a little harder to curb Adminius's dealings with Caligula, who he thought was just a shade away from complete madness. Caligula had almost invaded on several occasions and the cancellation of each action drove Adminius into a despairing rage each time. But, short of killing Adminius, Ahearn also knew there was nothing constructive he could do about his dangerous relationship with the emperor. Besides, other than the Cantii chief's beautiful but equally cold daughter, it was the only source of interest in this dump.

Although Adminius's influence in Camulodunon was not what it was, there were a small number of sympathisers in Cunobelin's court willing to help where they could in return for a few silver coins. And of late there had even been support from an unexpected quarter much closer to home.

And so, barely an hour ago, a messenger had swept into Durovernon on a sweating horse. He brought word from the Catuvellauni capital that Caradoc had captured someone with explosive information, starting the whole cascade of events that Ahearn now found himself teetering on the brink of.

The information alone was worth far more than the trinkets Adminius was stuffing into his sack. If Ahearn's suspicions were correct, it would not be long before Cunobelin would order Adminius's seizure — if he had not done so already.

Ahearn knew that anyone allied to Adminius would be swept up and destroyed with him. He did not fear an honourable death in battle, but a passage to the next life after a long period of suffering and torture was not of appeal. The information was scant and possibly misleading but nevertheless it had to be acted upon in all haste. There was simply too much to lose.

So Ahearn immediately set about putting his escape plan into action. It was not hastily conceived but premeditated, thought through and refined. He had paid well to have a ship permanently waiting at Fordeuuicum for them. Although the river flowed through the middle of Durovernon, access to the deeper channels of the Stur would be gained much faster from Fordeuuicum. The port was just a short sprint for the horses, which would barely break sweat with the effort. The vigour of the Roman welcome was the only thing Ahearn could not plan for, but it was sure to be warmer than that Cunobelin was likely to offer.

Adminius's rotund wife and three snivelling, snot-bound children were already aboard the ship, as were a few of their belongings. They were too frightened of Ahearn and his men to resist being dragged aboard.

"My lord, when will we be leaving?" asked a rider, rain dripping off him.

The bravest of the retinue of ten mounted warriors who waited to escort Adminius to the ship and over the Straits had ridden forward to speak to Ahearn. He looked nervous at interrupting the scarred man's thoughts.

"Soon," Ahearn hissed through gritted teeth.

The rider nodded and gratefully returned to the sodden group.

Time was moving on and Ahearn knew the warrior was right. They should leave now. He was sorely tempted to abandon the stupid man to his possessions. So many times he had taken a turn in life that put him into the jaws of rivalry and conflict when a move in the opposite direction would have surely led to comfort and success. Here he was at another of these points. But Ahearn was nothing if not loyal, even if his dependability went unappreciated on so many occasions.

So, as always, the decision was an easy one and he took it readily, choosing strife over simplicity. He turned around and went back into the roundhouse. Adminius was still scrabbling around in the dirt, part way through filling a second sack.

"It was not supposed to happen this way!" he shouted.

Adminius's vision had been to use the Romans to thrust his father off the Catuvellauni throne, destroy his brothers and fashion his own glorious and righteous sweep into power. It had all seemed so easy and none of it had meant leaving these shores. But now the time was here he was finding it hard to make the decision to turn his back on his land. He was desperate to be taken seriously in Rome and his fine possessions would, he believed, achieve his aim.

"We need to go, lord. Now," Ahearn said, interrupting Adminius's panicked thoughts. He looked up in surprise. It was rare for Ahearn to use any sort of title.

"I am nearly ready, I am sure we have plenty of ..."

Ahearn punched Adminius squarely on the jaw. He held back somewhat on the strike; despite his present irritation Ahearn had no desire to kill Adminius. Still, the tingling in his fist felt good and Ahearn grinned at the release of some tension.

As he was about to heft Adminius up something caught his eye amongst the scattered items, drawing him across the roundhouse for a closer look. Ahearn picked it up and held it at arm's length. Although only a simple piece of cloth it was of greater significance than all of Adminius' possessions put together, but he was unsurprised it had been ignored. In exasperation, Ahearn stuffed the article underneath his sodden clothes, to rest warm and secure against his heart.

Then he stooped and bore up the dead weight of his prince on his shoulder. Ahearn knew he would be in trouble for his actions later so as a counter he picked up one sack full of Adminius' junk and carried the both of them effortlessly out into the unabating rain. None too gently, hoping some of the items would break, he flung the sack to one of his men before dumping Adminius onto the back of the horse then climbing up himself.

"Ha!" he shouted and his horse galloped out of Durovernon, eating up the short distance to Fordeuuicum and the ship in a matter of minutes.

Ahearn carried Adminius aboard and then returned to stand on the short wooden jetty that protruded out into the river and marshal the men aboard. Several of the horses skittered nervously at the unnatural rocking of the boat as they stepped off the gangplank and onto the deck. Precious minutes were lost calming the beasts before they could be secured below with bags over their heads for the journey into another dominion.

"Cast off!" the captain ordered.

Ahearn was the last of the warriors to embark. He kicked the gangplank into the water. In his impatience he grabbed an axe and chopped through the ropes with brief, powerful swings. Wisely, the crumpled old captain did not protest at the deep cuts carved into the gunwales.

As the ship swung lazily out of the harbour and into the choppier waters of the mouth of the Stur, Ahearn watched men ride through the small town and to the edge of the harbour in a frantic search of the area. Except for the crew and himself everyone was below decks.

The rude ship looked just what it was — an inoffensive Gaulish trader. The vessel moved away quickly with the tide and the searching men took no notice of it.

When they were well out into the Straits, Ahearn heard from below Adminius's livid shout as he awoke and realised where he was, and the shrill shriek of his wife in response. But they were safe and heading for a new life in Rome.

Ahearn sighed and leaned back against the bulwark. He was sure he was going to hate every last minute of it.

## IV

Caradoc anticipated that his father could do nothing but give the command to take Adminius so both horses and warriors waited impatiently for the order to ride. When it came the comitatus surged out of Camulodunon like the hounds of the war god Camulos himself.

The journey to Durovernon was a punishing one, even at the best of times. Two major rivers, the sluggish black depths of the Tamessa and then the faster flowing, honey-coloured

Meduuuæian, had to be negotiated. Then there was the dense Blahwōn Forest, a mass of hornbeam and hazel that stretched for miles like a blanket across much of the poorer soils of Cantium. However, in their favour the route south was in the main heavily used and well worn. Two major track ways led in and out of the area and in places, along the Dūn, the passage was wide enough for an army to march.

The overall speed which they were able to maintain was a respectable one, even for Caradoc's tastes. He pushed his sweating horse hard and the comitatus struggled to keep up with his fierce pace, whipping their horses constantly in an attempt to at least narrow the gap between themselves and Caradoc and so avert his wrath.

Nevertheless he chafed to be in Durovernon. During their final resting of the horses they ate a brief meal and the Catuvellauni prince outlined his plan, forcing home his points with fierce chopping motions of his arm. He wanted no room for error and was barely able to eat anything. He slept little, pacing the floor instead while the others snored.

But at last they reached the town and paused briefly at the crest of the shallow hill. As Caradoc carefully surveyed the layout of the land below a few of the comitatus took the chance to stretch tired muscles or wipe the dust and dirt from their faces. All felt the exhilaration of the task ahead after the exertions of the journey behind them.

At the valley bottom lay the Cantium capital. Smoke curled lazily upwards from the huts, barely disturbed by the gentle wind.

Fionn's first impression was of a relatively poor-looking market town, certainly in comparison to the other great towns of Camulodunon, Verlamion and Calleva. Over the years Durovernon had grown at the expense of a fortified town, Bicanbyrig, where the Cantii capital had previously been located. But lately the fort had fallen into disuse and disrepair. Fionn was surprised to see the town unprotected; there were none of the massive ditches and earthworks that surrounded other major settlements. It appeared willing to survive on trade, rather than defence.

Durovernon was bisected by the Stur, an artery that brought this business directly into the heart of the town. Fionn noted the wooden jetties jutting out into the river, to which small boats, really just river craft, were attached and bobbed gently in the current. A ford allowed ready access between the halves of the town.

A market area had sprung up next to the river where all manner of goods, from food and pottery to slaves and metalwork, were sold. It looked relatively small and Fionn imagined the goods would be of low quality. Business here with the Romans was unlikely to be anywhere near as strong as in other parts of the region and money would consequently be less plentiful.

It was early morning but already Fionn could see activity as people milled along the wide roads between the clusters of roundhouses rising gradually upwards and outwards from the river. Some of the houses were clearly dwellings. Others contained industry such as a smithy, an ironworks and potters, and a number would be food stores or for protection of livestock.

They stared at the section of Durovernon on the far side of the Stur from where they stood. Here was the largest roundhouse in the settlement, surrounded by a banked ditch within which Fionn saw suspiciously little movement. He glanced at Caradoc who, by the angry look on his face, appeared to have made the same judgement. The ditch was not to protect against those on the outside but to keep the horses safe, the key to a warrior leader's continuing power and prestige.

"The horses are gone," Fionn said.

Caradoc swore. "He has flown!"

He kicked his horse into a breakneck gallop, closely followed by the electrified comitatus, all thought of aching muscles and hunger forgotten. Fionn unfurled Caradoc's standard and it fluttered strongly as they rode. It was a rectangle of white cloth on which was depicted a black eagle, its wings spread and talons extended in the process of attacking its prey.

People looked up at the clamour of many hooves, quickly leaping out of the way to avoid being trampled. A woman pulled a child back by the scruff of the neck from where she had been playing in the street, a hoof barely missing crushing a leg. A man was sent flying as a horse clipped him, throwing pottery up into the air to shatter into countless pieces on the ground.

The horses checked briefly as they splashed through the ford, the water up to their haunches. Within moments they reached the compound. The gates stood open and unguarded. Caradoc leapt off his horse and drew his sword before thrusting his way into the dominant roundhouse.

"Brennon, search the other buildings!" Fionn ordered, sending ten men to spread through the compound. "Hueil, take the rest of the men and search the area. Durovernon first and then the surrounding countryside."

Hueil, powerfully built and as angry as ever, nodded in response and turned his horse away. He pounded back out of the enclosure again. The warriors in his wake searched the town none too gently, barging into the roundhouses in case Adminius was cowering there.

Nemausus, a small man who lied and cheated at every opportunity, glanced around as he spotted a few silver coins half trodden into the mud. No one was looking so he grabbed the coins, stamped with a hippogrif and Adminius's name, along with a handful of dirt. He grinned, showing blackened teeth, quickly shoved them into his pocket and resumed the search of the compound.

Fionn entered the roundhouse which was cold, dark and uninviting. Glancing around briefly, it was immediately obvious that the building was devoid of life, scattered and smashed belongings a sure sign that the departure had been hasty.

"They have been gone for hours," Caradoc said, poking at the fire, which had burnt down to mere dull glowing embers. He sounded tired.

"We were so close," Fionn said.

"Close is not acceptable," Caradoc replied fiercely. He looked ready to say more but stopped at the nearing sound of horse's hooves.

A small group of riders, led by a warrior carrying a flag displaying a black raven, entered the compound. Caradoc's men emerged from the surrounding buildings, swords in hand, but he signalled for them to hold. The raven was a familiar symbol.

One warrior walked his horse forward from the group. He had shoulder-length brown hair and an almost perpetual sneer on a cruel mouth. Cold, piercing dark eyes blinked at Caradoc and then flicked to Fionn, instantly appraising the situation. He dismounted.

Fionn knew the man by reputation, which was a mixed one at best. Weland was the Cantii tribal leader, or had been until Adminius had been imposed upon him by Cunobelin. He was disliked by many and loathed by more, but his loyalty to Cunobelin was without question and that was more highly prized by the king than any questionable personality trait.

But moving Adminius to Durovernon had not been one of Cunobelin's smartest decisions. Adminius and Weland were equally stubborn and abrasive. The four years Adminius was in residence were marked by bitter disagreements followed by long periods of silence. Fionn could not imagine that Weland would be upset to see Adminius gone.

"It is good to see you, Weland," Caradoc said, to which he received a bare grunt.

"We need to talk," Weland said over his shoulder, re-entering the roundhouse.

With undisguised pleasure Weland tossed some of Adminius's belongings onto the fire and poked at it hopefully until a thin flame flickered into life. He kept his attention fixed on the fire as a tall, painfully thin man pushed through the fur hanging over the doorway. He removed his helmet to reveal a young but gaunt face that looked as if it were shy of food. He was followed by a much shorter warrior whose helmet remained firmly in place.

"Bearach, my witless son," Weland said, pointing to the thin young man.

There were rumours that Weland's wife could not stand to be near him and that there was little family likeness between father and son seemed to confirm this. The only similarity seemed to be the same style of hair and beard, as if the son were trying to make the father see something in him. Fionn grinned; Bearach meant spear and the young man looked willowy enough to be thrown aloft with ease. Bearach's lively eyes quickly took in the room with some amusement, briefly resting on Fionn and Caradoc apparently ignoring his father's comments. But his half-smile hardened as he mistook Fionn's laugh for something else.

"Take your helmet off, girl!" Weland barked in a long-suffering tone, addressing the second, shorter warrior. "My daughter, and bane of my life, Etain. She gets more like her mother, the bitch, every day."

Etain took off her helmet, allowing a cascade of silken blonde hair to fall about her shoulders. There was a challenge in her sparkling blue eyes that demanded she be accepted as an equal, and her pursed lips betrayed her displeasure at her father's words.

For a moment Fionn was unable to breath. She had a look he had never seen the like of. Etain caught his open-mouthed stare and laughed brightly at him, much to his embarrassment. He looked away and studied the items scattered on the floor instead.

"Adminius is gone," Weland said, still poking at the fire, trying to drive some of the chill out of the room.

"We worked that out for ourselves," Fionn said tersely, still burning with embarrassment.

"Then you no longer need me," Weland said and stalked towards the exit.

"Shut up, Fionn. Weland, we need your information and your help," Caradoc appealed.

Fionn's face suffused with anger, which he tried hard to swallow. Weland smirked at his unease.

"I learnt that he took a ship some hours ago across the Straits to Gaul. We could do no more so came back here."

"Can he still be caught?" Fionn asked.

Weland raised his eyes to the heavens at the boy's obvious stupidity.

Caradoc shook his head. "Very unlikely. My brother is as slippery as an eel. Adminius will be too far away now and probably even in Roman hands."

"It does not sound like you tried very hard to stop him," said Fionn, trying to provoke Weland after the earlier insults.

Weland shrugged. "I am glad to be rid of the fool. He did little of consequence other than brag and drink. I did all of the work whilst he lived at ease. He achieved nothing for my tribe except make us a little poorer and Belenos knows we were hardly wealthy to begin with.

"But I would have preferred to see him executed and left for the birds to pick at his decaying body than living in Rome. Either way, he is out of my life."

Fionn opened his mouth to reply but Caradoc cut in before the disagreement turned into something more. Weland had a knack for inflaming even the simplest of situations and without Adminius to attack he was bound to be looking for an alternative target. Caradoc was too tired and deflated to be bothered with his games.

"We need time to rest the horses and ourselves before we return to Camulodunon," he said.

"I will see to it. We have plenty of room now after all. The horses can be kept in the enclosure and your men too. Bearach, look after our young guest here." Weland inclined his head towards Fionn. He eyed Etain balefully. "You can go too, daughter."

Fionn's heart began to hammer in his chest again as Etain smiled immodestly. The day was at last beginning to improve. What a challenge lay ahead of him, with the prize such a fantastically beautiful girl.

Once Fionn was out of earshot Weland immediately turned to the weary-looking Caradoc. "Why do you rely on that young fool so much?"

Caradoc sighed, he had heard it all before from Togodumnus. "He is more capable than you think. He is also blood."

"He will be your undoing," Weland predicted.

"I cannot be bothered sparring with you, Weland. Can we talk about something more important than your views on my cousin?"

Weland shrugged, all thought of Fionn already banished. There was much to do but he was already a long way down the path in defining what lay ahead for him. He grinned inside at the shock that was coming Caradoc's way.

# V

## March AD 40

"He wanted to slip away but we have fought to keep him alive these past three days," the healer said. She bobbed her head at Caradoc to gauge his happiness with her efforts.

The old woman held a bunch of herbs in her hands, about to make another draft for Cunobelin. A pot boiled on a fire in the corner. Caradoc wrinkled his nose at the vile smell that issued from the steaming brown liquid the herbs were destined for.

"Thank you for your efforts," he said. A delighted smile spread across the healer's lips and she bobbed her head again and felt able to move onto the more difficult subject.

"We think we may be able to help him recover."

"How?" Caradoc sounded hopeful.

"We want to bore a hole in his skull to let the bad air out. Otherwise we think he will die."

"So why do you not proceed?"

"We are afraid he may be too weak to survive the procedure, which is difficult for even a young man to bear."

"That is very useful," Epaticcus snorted. "Whatever you do Cunobelin is likely to die and you are proved right whatever the outcome."

The healer looked mortified.

"That is not true!" she protested.

Epaticcus laughed derisively. "I shall see the king for myself and make the decision," Caradoc said, to the healer's relief.

The hushed tones of the occupants and their downcast eyes gave the impression Cunobelin was already dead rather than grimly clinging to life.

"He is still asleep," Fionn advised Caradoc quietly.

"Where is Togodumnus?"

"Dealing with a problem."

"He enjoys your father's illness," Epaticcus said, none too quietly. Some in the room shook their heads in displeasure at his words.

"I am sure it is important," Caradoc said, moving towards the sickbed.

Caradoc did not believe it was the healer's efforts that kept Cunobelin alive; he knew full well how stubborn the old man could be and could not imagine he was ready to die. But when he squatted at eye level with the atrophied body he began to have his doubts. Even in the short period of time since he had seen him last his father looked decidedly worse.

The king lay in his bed, propped up at a shallow angle and cocooned by a mass of furs which served the dual purpose of providing warmth and holding him in place like a newborn child. On his pallid face flickered the flames from the nearby fire, which gave the room a searing heat, but Cunobelin's skin still felt corpse like to the touch. Caradoc was momentarily pleased that Cunobelin slept as he could not stand to see the old man mumble incoherently. Immediately, however, he felt ashamed at his self pity.

It had all begun with Caradoc's furious return from the abortive attempt to capture Adminius. Debate and condemnation circled in court for days afterwards, but Cunobelin did not get involved. Instead he retired to his bed, a space he had rarely occupied in the past. The old king thereafter spent his time fitfully sleeping or drinking heavily. The food he was given lay largely untouched and alcohol seemed to provide his only sustenance.

At the same time he lost interest in the daily goings-on of the tribe. None of the repetitious troubles of his subjects mattered to him and anyone disturbing his reverie, including his sons, was sent away with a blunt and obvious threat. Eventually no one troubled him at all and the king seemed finally to find happiness of a sorts.

But then a servant discovered Cunobelin half out of his bed, drool running down one side of his face and a patch of dried urine about him. After the servant dragged Cunobelin from the floor and back into bed he found it difficult to understand what the king was saying.

The healers were immediately called and when they examined the old man they found that one side of his body, from toes to head, was frozen and immovable. His speech was slurred and, although his mind was still in perfect working order, Cunobelin could communicate little of substance.

Although Togodumnus had been acting on Cunobelin's behalf since his withdrawal from court, news of the king's incapacity soon spread, creating ripples of disturbance across the realm. Envoys besieged the court, trying to discover the true nature of his condition. Despite Togodumnus's assurances, most left worried and unsure as to what the future held. The truth of the situation could not be avoided for much longer and so Togodumnus sent for the tribal leaders to debate what should be done next. Caradoc had come as bidden.

Caradoc closed his eyes, hoping that when he opened them he would see his father in his true form again. But all he saw was the same old, drawn face steadfastly asleep. He stood and the group naturally broke up and drifted away, a few mumbling platitudes and apologies. He left the room last. Other than two servants attending his bedside, Cunobelin was left alone to continue his fitful slumber.

Caradoc stepped outside. The sun, low and angry in the evening sky, seemed to reflect his feelings. He stared into its rays, feeling the gentle warmth on his face. He felt a little lost. Cunobelin had always been present, always larger than life and the driving force behind his family's fortunes, good or bad. Without his father, Caradoc knew it was time for others to take up the reins. He offered a brief prayer to the gods for guidance.

Fionn settled onto the thick rug which softened the hard floor and stopped the sapping of heat into the cold earth. A fire crackled nearby, spilling out the only light in the room until the slaves began to light the oil lamps. The yellow flames guttered and issued an oily, smelly smoke that soon filled the air.

Togodumnus held out his goblet for wine. The slave poured the liquid steadily, then moved to Caradoc and finally to a frantically-beckoning Epaticcus who drained his goblet in one draft.

"Get back here and refill this," Epaticcus barked. The slave proffered the amphora to pour more but Epaticcus grabbed the vessel, filled the goblet himself and planted the amphora next to him, glaring at the slave defiantly.

Kynthelig waved the alcohol away. He settled instead for an infusion of herbs but somehow managed to spill the steaming liquid into his lap. He jumped up in pain and embarrassment, trying hard not to curse. The slave moved to help but the druid dabbed himself dry.

"Did you see that? Hilarious!" Epaticcus laughed and nudged Weland, who sneered at the drunkard before turning his back on him. Epaticcus shrugged and carried on giggling to himself.

Caradoc was immune to Kynthelig's difficulties. He sipped his wine as he looked at each of the men Togodumnus had called to attend. In this room were the real wielders of power in the Catuvellauni kingdom, the only ones that mattered in all the thousands that Cunobelin governed.

Once the goblets were filled and the food spread out on the table the slave servants slunk back against the walls to hide in the shadows. To all intents and purposes they did not exist; they were mere pieces of furniture until needed again.

Togodumnus paced around the room, unable to stay in one position. He realised the others were waiting for him. He leant momentarily against the hearth, absorbing the heat of the fire.

"It is very unlikely the king will make a full recovery," he said to the gathering. "We have to decide how we deal with this situation."

"The healer told me she believed our father could be saved," Caradoc challenged.

"You have seen the difficulty he is in, how he cannot use part of his body. He is incapable even of meaningful speech. He cannot even piss for himself."

"I knew the healers were lying," Epaticcus said, then belched loudly.

"There are growing whispers that this is the end of the Catuvellauni," said Malvyn, the gnarled chief of the Trinovantes.

"Never!" Epaticcus thumped the table, rattling the crockery.

"People are worried about what the future holds so naturally they debate what is best for them. It is entirely possible that before long the tribes on our periphery will begin to question whether we are strong enough to survive. We must not let the whispers become shouts," Malvyn said.

Malvyn had fought many campaigns with Epaticcus, his boyhood friend, in pursuit of Cunobelin's goals. The two tribes had such a long-running and deeply-intertwined relationship that these days they were almost impossible to separate. Malvyn was an old man, infirm and incapable of much more than a shuffling walk. He had not been outside Camulodunon for almost ten years.

"You speak as if he is dead already," Fionn said.

"I merely point out the situation we are in," Togodumnus said. He had moved again and taken a seat at the end of the long table, but jiggled as if he could barely contain himself.

"He will get better," Epaticcus said fervently.

"Whatever we believe will or will not happen, at the moment Cunobelin is not fit to rule," Kynthelig said. "Let us hope he gets well again but I agree with Togodumnus — we have a problem that needs dealing with."

"What do you suggest?" Caradoc asked.

"We need to send a message to the crows that are circling, waiting for our death, and ready to descend and pick over the bones," Togodumnus said. "We need to show them that we have teeth, we have muscle and we are alive and strong.

"The king has been too long involved in Roman concerns. We have been complacent and spent much time looking outwards. But it is time to look inwards again and towards our borders."

Epaticcus nodded fervently. "Yes, that bastard son of a diseased whore, Verica, continues to cause trouble. One day I would like to drive him out all together."

The two men hated each other with a burning passion that went back to when they were young men. This antipathy had reached a crescendo four years ago when Epaticcus drove Verica out of Calleva and south to Seolesiae. After settling in Calleva Epaticcus was ready to finish the task but then, after twenty-five years of continual annexing of territory, Cunobelin decided that all further expansion must cease. Epaticcus, much to his chagrin, was told to leave Verica bottled up in his remaining land. What resulted was an uneasy and vague alliance, maintained, it was said, simply to appease Rome. Despite this the two tribes had often clashed since in bloody but indecisive skirmishes. One would only rest when the other was finally buried.

"We have just received another envoy from Verica probing our intentions. I sent the man back with assurances that the alliance stays as firm as ever and we will categorically not attack him."

"His men cross into my lands. They steal my livestock and kill my tenants," Epaticcus said. "I have every right to attack him!"

"I told the envoy that Verica must stop the raids. He claimed they were small groups of mercenaries not affiliated to him and I was given assurances they will be found and executed."

"That old woman should have been put to the sword years ago. He is an enemy that needs to be destroyed. Verica may be weak but he can still harm us," Epaticcus persisted.

"Verica is a friend of Rome," Weland said.

"My point exactly."

"No, what I meant was..."

"...that he should not be trusted," Epaticcus interrupted before he could finish. Pleased that his argument was so easily won Epaticcus drained his goblet of wine in celebration.

"We will leave Verica out of this for the moment," Togodumnus said, raising a hand to stop a further outburst from Epaticcus, who sat open-mouthed, seeing defeat at the jaws of victory. "We do not want to make an enemy of Rome just yet."

"So who do you suggest?" Malvyn asked, whilst Epaticcus downed more wine.

"We have traded with the Dobunni for many years," said Caradoc. "However, Eisu's northern faction is starting to become bolder. Eisu is a trader and not the strongest of leaders. It seems his subordinates are forcing him to show his mettle and so they have begun encroaching into our territory. We must stop this. I propose that Epaticcus and I invade the northern Dobunnic territories and we take the land for ourselves. When the time is right, then we will face Verica."

"Do you wish the opinion of the druids on this proposed venture?" Kynthelig asked, his voice dripping with disdain.

"Not particularly, but I'm sure you will give us the benefit of your wisdom," Epaticcus replied with equal sarcasm.

"Do you, Kynthelig, and the Druid Council support this decision to go to war with the Dobunni?" Togodumnus formally requested.

The elderly druid received the request with a stately nod of the head, then mused for a while. In a deliberate, and successful, attempt to raise Epaticcus' blood pressure, he appeared to consider the merits of the plan, although he had already made his decision.

"I give my consent," he said eventually.

Epaticcus laughed uproariously, already looking forward to the battle, the conclusion of which would bring him one step closer to finishing off his old enemy. He pulled Caradoc to one side to start planning what would need to be done before the campaigning season opened.

The old druid had absolutely no interest in the detail of battle. He rose from the table and left the others to it. He glanced at Weland and was intrigued to see him sitting back from the discussion, apparently deep in thought. But Kynthelig shrugged to himself. As long as his plan was in motion, those of others did not matter.

# VI

"What?" Epaticcus struggled with the concept. He paused in eating his breakfast and glanced at Fionn and Brennon, who looked equally bemused by the suggestion.

"Chariots," Caradoc repeated. "That is how we will get into Corinnion."

"So Eisu will let us just ride into his town, will he?" Epaticcus spat food as he chuckled.

"Of course not. They are the tool we use to open up the town."

"Throw the whole plan at us, Caradoc," Fionn said. He put his food down on the ground, unable to eat it now.

As the sun rose Caradoc outlined his strategy. Eventually, even the sceptical Epaticcus started to see a glimmer of hope in it.

"But it is dangerous," was all he was able to say, licking his fingers.

"Do you have any better suggestions? If so let us hear them. I would be delighted to find another way but at the moment I cannot think of one and we just do not have the time. The men are going to starve soon and we have to take action. Now, not next week."

There was silence for a minute.

"So we are agreed," Caradoc said, taking the lack of argument for assent. "Fionn, this is what I need you to do..."

Epaticcus began to manoeuvre the army in the early evening, just as the light was beginning to fade. Torches flared as they were lit to illuminate the path. The men grumbled at the stupidity of moving when the visibility was limited. They stumbled over rocks and roots and cursed as equipment jingled, rattled and bruised.

As the infantry relocated the responding sound of horns echoed from inside Corinnion. Dobunni soldiers flocked to the walls and watched curiously as the invaders marched noisily from their position in the centre. There was elation at first, speculation that the Catuvellauni were withdrawing, but this turned to disappointment as they simply moved around the hill to a position opposite the eastern gate.

As all eyes were on Epaticcus, Caradoc withdrew silently about a mile to a clump of trees, within which he hid. With him was a small contingent of warriors and the comitatus. Epaticcus had grumbled, saying he felt naked without his men. but grudgingly accepted the plan would only work with a combination of speed and distraction.

The Dobunni stayed on alert all night as Epaticcus loudly marched small groups of men with torches around the exterior of Corinnion whilst the rest of his army slept. When dawn broke the Dobunni were tired, drawn and on edge. As light spilled over the countryside Eisu, feeling bone-weary and with heavy black bags under his eyes, glared over the battlements. Beneath he saw Epaticcus's army ranged in front of Corinnion, looking as if they meant business.

For the rest of the day Epaticcus periodically sent sorties of men forward, testing the defences. A party headed towards the eastern gate and were driven off by a hail of sling stones, inaccurate but numerous enough to be dangerous. Others attempted to navigate the ditches and were faced with spears and arrows as they climbed. As each threat arose, Eisu sent warriors to deal with them and he constantly roved the defences, watching keenly for where the next attack might arise. It was a long, hard day.

Night fell and the moonless sky was clear, with the exception of a rare cloud that skittered quickly across in the wind. It was perfect for their intentions. Epaticcus heard a struggle and an animal yelp in the darkness behind him. In the silence that followed he thought of the battle ahead. He offered a prayer to Camulos for their success. A minute later he prayed again, asking the god for an opportunity to fight Verica before he died.

*No harm in trying*, he thought.

"Do it," Epaticcus whispered, votives delivered.

A warrior nodded and stood. He placed the arrow against his bow and offered it to be lit. When the flame was burning strongly he drew his bow taut and shot it high into the sky over Corinnion.

"Attack!" Epaticcus shouted again and again. All along the line of assembled warriors, carnyx blared balefully.

At the signal the Catuvellauni surged forward in a broad line, some heading towards the gate, others for the bank. Inside Corinnion the slumbering guards, at last getting a break from the onslaught of the day, jerked blearily from their sleep and shouted the alarm. Dobunni warriors surged towards the ramparts, gathering weapons as they ran. Slingers reached down to the piles of stones collected from the seashore and rounded by the pounding of the waves, and fitted them into the pocket of the leather sling. At first they threw blindly into the night, their vision lost from standing by fires.

A group of Catuvellauni soldiers ran towards the gate with burning brands in an attempt to set them on fire. But they were quickly felled as they sprinted down the narrow passageway, leaving the brands to burn impotently on the floor next to their corpses.

Eisu joined his men on the ramparts and stared downwards at the bodies. He turned to his assembled warriors.

"Let them dash themselves against our defences! Let them suffer and die by our hand!" he shouted. "They cannot breach Corinnion, even with countless men at their command!"

His men roared their approval and renewed their defence. Eisu perched on the ramparts and watched his men kill Epaticcus's at last, laughing as his enemy impaled themselves on his walls. He had been right not to face the Catuvellauni in open battle, and now they would pay the price for their arrogance.

"Set the chariots," Epaticcus ordered once the battle was in full motion. From all around him came the clamour of war.

The five teams started forwards. There were two men in each chariot, which was filled with tinder dry wood and soaked with pitch. The smell was overpowering. The horses moved slowly at first, their progress unseen in the dim light by the Dobunni. But then, with a shouted order, the horses were whipped and the chariots sprang forward, dashing towards the corridor that guarded the eastern gate. The mounted warriors hung on grimly to avoid being thrown in the tumult.

The chariots were upon the defences so quickly that the Dobunni had little time to react. Before they knew it the chariots were being drawn up before the gates and unhitched by one warrior while the other tried to calm the wild-eyed horses. All five chariots were pressed up against the gate. Suddenly the Dobunni countered and a hail of arrows, stones and spears rained down onto the Catuvellauni.

Horses and men alike were mown down.

A warrior raised a shield over his head. His shoulder streamed blood from an arrow impaled almost down to the feather. He was unable to turn his head too far as the arrow pressed against his cheek. With a supreme effort he cast the brand into the nearest chariot. The wood and pitch caught immediately and the flames roared against the gate. The warrior fell back from the heat and lay on the ground panting, his life bleeding out of him.

Eisu ran to the rampart and stared in disbelief at the gates. They were engulfed in roaring flames, like a beacon, the fires too strong to be dealt with by the warriors, who nevertheless ran desperately to get water. For the first time he began to doubt Corinnion's defences.

Caradoc crept along the battlements. Behind him were arrayed another nineteen men, his best warriors. Fionn kept close to Caradoc, knife in hand, Brennon beside him. Fionn turned at a snigger from one of the men. He was unsurprised to see it was Nemausus. The little thief grinned and showed a black space between his lips where his teeth were. He raised a hand to feel the puckered scar on his forehead, a trophy from a fight when only a child.

"Be quiet, you idiot," Hueil hissed. "Do you want them to hear us before we are anywhere near?"

"I am looking forward to trying the Dobunni women!" he whispered. "Anyway, they will hear you snorting like a pig from miles away!"

Hueil, a brute almost as powerfully built as Brennon, was the angriest man Fionn had ever met. His forehead was permanently fixed with a frown and his cheeks red as if always on edge. The only time Hueil released his pent-up rage was in battle, where he was a sight to behold. His nose was a smashed piece of gristle spread across his face from the many fights he had been in, and he could only breathe by gulping air via his mouth.

Stealthily the group climbed the ditched defence, the incline difficult to work against despite leaving most of their armour and weaponry behind — if they were discovered a few extra pieces of metal would not save them. Being able to move quickly, lightly and most of all quietly was more important.

Caradoc had expected the scree to pose a problem but weeds had grown through the stones, making them much firmer to walk on than intended by the builders. They made barely a scrunching sound as he stepped on them. Finally they scaled the battlements by hitching and pulling each other up on straining arm muscles.

Caradoc paused to listen. From the other side of the town was the roar of battle. Flames licked above the height of the wall as the fire engulfed the eastern gate. The light from the conflagration illuminated the men spread along the ramparts, busily attempting to repel Epaticcus's warriors and douse the flames.

Below him lay a spread of roundhouses and then the central compound, protected by the second ditch. Inside it horses stood calmly despite the noise. To the right was the prize, the western gate. Fionn touched Caradoc on the arm and pointed. A small movement indicated a guard. Doubtless there would be others. At a sign the group descended, daggers unsheathed.

The plump guard kicked at a stone in boredom. It skittered across the road and hit something in the darkness with a muted thud. The sounds of fighting carried easily to his ears. He winced as a scream rent the air and he wished he could be in bed next to his plump wife with only the sounds of everyday life about them.

"I am glad we are nowhere near that!" the guard said to his colleague, a much younger man than he and overly keen in his opinion.

The young man grunted in response, hoping he would get his chance in the battle before the Catuvellauni were driven off. He looked up at the sound of movement above them and momentarily froze at the unexpected sight. Men were inching towards them in the darkness!

"Intruders!" he shouted and drew his sword, but before he could raise it in battle a hand was pressed over his mouth. He tasted the sweat and dirt on it. The young guard struggled to resist the pull backwards that exposed his neck to the knife which sawed and bit into his windpipe, choking off the sound of his bubbling scream.

Fionn dropped the guard to the floor. Already a slick pool of blood was forming around his body as it gushed unabated out of a slashed artery. The other guard lay dead too, by Nemausus's hand, sightless eyes staring up into the night sky. But the strangled shout had brought others.

"Kill them!" Caradoc ordered as more guards, stunned by the presence of the enemy inside their walls, rushed froma nearby building, ready with swords and spears.

Despite being better equipped the Dobunni were tired, scared and clumsy. They died easily. Brennon lay about him with his axe, chopping at limbs and torsos. Hueil raged as he grabbed a guard then twisted and broke his neck with a sickening crunch, as if he had wrung a bird's neck. Fionn stepped inside his attacker and lunged upwards with his knife, ripping the man's stomach open into flopping folds of skin. The man shrieked and stepped backwards, desperately trying to hold his intestines as, like a handful of snakes, they wriggled and pulsed in his grip. He collapsed to the floor and watched his life ebb away into the dirt.

The remaining guards were quickly despatched. Only one of Caradoc's men had been lost but seven Dobunni lay dead — the rest had turned and run from the ferocity of their attackers. Brennon wiped his axe on one of the corpses, tutting at the notch in the blade. Nemausus was already crouched and searching through the folds of the dead men's clothes.

Caradoc stepped towards the gate. A huge horizontal beam lay across it, held in place by supports.

"Help me," he said.

Brennon, Hueil and Fionn heaved at the bar with him. With a thud it fell to the floor and was dragged out of the way by Hueil and Brennon, as easily as a normal man would carry a branch.

"Come on, open it!" Nemausus urged, the slight man keen to unleash himself on the town's occupants.

Hueil glared at him. The ferocious look would have cowed most men but the little thief was unmoved. He pointed again to the entrance. Hueil and Brennon each shoved a gate open to offer Corinnion to the mercy of the Catuvellauni. As they did so Fionn shot a flaming arrow into the sky. Within moments he could hear the sound of horses' hooves and stood out of the way as the comitatus entered through the gates, each carrying an extra man behind him.

"Sound our entrance," Caradoc said, and the carnyx blew as the infantry dropped off horseback. Nemausus snickered wickedly to see them.

The Catuvellauni were inside Corinnion and they surged through the town hunting the enemy, adrenalin roaring in their ears.

Eisu turned, puzzled at the sound of the carnyx. It was behind him, not in front where it should be. He leaned over to get a better view, his concern growing as he saw some of his men running from inside the town towards the wall and shouting. One man fell as an arrow buried itself in his back.

Screams erupted from within the town's streets. For a moment Eisu's mind refused to take it in, then his stomach dropped as the reality bit home. Somehow the enemy had broken through and were already deep in Corinnion, slaking their thirst.

"We are breached!" Eisu bellowed. "Look to your rear!"

He pulled at his men, dragging their attention away from the activity outside the walls. The Dobunni warriors turned, equally stunned that their defences had been compromised. A shiver of fear coursed through them, well aware of what would happen to those that did not surrender to their besiegers straight away.

Many defenders dropped their weapons and dashed into the town to save their families, or over the battlements and into the night to save themselves. The braver Dobunni fought in small groups, survival now most important, but they were mercilessly hacked down as the Catuvellauni warriors boiled over them, taking out their weeks of frustration.

Eisu fought grimly, killing one warrior, then another, but slowly his men were slaughtered by the greater numbers of the Catuvellauni. A huge bearded warrior hefted a terrifying large axe.

"Fight me," the man said with a rumble deep from his core.

But Eisu, numbed to the core, knew it was over. He lowered his bloody sword. Brennon obliged the Dobunni chief, stepped forward and removed Eisu's head in one easy swing. His torso sagged to the floor. Brennon stooped and as he stood again hung Eisu's decapitated head from his waist belt, where it dripped warm blood down his leg.

Caradoc stood above the burning gates, ignoring the sting from a cut on his arm delivered by a desperate

Dobunni warrior, who was now growing cold and stiffening. The carnyx wailed again and again declaring their victory. With the exception of clearing out some pockets of resistance, the battle was over. Corinnion was theirs and the Catuvellauni warriors would drink their fill of the town tonight. Already he could hear the screams of desperate women echoing.

"Caradoc!" Fionn shouted from beneath him. "It is Epaticcus! Come quickly!"

Caradoc went cold. He leapt over the battlements and skidded down the slope after his cousin.

Epaticcus's breathing was ragged as he struggled to pull air into his punctured lung. A sword had been placed into his left hand and he gripped it tightly, all his energy directed into holding the weapon beyond the last moment. Fionn knelt by his side, supporting his head. Caradoc knelt opposite him, staring into his uncle's eyes.

"A lucky shot," Epaticcus laughed and began to cough, blood at his lips.

Epaticcus customarily led his men into battle and was in the thick of the fighting throughout. The old warrior stood unscathed as all around him men fell and he laughed at his good fortune. But then, even as the victory carnyx blew inside Corinnion's walls, Epaticcus was struck by a spear, hitting him in the chest and boring into vital organs.

As he lay on the ground Epaticcus ordered that the spear be dragged out. He cursed long and loud at the man who stepped forward to carry out the demand. The wound was wide and gaping and there was little that could be done other than to make the old man comfortable as the inevitable approached.

"Do not be sad," Epaticcus said to Fionn. "I have had a long life and I go to the next one a happy man. Better to die here, with a sword in my hand, than incontinent — bed ridden and soaked with piss — or bitter and full of regret like that old fool Verica!" He laughed and then hacked again, his face drawn in agony.

"Bury me with our family in Camulodunon," Epaticcus requested.

Fionn nodded in agreement, unable to bring himself to speak.

Epaticcus looked over at Caradoc. "Swear to me. Swear to me you will rid this land of Verica. Take my place at Calleva and finish what I started. Swear it!" He coughed again with the exertion, deeper and longer this time.

"I promise, uncle," Caradoc said when the racking had subsided.

Epaticcus smiled. "Good boy. I knew I could trust you. Verica has outlived me, the bastard. Make sure it is not for long."

And then Epaticcus sucked a last rattling breath and died, his fingers still gripping his sword.

# VII

**June AD 42**

The gathered crowd was hushed as the warrior walked resolutely forward holding the battle standard aloft. The wind whipped at the fabric and, as if the hand of a god had reached down, tugged it out to its full extent to display the vicious hound, all teeth and muscle, in mid-leap, primed and ready to bite and tear its enemies.

Those nearest the procession took a step backwards, forcing the row behind to do the same, so crowded were they. The motion rippled outwards as if a stone had been thrown into a lake, creating a narrow, temporary opening in the ocean of bodies, which closed again as soon as the litter and the following dignitaries passed through. A keening sound issued from the crowd as men and women wept and wailed for the loss of their king.

Caradoc, Togodumnus and Fionn carried the shell that had been Cunobelin, hound of the Sun God Belenos, his battle with old age and illness finally lost, to the great mound within the defensive ditches of Camulodunon.

His thin body, wasted and weakened from being bed-ridden for over a year, had been placed in his finest armour, a suit of chain mail and a winged helmet, giving the waif-like corpse and the litter at least a little weight. Cunobelin's hair and beard were trimmed, combed and neatly tied. His hands were clasped around his ornate sword, which lay on his chest.

The barrow which was to be Cunobelin's last resting place was a hollowed-out mound one hundred and fifty feet in diameter and towering fifty feet high. It was far greater in scale than any other in the graveyard where the honoured dead of the Catuvellauni were buried. Nearby laid Cunobelin's wife, two of his children who had died at an early age and Epaticcus, his grave not long sealed.

The gathering in Camulodunon was enormous, the largest assembly in one place for a single purpose for generations. People from all walks of life, all strata of society, had travelled from far and wide, tribal leaders, farmers, peasants, merchants, craftsmen, seers, warriors — the list went on and on.

The public had descended on the town in advance of the burial, filling it to capacity, spilled outwards into the surrounding countryside. As well as the common men and women, official contingents arrived from most of the tribes south of Caledonia, whether they owed fealty to the Catuvellauni or not. Some came out of respect, some out of curiosity, many for selfish reasons.

The granite men of the Silures, their distinctive dark, wavy hair a relic from their northern Iberian ancestor's centuries before, and the Ordovices, who had left behind their remote hill forts — both journeyed from their craggy lands far to the west. Their guttural language made it hard to understand what they said giving the excuse to avoid the hard looking warriors. The Cornovii from the Midlands that bordered onto both tribes had some skill in the dialect and were able to interpret, but most chose not to do so.

The hill fort-dwelling Durotriges, suspicious and withdrawn, travelled from the West Country. The Dobunni, lead by their newly-installed chief Cullen, arrived as late as possible for the ceremony, still reeling from their defeat. They crept around

Camulodunon in discrete groups, like recently chastised children.

The Iceni and the Corieltauvi, both agricultural societies from the north of Catuvellauni lands, were also present. The Iceni queen, Boudica, looked cold and haughty on the arm of her older husband, Prasutagus. They mixed easily with their far-flung neighbours, the Brigantes and the Parisi. Cartimandua, the Brigantian queen, held sway over the tribe, not her husband, Venutius, who followed everywhere in her wake, looking none too pleased.

Even the druids, their dislike of Cunobelin's stance towards Rome temporarily put to one side, made the punishing journey from their island in the west, Mona, travelling even further than the Silures and Ordovices.

Only a few tribes, those in the farthest reaches of the country, were unrepresented. No word had been received from the introverted Dumnonii, an isolated and wild tribe from the south-west extremities, and the Demetae. None of the feral tribes from the northern wilderness had attended either — whether because of a lack of interest, trust or knowledge, no one knew.

On reaching the immense burial mound the bearers hefted the litter off their shoulders to carry it at waist height. Caradoc needed to duck to enter the low opening that led into the barrow chamber. The air inside was musty, the dank smell of earth still present despite the burning of sweet-smelling woods and herbs. It was a not-so-subtle message from the gods that the soil would hold Cunobelin now.

The old king was gently, reverently shifted from the litter into the centre of the chamber which, although about twenty-five feet square, was crowded, leaving little room for the dignitaries to stand and they shuffled to find a space. Caradoc and Togodumnus stepped away from the litter whilst Kynthelig moved to stand above Cunobelin's head. He looked over his body and across the chamber. Fionn squeezed through to stand next to Etain. Hidden by the folds of her robe she sought out his hand and squeezed it, bringing a grateful smile to Fionn's face.

Over the previous days slaves had carried goods and materials that reflected Cunobelin's vast wealth into the compartment. The Catuvellauni battle flag was fixed to the wall. Cunobelin's shield was propped up against his bed, within easy reach should it be needed. A medallion hung about his neck, glinting in the lamplight. A multitude of amphorae holding wine (which Epaticcus would have denounced as an utter waste), food and grain were stacked neatly around the walls.

Piles of coins, silver, gold and bronze, were lined up on a hammered bronze table. There were metal goblets, statues, effigies, exquisite imported pottery, a chest full of clothes and bronze bowls. A whole host of honours obtained in battle and the heads of many enemies were arrayed to stare in supplication at Cunobelin's body. The chief's beloved hound, killed the day before, lay curled at his feet beneath the litter.

Kynthelig lead a prayer to the god Cernunnos, requesting safe carriage of Cunobelin's soul to be reborn into the next life. Then wine was handed around to each attendant and drunk in memory of the deceased king. The goblets were swapped for a grave good — a statue, a bowl, a spear — one for each person in the chamber. One by one the items were broken and dropped to the floor as the attendants said a farewell to Cunobelin and departed.

Caradoc was the last to leave, nodding to thank Fionn for the comforting pat on his shoulder. He turned and took one final look at his father's body and the grand array in his chamber before stepping back outside.

As the chamber was sealed the wind dropped and the bleak winter sun shone down, as if Cunobelin's soul had been borne to its destination and the weather could rest. Caradoc had never known the like of it. It was a sad time. But it was also a new beginning. He knew many were worried by the change; Cunobelin had brought a great prosperity and political stability to the kingdom, and that could all be undone in a heartbeat. Some saw it as a breath of fresh air and others as an opportunity to be embraced wholeheartedly.

He turned away from the barrow and, with the thousands of others, left Cunobelin to his rest. He wondered which of the choices about the future were his to make.

The next day the congregation gathered again, this time centred on the plain woodcut platform constructed solely for this occasion. The sacred location on the outskirts of Camulodunon sat on the apex of a gentle slope and had been used for centuries to witness ascension.

Off the platform to one side stood a cauldron atop a fire. Inside it water boiled, steam curling off its bubbling surface. A path to the dais had been marked out by equally-spaced, simple wooden poles. A fine, misty rain had started an hour ago and the throng was getting steadily wetter. But no one left.

Family members, the prominent and powerful were arrayed closest to the platform. Then came the less important people in the subsequent rows, the order a precisely controlled demonstration of favour and status, right to the back where the general public stood with, at best, a dim view of proceedings.

Fionn stood with Caradoc and his perennially happy wife Ula and their three children. The middle child, Euergen was a twelve-year-old tomboy, her blonde hair always snagged and dirty, even today when it had been brushed especially. Caradoc shook his head at the smudge of dirt on her face.

He had laughed years ago when Kynthelig told him she would be a very important religious figure in later life, as would the rest of his offspring. But the old druid was deadly serious and made

Caradoc swear to protect them (an easy task anyway, they were his children), and only then did Kynthelig calm down.

Euergen jiggled her leg, eager for this to be over so she could run and play with her new friends. That there had not been a crowning for thirty-two years meant nothing to her. She pulled a face at a skinny boy in the crowd who returned the gesture and looked away as Euergen sniggered.

"You are going to get yourself into trouble. Again," Brennon warned in a whisper. "Etain looks like a problem."

Fionn kept his eyes on Etain, who finally relented and smiled slyly at him before glancing away, deliberately fixing her attention on a handsome warrior.

"I know," Fionn grinned. "It is fantastic."

"Do not expect me to help you out of it."

"You will."

Brennon shook his head in exasperation. "When it comes to women, you never listen to me."

"She is like a wild horse waiting to be tamed."

"Even wild horses eventually turn into old nags," Brennon said sagely.

"Do you have a single romantic bone in your body?"

Brennon snorted.

Weland, as if party to the hushed conversation, gave Fionn a blank, unimpressed stare, which was returned in equal measure. To Weland's right Bearach looked utterly bored with it all and stared at the ground as if he would prefer to be anywhere else but here.

Verica tapped his foot nervously, loath to be without the protection of his comitatus but unable to buck the positioning. Bringing his wife was out of the question, so he stood alone and aloof. The part of him that liked to preen was pleased to have been invited but the other part of him, the seditious side, was disappointed not to have been snubbed, seeing it as an opportunity for a future revenge missed.

Since Caradoc had replaced Epaticcus in Calleva, tension on their territorial borders noticeably relaxed. Verica was unsure what to make of this and the ambiguity made him nervous. At least Epaticcus had been utterly transparent in that respect, he mused.

The chatter ceased at the whinny of a horse. Kynthelig led a stallion, so white it seemed to glow, down the narrow corridor followed by two massive warriors, stripped to the waist.

The horse's skin shone with the lustre of a beast in its prime. It was a champion horse, the best in the land, and it showed in its superb musculature, which rippled and flowed as it walked majestically to the pinnacle.

Kynthelig stepped onto the dais and then men and horse, its hooves beating a loud tattoo on the wood, turned to face the way they had approached. The horse tossed its mane and bared its teeth. Kynthelig moved away slightly, wary of another bite.

The man who was to be crowned walked towards the dais. Heads turned again to watch his progress. People whispered, fingers pointed. The grass was wet and soft underfoot as he made his way up the slope. When he reached the platform he stepped onto it, the dry wood rough and hard to the touch.

Togodumnus, shrouded in a fine cloak, stood elevated above his people, surveying them. He turned full circle, seeing the smiling faces of his family, friends and subjects. But Togodumnus had no wife or offspring to witness his achievement. b

Both were dead, cruelly lost three years ago during childbirth, and for a moment the unwanted recollection stole the rare half smile from his face.

Kynthelig walked to the edge of the platform and raised his arms.

"The kingdom of the Catuvellauni is without a King!" he shouted, his voice echoing. "The line must continue lest we fall into disrepair. I stand before you to proffer a new ruler of this realm!"

The druid bowed to Togodumnus as the multitude bayed their acceptance. Kynthelig brought a razor sharp knife out of the folds of his robe and raised it into the air.

"The Goddess Epona! With the blood of your noblest subject I ask you to bless the ascension of our King, Togodumnus."

Kynthelig, with a quick movement to his right, slashed at the stallion's throat, nicking an artery. The horse whinnied keenly at the unexpected incision. Blood spurted in a bright arc from the wound, painting Togodumnus' white cloak with a livid red gash. Kynthelig stepped back as the warriors fought to hold the thrashing mare, as her life pumped from her neck. She tired quickly as the blood pooled on the platform beneath her hooves. As the horse's brain and organs became starved of sustenance the thrashing lessened. Her head bowed and then she dropped to her knees, first her front legs, then her rear before rolling onto her side, panting. Still the blood pumped; there seemed no end to it.

The warriors took up an axe each and hacked the dying horse to pieces with brief but powerful swings with a sound like chopping rotten, wet wood. Quickly the animal was converted into an unrecognisable pile of bloody lumps. These were gathered up by slaves, the gore soaking into their clothes, and thrown into the cauldron, each portion splashing water from the pot as it hit the surface. The boiling water immediately went from clear to a deep pink. The meat was allowed to briefly cook before it was scooped out and placed steaming onto large platters. The slaves threw water onto the fire and with a hiss the flames spluttered and died.

Two slaves struggled to carry a heavy bath up the hill between them. Finally, hot and sweating despite the cool rain, they reached the platform. After the briefest of respites they levered the bath up onto the dais. Using cloths to protect their hands they grasped handles on the side of the cauldron, lifted it and tipped the rapidly cooling water into the tub.

"Step forward, lord," Kynthelig motioned to Togodumnus, the water deemed bearable after he had dipped his fingers into the liquid.

Though the throng watched impassively a barely discernible vibration passed through those assembled as Togodumnus slipped off his cloak and stepped into the water, clothed only in the torc that was about his neck. He kept his face impassive as he sank into the water, although he wanted to wince at the heat that stung his skin, turning it red on contact.

"By consuming the animal that is all powerful, so our king gains strength from it!" Kynthelig intoned.

A slave stepped forward and offered a platter of the horsemeat to Togodumnus. "My King," he said and bowed deeply, keeping his eyes firmly on the bloodstained wood of the platform beneath his feet.

Togodumnus selected the uppermost segment of the white meat and bit into it, grease smearing around his mouth.

"Let its strength be given to all!" Kynthelig shouted, and at his signal a band of slaves moved among the honoured and powerful observers, who each took a chunk themselves until none remained.

"The King drinks of the horse's blood, Epona's child, and by doing so gains its wisdom, speed and grace!" Kynthelig said once the entire mare had been consumed.

Togodumnus dipped his face into the bath and sucked the bloody liquid into his mouth. He swallowed some of the unpleasant brackish water, which had a salty, iron tang to it.

Horse and king were now one.

Caradoc stepped onto the platform. He experienced a brief twinge of jealousy, thinking that but for the accident of birth he would be king and not his brother. But he squashed the emotion as soon as it appeared; his duty was to his brother and none should be happier for him.

"My King," Caradoc said as he knelt. He took Togodumnus's outstretched hand and pressed it against his forehead. "With my life, I defend yours. My possessions are your possessions. My sword arm is yours to direct and my horses yours to command."

Ula and the children followed suit, then Fionn as immediate family. One by one each of the nobles, whether they had sworn fealty to Cunobelin or not, took the proffered hand, touched it to their forehead, swore an oath to their new ruler or peer and stepped down to let another take their place.

When it was Verica's turn he stepped onto the platform. After a brief hesitation he took Togodumnus's hand but spoke in a mumble that could not be heard beyond the dais. Caradoc looked at Verica with interest as he retreated. It was more than he had expected from their old enemy.

At last, when all oaths, promises and vows had been sworn, Togodumnus stepped out of the bath, his skin shadowed with the blood of the mare. The water had gone cold long ago and he tried hard not to shiver in the wintry air. But he stood tall as Kynthelig wrapped his cloak about him and fixed it in place with a fine gold brooch.

Togodumnus knelt, one knee on the floor. He bowed his head and the druid placed a narrow circlet of gold about his head. After a moment Togodumnus got to his feet again.

"Behold your King!" Kynthelig pronounced to a roar from the masses.

Togodumnus arose and listened impassively to the din. He was King of the Catuvellauni.

Kynthelig undressed slowly. He was bone-tired, his body ached and he desperately needed some long-awaited sleep. He deserved it like no other. However at the same time the druid felt an unstoppable surge of feelings — light-headedness, elation, ecstasy — all competing and coursing through his core.

Almost everything he had striven for over recent years had come to fruition. Adminius the lover of Rome driven out. Cunobelin replaced by a king with a stronger antipathy towards the Romans that could be exploited, with another waiting in the wings should the worst happen. The Dobunni cowed.

Verica was old, weak and friendless. His succour from Rome was largely an illusion these days, held up for all to see but without substance or presence. The old man was isolated and all but vanished from these shores. His ejection was just a matter of time, Kynthelig knew, the last piece of the puzzle ready to be fitted into place.

Once Verica was gone — or, better still, in the earth rotting — and the remaining Atrebates were finally absorbed into the kingdom the job would be complete. The last stronghold of the druids would be secured.

Forever.

Kynthelig slid into his bed and allowed himself to relax. The risks he had taken had been worth it in the end. The most hazardous, deceiving the Gaulish trader Barick, had brought Kynthelig dangerously close to the edge. When Caradoc had dragged the man into Cunobelin's roundhouse Kynthelig almost had a heart attack in fear of being recognised. But, thankfully, he got away with it.

The druid fell into a deep and peaceful sleep, free of the intruding nightmares of his youth. It was the best sleep he'd had for a long, long time.

# VIII

**August AD 42**

"Why did you return without an answer?" Verica ranted.

"Togodumnus refused to see me! What could I do?" The diminutive man cowered, his face bloodless with fear.

"Then you should have stayed until you were granted an audience, fool!"

"But I had been there three days already. I thought..."

"You thought? I did not send you there to think but to talk!" Verica lunged at his envoy and slapped him in the face, sending the far smaller man spinning to the floor. "Get out of my sight!"

The envoy picked himself up. He held a hand to his stinging cheek, but felt relief. He had been lucky, compared to some. He quickly backed out of the room in case Verica changed his mind.

Verica paced back and forth, as if he was trying to wear a rut in the floor. He paused and tugged absently at his grey beard. Even at the best of times Verica was an angry and bitter man but for weeks he had terrorised the Atrebatean court with his outbursts, which grew in intensity and vitriol with each day and the return of each snubbed envoy. Those courtiers who could stayed out of Verica's way and sent others less fortunate to do their bidding. Where Verica could not be avoided his attendants were as obsequious as possible in his presence.

"Was that really necessary?" Oifa asked bitterly.

Verica stared at his wife, as if only just realising she was in the room. She was much younger than him, with flaxen hair and cornflower-blue eyes that had enchanted him when they first met. However, far more important to Verica was the influence that came from marrying Eisu's daughter. That was until the Catuvellauni had killed the Dobunni chief. Now Verica struggled to see what use the frosty woman was. She had not even been able to give him children — his basic right and the sole purpose of a wife. Now he knew why Eisu had been unable to marry her off. Verica had thought she was being saved to achieve the optimum political benefit. Clearly he had been mistaken.

"What did you say?" Verica asked, delighted to be given another chance to lash out.

He had raged at many an unfortunate slave or subject of late;

Verica was still a powerful man despite letting himself go years ago. However no one, and especially not Oifa, could mention his failing physique and expanding waistline without feeling Verica's wrath.

"Nothing," Oifa said, before adding a reluctant "My lord."

"I thought so," Verica spat, pleased to see his wife with her head bowed.

He resumed his pacing , banishing Oifa from his thoughts. Surprisingly, he had liked the respite in hostilities after Epaticcus's death. Verica enjoyed a renaissance with Caradoc, his new neighbour, and with time on his hands had unexpectedly found pleasure in things other than constantly plotting moves against Epaticcus.

He had begun to think that perhaps his struggle against Cunobelin and his family had gone on for far too long and that it was time to bury it. Some welcome happiness and humour returned to the Atrebatean court after an absence of many years. Verica even started to enjoy Oifa's company, despite her barren womb, and she blossomed as a result of the attention.

But then Cunobelin died and Togodumnus ascended to the throne. Relationships with the Catuvellauni cooled significantly, to a level even frostier than that between him and Epaticcus. Verica was worried, very worried. In hindsight he wondered whether his judgement had been wildly off the mark again. Maybe it was no renaissance but simply a lull during which the brothers had dealt with other priorities.

So, in desperation to learn the truth, Verica sent a representative to Togodumnus. But the man had returned with a vague and meaningless response. So he continued to probe, sending envoy after envoy, initially to Caradoc in Calleva, as Verica assumed there would be a better reception here, and then again to Togodumnus when the approaches to Caradoc failed.

But, just like the first, every envoy returned to Seolesiae after suffering a three-day wait, with the barest of platitudes. And now this latest — a summary dismissal without the merest sniff of an audience. Not even a lame excuse to justify it. It was another step in the wrong direction.

"Rome," Verica mumbled to himself as the thought occurred to him.

"Pardon?" Oifa asked, looking up from her weaving.

"Nothing!" Verica snapped, embarrassed at being caught thinking out loud.

Oifa looked back to her work again and tried to make herself invisible.

Rome was a good idea, Verica thought. If those within his homeland could not or would not help, perhaps others would be willing. Having visited Rome on several occasions Verica had known Caligula well enough, but now the mad emperor was dead, murdered by his own men last year. His tenuous grip on reality and insane actions finally became too much even for his people to bear.

Caligula's replacement was therefore a completely unknown quantity. Verica understood his name was Claudius. It was said that the new emperor was indecisive, weak and sickly. Mention had also been made, albeit a whisper, that Claudius was somewhat deranged and merely a convenient figurehead for the real but shadowy wielders of power. But Verica was secure in the knowledge that being a friend of Rome meant something, whether a lunatic or a hypochondriac was on the throne. Had Verica not sent his own son to Rome for an education? That in itself must count for something.

He nodded to himself, his mind made up.

He would send an envoy to Rome. There was plenty to tell them and maybe a favour to ask. All Verica needed to know now was the price he would have to pay for their help.

# IX

**September AD 42**

The rider bent low over his horse as another arrow whistled past his ear. His pursuers were falling behind and the accuracy of their arrows was waning. They were good, but so was he, and he knew the landscape much better. He ignored the pain from the shaft that was buried in his shoulder. The pounding of the horse's hooves over the rough terrain constantly worked the wood in the wound, kneading the raw flesh.

But he must get back to Seolesiae — the others needed to be warned. He kicked the horse's haunches again. An enemy had broken through and were not far behind.

"Raze it to the ground!" Brennon shouted.

The warrior band he had led into Seolesiae charged through the streets, casting burning brands onto the thatched roofs, tinder-dry after a distinct lack of rain for two weeks and the hot sun that had beaten down on them. The flames immediately caught and within a few minutes a multitude of roundhouses, in a random pattern, were ablaze. The conflagration ripped through the dwellings from the top down, turning them into raging bonfires. Bright sparks rose into the half-light of the dawn, its first fingers just about to lift over the horizon.

The residents of Verica's capital were caught completely unawares and spilled out of the buildings to escape the inferno, only to be met by the Catuvellauni warriors, their weapons free to cut and slash at anyone that opposed them, and many that did not. Half-dressed people ran left and right, screaming. Against the backdrop of flames women gathered children, animals were ignored and ran free, adding to the chaos and clamour. The Catuvellauni riders coursed through the crowd, cutting, slashing and stabbing, like wolves among livestock, unsure which choice morsel to snap at next. A lucky few, not caught up in the panic and on the outskirts, escaped into the surrounding countryside.

"Leave them, Nemausus," orderedBrennon, putting out a restraining hand, his fingers pressing hard to feel bone beneath the flesh. "There will be time to go after them later. Stick to the task at hand."

Nemausus nodded. "As you command," he said sarcastically, irritated at losing the opportunity for easy pickings. In the dark of the open spaces there would have been no one to witness his actions. With a scowl he turned back to the fray and took his anger out on a cowering old man who screamed as the warrior with the black teeth advanced.

Brennon raised his axe and touched the blade, asking for a blessing from Esus. He was ready to dirty it with Atrebatean blood. There would be time enough later to loot and take slaves. Now it was about noise, chaos and destruction.

"For Caradoc!" Brennon yelled as he spurred his horse towards a group of warriors hastily arranging themselves in defence.

As Atrebatean warriors sprinted towards the centre of the battle a smaller group rode in from the east, unseen and ignored in all the disorder.

A broad river separated the promontory of Seolesiae from the mainland. A series of hills to the north of the stronghold had been fortified with three separate sets of ditches and dykes that Verica thought strong enough. He had been wrong.

The Catuvellauni quickly overran the defences, and last of all the guards that controlled the river crossing point, leaving the town open to attack. A contingent, on horseback for speed, raced towards Seolesiae before word reached the town of the defences falling.

Caradoc paused for a moment to take in his surroundings. He did not know Seolesiae well. For a few bronze coins a smelly trader had described the town from the harbour upwards, but it was scant information at best, particularly regarding the periphery. There was only one road into the town. Then, once habitation was reached, it radiated outwards into a series of tracks, like the spokes of a wheel, across the settlement which was smeared along the shoreline. It was the central compound they wanted, near the harbour.

"Over there, I think," Fionn pointed to their left.

"Remember, we stick together. We kill anyone who gets in our way. All I want is Verica. When we find him we take him alive at any cost," said Caradoc.

"Hold them back, whatever the cost!" Verica ordered the commander of his guards desperately. The white-faced warrior bowed and turned away, sword in his hand, shouting for his men.

Verica stooped down. "You did well, thank you."

The wounded messenger sat slumped against the wall smiled, his life leaking out of the ragged wound at his shoulder. Verica clasped the man's hand and then stood. He turned to his aides, the dying messenger's sacrifice already forgotten.

"To the boat," Verica ordered. "Quickly."

Caradoc's group of riders pressed into the town, the tang of sea air drawing them on. The light was spreading, revealing more of their surroundings. Weapons drawn, the warriors rode carefully along narrow, weaving streets where the roundhouses were packed well together. Fionn wrinkled his nose in distaste at the strong smell of smoked fish which issued from one building.

The outer town was separated from the harbour and compound by a wall and ditch. The entrance was unguarded and the group warily entered.

"I do not like this. It is too quiet," Fionn whispered.

Suddenly, as if on a signal, Atrebatean warriors ran screaming towards Caradoc and his men. They fought hard and progress towards the harbour was slow and bloody. Caradoc hacked about him as he fought three guards who pressed in from all sides. He deflected a sword strike off his shield and struck back, catching the man in the shoulder. The commander screamed as the sword cut flesh and shattered bone.

Fionn lunged upwards and caught another in the stomach. He gurgled and fell backwards. The third guard ran. The Catuvellauni kept pressing forward. Each inch had to be gained at a price. But then the Atrebateans broke, their taste for the fight gone with their leader dead and knowing Verica had already fled. They melted away, unwilling to pay any more than they already had.

Within minutes of making the decision Verica was stepping aboard the rocking boat with his closest aides and three of his best warriors. Another five had been left on the harbour and were smashing holes in the bottom of every ship bobbing on the surf or drawn up high on the sand.

The boat pushed off, fighting against the tide. The gap between it and the shore opened agonisingly slowly. There had been no time to find Oifa, and for a second Verica wondered what had become of her. He was sure it would be unpleasant. Numbly he stared back towards Seolesiae and his heart sank as his capital burned fiercely. The sound of his people screaming carried clearly to him. He tried to close his mind to it but even with his fingers in his ears the pain and horror cut through.

With sword arms aching, bruised and cut from the fighting, Caradoc's men reached the harbour, having slashed their way past the five strong rearguard who, although brave to a man, lay dead and open-mouthed in the shadows. Fionn pointed out to sea, to where a small boat was being rowed away.

"Look for another vessel! We cannot lose him!" Caradoc ordered, his face contorted.

Fionn checked one and then another. "They are all holed. We would sink before we got ten yards."

Caradoc swore and threw down his bloody sword in frustration. Verica had escaped.

When only yards out to sea Verica saw Caradoc and his men sweep down into the harbour and engage with his men that remained along the stone and wooden walls that reached out into the lapping waves. He was glad he had left immediately. Any delay in fleeing would have meant his death, he knew for sure.

He collapsed onto a seat, numb. Around him men strained at the oars. Later — he did not know how much later as the crossing had been a blur — the ship bounced as it rode up a beach. Verica, still lightheaded, stepped ashore in Roman territory, a refugee from his own lands.

# X

The slim, balding man closed the door to Claudius's bedroom and shooed away the supplicants that crowded around, ever eager to serve.

"The emperor is incapacitated from another bout of stomach pains and does not wish to be disturbed," Narcissus said primly. Suitably dismissed, the attendants, hangers-on and opportunists drifted away to other parts of the palace, disappointment etched on their faces. But they knew there would be other days.

Narcissus sighed. He gathered himself for a moment, then walked into his office and closed the doors gently behind him with a soft click. He was a man who made little fuss or noise and lived in the same fashion. The room was simply furnished, with little of the finery that pervaded the rest of the palace. It was usually dominated by a desk, its ever-present piles of communications neatly stacked and ordered, writing implements and a lamp always lit whatever the time of day. Narcissus liked to keep the drapes drawn over the towering windows — they let in far too much light for him.

Narcissus was grandly titled the De Facto Chamberlain to the Court. In short, this meant he was Claudius's secretary, but this simple description belied the tremendous influence the freedman wielded. Each and every document that needed the emperor's attention, and many that did not, passed through Narcissus's hands. He selected those that Claudius needed to see and action, often with a word of advice on how they should be handled.

Claudius trusted Narcissus implicitly, even if few in the Roman court felt the same way, and allowed his secretary to make a multitude of decisions when he was absent from illness, which was often. Narcissus, of course, issued every decree in the emperor's name.

Such was the snobbery regarding ancestry in Rome that his upbringing as a slave would never be forgotten. But, ironically, Narcissus had become richer and more powerful than many of those that looked down their noses at him. Both, however, were facts he preferred to make little of publicly. Narcissus could exercise a long reach if he wanted to and he had to be carefully negotiated by suitors. Sometimes he could be persuaded to make certain documents rise to the top of the pile and others fall to the bottom, all as a result of generous donatives from interested parties.

But these days Narcissus faced a fresh challenge, so the desk was moved to one side and pressed up against a wall, still with the cascade of papers upon it. A large table had taken its place and become the central focus in the room. His new work surface was still covered with documents, but of a different kind — maps, reports and plans, military rather than mundane, strategic rather than administrative.

"Is the emperor going to join us?" asked a man who leant over the table, apparently absorbed by its contents. His tone was casual.

He held a very full glass of wine in his hand. A few weeks ago Narcissus would have panicked, convinced that some of the contents would spill and make the ink run on the carefully-prepared papers. However, he now knew that Adminius had a knack (although the Briton would doubtless refer to it as a talent) for never spilling a drop of alcohol.

Where Narcissus was slim, Adminius was fat, so much so that his extra weight hung off him in folds. Life in Rome had been good to Adminius, too good. He adjusted his toga and made a mental note to replace it, and to have the slave whipped as it seemed to have shrunk again when washed.

"He apologises and asks us to continue without him," Narcissus said, removing the glass from Adminius's hand and receiving a hard look as a result. "As I have said before, he is confident in our abilities."

Adminius smiled at the compliment and looked forward to the day he would finally meet the most powerful man in the world.

"News has reached me," Narcissus continued, "that Verica is being brought to Rome as we speak."

"Why, what has happened?" Adminius retrieved his wine from where Narcissus had left it only moments before, ignoring the secretary's glare. He took a quick sip and savoured the fruity flavours. The Romans made excellent wine, he thought, little knowing it was imported.

"Your brothers sacked his capital. Doubtless they would have killed Verica had he been captured."

Adminius snorted. "I told you! How many times have I said that they cannot be trusted. With my stupid father dead they will be planning to spread their control ever wider. Believe me, this is just the beginning."

"That is why we plan, Adminius," Narcissus said quietly, as if admonishing a forgetful child. "However, the stakes have now been increased so we must bring our considerations to Claudius's attention. Your brothers have become a problem — we appear to have a serious aggressor on our borders."

Narcissus began to pace the room as he spoke, his usual cool demeanour temporarily punctured.

"In the past nothing pleased Rome more than the winning of new lands and riches. Conquest made heroes of the victors. But Tiberius stopped the expansion of the empire years ago. Claudius, however, desperately needs a political success. He is unknown to his people and has enemies ready to spring on his every weakness, which at the moment are many. Surviving Roman politics is a dangerous balancing act. One slip in the wrong direction can send you tumbling into oblivion."

Adminius wondered whose survival Narcissus was most concerned about. More than likely Narcissus's, rather than his own.

"So you need a justification," Adminius said.

"Well said," Narcissus agreed. Adminius raised his goblet in a salute to himself and gulped some wine.

"If we are not careful Britain could become a garnering place for dissidents and enemies of Rome. So, we have a serious threat right on our borders, which is always a stimulus to the Senate, who witter and worry about their own safety like old women. Also, Britain is rich in mineral resources and has a prosperous agricultural economy. There is wealth to be had there, a significant incentive to our soldiers."

"It sounds like you have thought this through."

"I have had little sleep recently," Narcissus admitted ruefully.

Adminius sniggered to himself. He hadn't either, but for very different reasons.

"We have several choices," said Narcissus. He raised his fist and counted the options on his manicured fingers, forcing Adminius to drag his attention back to the secretary. "One, we could do nothing. Your brothers may simply consume themselves pursuing expansion across their own country and never think about crossing into Roman territory."

Adminius laughed at the suggestion, taking another large swallow of wine. "Or, equally, they may not." He wiped his mouth with the back of his hand but several drops marred the white of his toga. "They hate Rome and everything about it. Whether now or later, one day they will think outside British borders."

Narcissus ignored the vitriolic interruption and pressed on. "Two, we could reinforce the coastal positions facing the Gallic Straits with additional legions and so keep the Britons hemmed in. But this will use up a lot of resources we do not have the luxury of wasting.

"Three, we invade, which would use a lot less manpower than bottling your brothers up. Caesar invaded with five legions plus some cavalry and managed to subdue the Britons. This feels like the best option." Having had extensive analysis carried out, Narcissus already knew this to be the case.

Narcissus stopped his pacing. "But before we go to Claudius we need to identify someone to lead this venture, someone credible who the Senate will believe is capable. Someone who has held a Praetorian rank and so has already been granted the right to command," He paused for a moment, apparently thinking, but in truth he had identified the right general days ago.

"Plautius is in Pannonia," he said slowly. "We have a problem there that I think we can use. The last serious opposition was seen off years ago and the area is relatively calm so the legions have little to do but maintain their barracks. A bored legion can be trouble and is always a worry for the Senate. Yes, that should be easy to play on."

"Who is this...Plautius?" Adminius asked.

Narcissus looked irritated at the interruption to his thought process. "A distant relative by marriage to the emperor," he answered sharply. "That in itself could prove useful. He's clever and resourceful. He was made a legate at the age of twenty-four, which is highly unusual."

Adminius shrugged, taking Narcissus's word for it. He had little knowledge of Rome's complicated process of promotion. Besides, it was of little consequence who led the invasion, as far as he was concerned, so long as it happened. He looked around the room for more wine and was disappointed not to see any. He half-considered asking Narcissus to call a slave then thought better of it.

"Yes, Plautius is our man. I will see to it that he is ordered to Rome immediately," Narcissus decided.

Narcissus stalked across the room to his familiar desk, pulled the chair from beneath it and sat down. He dipped his quill pen in ink and started writing orders on parchment paper for Claudius to sign in the morning.

Adminius put his goblet down. He could hear the scratch of pen on paper as Narcissus wrote, then a brief pause as he dipped it in ink and started writing again. He glanced at the table and pulled a map of southeast Britain towards him. The Roman plans were certainly of benefit to him, but they were only in partial alignment with his own.

Had Narcissus chosen then to look over his shoulder he would have seen just a bored, blank look on Adminius' face. But the ordinary expression masked a furiously working mind.

# XI

**January AD 43**

The night was pitch black, so completely free of light that it was difficult to see his hand when he held it in front of his face. The moon was out but it and the stars were hidden behind a dense bank of cloud.

The night was bitterly cold. He pulled his cloak tighter as he waited, first tugging the hem free of a snag on which it had caught, some unidentifiable bush loaded with spikes. Normally an escort of guards accompanied him everywhere so the novelty of getting here alone was intriguing, like a long-forgotten skill buried somewhere in the past that had to be resurrected. But once he was waiting here in the biting wind the freshness of being on his own was quickly carried away on the breeze. He was getting bored and his inability to see far, to be unable to plan ahead for any eventuality, was unnerving. It would not be something he would repeat in a hurry, he decided, if ever.

He froze at the prick of a knife at his throat, the cold touch of the metal unmistakable on the artery where a simple nick would mean an unstoppable flow of blood and certain death. He knew that before his hand could travel even the short distance to his weapon the knife would cut. It's what he would have done were roles reversed.

Suddenly the knife was gone and he was pushed hard by a hand in the middle of his back. He went to ground and rolled, then stood upright and ready with sword in hand. Briefly the cloud rolled back from the moon and revealed his attacker. He was a giant of a warrior, his hands clasped on top of his thighs as he bent over double, barely able to contain his laughter. He wheezed as he tried to suck air into his lungs.

The man sheathed his sword, walked over to the still-laughing warrior and punched him hard in the face. It felt like hitting a piece of old, gnarled wood and had about as much effect, other than generating a sharp shooting pain in his wrist and hand.

The big man was grinning. He straightened, wiping away a line of blood that ran from his split lip. "I will let you have that one," he said. "I suppose I deserved it."

Both laughing, they embraced warmly.

"You are getting old," said the giant. "I was not particularly quiet yet I was able to get right up to you. You went as stiff as a post when the knife touched you — I thought you had pissed yourself. It was difficult not to laugh in your ear and spoil the joke."

"Perhaps I am getting old," he admitted. "By rights I should have been dead years ago. It has been a long time, Ahearn."

Ahearn nodded in agreement. "And not always fun. What is life without fun? Living with foreigners and their dirty ways, laughing at their stupid jokes spoken in an incomprehensible language — it is hard not to spit in their faces."

"How is the old woman?"

"He has loved every minute of it. He is permanently pampered by servants, who appear to provide for his slightest whim. He eats the best food, drinks the best wine and visits the best whores in the city. He claims to count the emperor as a personal friend but somehow I doubt that when he visits the palace he spends any time with Claudius at all. His biggest achievement is his waistline, which increases in girth every day. He can hardly see his feet now, although he claims to be as fit as ever."

"Are they still coming?" the other asked, comparatively uninterested in Adminius and his diet.

"Yes, and soon. Plans have been drawn up and then torn up on many occasions but finally there is one that seems to satisfy them." Ahearn shook his head, "The manpower taken to design this is unbelievable. If you and I had half their resources at our command we could rule all of Britain."

"Tell me about the arrangements. I want to know how I can help."

"Is that why you asked to see me?"

"Yes, old friend. I know I can trust you."

"What has changed your mind? So many times their people have been over and on each occasion you sent them back."

"I have no love for Adminius, Belanos knows, but my voice carries little weight in the new order of things."

"Has that not always been so?"

"It has worsened. At least Cunobelin saw the strategic benefit of my tribe but now the brothers do not care. They think of themselves and expansion again, of accumulating more wealth for a land already over fattened and greedy. It is time to redress the balance, to regain the status my tribe deserves, that it lost long ago. I have no future under the brothers, what you offer seems much more."

"The Romans are harsh masters."

"It cannot be worse than it is now."

"Do you not see the irony in this, old friend?"

"What do you mean?"

"You look to the Romans to restore the tribe's position when it was they that took it away."

"No, that was Cassivellaunus!" the man remonstrated, then paused for a moment, casting his mind back. He remembered the stories his forefathers had told, passed from generation to generation, the hurt never quite buried.

"The deal he struck with the Romans destroyed my tribe, forced its subjugation. Now his ancestors look to finish the job. That is why I do this — not for Adminius, or for you or for the Romans, but for my people!"

"Your reasons are your own. All I care is that you help. Your involvement is key and Adminius will not forget that. If all goes to plan he will be very generous to those that aid him."

"I know and that is what I count on. The risk is huge. If I were to be found out..." he shuddered at the thought.

"But the reward is far greater."

After a pause the other said, "Tell me what I am to do."

Ahearn spoke without break. In the growing light his friend could see the livid birthmark appear, seeming to glow the same bright colour as the emerging dawn. When business was concluded and agreements sworn the two of them parted with a clasp of hand on opposing shoulder. They rode away separately without a backward glance, both deep in thought about the future and the roles they were to play.

# XII

**April AD 43**

Barick swore as a wave burst over his small vessel, flinging icicles of sharp, cold spray over the bow of the ship and into his face yet again. He blinked the salty water out of his eyes, unwilling to remove even one hand from the tiller for the merest of moments. He was wet and cold but at least he was too numb to feel the stinging spume any more.

His stomach lurched as the ship pitched over the white-flecked peak of a wave, then dipped into the trough before climbing the other side to repeat the tiring process all over again. Even though the design of his ship, flat-bottomed and wide in the beam, had been adapted over many years by trial and sometimes serious error to suit to the environment, Barick needed to battle to keep it in a straight line. Again and again the tiller bucked in his hands as successive waves pounded the vessel as if the sea were eager to claim him.

"Good girl," Barick commended his ship, Raven.

He knew these waters well. They could vary from flat calm one moment to vicious the next. The tides were strong, able to sweep the unwary well beyond their destination, unstoppably. Fog seemed to roll in at the most inconvenient time, masking the land and any reference points. On many occasions Barick had been forced to drop anchor and wait for the miasma to clear. So he did not need the heavy feeling in his gut to tell him that this was just the beginning of what could turn out to be very, very bad weather indeed. He wanted to find land, and quickly.

Barick had the apparent ability to step into danger and difficulty with monotonous regularity. However, the most important people in his life seemed to appreciate the rewards this brought. His wife had plenty of money to spend and at last a status she felt she deserved. And the men that made up his crew were the reckless ones that enjoyed the tension and stress Barick's decisions put them into. Those of more tender temperament left the ship at their earliest opportunity. But this did not cause Barick a problem as there always seemed to be willing replacements. Yet at this instant he was regretting that his desire for profit and advancement had blinded him to risk yet again. The gods howled their agreement in the wind and Barick swore at them.

The fine Roman goods Barick had received in payment for this latest escapade were being bounced around unceremoniously in the hold and he wondered whether there would be anything left to trade even if he did get out of this bind.

Strangely, it was not the weather that troubled Barick but his second cargo - six men going from Gaul, across the Straits and into Britain. Their horses, wide-eyed and increasingly nervous, were tied to rings embedded in the deck of the ship. Barick conceded that at least the crashing waves were washing away the excrement they had ejected in their fear. Fate could be a strange master.

The old man, his hair and beard completely grey, claimed to be their leader. He had been little in evidence during the trip, retiring below decks before they even left the harbour and only making only rare appearances on deck. Barick had barely got to know him. But it was clear he was immensely proud and used to having his commands quickly followed to the letter.

In truth, however, the men seemed to look to another of their party for leadership even when the old man was around. Right now he stood clinging to the mast, peering intently over the high sides of the boat. Barick wondered what he was looking for. He was a giant of a man. His bulk alone would be enough to make anyone think long and hard about crossing him. The two swords strapped across his back, the carved hilts poking above his shoulders, added to the sense of danger. His long hair, tied back to stop it whipping about his face in the wind, framed a face which spoke of a hardness, an ability only to compromise when there was no other option. Barick had unwillingly spent enough time in the giant's presence to sense an ever-present menace just below the surface, tensed and ready to unleash itself at the instant it was needed.

But it was the livid pink birthmark which disfigured half the warrior's face, the skin puckered up as if it were about to burst at any moment, that was the most shocking. When they had first met the sight of the scar had made Barick pause before speaking. The man's eyes searched Barick's face, challenging him to say something. Barick suspected the blemish was more than skin deep and he made sure he was courteous to the giant at all times.

Barick said a prayer to Lugus, the god of trade, for safe delivery from the giant. If he was to die, let it be at the hand of the malevolent sea. But The Shadowy One could be a trickster, existing in the place between light and dark, equally willing to select either good or evil outcomes for the traveller, and it seemed that the god's decision was yet to be made.

Barick could live with this uncertainty. His fortunes had dramatically improved since accepting Lugus into his life and the pendulum of fate had swung the other way for him. To further reinforce his bond with Lugus, Barick had named his ship Raven after the god's own bird. He even had a flag made with the bird stitched into it, which always flew at the top of the mast. Barick figured that Lugus would never sink one of his own. But when Barick raised the flag up the mast for the first time his men crossed themselves and muttered dark comments. It took weeks of constant reassurance that this was Lugus's raven, not Babdah that feeds on the dead.

"Land! Land!" The shout from one of his crew shook Barick from his absorption with the tiller and his god.

The crewman gesticulated wildly ahead, a grin of relief plastered on his face. It was just a dark smudge low on the horizon, difficult to see where the cloud started and it began. But nevertheless it was Britain and Barick yelled for joy.

"More speed, my brave men! More speed!" Barick bellowed over the howling wind.

He was willing to take the additional risk, keen to get the giant and his men off his boat as quickly as possible, even if that meant lost profits as the precious items below smashed in the heavier waters. Some things, even to Barick, were just not worth it.

Barick skirted along the coast looking for the place he had been told to deposit his cargo. The waves were coming at him beam on now and the ship was developing a sickening rolling motion. Then Raven rounded a headland and a gently curved bay appeared. The surf seemed gentler on the shoreline, the sting taken out of the waves. Barick ordered the anchor dropped and the sail furled.

"Why do you not land?" The scarred warrior spoke surprisingly quietly.

"The tide has not yet turned. I do not want to get stuck high and dry ashore," Barick said. "It will not be long, an hour at most." He would have preferred to wait more than an hour but doubted the giant would accept any longer.

"You will land now."

"I have told you, we cannot."

The warrior glared at Barick and moved to draw a sword.

"You and your men are welcome to try and beach the ship," said Barick, his voice firm despite the quiver in his stomach. "But it will be torn apart and the horses will drown, probably some men too. Do you want that?" Barick raised a questioning hand, ready to signal for the crew to raise anchor.

The warrior glared at Barick. He was about to snarl a reply when the old man emerged from below decks. He looked from man to man, sensing the tension between them.

"What is the delay, why have we stopped?"

Barick explained their situation again. "An hour at most, lord," Barick reassured him. "One hour and then we can go ashore."

"Sixty minutes is not long to wait, would you not agree, Ahearn? After the time we have been away a little more hardly matters."

Ahearn turned away and leant on the rail so that the grimace on his face was hidden. For the moment he needed the old man so he swallowed the retort.

Satisfied that, thanks to him, the decision had been made the old man nodded at Barick and returned below to get out of the wind and rain.

It was a nervous hour for Barick. The time it would take for the tide to turn was a rough estimate. He knew he would be close but he hoped his guess was accurate enough for Ahearn. As the minutes crawled by the huge warrior grew more restless and his scar seemed to flush increasingly crimson. In response, Barick's nervousness grew. But at last, just when Barick was getting desperate, the sea began to flow towards the shore. Barick blew a huge sigh in relief then grinned at Ahearn, as if he had never doubted his judgement.

"I told you, one hour!" he said smugly. Ahearn just glowered.

"Take her in," Barick ordered his first mate, who looked mightily relieved himself.

Once the barnacle-covered anchor was hauled up the oarsmen paddled the ship slowly forward, inching towards the shore. A keen-eyed lookout stood in the bow and another atop the mast in an effort to avoid any sandbars or submerged debris, a difficult job given the rain that still beat down making the visibility poor.

Barick had been told that there were no farms nearby and little chance of anyone likely to observe the landing even on the warmest of days. He could not imagine anyone being foolish enough to venture out in weather like this. Nevertheless he had a story ready, just in case.

The old man came above decks and smiled broadly at the sight of land within touching distance. "Now it begins," he whispered exultantly to himself.

"Raise the oars!" Barick shouted as they neared the beach.

Raven nudged up onto the sand which rose gently to meet the marshy land behind. She had to be beached to get the horses off but Barick had a limited window to do so before the tide again turned. A crewman was waiting with a broad gangplank which splashed down into the surf as soon as the ship halted.

"Come on, you lazy bastards!" Barick yelled at his men.

Four men worked as quickly as their numbed fingers would allow untying the horses, who were then led down the ramp and into the surf. Ahearn followed them without a backward glance, the plank bowing under his weight. The old man stood on the gangway for a moment, breathed in the fresh air of home and then stepped ashore.

Verica spread his arms out wide and tilted his face upwards to the sky to let the icy rain fall onto his face and wash away the stench of Rome.

"At last!" he said, and knelt in the sand, letting the fine grains cascade through his fingers.

Then he stood, the wet sand still clinging to his knees, and strode purposefully to his horse. There were some tribes that were unhappy to have the Catuvellauni for neighbours or masters and the old man had an offer for them.

"Raise the ramp!" Barick ordered as soon as the old man stepped off the Raven. "Let us get out of here."

The oarsmen rowed back, difficult work against the tide. Barick's relief at getting rid of Ahearn and his men was palpable. But, for a split second, he wondered if there was an additional profit to be had from this exploit and he leant on the side of the ship, looking to shore. At that moment, Ahearn twisted on his horse to look at Barick, his black eyes boring into the master of Raven as if guessing Barick's half-formed thoughts.

"Maybe not," Barick mumbled to himself.

He waved to Ahearn, who ignored the gesture, kicking his horse and riding after the others.

Barick swallowed hard and forced the idea of treachery out of his mind. He had been well paid and for once his instinct warned him that he would never be able to sleep easily again. He guessed, rightly, that revenge was a natural part of Ahearn's world.

At Barick's order the sail was unfurled to fill with the gusting wind again. He turned the tiller to send the ship into a slow, wide turn as the tide tried to push them back ashore. Barick kept Raven hugging the coastline, keeping just enough distance so as not to be swept onto land but seeking familiar sights in the gloom as he headed east. The oarsmen were allowed to rest as the currents and wind enabled the ship to pick up speed.

After what seemed an age Barick saw the southern mouth of the Uantsumu channel. He had gone as far east along the coast as he could; any further and they would be back in the Gallic Straits sailing towards the continent and leaving Britain behind. At less than a mile wide the Uantsumu separated the mainland of Britain from an island called Tanneton. The gullible among the Britons held a mystical belief about the place. Supposedly the souls of the recently-deceased rowed from Gaul during the night to rest for eternity on the island, the empty boat returning at dawn from where it came. It was a superstition Barick publicly scoffed at but nevertheless he offered a silent prayer as the low-lying hump of the Isle of the Dead hove into view.

Barick swung out briefly to avoid a shingle bank which forced ships entering to take a narrow line into the channel. He made sail now the wind had dropped and turned the tiller to send the ship in a northerly direction. To the right of Raven was the eight-mile long finger of Stanora, a narrow strip of land bordered by a stony beach that extended straight down from the broader mass of Tanneton. To their left lay the mainland, from which a little blob of land called Rutupia jutted out to loom over the channel mouth.

Stanora and the shingle bank worked in concert to take the sting out of the rough seas which characterised the Straits. The rise and fall of the Raven decreased noticeably as the ship passed into the sheltered waters, and Barick heaved a sigh of relief.

After a few minutes sailing, the narrow channel widened significantly and Barick took Raven on a dogleg course, continuing to follow the low-lying coast to his left. He used the white chalk cliffs as a guide in the lashing rain until he came to a river mouth from which the Stur rivers exited into the Uantsumu.

Barick aimed Raven at the largest of the pair of waterways which led to the port of Fordeuuicum some five miles inland. As he handled the tiller, now passive in his hands, Barick again turned his mind to alternative methods of profit, the scare he had had from the big warrior more distant than the upcoming meeting.

# XIII

Three men waited in the blacksmith's workshop, out of the pouring rain where at least there was some semblance of warmth. Two stood patiently, the other paced back and forth, irritable and edgy.

Fionn watched with interest as the smith hammered into shape a piece of metal that glowed a dull orange. With each clash of hammer on anvil the lump of iron thinned and widened so it more closely resembled the sword it was going to become. The sound reverberated across the port and carried to the edge of the village where ten of Weland's comitatus stood, near enough to be in place quickly should their charges need protection, but far enough away to have no clue as to their discussion. After a few minutes of hammering the smith plunged the hot metal into a bucket of cold water. It hissed, issuing billows of steam that filled the immediate area.

A peal of thunder rattled from the heavens, as if a blacksmith in the sky above were forging swords for the gods themselves. At another large clap, much closer this time, one of the horses skittered sideways a few feet until its rider brought it back under control.

Weland grimaced at the rain. Water had soaked through his clothes on the journey to Fordeuuicum and found its way into every conceivable nook and cranny. He was soaked to the skin and distinctly unhappy. He had never liked being wet but being wet and waiting were unbearable. To relieve some frustration he kicked at another stone. It skittered over the uneven ground and splashed into the river.

"Foul weather you have in this part of the country," Caradoc said.

Weland grunted in reply whilst looking for something else to kick.

Fionn looked at Caradoc and shrugged. He returned his attention to the smith, who sweated profusely in front of the fiery furnace as he heated the partially-made sword ready for another beating.

No further words passed between the men and whilst they waited the thunder gradually receded until it was no more than a distant rumble. Then, at last, an old boat hove into view. The sail had been furled but the flag displaying a black bird fluttered atop its mast. Oars dipped gently into the water as Raven made its way up the river to Fordeuuicum.

"About time," Weland growled. There were no stones left within yards of the smithy's to be kicked.

With a display of seamanship and a lot of shouting from the captain, the ship headed towards a jetty. As it bumped into the wharf two bedraggled men leapt over the sides and tied Raven to slick wooden posts that jutted out of the water. As this was intended to be just a brief stop the slack normally allowed to allow the ship to ride the coming and going of the tide was ignored. As soon as he could, Barick wanted to get what was left of his precious load up the coast to Camulodunon, where there was more money to be had,

Barick, normally a jovial man anyway, looked extremely pleased with himself as he stepped ashore. Already soaked to the bone, he paid no attention to the persistent drizzle the storm clouds had left in their wake. He paused briefly at the post and cast a critical eye over the makeshift knot that held his ship in place. He shook his head slightly in annoyance then, as quickly as a man of his bulk could, he waddled up to meet the trio who had moved onto the river bank whilst the ship was being moored.

"Where have you been?" Weland demanded.

"And my greetings to you too, Weland!" Barick laughed expansively at his welcoming committee. "I have been fighting with the seas! My apologies for being later than we arranged, but the weather is foul out there. I would not normally travel at all in conditions such as but as it is for you Weland..."

Barick looked at Weland's companions for some appreciation from them for his exploits. The blood drained out of his face as he recognised Caradoc and Fionn. Old, evil memories came flooding back. He had not seen either of his torturers since their fateful meeting, dealing instead with Weland and another contact in Camulodunon. Caradoc remained impassive, as if this was their first meeting, but Weland took offence to the pause.

"I suggest you tell me what you have now, trader, or I will have my men cut it out of your fat belly!" Weland jabbed a thumb over his shoulder towards the comitatus.

Barick recovered quickly; perhaps Caradoc and his friend were not there to torture him again, he decided. He grinned once more, wider than ever. "I am pleased to see you are in as good a mood as always!" he laughed. "But as you are old friends..." Barick paused dramatically. Weland growled.

The trader laughed again, his composure fully regained.

"Always the impatient one, Weland! You need to cultivate a sense of humour!" Barick then changed his tone to one of deadly seriousness. "If you must know, the Romans are too scared to sail. They are still in port and unlikely to cross the Straits."

Weland shot a searching look at Caradoc. In the past Barick had proven incredibly adept at gleaning important knowledge and this would not be the first time he was used in this way. But it was hard to accept this blunt information at face value.

"How do you know this?" Caradoc asked.

"There is a great army, thousands upon thousands of men and animals, assembled in Gesoriacum. They have been there for months! Soldiers like to spend money and when they are drunk they talk. The fleet was ready to set sail and at the last moment they again failed to leave. But this time their emperor was not there to collect seashells with his men."

"Why?" Fionn asked.

Barick shrugged, as if it were obvious to anyone with even the barest knowledge of the sea. "The Romans are like cats: they hate water."

It made some sense to Caradoc. He recalled how Caligula had planned to invade Britain four years ago but Romans soldiers were notoriously poor sailors. They preferred solid ground to unstable water; even mere lakes were a concern to the average legionary. On top of this heading across the Gallic Straits meant travelling outside the known Roman world and into the complete unknown, a frightening prospect to a people of such certainty, but one which made Caradoc shake his head in confusion when he heard it.

So Caligula's legionaries bluntly refused to board their ships and no amount of threats from the emperor, his eloquence all but destroyed by the madness, had swayed the soldiers. So, in a fit of pique, the emperor set his men to collecting shells from the shore instead. He even ordered a statue erected to himself commemorating the 'invasion', much to the amusement of the rumour mongers and gossips back in Rome.

Two years later Caligula was dead, assassinated by the Praetorian Guard, the very unit supposed to protect him from harm. It was they who selected Caligula's uncle, Claudius, to rule instead. Apparently, he was an unstable character too. Caradoc wondered at a society that would elevate lunatics to rule them.

"What do you think?" Fionn asked.

"It is possible," Caradoc ruminated.

Caradoc suspected that perhaps the invasion was again doomed to failure. Barick's information fitted with quite a few pieces of flotsam and jetsam of rumour and supposition that had reached the tribal leaders from any number of sources, but this was the most credible of them all. He chewed on this cud of data, digesting it along with everything else he knew and suspected.

"You can be on your way now," Caradoc ordered.

Barick, emboldened after his initial shock, held out his hand. He still found it difficult to close it into a fist — the scar tissue on his fingers was tough and hard as leather — but for Caradoc he would try.

"It is not your thanks but your money that I want," Barick said bluntly, all traces of humour sunk to the bottom of the Straits.

Caradoc laughed and dropped some coins into Barick's palm. They were rapidly secreted into some dark place in the fat man's robes.

"Until the next time." Barick nodded his head in leave-taking and trotted to his ship without looking back. He clambered aboard with surprisingly agility, and whipped his crew up for the trip back into the Uantsumu and on to Camulodunon.

"Good news my lord?" asked one of the escorts as Weland clambered onto his small stocky horse. Weland looked irritated for a moment then suddenly, and uncharacteristically, grinned. He kicked his mount into a gallop, leaving the others to catch up.

Things could not be better, he thought.

# XIV

The horsemen urged their mounts in a mad dash over the three miles to Durovernon. The persistent rain had created a welter of puddles, some of which were wide and shallow, while others hid potholes deep enough to throw horse and rider in a whirling tumble of limbs. Despite the urgency all were safely negotiated, but by the time they reached the town riders and horses were spattered with grime from head to toe.

Weland entered the ditched enclosure first. He dragged his horse to a halt at the last moment, leapt off and left the animal to its own devices. He stalked towards the largest roundhouse, where two warriors stood either side of the entrance. Weland blanked the men, who stiffened at his approach, and the severed heads of several defeated enemies which hung around the doorway, grotesque expressions drawn on their faces as the skin tightened and desiccated in the sunlight. He stooped to enter the hut, wiping the encrusted dirt from his face as he did so. Weland was inside when

Caradoc and Fionn drew up with the rest of the escort, the horses blowing.

Caradoc was struck by the heat in the room after the relative cold outside. A charcoal fire crackled in the centre of the room, the only sound to punctuate the oppressive silence apart from the rain that beat on the roof in an irregular tattoo. A large number of armed men stood in carefully selected pockets around the interior. They had been engaged in impatient small talk until it was broken off with the influx of the new arrivals, to which all heads were turned.

Caradoc looked at how the tribes represented arranged themselves, who stood with whom, and mentally shook his head at how little some things changed, despite the passage of time and their latest dilemma.

Stories told that there had been regular and bitter tribal and inter-tribal rivalries, mostly because the tribes took great pleasure in bickering and fighting with each other. Incursions and subsequent bloody retribution were commonplace as one tribal leader tried to upstage, outwit or even oust another.

But all that had been challenged when the general Julius Caesar invaded almost one hundred years ago. The tribes decided they hated the Romans more than they hated each other — it was their country, their land and for no one else to take it away. The tribes were, at a stroke, handed a common cause to unite behind, but they needed a leader. They looked no further than Cassivellaunus, Cunobelin's grandfather, a strong-willed, outspoken and ruthlessly ambitious man who willingly accepted the offer.

Cassivellaunus avoided open battle with Caesar — his army was unsuited to it — and instead resorted to a grinding guerrilla warfare. Eventually there was a halt in hostilities that suited both men, and on the back of which the pair struck a deal. The Catuvellauni were granted a trade agreement that would bring with it great wealth and power. Caesar believed allies were needed in Britain, in particular to bolster his appeal at home, and what better way to gain favour than by making those same people rich?

With the pact struck, Caesar left British shores, never to return again. Cassivellaunus was a hero and the inheritor of a fledgling empire. But for the Britons the world changed forever. Its inhabitants began to look outward, beyond tribal boundaries. Cassivellaunus recognised that with numbers came strength and he wondered at the power of Rome should they return. So the new king, and then his descendants, worked hard to forge the assemblage of tribes into a cohesive group to better face the potential threat. Some came willingly, but others had to be annexed violently.

And much of the southern and eastern lands of Britain did indeed grow fat and prosperous through Cassivellaunus's trade agreement. Nevertheless there was a bile that caught in the throats of those tribes that had not benefited, corrosive and almost impossible to swallow. Every now and again it rose to the surface and needed to be cut out if peace were to be restored. Not every tribe in the south was happy to witness the growing power of the Catuvellauni.

A condition of Caesar's bargain was his refusal to allow the Cantii, who had led the resistance to his invasion, and the Atrebates, whose chief was Commius, a former ally of Caesar who had turned against him, to partake in the trade deal. The prestige of both tribes fell and their power waned.

Overnight they became financial backwaters.

But, after all the years of inattention, the Romans had recently grown interested in their country again. The rumour of invasion and subjugation had swollen. Togodumnus asked the tribes to look outwards again, to shelve whatever rivalries existed, but unfortunately not all proved capable of doing so. The Dobunni, despite offering men, were so far not forthcoming and their warriors were absent from the throng. The Durotriges and Iceni flatly refused, preferring to remain neutral for the time being until, so the rumour went, the eventual winners could be predicted.

The army of 90,000 men, raised from those tribes that were left, was on the outskirts of Durovernon, nearest to where the invasion was anticipated. It was a much smaller force than they would have liked, raised only from the Cantii, the Atrebates and Catuvellauni, but it would have to suffice.

"Be seated," Togodumnus said to the war council and took his place.

The warriors followed suit, organising themselves in a fashion that reflected the seniority of the tribes and individuals, the most powerful closest to the king.

"What news did the trader bring?" Togodumnus demanded. He lifted his hand and felt the narrow band of gold that encircled his forehead, a recently developed habit.

Weland did not immediately reply. He had not sat down with the others and instead was taking off his dripping wet cloak, which he tossed to a slave. He moved towards the fire to dry out and rid himself of the sapping chill in his bones.

"As I expected, your hospitality remains poor, Weland, "demanded Urien of the northern Atrebates. "We are all tired of waiting. What are the Roman plans?"

Weland snapped around. "Why do we allow this weakling into our midst?" he asked loudly of the assembly, spreading his hands to include them all in the question. "He contributes the smallest number of men, all of them ill-equipped, backward farmers, and then all he does is complain about the rest of us!"

Urien was a small man but stocky and powerful with a volcanic temper. From their first meeting the pair had struck up an immediate and mutual hostility. Weland correctly perceived Urien's short fuse and from then on took great pleasure in goading him into an explosive reaction at every possible opportunity, the more embarrassing and public the better.

Urien did not disappoint. He sprang to his feet and advanced menacingly towards Weland, drawing his sword in one smooth motion, the blade grating across the scabbard. Three of his men leapt up to back him. Suddenly there was a melee as warriors from both camps rose to face each other, revealing rifts and enmity. All the time Weland remained impassive in front of the fire, hands outstretched towards the warmth as Togodumnus and Caradoc shouted for calm.

Once composure of sorts was restored Togodumnus stood in front of the council, his face like thunder. Caradoc, thoroughly fed up of acting as a mediator between the quarrelling men, wore a look that spoke volumes.

"We do not have the luxury of being able to fight each other," Togodumnus said. "Enemies stand at our gates and yet you insist on quarrelling like children! Do you want to see your family dead and your lands burning? Because that will happen unless we stand together! If we are divided we will certainly fail. Every man here is needed and welcomed equally, but whoever is not with me should declare themselves so now!"

No one spoke, no one protested. The fire popped and crackled and steam rose off Weland as he steadily dried out. He shrugged half-hearted agreement at Togodumnus. Urien, seeing Weland's action, stepped back and motioned for his men to stand down. Swords reluctantly rasped back into scabbards, problems shelved for the moment.

As he turned, Urien saw Weland's barely disguised smirk but rather than react he mentally filed the insult away, along with the many others, for a future settling of scores. Steadily the placated council took their seats again.

"No more games, Weland. Give us your information now," Togodumnus ordered, suddenly feeling dreadfully tired.

"As you wish, my lord," said Weland, the words deliberately tinged with obsequiousness that bordered on the sarcastic. Togodumnus bristled but held his tongue for the moment. "We met my man, Barick. As usual he was in irritatingly high spirits and overflowing with useless news, but eventually I managed to tease out of him the fact that the invasion has foundered."

There was a buzz in the room as the revelation was digested.

"Caradoc?" Togodumnus asked, having to raise his voice to cut across the hum of many voices.

Caradoc stood and spoke loudly. "Barick is one of many traders we use to gather information from across the water but he has been particularly valuable to us in the past, as you all know. He seems to have a knack for fishing out fact from gossip and innuendo. He clearly believed what he was telling us, I saw no subterfuge in his eyes. Even more compelling is that the rumour fits with others that have reached us of late."

"And so your conclusion is?" Togodumnus pushed.

"I have to agree with Weland," Caradoc said after a moment's pause. "It appears the Romans will not invade."

The news pulsated around the room. Togodumnus sat back in surprise. The tribal army of the Britons had been in place for weeks and was growing restless, for two reasons. First, most Britons had simply never met a Roman and knew nothing about them. The apparent threat seemed distant and unreal; events that concerned the invaders were long in the past and told as stories late at night to scare children.

Second, many of the foot soldiers were farmers or traders and wished to return home to look after their livelihoods and families, their presence vital to generating income and therefore survival. The disclosure that they may be able to finally do so would be a powerful one and difficult to resist.

"What if this Barick is lying? What if he has been paid to tell us what we want to hear?" Urien's shout cut through the noise, which fell audibly as he did so.

"Barick has nothing to gain from telling us anything but the truth," Weland argued, venom dripping from his words. "I have known him for years. He does not earn his living by selling information, it is a mere sideline. He likes being part of what is going on and being the centre of attention, it makes a small man feel important. Helping the Romans, as you suggest, would cut off his major source of income — us. Besides, he also knows I would hunt him down and kill him and his entire family if he betrayed us."

"Even so..." Urien said.

Togodumnus cut Urien off. "I want to hear all of your views. Speak freely."

So one by one all present stood and, if they had something to say, made their comments to the assembly. Those for keeping the army in place argued first. Brand, a local Cantii chieftain from the west of the territory and subordinate to Weland, stood up to speak. He was quiet, tough and well respected. He gave eloquent reasons for remaining on hand. Caradoc followed. Urien, too, added his weight, despite interruptions from Weland. Finally Fionn urged caution.

"We must stay. It would be nonsense to leave!" he argued.

"And what would a pup like you, barely off your mother's teats, know about matters such as these?" Weland challenged.

Fionn growled in anger at the insult, rising to his feet. "More than you, old man, stuck in your flea-ridden town miles from anything of consequence!" he spat in response.

Weland sprang up, veins standing out in his neck, and stood nose-to-nose with Fionn, the younger man looking down on the elder.

"You are a young fool! Like your father but with none of his limited good points!" Weland taunted.

Fionn lashed out at Weland, catching him with a sharp uppercut. He stepped back and drew his sword as Weland, flat on the floor, rubbed his aching jaw.

"You will regret that, boy," he promised as he clambered to his feet, unlimbering his own sword, which he held easily.

"Gladly."

Caradoc placed himself between the pair. "Enough of this! Yet again, Weland, we do not have time for your taunts. The pair of you will sit down or be ejected from this assembly."

Reluctantly Fionn backed off and returned to take his place but kept his gaze locked on Weland.

"I keep my promises," Weland said.

"So do I," Fionn replied.

Weland finally sat after a flat look from Togodumnus, finally breaking eye contact with Fionn.

After the petulant interlude it was the turn of those who argued for breaking up the army and returning home, of which there were many voices. Weland in particular lent heavy support, primarily, he claimed, as the

Cantii were struggling to feed all of the men on his land.

"We need to return to our homes," he said. "The growing season is almost upon us. We must plant crops or our people will starve." A murmur of agreement rippled through the assembly.

"We have waited here too long already. The Romans are afraid of us..." — the assembly roared its pleasure at these words and Weland had to shout to be heard — "...and they are afraid of the sea! But it is time to go home. We must look to our own lands, our own problems. If we stay alert to their threat we can quickly reassemble if we need to in the future."

"I disagree with Weland," Kynthelig said when the cheering died down, dumping cold water on the celebratory flames as was his style and receiving a groan in reply. "The Romans will not give up easily — I know from personal experience. I do not think we have seen the last of them. But our men have already started to drift off back to their land already, and this latest news will spread like wildfire and the movement home will just become even stronger. Practically I do not think we can hold them here any longer and I reluctantly agree it is best to break up the army and return to our homes."

Weland pounced on the opportunity. "The Cantii will keep a close watch on the Straits. The beacons will be kept stacked and manned day and night whatever the weather. Messengers will be constantly ready to bring word to you all should we hear of the Romans assembling again. I pledge that my men will be ready to go to wherever they are needed, whenever they are required."

"Are there any more opinions?" Togodumnus asked and received many shakes of heads, much said already. It had been a long day. "In that case I need some time to think this over."

He stood, asked Caradoc to join him and stepped into the cold outside.

"What do you think?" Togodumnus drew his cloak around him.

"Although I hate to say it, Kynthelig is right." Caradoc smiled at a little girl as she ran past, chasing an equally young boy, perhaps her brother. "I think we would be wrong to leave but I do not see how we can realistically hold the army together. Many of the chieftains have already made their minds up — you can see that for yourself. We will need their support in the future and forcing them to chase what they will see as a foolish errand now will simply undermine us later."

"I agree. I also believe that for the moment the Romans will not be troubling us. Too many facts seem to tell us this. I will disperse the army."

The decision made, Togodumnus turned back to re-enter the roundhouse. With a heavy heart Caradoc followed but could not bring himself to go inside and instead stood on the threshold. Within moments there was a cheer from the interior as Togodumnus delivered his decree.

But Caradoc did not share their enthusiasm and, as the two children ran past him again squealing, he wondered what the future held for his country.

## XV

The sound of carousing that issued from the roundhouse was deafening. Although it was well into the small hours the celebration was still in full swing and few in Durovernon were able to sleep.

Slaves had spent the rest of the day preparing a feast. Cows, pigs and a deer had all been slaughtered and roasted slowly over great fires, the fat bubbling out to fall into the flames with a hiss. The smell of cooking meat had pervaded the town all evening but only the bones of the carcasses remained now, many scattered on the hut floor. Amphora after amphora of wine had been consumed, along with eye-watering quantities of beer.

The usual entertainment accompanied the flowing drink. Many songs boasting of bravery and honour were sung in cracked or slurred tones, often accompanied by mocking catcalls from the spectators. Even Kynthelig had allowed himself to be drawn into singing of the druids. He possessed a surprisingly good voice for one so wizened.

But Fionn thought both the entertainment and provisions poor. The storytellers were limited in their tales and not particularly humorous, even with a skinful of alcohol inside him. The meat was stringy and the wine a little sour. The beer, locally made, was presentable though. At least the Cantii could get something right, he thought.

Urien had left immediately after Togodumnus ordered the dispersal, refusing Weland's half-hearted invitation to stay. Fionn was certain there would have been trouble between the Cantii and Atrebates and strongly suspected Caradoc had a hand in arranging the departure. Fionn knew enmity when he saw it and supposed the pair's argument would rumble until one day it was settled once and for all. He knew, however, that he now shared the same ground as Urien after his earlier altercation with Weland. But he would not be leaving, he had other things in mind.

The inevitable fights broke out a few hours into the celebration, started for a variety of reasons — to settle old scores, for the pure fun of it or for simply selfish reasons, to impress the leaders. Arm wrestling was another popular contest as a show of strength.

Fionn challenged Bearach just to witness his reaction and had been taken aback when it was accepted. He was even more surprised when Bearach soundly beat him, several times and convincingly. However, despite the public embarrassment, it was a good way to get closer to Etain who looked on from the fringes of the contest.

Bearach had collapsed into a drunken heap hours ago and been carried away to his bed. Fionn may have lost the test of strength and leverage but he possessed the thicker skull. Their scores were equal and he would tell Bearach so whenever the chance arose.

"Look at him," Fionn slurred, having added further weight to his claims of superior drinking ability. He gestured at Togodumnus. "A happy circumstance and yet still he is capable of being even more morose than ever."

"You should not be too hard on your cousin," Caradoc replied. His eyes crossed as he tried to focus on Fionn. "He has never been the same since Nara died giving birth."

The object of their discussion sat slumped in his seat. In his right hand he held a goblet of wine, which was tipped forward allowing the contents to steadily seep onto the floor. He stared into middle space, apparently seeing nothing and oblivious to the raucous behaviour all around him.

"Drunk or depressed?" Fionn asked.

"Probably both," Caradoc confessed. "Unlike Kynthelig."

The druid stood faithfully at Togodumnus's side. As Caradoc correctly deduced, Kynthelig was utterly sober, having not allowed a drop of alcohol to pass his lips all night. Instead he was deep in thought, wondering what the future held for him and his kind.

"What now?" Caradoc asked as another commotion broke out.

A pair of men were fighting in the centre of the room. It was Brandan and Brennon. They flailed at each other, throwing wild and wide punches, unsure which of the three faces their opponent had was the real one, so striking all at once. After a few minutes of thrashing Brennon finally landed a solid blow, which threw Brandan into Caradoc and spilt his goblet of wine all over him.

"Bloody fool!" Caradoc swore and kicked Brandan, who barely noticed the blow. Brandan got unsteadily to his feet, apologised to all of the Caradocs in front of him and then struggled to focus on Brennon who staggered in to continue the contest.

"More drink!" Caradoc shouted, waving a hand in the air and nearly falling off his chair as he did so.

A slave eagerly ran over to Caradoc with an amphora in hand. At that instant Brandan flung a punch, missed Brennon by a substantial margin and smacked the slave solidly on the jaw. The slave crumpled into a ragged heap and the amphorae shattered on the ground beside him. Gales of mirth rang out . The fight broke up, the opponents laughing too heavily to do anything other than hold each other up.

"A draw!" Brandan shouted and left the floor, his arm around Brennon's shoulder. Another pair of dishevelled warriors willingly stepped in to take their places and started swinging ragged punches at each other.

"Oh well," Caradoc said as he watched the wine seep away. "I need to stop drinking anyway. Kynthelig will have us up early to get back to Calleva. He despises Sucellos."

Sucellos was the god of alcohol and a lifelong friend to Epaticcus. Caradoc raised a final goblet of wine to them both and drained the last few drops from it.

"Kynthelig is an old fool," Fionn said. "Anyway, I will be staying here,"

Caradoc blearily followed Fionn's line of sight to Etain. Weland stood protectively by her side, a hard glare halting anyone who remotely indicated an interest in his daughter.

"You are walking on dangerous ground."

"I know, but the reward will be worth it."

Etain caught Fionn's eye, smiled and glanced away.

Caradoc laughed. "Your father would have been proud, but she is not as innocent as she looks that one, I would bet!"

"It will be fun finding out," Fionn said.

"I suppose I can spare you for a few days," Caradoc said with mock severity. "Is there anything you need?"

"Just let me have Brennon and two of the comitatus," Fionn asked. "I will be here no more than a week. I am sure I can convince Weland in that time that I am a good prospect for his daughter."

A sly thought occurred to Caradoc, even through the alcoholic fug, but he managed to stop all but a flicker crossing his face.

"It will be less if Weland has his way. You have made a bad enemy there, Fionn. Watch yourself."

"I can handle myself."

"I know you can, but if you come back with your tail between your legs do not say you were not warned."

"We both know you will remind me if I do."

"I am off to bed." Caradoc stood up, swayed briefly then fell over in an uneven heap and promptly started to snore.

Fionn looked over at Etain again. She whispered something into her father's ear and as she did so looked sideways at Fionn. Weland nodded and then kissed her on the cheek. As she left the roundhouse Etain paused and glanced over her shoulder at Fionn, a half smile on her lips.

"I need a piss," Fionn said loudly to no one in particular, stretched, and then walked unsteadily across the room, ignoring Weland's withering stare, and stepped outside.

Fionn was unsure of his surroundings in the darkness. He stood still for a minute to let his eyes adjust to the relative gloom. Even then Etain was nowhere in evidence. He walked around the enclosure, seeing no one, hearing only the roar of the celebration. After another five minutes of searching Fionn swore, convinced he had been fooled and angry with himself for falling for her tricks. He decided to go back to the merriment, but as he walked past a building a pair of arms encircled his waist and drew him into the shadow. A pair of full lips kissed him solidly.

"What will your father say?" Fionn asked when he had chance to draw breath. His heart hammered in his chest and Fionn told himself it was just a shortage of air.

"What does it matter?" Etain said carelessly.

"I am not exactly your father's favourite right now."

"I know, that is what I like about you," Etain said and she drew him into another embrace that lasted even longer than the last and made spots swim in front of his eyes.

Fionn awoke beside Etain early the following morning, his bladder screaming for release. For a moment he was unsure where he was, his surroundings unfamiliar and the room incredibly dark. He sat up to look around and immediately regretted it. His head pounded and his mouth was as dry as bark. He needed to drink something, anything other than beer. The very idea of alcohol passing his lips made brought the acid taste of bile to his throat.

Etain stirred and rolled over. With a smile, Fionn, remembered the last few hours. He drew on his breeches for some modesty. As he stepped outside the moonlight fell on Etain, making the hair that cascaded down her bare back glimmer like precious metal. He marvelled at how good it felt to be around her and how natural the new emotion was. Fionn felt a knot tighten in his stomach and he left the roundhouse grinning from ear to ear, never wanting the memory to fade.

It was much later in the morning before Fionn was up and about and searching for Brennon. He found his best friend down by the river, washing his face and hair in the bitterly cold water in an effort to clear his head.

"There you are," Fionn said, laughing at Brennon's bloodshot eyes. He looked grey and ready to be sick at any moment. A bruise was colouring on his cheek. "You have never been any good at holding your drink and today is no exception!"

"Unless you have some useful advice, like a quick cure for a stinking headache, leave me alone to suffer in peace," Brennon complained, immersing his head in the water again and listening to the swirl of water in his ears.

"I do have a suggestion," Fionn said when Brennon lifted his dripping head out of the river, panting heavily. "We go into the forest up there," he pointed towards the Blahwōn, "and we hunt. Etain tells me the sport is good here, lots of deer, apparently."

"So your idea is that, with a raging hangover and an upset stomach, I get onto a bouncing horse and chase down animals."

Fionn grinned. "Something like that, yes."

"Best idea you have had for weeks. When do we leave?"

An hour later the four of them were coursing up the shallow hill. Brennon had forced himself to throw up and felt a lot better, but his head still thumped as Sucellos rattled around in his skull and took his revenge. But a drink of beer had helped the god withdraw his talons a little. At the rear shambled a distinctly unhappy Bearach, encouraged along by his sister. He hated horses and rode poorly, with a distinctive rolling gait as if he were on a ship's deck in heavy waters. It was a constant source of embarrassment to him.

"Oh, cheer up Bearach. You may have some fun for once!" Etain chided.

"I am only here because father told me to keep an eye on you two," he sulked.

"It is a bit late for that," she said archly.

Bearach flushed crimson. "Father will not be pleased. He does not like Fionn."

"Our father dislikes anyone who comes near me. Besides, I am old enough to make my own choices."

"You should have married long ago."

"Yes, but to ugly men I hated."

"To men with power that would have helped the Cantii."

"What do I care for politics? Besides, Fionn is a prince. He is cousin to Caradoc and Togodumnus. He is a very powerful man."

"Father thinks not."

"Maybe not now," she confessed. "But he will be one day."

Bearach ducked to avoid a low hanging branch. Etain cursed inwardly — she had seen the limb and distracted her brother, hoping it would sweep him off his mount's back. But the joke went untold. What a pity, she thought. I could have laughed at that one for years.

"Enough of the elder brotherly advice, you know it is wasted on me. Let us hunt!"

Etain spurred her horse forward and Bearach reluctantly did the same, caught between his dislike of the sport and the stern order from his father to stay with Etain. Not that he would be able to make any difference when it came to his sister's decisions. Fionn was a strange choice, he mused. He was loud, confident and clearly had an eye for women, but Etain liked him and he knew she was a sharp judge of character and did not suffer fools gladly. With a sigh he tried to stay on his horse as it galloped after the others.

They moved quietly through the undergrowth. The horses were tied up a long way back. Fionn, with Etain, was slightly in front, an arrow nocked and his bow partially drawn. Brennon, despite his ineptitude with the bow, was off to the left in a similar stance. Fionn had told him to scare the quarry his way. Bearach, as he had all day, lagged behind. He had offered to look after the horses but Etain had told him she would enlighten Weland with the fact that Bearach had failed in his duties, so he trailed the party carrying his favourite weapon, a spear, despite the scorn heaped upon it by Fionn.

The group were stalking a deer. It nuzzled at some long grass, cropping away diligently at the stiff blades. Every few seconds it would raise its head, listening and looking for danger, before returning to the succulent green sward. Fionn lifted his left hand in a signal for the others to wait. He returned his hand to the bow and gradually drew the gut string back. He could feel the smooth wood of the bow, the rising power hidden in the string ready to be released into the metal tipped arrow fletched with the black feathers that Fionn preferred. Just as he was about to release his breath and then the arrow, something made the deer jerk its head up in alarm and dash away, swallowed up in the undergrowth in seconds. Fionn let fly but the arrow missed by a considerable margin. He swore in disgust.

"Did one of you move?" he shouted.

Before anyone could do more than shrug there was a loud rustling in the scrub, a sound like a chariot being dragged by wild horses, and a boar burst out. It ploughed to a stop. Its small eyes, black and as deep as a chill pool of water, bored into Fionn. The thing was huge, taller than a hunting dog. It had a wicked pair of tusks, behind which hulked a powerful package of muscle and sinew, tensed and ready to charge, but the beast appeared unsure whether to lunge at Fionn or Etain.

Fionn dared not move. He knew he would be unable to extract an arrow from his quiver and fire it before being gored. Any hunter with the slightest of experience knew you only got one shot at a boar. Its thick hide and incredibly strong bones meant anything other than a fatal blow, a hit to the heart, and the boar would keep going, on and over you, the sharp tusks likely to tear out a significant chunk out of your body before you could able to get out of the way. He had seen it happen to an unfortunate dog whose side was torn open. It had had to be killed to put it out of its misery.

The boar snorted, tossed its head and pawed at the ground, as if reminding them of its presence. Brennon was an awful shot with the bow, more likely to hit Fionn than the charging boar. But something needed to be done to break the impasse. Fionn decided he would have to go for his sword, which was nearer, and risk it. Perhaps Etain could help and he glanced over at her. She looked pale but determined and returned his look with a nod.

Man and beast tensed, one to charge, the other to snatch at his sword. But before Fionn could move the boar squealed with a high pitch, ear-shattering keening. From its chest protruded a spear that had sunk deep into its body. Blood coursed along the length of the weapon and pooled in the grass. The boar's eyes went wide with shock. It fell to its knees and then on its side, its great heart pierced but still pumping.

Whilst everyone else stood rooted to the spot, Bearach dashed to the boar and cut its throat with a dagger, splashing even more gore onto the ground. He planted a foot on the animal's chest and with some difficulty pulled the spear out, using its body as leverage. It was all over in seconds. Etain broke the spell. She ran to Bearach and gave him a huge hug and kiss on the cheek. Brennon grinned at him.

"Thank you," Fionn said, stunned by how fast it had all happened. He clasped hands with Bearach. "I owe you my life."

"Any time," Bearach said and, to his surprise, realised he meant it.

Later, as they rode back to Durovernon, the boar their only kill slung over a spare horse, Bearach chattered animatedly. Then a sudden thought struck him.

"My father will be very unhappy with me," he said, sounding worried.

"Why?" Fionn asked. "You were a hero today."

"Exactly...he will tell me I should have let you be killed!"

# XV

Aulus Plautius stood at the prow listening to the mesmeric regularity of oars cutting into water. Since the storm three days ago the wind stayed low. The sea was as flat as unleavened bread and instead muscle was being relied upon to make headway, the ineffective sail having been furled.

It was a beautifully clear night. A multitude of stars shone out of the inky black sky and the near full moon cast a long shadow of the mast onto the water. Plautius pulled his purple cloak, fixed at the shoulder by a large brooch, tighter about him. At this time of the year the temperature usually dropped considerably following nightfall and tonight was no exception. The expanse of water had sucked any heat out of the air long ago.

He could pick out the dim lights fixed to the mast of the other boats in the convoy; they looked like paper lanterns on a pond. A sailor had shinned up the mast earlier and now stood atop it looking for landfall and to ensure no other ship approached them too closely and risked a collision. This would be repeated on all of the ships in the fleet in the dark, unfamiliar and treacherous waters.

Most of the hangers-on — the idle rich looking for excitement or profiteers who set sail with them — had fallen behind soon after leaving port. They were a superfluous distraction but Plautius knew they would reappear. Following in a legion's footsteps was good business. The soldiers were all too keen to spend their pay on cheap goods, poor wine and infected whores.

"Sir?" The curt question broke into his thoughts.

Plautius turned and noted with disapproval that it was the centurion of the Praetorian Guard, who looked none too pleased to be sent on this errand. Plautius did not care about the man's feelings.

"Yes, what is it?" he said, equally terse.

"Narcissus requests the pleasure of your presence in his quarters."

"Inform the secretary I will be there shortly." Dismissed, the centurion turned abruptly and left without a word.

It was a surprising turn of events and one that still deeply puzzled Plautius. Immediately prior to the departure of the invasion fleet the emperor's private secretary had insisted on travelling along with them. Resistance from Plautius was nullified when Narcissus produced a letter from Claudius commanding anyone to whom the document was presented to give its bearer whatever was required.

Plautius had clamped down on his reply and instead suggested the secretary travel on his flagship. Narcissus maintained several times thereafter that he was merely at hand as a bystander, but Plautius suspected there was another purpose to his presence — he just did not know what it was yet. As a man who planned in intricate detail and believed in understanding in advance every facet of a campaign Plautius found this new and unknown factor disturbing.

He waited a few minutes before he left his place at the bow. Despite the letter the secretary was not in charge as far as Plautius was concerned and he had no intention of leaping to his every command. He knew, however, that impudence could only be pushed so far. The general had survived these last fifty-three years by knowing when to push and when to be pushed.

He barely noticed the rise and fall of the ship as he descended the stairs and into the bowels of the ship where Narcissus nestled in his cabin, like a mouse in his nest. Plautius knocked and then, without waiting for an answer, entered the plain room made entirely of wood. He could see the seasickness on Narcissus's pale face and his nose wrinkled at the stink of vomit in the confined space.

Narcissus hated sea travel as much as the next man. He disliked being away from Rome and its familiar politics, so he had attempted to bury himself in his work to give him a semblance of reality. His small, thin form, simply dressed in a toga, huddled at his desk. He scratched away at a parchment by candlelight ,trying hard not to feel sorry for himself. But he had to admit that so far it had not really worked. Narcissus still knew he was on a ship in the middle of a black ocean and the thought frightened him to his core.

"Ah, Plautius. I hope you are faring better than I?" Narcissus asked, smiling weakly, putting down his writing implement.

"I believe we both suffer," Plautius replied.

Narcissus twisted in his chair and indicated another seat opposite him.

"You are being generous, Plautius. For a man who has spent so much time on the water for the benefit of the empire I cannot believe you even notice it any more." He received a nod of assent from Plautius and grinned at his perception.

"These ships are not really designed for comfort, are they?"

"No, sir, but they will get us to where we need to be. You asked to speak to me. I assume it is not about the quality of your quarters?" Plautius's brown eyes hardened. He was keen to understand what Narcissus wanted. Maybe he would learn why he was here at all.

Narcissus instantly dropped the smile.

"No, I did not. As you know I am just here as..." — he searched for the correct description — "an observer."

"Is that why you have the Guard?" The messenger was still very much on his mind, but as soon as he spoke the words Plautius cursed himself for his loose tongue. But it was too late, it was done.

Narcissus pursed his lips. "I grant it is unusual but the emperor thought it a sensible precaution that I was well protected during this time."

"Are my troops are not good enough?"

"If your troops were insufficient they would not be on this voyage. Besides, it is only a century of eighty men, hardly enough to matter in the greater scheme of things."

It was not so much pride that had prompted Plautius's outburst as concern at having an independent force, no matter how small, outside of his control. Also, it was not as if he could have them thrown off the ship into the middle of the sea. Plautius did not like having limits placed on his choices, particularly when in unfriendly territory.

"I cannot have passengers on this venture, Narcissus. The Guard are soldiers as much as the next man. If the situation arises where they must fight, it will be so."

"I am sure that will not be the case, but if it happens you have my word that they will be yours to command."

Plautius felt relieved. Narcissus seized the opportunity to change the subject. "You are aware how important the success of this venture is for the emperor?"

Plautius nodded. "Of course. It has been made very clear to me on many occasions."

But Plautius also knew there were those that wanted the invasion to fail, and expressed their opinions as such to him. But he did not repeat their views, as therein lay danger.

"My future is inextricably tied to that of the emperor — his failure is my failure, and vice versa, so it was my suggestion that you be placed in command of the invasion." Narcissus was pleased to see the look on Plautius's face. "I needed a good Roman to lead us, someone who would want and strive for success. Someone such as you. That at least should be no surprise?"

Plautius did not reply, his mind whirling with the unusual variety of demands and constraints the invasion and its politics were placing upon him. The silence stretched.

"No matter," the secretary shrugged. "I am sure you understand me plainly enough already. So, now I have been completely open with you, please remind me of the plan."

Plautius was well aware that Narcissus knew the intricate scheme and all its facets intimately. But as most soldiers do he decided to sidestep the politics and take the safest course of action — obey orders.

"The first stage is the most critical. We are assuming the Britons will be well aware of our coming. Therefore the landing is our biggest risk. It is here we could founder, so the plan anticipates they will attempt to stop us at the beachhead.

"However, all we need is a toehold on the mainland. If we can achieve that we will be in a much stronger position. Any surprise we can obtain, however slight, is essential, and hence the night-time sailing, despite its adverse effect on our soldiers."

Narcissus interrupted. "I may have sown some seeds of doubt with the Britons that could help our cause."

"How?" Plautius was puzzled and wondering whether to be angry.

"We have been sending false information along established communication routes to the Britons in the hope it gets back to Togodumnus. The last message was sent only a few days ago."

"Why was I not informed of this?" Plautius demanded.

"Would it have altered your plans at all?" Narcissus asked, his voice calm, gentle and oily. "As you say, we assume the worst and that is considerable resistance when we land. This diversion has a small chance of succeeding at best. I saw no need to distract you with a probable false hope, but nothing is lost in the trying."

Plautius opened his mouth to speak, but Narcissus waved away further comment. "Anyway, it is done. Continue." Narcissus kept Verica's mission to himself, for now. It would only complicate matters even more with Plautius, he told himself.

Patiently, Plautius again ran through the invasion plan...

The strategy had been assessed, proposed and reworked countless times and down to the tiniest of details. The constant filtering of information resulted in a plan that called for the strength of four legions — the II[nd] Augusta, IX[th] Hispana, XIV[th] Gemina, and the XX[th] — totalling over 21,000 legionaries and supported by another 15,000 auxiliary soldiers. Cavalry were also called for and a force of 5,000 deemed necessary, all of who needed horses.

On top of this, immunes were essential — men with specific skills such as engineers, doctors, cart and mule drivers. Then there were the inanimate objects, such as artillery, several tonnes of food, carts and baggage. Pack animals — some ten thousand mules and oxen — were needed to pull these heavy items. There were even river barges being brought over, which Plautius intended to utilise along the many rivers in the area to cut into the heart of Catuvellauni territory. Such a venture resulted in almost 50,000 men and 15,000 animals being transported on over 1,000 vessels. It was a massive mobilisation of forces and the Romans excelled at it.

The invasion had to take place in the south-east corner of Britain. The strongest tribes were located here and the planners knew it was key to take out the most effective resistance first. But there were few credible invasion points in the area. One option lay to the west: a large shallow bay, fed by the river Limana, its gaping maw several miles across. Entering the bay was extremely hazardous, as there were large sand bars and shingle beds scattered at irregular intervals. It was highly probable that at least some of the fleet would founder on these obstacles, weakening the strength of the overall invasion.

Two further rivers fed the bay, generating at low tide a confusing mix of creeks and mud flats that could trap even those with local knowledge. Behind the inlet lay miles of swampy marshland, which ran until they met the formidable Coed Andred, named after the Goddess Andred whose darker side revelled in war and victory.

The densely-packed oak and hornbeam of the forest choked the land until it was overwhelmed by the one hundred and twenty mile arc of the northern segment of the Dūn, the rolling chalk hills on the far side of which nestled Durovernon. Even if the force was able to land unscathed, getting to its target was impractical and this option had been discarded.

Instead the fleet was aiming for almost the most south-easterly point of Britain.

"The landing force is split into three divisions, specifically so we can deal with the expected resistance and the limited landing points," Plautius explained. "The first division of two legionary cohorts of the XX[th] plus cavalry is being led to Tanneton by Gaius Hosidius Geta."

Plautius's ebullient second-in-command was aiming for the western side of the bleak peninsula. The general pointed at a map to show Narcissus where this lay. Ironically the XX$^{th}$ would be guided to the island by a beacon which shone out from its highest point. Its purpose was to warn ships away from the nearby treacherous sand bars that hid just beneath the surface, even at high tide, but this night it would instead draw disaster to the isle.

"The administration centre will initially be created on Tanneton," Plautius continued. "In parallel, Geta and his men will clear the island of any enemy threats. Based on intelligence we expect these to be few and weak. The Stanora peninsula is of sufficient length to beach most of the ships which are not being used to patrol the channel between Tanneton and the mainland."

"But Tanneton alone does not give us Britain," Narcissus pointed out.

"Correct. Tanneton merely gives us a jumping-off point. A foothold on the mainland is crucial. So whilst Geta is subduing the island our division will land at a promontory called Rutupia." Plautius slid his finger acroos the map the short distance from Tanneton to the mainland. "We will have half of the II$^{nd}$ — 2,640 men — plus a cavalry alae. The legate Vespasianus will lead them.

"The initial stratagem for both divisions is to dig in and so secure the entrance to the southern waterway of the Uantsumu Channel which separates Tanneton from the mainland. We have sufficient provisions for two weeks so we only have a limited window in which to gain an advantage."

"Why so little food?" This was a stratagem Narcissus had struggled with throughout the planning period.

"Bringing more provisions means more resources, and more ships. This way we all have a greater incentive to ensure we do not fail. Besides, if we cannot break onto the mainland in two weeks we never will." Plautius shrugged matter-of-factly, and moved on. "Once we control the Uantsumu and have a strong position at Rutupia the third division will be ordered from Gaul."

The final segment of the invasion force would bring with it animals, armaments and supplies. Enough to give the Romans Britain.

"It is a good plan," Narcissus said.

"Of course. But often plans do not go as smoothly as anticipated in situations such as these." Many a time Plautius had had to make hurried decisions on too little information to rescue perilous situations before they completely unravelled.

"It will not take long to crush the Britons underfoot," Narcissus said confidently.

"That may be so at first, but I think it will take many years to subdue them completely."

"Why do you say that?" Narcissus looked offended.

"They are like the Gauls. They have many centres of power, many tribes to subdue. We will have to defeat them one by one, as Caesar did."

"It will be done, I am sure. You will do it for Rome, Plautius."

"The landing is the key," Plautius said again, barely hearing Narcissus's platitude. "We also know the Britons are highly mobile — their skill with the horse is excellent — so I expect their chariots and cavalry to form formidable opposition. We will need to find some way of nullifying this during the campaign. There is a lot to achieve and there is a lot that can go wrong."

"How long before we disembark?"

"Soon. A few hours at most, I would expect."

"Then I will not keep you from your important duties."

Narcissus swivelled back in his chair and bent to his paperwork in the weak candlelight. Plautius blinked in surprise at the sudden end to the audience. He mentally shrugged, stood and left the cabin. He closed the door quietly behind him, suppressing an urge to slam it, and retraced his steps back onto deck in search of his staff, keen to check a few last minute details. Part of his mind was on the landing, but part also thought of his wife whom he had left behind in Pannonia, heavily pregnant and about to give birth to their first child. He hoped it would be a boy so his name could carry on.

As the oars rose and fell, Plautius wondered how old the child would be before he was first able to lay eyes on it.

# XVII

"This is an insult!" Adminius raged, spittle shooting in all directions. The legionary grimaced as some landed on his breastplate, ruining its sheen. He would have to remember to clean it off later or his optio would be sure to put him on a charge — if he was lucky.

"Why are you preventing me from meeting with Narcissus and Plautius? I have every right to be there. I helped design the invasion plan!"

The legionary did not reply and stared impassively straight ahead into the middle distance, blocking the hatchway to the ship's bowels, as he had been ordered to. He was far more afraid of crossing Max than upsetting the fat foreigner.

Adminius resorted to shouting even louder, in case the man was hard of hearing. "I am a friend of the Emperor, Claudius. He will be most upset to hear of this!"

It was about as effective as ranting at a piece of wood and finally Adminius recognised the futility of his efforts. There was nothing practical he could do about getting past the guard himself. If only Ahearn were here, the legionary would be over the side of the ship in moments if he so wished it!

He stalked off and furiously kicked the side of the vessel several times. Even this relatively small effort, coupled with the anger suffusing his body, made him gasp heavily and so he contented himself instead with glaring at anyone he could fix his eye on, catching his breath ready for another assault. But the legionaries had been shouted at by professionals and Adminius did not even come close, so they simply ignored him, treating him like the passenger they knew he was and fanning the flames of his ire even further.

Adminius's actions had not gone totally unnoticed, however. With an angry growl, the optio went for his sword — for at least the third time in as many hours.

"Do not be a fool, Anatolius," said Max as he stayed his arm.

Anatolius shrugged off the restraint of his commanding officer. "It is bad enough having to put up with these...*barbarians* as it is, Max," he spat. "But having to listen to that pompous, pampered idiot bleat about his imaginary status makes me want to stick my sword into him, give it a good, slow twist and then dump the fat bastard overboard with the fish."

"I know, I know. He is an idiot, but he comes as part of the deal with Narcissus, who I am sure would be very upset if you killed his lap dog." Max held his hand up as Anatolius tried to speak, his dead grey eyes hooded. "Or beat him up."

"Even if it was just a *little* thrashing?"

"Of course! For the moment you will have to keep your gladius in its scabbard. Wet it on some Britons instead."

"Well, I do not like it. We should be in Rome, where we belong. I cannot understand why we have been sent into the field."

"It does little for me too, but orders are orders. The emperor says we protect Narcissus, so here we are. Anyway, I do not think Plautius likes us being here any more than we do, from the looks he keeps giving me."

Less than a month ago Max had been called to an audience at the imperial palace on the Palatine. There and then he was given the highly unusual order to accompany Narcissus to Britain, unusual because the Praetorian Guard rarely served outside the city and existed solely to protect the emperor. Max was given just one day to organise his century of eighty men before marching from Rome with the secretary to Gesoriacum and straight onto the ship, which now weaved its way over the Straits and into the unknown.

Max had been born in the slums of Rome but never knew his father. He had been a drunk, according to his mother, and left before she came to term. The wiry little boy grew up quickly in the back streets of the city, carving out a place for himself with his quick fists and smart mouth.

But he had been hungry for more than a life of servitude, so at the earliest opportunity, his eighteenth birthday, he joined the Praetorian Guard. Its familiarity with the upper echelons of power and the manner in which the legionaries carried themselves, full of vigour and confidence, appealed strongly to Max. Even though he was already hardened by his upbringing, twenty years of service in the Guard added further mental armour, to the point where he became equally capable of combating people or politics. Max had dragged himself out of the gutter and, with a single-mindedness bordering on obsession, took every opportunity to force himself further and further away from his humble beginnings.

He had little time for friends and Anatolius, a bulky, powerful man of average height, was probably the closest thing to one. He had reported to Max for most of his fifteen years in the Guard and his rise through the ranks had been as a direct result of following in Max's wake. His position of optio made him second-in-command of the century, appointed by and answerable only to Max. Where Max was subtle and scheming, Anatolius was a blunt weapon that would swing with abandon if left unchecked. He had a cruel streak and was intensely disliked by his men, something Anatolius enjoyed immensely and keenly reinforced whenever he could.

"Look at him." Max nodded at Adminius. "He is fat, weak and effectively powerless. Not much, you say. But I have been told by a credible source that, as implausible as it sounds, he will be installed by Plautius as the client king once we beat the Britons. So where you see a whipping post, I see a pot of gold. This is one of the best opportunities we have had in years to gain favour with Narcissus and maybe get a bonus from Adminius, and I am not about to let you kill it." He gave Anatolius a cold smile.

Max had proven many times to have an uncanny knack of spotting opportunities that furthered either his finances, influence or, preferably, both. In Rome, status and therefore power was inextricably linked with money and favour. Even though Max's instinct told him that Narcissus should not be fully trusted, the freedman had both of these properties in abundance,and so the threat was outweighed by the potential reward. Adminius, on the other hand, was an altogether more straightforward prospect. Max simply loathed him and would take him for all he could get.

Anatolius was disappointed to miss out on the prospect of violence but he trusted Max's eye. He dropped his arm to his side, away from the hilt of his sword. Still, he mused rubbing his square chin, maybe a chance to kill the fat man would arise at some point. He smiled at the thought.

# XVIII

Despite Ahearn's initial reservations Verica had, in fact, been well received in Seolesiae. A celebration had even been hastily organised to welcome the travellers that rode into the town as the sun was at its peak. Although the fare had been poor, Verica ate and drank as if it were the juiciest of meats and finest of wines.

Amon, the Atrebatean leader installed by Caradoc after Verica's ejection, seemed happy to have the old chieftain back despite what could be his own resulting demotion. If anything, Amon looked relieved at the prospect of being able to hand the reins back to the old man.

Ahearn watched Amon throughout the celebrations, saw his sharp, calculating eyes and the habitual licking of his lips. He concluded that Amon was a sneaky, slimy little rat, little more than an urchin, suited to a hovel rather than a chieftain's hut. A man that would more than likely stab you in the back for the price of a bronze coin, or for nothing at all if the mood so took him. But Ahearn was pleased. In this instance a double-dealing ruthlessness would be an attribute of distinct value.

Then the negotiations started. Verica's approach, using persuasion and platitudes, proved completely alien to Ahearn. His own method was simply to tell people what he wanted, and most of the time his demands were obeyed, or else people died. He found the extensive and incredibly circular discussions immensely irritating. First Verica would make an offer, and Amon would want more. Then Verica would be pleasant and partially accept the increased stakes before the process repeated itself again. And so it went on.

But at last the pair came to an amicable agreement and Ahearn breathed a sigh of relief. Amon produced a wide grin that revealed incisors so sharp they almost looked as if they had been filed to a point. Ahearn began to think that perhaps Amon's initial reaction at their arrival had not been relief but the prospect of profit, which had been satisfied.

The following morning they made ready to leave. Ahearn thought he could hear Verica's bones creak as the old man climbed into the saddle.

Amon bowed deeply. "Let me have the honour of providing you an escort through our lands," he said in his singsong voice.

"I accept with gratitude," Verica said then bowed himself. "Until the next time we meet, Amon."

The party rode out of the town to a fanfare. Ahearn thought the Atrebate 'warriors' surrounding them looked spindly and weak, like undernourished cattle, but to have refused their presence would have been an insult that Verica could not have stomached. Nevertheless, Ahearn kept his hand near a weapon at all times, still not convinced he knew where Amon's loyalties lay. Despite his fears the Atrebatean escort were just as relieved to be able to leave their charges at the border as Ahearn was to see them go. With barely a glance they turned and galloped for home.

At last Ahearn could turn his focus to the next stage of the plan. He kicked his horse into a trot, keen to get to the Dobunni.

# XIX

Plautius stared up into the weak yellow sun that was already well up in the sky. The first rays had peeked over the horizon an hour past and still the convoy had not reached the land that was so tantalisingly close. An unexpected stiff current flowing off the coast had considerably slowed the fleet's progress. The men were thrashed to put their backs into heaving the heavy wooden oars through the sea and drive the ships forward. But for all their efforts, the fleet made insignificant headway and the oarsmen were stroking more gently now, holding their position.

A breeze blew across Plautius's face. He looked up to see the flag atop the mast expand to its full length as a wind suddenly gusted. He shouted for the sail to be dropped and the oarsmen to strike hard for shore. The ship surged forwards and, under the additional impetus, finally broke free from the restraining hand of the current.

But the hoped-for advantage of a dawn landing had been shattered. Plautius would only know if the delay was decisive and whether the Britons had mustered when his ships were about to land and he faced their massed ranks. But as the fleet entered the mouth of the Uantsumu Channel and closed in on the Rutupia headland, he was amazed to see that the cliffs were empty. Not a single man was visible to oppose the landing, never mind the anticipated army. Even at his most optimistic Plautius had expected at least some resistance and a stiff battle to gain a foothold.

"You were wrong, Plautius," Vespasian said.

"Yes, thank the Gods," Plautius laughed. "Mars smiles on us today."

He had been holding his breath and let it out in a great whoosh as he realised Vespasian was correct. The biggest challenge to the invasion, just getting ashore, was to be avoided and in such an unbelievably fortuitous manner.

Vespasian stood at the ship's rail next to the general, poised to lead his II[nd] ashore. Plautius liked to know about the men who reported to him so he had spent some time investigating Vespasian's background. He had uncovered no real enemies to speak of — in fact, everyone seemed to have a good word to say about Vespasian, a particularly powerful survival skill in Roman political circles, and one which Plautius envied. He came over as an unassuming character with an inoffensive nature.

It appeared that Vespasian at first refused to join the privileged ranks of Rome, preferring instead to work the family farm in the barren countryside north of the city, and leaving the social climbing in the hands of his older brother, Sabinus. But his ambitious mother did not want a farmer for a son. Maternal pressure finally told and Vespasian steadily, albeit reluctantly, began his rise through the ranks, culminating in his most recent promotion two years ago to the position of II[nd] Augusta's legate, based in Germania.

What initially concerned Plautius was the source of Vespasian's promotion — Narcissus — the whisper being that the secretary had influenced Claudius's judgment. The charitable among the rumourmongers pointed to the scandal of Vespasian's marriage, well beneath his social class, to the daughter of an equestrian and former formal mistress to an African knight. That he married for love was inconsequential and they assumed the major factor to be that Domitilla was, like Narcissus, a freed slave and that he looked kindly on Vespasian as a result. If so, it was an amazing piece of good fortune.

So Plautius decided that the best option was to be cautious around Vespasian whilst soaking up as many facts and rumours on the man as he could and balancing them against his own experiences. During the campaign build-up in Gesoriacum and on the crossing Plautius discussed some of his plans and tactics with Vespasian and found him to be solid and dependable, with a quick mind. He liked what he saw, but knew that Vespasian's only experience in his career as a soldier was as a junior officer quashing an uprising in Thrace. Fighting the Britons in a command position would be a much sterner test.

On Plautius's other side stood Martius the aquilifer, a hand-picked gnarled veteran with skin the colour of mahogany, developed through over twenty flawless years' service in the army, which had earned him the proud honour of carrying the aquila standard. In his right hand Martius held a wooden staff four feet long and topped with a T-shaped gold podium. Atop the podium and above Martius's head perched a golden eagle, lightning bolts radiating out from beneath its claws. Jupiter, the king of the gods, embodied Rome's given right to rule the nations of the empire and the eagle was his bird, the generic symbol of Rome's might. To lose an eagle was the ultimate disgrace, which would stain the history of the legion forever, and Martius would fight to the death to defend the aquila, as would any other soldier in the legion.

Besides his standard short gladius sword strapped onto his left hip and pugio dagger on his right, Martius was intentionally dressed differently to other soldiers. On his torso, rather than the interlinked iron bands of the standard legionary armour he wore a lorica plumata of silvered bronze scales, which extended to the waist, below which hung vertical overlapping leather strips down to his knee. A small, flat circular shield, which could be attached to his arm in battle should his hands be full with standard and gladius, was strapped to his back.

Martius stared forward impassively at the nearing shore, as if he had seen it all before. He absent-mindedly raised his spare hand to scratch at his bare head — aquilifers went into battle without a helmet.

Each legion was identified individually by its own standard, and behind Martius stood the II$^{nd}$'s signifer. He carried a six-foot long spear to which a red piece of luxurious cloth was hung. On it, picked out in gold, was the symbol of a capricorn, the birth sign of Augustus who had raised the legion, the winged horse Pegasus and Mars, the God of War and the father of Romulus and Remus who had founded Rome itself. The signifer wore armour and weaponry that was similar to Martius's but on his helmet was tied a bear skin, its dead eyes staring out over the British coastline.

The men aboard the flat-bottomed boat staggered as it rode up and settled onto the sandy, shallow beach. Plautius stepped into the bitterly cold water swirling about his feet. Behind him he heard following splashes as Martius and Vespasian came ashore. The aquilifer, suddenly energised and bright eyed, marched up the slope past Plautius and, using the metal spike at the base of the standard, rammed it into the ground so the aquila stood proudly looking inland. The signifer followed suit. Two legionaries formed a guard either side of the standard bearers — they would stay until the camp was constructed and the standards moved again to a place of honour.

With the ritual complete, Plautius walked with difficulty over the soft, wet sand, the faint smell of seaweed and salt in the air, to its highest point only tens of feet above sea level. He looked inland. Rutupia had been deliberately chosen as the landing spot because of the relatively narrow strip of land that coupled it to the mainland. As a result, the manoeuvres of any force attacking Plautius's men would be restricted within this ribbon, which would afford a degree of extra protection to the Romans behind it.

Beyond the headland the ground this side of the Dūn was very flat, running on for miles in a plateau broken only by irregular banks of trees. Plautius could not see anyone. There were none of the clouds of dust raised by a marching army, not even a solitary rider, just the call of sea birds that circled high above. He shook his head in wonder.

Plautius turned to watch as the legionaries, in battle order wearing full armour, followed in his path and spread out through the immediate area.

Quickly and efficiently the remaining ships in the division pushed onto land in a tight row. A freak wave caught one ship and it slewed around, threatening a disastrous encounter with another already beached craft. But the man at the tiller reacted quickly to avert a collision and the ship landed safely, albeit skewed. Plautius made a mental note to find out who the man was and commend him later.

Men jumped from the ships to fasten them in place as gangplanks were laid. Later the ships would be pulled higher on the beach as protection from the forces of nature, but for now they were too heavy and had to be unburdened first. From one ship the horses of the single cavalry ala that accompanied the legionaries were carefully guided off by their riders, hooves clattering on the wood. The mounts tossed their manes and snorted at the unfamiliar smells. From other vessels centuries of eighty men marched off. Equipment, food and baggage were unloaded as officers shouted, cajoled and whipped their men into frenetic but ordered activity.

Plautius expected that Geta would soon be landing on Tanneton to begin building an almost identical facility to protect the fleet when it was aground. It also meant there would be a defensible position on the island to fall back to and regroup should serious resistance be encountered on the mainland. Plautius knew the Britons had little in the way of an armed fleet and nothing that had a hope of seriously resisting the Classis Britannica and threaten the Stanora supply base. Even so, a withdrawal would be the last option as, if they were ejected from the mainland, returning would be extremely difficult.

The first and primary task of the II[nd] was to set up a barrier to any hostile forces, even though none were in evidence, so work would soon start on constructing a temporary camp. The mild title belayed its real nature, which was more of a fortress. A quarter of Plautius's force would form a human shield behind which the camp would be built by the remainder. Once the division was safely protected small cavalry detachments would be sent out to roam the immediate area and locate the enemy. As this was just the initial base, Rutupia being be far too small to handle the influx of the third division once it landed, a larger camp would then be built a little further inland.

Plautius shook his head as he caught himself going too far ahead into the future. First things first.

"I am very glad to be off that boat," Narcissus panted as he reached Plautius at the top of the beach, breaking Plautius's thought process anyway. He looked pale, bedraggled and still weak from seasickness. Max was at his shoulder and Plautius was inwardly pleased to see the Praetorian looked a little green himself.

Plautius turned at a sudden commotion by the water's edge. There was much shouting and arguing followed by an almighty splash. Adminius was face down in the water and struggling to right himself, with an enraged Anatolius, who looked ready to explode, drenched to the skin beside him. Max hurried back down the beach to deal with the situation as Adminius, with the aid of one of his soldiers, pulled himself up to turn on Anatolius, his temper not helped by the gales of laughter flooding from the ship he had fallen off.

"He is a fool," Plautius said, disliking the distraction at such a critical juncture.

Before Narcissus could respond, Plautius twisted away and stalked towards Crispus, the tribune responsible for building the camp. The bald but bearded man was engaged in an animated conversation with several immunes as they surveyed the area and referred to a plan, which flapped in the sea breeze. Crispus looked up, surprised Plautius was joining the conversation. Ordinarily Plautius would leave the camp construction to his tribune but he wanted a diversion from Narcissus before he said something he would later regret. Crispus was the closest excuse at hand.

Narcissus trailed uncertainly behind, listened to the foreign language of construction for a few moments and then decided to stand off to one side and watch the activity all around him. He was in very unfamiliar territory, which was getting more alien by the minute and he was trying hard, but unsuccessfully, to disguise how uncomfortable he was.

Before long the immunes broke away from Crispus and were marking out the scope of the site. The debate had been where to place Narcissus and Adminius, their presence causing a temporary upset and forcing a careful reworking of the preparation, but between them they managed to find somewhere adequate.

A flag was placed in the centre of the plot. The right angles of the rectangular camp, its length a third longer than its depth, had been measured already and large flags were being carried to mark its corners and the location of the gates.

The inner sections would be constructed to a precise arrangement following a strict routine of status. First and foremost was the fixing of the praetorium, the position where Plautius's imposing tent, as commander of the entire invasion force, would be positioned. Once established, the standards would be planted in front of it. A straight line was being drawn for the placement of the tribunes' tents, parallel to which would be the encampment area for the troops. A road would be constructed to join the main gate, which faced inland, and the rear gate, which faced towards the sea. Another road would also be needed to join the two side gates, thus a street plan of the interior that was essentially a cross. Finally a road also ran the full circumference of the camp, joining all the areas together.

For each century a fixed amount of space was allocated, delineated by coloured flags, which indicated positions for the troops to take up on arrival. In the centre of this area the men's baggage was gradually being piled in a circle around the markers, for ordering later.

Vespasian's veterans of the first cohort, his toughest and most experienced men, were entering the camp first to take up their places in the front of the camp, the praetentura. This ensured the strongest troops were ready to engage any attackers ahead of newer, less experienced soldiers, who were placed with the rest of the force, roughly half of it. The cavalry were at the rear of the camp, in the retentura.

One by one the centuries found their prescribed areas. Narcissus watched the legionaries take off their equipment but ensure most of their arms were stacked close at hand. First the men rammed the iron handled pilum spear into the ground. Against this they leaned their shields and tied their helmets on the shield to prevent them blowing away if the wind arose. However, the legionaries kept sword and dagger strapped to their waist. This was enemy territory.

Once the weapons had been placed it was time to dig. Pickaxes and shovels were handed out. A legionary spat on his calloused hands, hefted a pickaxe and swung it with all his might to gouge a hole in the ground, which, thankfully, was relatively soft.

The trench was planned to be five feet wide and three feet deep. Narcissus was surprised to see such quick progress and at this rate it would not be long before the first ditch was completely opened up. The spoil produced from the digging was thrown behind the line of toiling men and inside the camp to form a rampart, doubling the size of the barrier. Wooden stakes were being carried ashore and stacked in bundles behind the growing rampart. The stakes had sharpened points at both ends to make them easier to drive into the soil and present a dangerous obstacle to any attacker. In the middle of the stake was a narrower section so they could be lashed together with leather thongs for extra strength.

The pace of construction was stiff and would not let up until the camp was finished. Narcissus turned as a centurion whipped a legionary with his vine stick, causing the man, who must have made some stupid mistake, to cry out as it smacked into his arm, immediately raising an angry welt. All over the camp centurions patrolled their own section to make sure it was not their men that fell behind and delayed completion.

Then the leather tents began to arrive, one for eight legionaries — a contuburnia — to share. The more senior the occupant, the larger the tent, and the belonging to Plautius was more a pavilion and almost opulent. The tents were pitched at least 200ft from the trench, far enough away to be out of range of any fire arrows or javelins cast in from outside by any marauding forces.

Narcissus got tired of standing around. Plautius had moved on and was nowhere in evidence, so the freedman walked back down the slope of the shallow beach to find his ship and his cabin. There was more work to do and with all the activity he felt like a diseased whore at a party — unwelcome and unwanted. It was not a sensation he was used to.

Further up the Uantsumu, a fishing boat banged into shore, nets forgotten and lost back in the channel. A father and son stumbled off, numbed by what they had seen.

"Take a warning to Durovernon," the father said. "They must know what has happened here."

"What will you do?"

"I will return to Tanneton for your mother and sisters."

The young man, barely a teenager, hesitated and his father gripped him by the shoulders, staring intently into his eyes.

"This is more important than you or I. Weland must prepare for battle. He must be warned." He shoved his son in the back and he stumbled forward. "Go! Find a horse and raise the alarm!" he shouted. The boy ran inland, his father's orders ringing in his ears and the responsibility weighing on his young shoulders.

The father pushed the small boat back into the channel and clambered aboard when the water was deep enough. He set the sail and tacked across the Uantsumu, all the time keeping a close look out for enemy ships. He prayed to the gods that he could be lucky twice and get home safely.

# XX

The first they knew was when a rider scythed through the river. His stolen horse was blowing, foam at its mouth and heavy sweat on its haunches. Although the journey was a short one it was not a beast that was used to being forced to run, a bare canter being more its style. Mud was splashed copiously on horse and rider, barely touched by the brief dousing gained at the ford.

The boy pushed the horse hard, his heels kicking into its ribs again and again, despite being so near to his destination. People and animals got out of the way, reforming in their wake, eager to learn what the fuss was all about.

The horse ran up the riverbank and to the roundhouse, which looked peaceful, smoke seeping gently through its thatched roof. The rider leapt off the horse before it had fully stopped and rushed towards the building. The guards at its entrance blocked the young man's way with muscled forearms, pushing him backwards so that he landed heavily in a puddle.

"Where do you think you are going?!" they challenged, laughing as the young man stood, covered in mud. As he poured out his story the guards listened sceptically.

"I tell you, it is true!" the young man said when he had finished.

One of the guards wrinkled his nose at the smell of fish from the boy's clothes. "Go and advise Weland," he said to the other. "Then we can rid ourselves of this...irritation."

He returned his attention to the young man, noting the wisps of hair on his chin, where he tried to grow his first beard. He scowled. "If you are wasting my time, boy, I will flog you myself," he said, as his colleague entered the hut nevertheless. The young man breathed a sigh of relief and for a moment his thoughts returned to his father and family. He hoped they were safe.

A moment later Weland poked his head out of the hut, his hair loose and wet. "Let him in," he ordered.

"In you go," the guard said, speaking as if it were his decision.

"Thank you," the young man said, and pushed past the other guard as he left the roundhouse.

After a minute of muted conversation the curious guards heard first one, then other voices inside raised in urgent discussion. Weland burst out of the roundhouse carrying a long, curved sword in his hand, followed by the young man,. He shouted at the guards, who now charged off, red-faced and urgent, their doubt in the young man's story banished.

"Move it!" they shouted, shoving people aside in their haste to get through the gathering crowd of inquisitive onlookers.

A horn rang out, echoing around the valley. The harsh sound issued from a long tube tipped by a brass figure in the shape of a dog's head. The cry of alarm snarled through its bared teeth, spreading through town as more warriors repeated the battle cry of the carnyx. Within minutes two messengers hurtled out of the town along its northern road taking the urgent news to Camulodunon and Calleva.

Warriors began to move through the town with a tense urgency. People dropped items they were carrying to lie where they fell; children were scooped up, weapons gathered. Prayers made to a variety of gods whilst swords were gathered to be sharpened in preparation for conflict.

Weland's men gathered in the enclosure, horses tossing their heads in nervous excitement as they sensed the tension. Fionn, intrigued by the commotion, made his way to the enclosure. The dependable Brennon, his childhood friend, sat ready in the saddle. The two others Caradoc had left behind, Hueil and Nemausus, sat beside him,.

About to order his men to stop Fionn accompanying them, Weland was distracted by Etain dashing into the compound. She untied her grey mare from a pole, slid a short sword into a scabbard on its side and climbed up.

"You are to stay here, Etain," Weland ordered.

She pretended not to hear Weland's protests and moved her horse beside Fionn, flashing him a brilliant smile. Weland snarled in distaste then gave up. Time was too pressing to waste on his daughter and her temporary infatuation. He strapped his sword to his waist, hastily flung on a heavy coat handed to him by a slave, clipped it in place with a gold brooch and then mounted his sturdy horse. Glancing around he made sure Bearach was already mounted before kicking his horse into motion. The group rode out of the town at pace, following the still mud-splattered young man who led the pack on a fresh horse, far superior to the one stolen from a farm. Again people and animals scattered out of his way.

The twelve miles to the coast was covered quickly but nevertheless it seemed to take an age. All the time thoughts raged through Weland's head as he pondered the fisherman's warning. He dragged the bit in the horse's mouth to draw it to a stop, its teeth baring as he did so. The party was slightly south of Rutupia, hidden from what they were here to see by a rare dense bank of trees. Weland sucked in his breath, the feeling becoming a reality.

Romans.

Rutupia, a small blob of land that jutted out into the sea, was joined to the mainland by a narrow strip of land. When Weland was a child it had been a causeway, only reachable when the tide was out. He had competed with his friends to be the last to cross the strip of land, the incoming tide lapping at his heels as he was screamed at. The Roman commander had chosen well, he grudgingly admitted to himself as he held a hand over his eyes to shield them from the sunlight.

Already the Romans had two ditches opened up, one of which ran the full length of Rutupia. Men in armour toiled with implements, working feverishly under the watchful eyes of the mounted officers who paced along the earthworks. Within the workings yet more men laboured, pitching tents taken from piles of kit that seemed bound to topple over. The one weakness, if it could be called that, was the entrance at the western side, a gap in the ditches where logs were being lashed into place to form a gate. Despite himself, Weland was more than a little awed at the speed with which such formidable defences were being created on his own land.

Single-sailed galleys bobbed in the water below. Some, however, were beached, and their cargo was being transported by lines of men, each piece handed from one to the other in long lines that stretched up to the building site. Horses and mules were being coaxed off one by one. Weland saw one beast break its reins and pummel up the beach vainly chased by its handler. On any other day he would have enjoyed the spectacle and laughed at his misfortune.

Weland swore long and loudly. "What a stupid mistake we have made."

"But all the information we had suggested they were not coming," Fionn said in disbelief.

"Well, you can see for yourself the truth in that," Weland replied sarcastically.

"We can achieve no more here," Weland decided. "We must return to Durovernon and prepare for battle." He started to turn his horse away.

"We should attack now whilst we can," Fionn said.

Weland turned in his saddle and jabbed his finger at the Romans. "With these few men you suggest we should take on all of them?"

"We could quickly gather a large enough band. This is when the Romans are at their weakest. If we allow them to become entrenched it will be like digging a wolf out of his lair."

"I have made my decision. We return to Durovernon. We can do no more here."

Fionn glared at Weland's retreating back, determined they should at least do something, even if Weland thought it futile.

"Brennon, we will ride at the Romans," Fionn said.

Brennon grinned, "After you, my lord!"

"Ha!" Fionn shouted and kicked his horse forward, out of the tree cover.

"I am not doing it!" Nemausus protested loudly to Fionn's rapidly disappearing rear.

"Yes you are!" Hueil scowled, grabbed the scarred man's reins and tugged his horse into a gallop to close the gap with the leaders.

His three men spread out beside him, Brennon on the right, Hueil and Nemausus to his left but a little behind, as they galloped towards the camp. Weland whirled around in anger at the shout, grabbing at Etain's reins to stop her following.

A horn blared out from the Roman camp. The defensive ring in front of the construction formed a square bristling with spears to ward off the horsemen.

Fionn rode along the front of the square and loosed off an arrow. It hit a legionary's ribbed armour on the shoulder but, rather than digging in as Fionn expected, it ricocheted off and caught the soldier in the throat. He fell to the ground with a choked scream and was dragged away by his comrades. Another stepped in to replace him, keeping the square tight and impenetrable. Nemausus and Huiel followed suit and a few more Romans fell.

They made two more passes and each time legionaries fell. But Fionn knew his four horses were insufficient to make even a scratch in the voluminous body that faced him. Cavalry could spend all day riding back and forth past a square and do nothing to dent it unless the line was broken, which he had little chance of achieving. Reluctantly he ordered Brennon and the others into a retreat. Behind them the Romans stayed in formation in case the Britons returned.

"You are a young fool!" Weland raged at Fionn once they had rejoined the rear of the group who had stayed to watch the futile demonstration.

"I wanted to test them," he said.

"Some test! What did you achieve?"

"We saw their strength and we killed some soldiers."

"Congratulations — a handful down, thousands left."

"It is far more than you did."

"I told you we were too few to fight them, that we should return to Durovernon and prepare. There was nothing we could have done against such overwhelming numbers and you have just proved that tenfold." Weland stared hard at Fionn. "I do not care who you are related to, even though that fact keeps you alive. Your words mean little in Calleva, less in Camulodunon and here, in Cantium, where I am chief, they mean nothing!"

A red-faced Hueil snarled in anger and pushed forward to redress the insult. Fionn and Brennon held him back. Nemausus looked disappointed that there was to be no fight. Weland ignored all of them and spurred his horse back to the head of the line and next to his daughter.

"Stay away from Fionn," Weland told her. "He is a danger to himself and so to you."

"I make my own choices father," she responded tartly.

"Then the pair of you are equally stupid."

Rather than replying with mere words Etain slowed her horse and dropped back from her father until Fionn was by her side. Her cheeks were crimson and her eyes flashed with barely suppressed anger.

"What was all that about?" Fionn asked.

"You, of course!" she hissed through gritted teeth. "My father thinks you are a fool."

"Tell me something I do not know."

"Well, for once I am in complete agreement with him! Do you have to try and prove yourself every time an opportunity presents itself?"

Fionn was lost for words, unsure how to respond. Etain fell into a fuming silence, staring straight ahead. Fionn suspected that whatever he said to Etain would be wrong, and if he denied her statement then it would be a lie. He looked helplessly at Brennon who shrugged.

Fionn's mind spun as the group rode back to Durovernon, leaving behind them a Roman camp that buzzed like a bees nest.

# XXI

Just over a mile away, across the Uantsumu, Hosidius Geta lead his men onto the Stanora spit. One after the other boats surged up onto the shoreline and soon they stretched out side by side in a row along the beach.

Given the choice Geta, a tough, no-nonsense man, preferred to be in the field with his men over anything else and he bore the scars to prove it. He had never been keen to get himself heavily involved in the administrative duties of camp life and with the increasing seniority of his position had long ago been able to give up the pretence. Instead, he ensured that he surrounded himself with people who were far more willing and capable in the role he was so keen to avoid. The stolid Sennius, his trusted second-in-command, was a perfect fit.

Geta compared Sennius to a cow placed in an untouched field of fresh grass. Once pointed in the right direction Sennius would munch continuously until the task at hand was completed and then stop to await new orders, whatever they may be. He even had the look of a cow, with little hair on his head and doleful eyes that rarely blinked.

Sennius's latest rich sward to crop was the building of the Stanora camp, leaving Geta able to climb into his saddle and join his men. He welcomed it like an old friend, comfortable and familiar compared to the ship he had recently gladly clambered off. His armour felt good and the weight of the gladius was reassuring. He patted his horse on the neck with a massive hand before pulling at the reins and leading the cavalry ala and two centuries of legionaries into Tanneton.

Geta knew Plautius would not like his decision, in fact Sennius had even told him so. The commander's expectation would be the completion of the camp before any action was undertaken, but Plautius was not here and Sennius's advice fell on deaf ears, as he knew it would. Geta was confident he could explain the reasonings of his actions, should the need arise. A half-plausible excuse had already formed in his mind and he knew the rest would be supplied with time, as it had on plenty of occasions before.

Geta knew exactly where the major villages and therefore potential sources of resistance were on Tanneton, and he was determined to wipe them out before they even became aware of the Romans' presence, never mind became capable of forming any sort of meaningful resistance.

Tanneton's highest point, a mere one hundred and sixty feet above sea level, was almost due north from the spit. Geta's force was able to cover the ground with relative ease as the incline was shallow and the ground firm, easy pickings for his well-trained men. Looking back from the peak he could see Sennius was already plodding through his task. Construction of the Stanora camp was well underway and none the worse for his absence. He nodded to himself, sure his decision had been correct now. Beyond the camp he could see Plautius's landing point at Rutupia. Further to the north and to the east it was all flat land and on the horizon the hump of the Dūn skulked.

The island itself was only eleven miles long by four miles across and covered an area of around forty-two square miles. Outside the villages it was sparsely populated with farmsteads like the one Geta now surveyed from the cover of a scrubby tree line. It looked no more than a rude huddle of poor roundhouses protected by a pitifully basic banked ditch. Whether they were confident in their abilities or simply naïve Geta neither knew nor cared. Cultivated fields radiated outwards from the central buildings where figures could be seen bent over and working the land with crude implements. The larger animals, horses and cows, were penned off nearer to the houses but fowl and dogs were allowed to run free and scratch in the dirt for morsels of food. Geta grimaced in distaste.

"This will be easy," he mumbled to himself.

He needed only to give brief instructions to his men. At Geta's signal the legionaries ran to the farm buildings and coolly butchered anyone they found, a swift stab and then move onto the next victim. At the same time the cavalry sprinted through the fields and cut down the labourers with a vicious back-swipe of their swords. Those that tried to run were easily caught; there was no chance of escape. Within minutes there were no human survivors left. Geta was glad that it was still too cold for there to be many flies.

Any additional food, no matter how poor, was welcome, so the animals were rounded up to be taken back to the camp, unaware of their change of ownership but their ultimate fate unchanged. Then the farm buildings were set alight and the skinny corpses tossed into the flames one by one.

No Roman losses had occurred in the assault. The only injury was a burnt hand suffered by a clumsy legionary when he had fired the buildings. Geta scowled at the man's stupidity and told the centurion to put him on report. At least ten lashes would be added to the lesion.

With the job well done Geta thought about the next assault. There was a larger settlement on the coast further to the east. He could imagine the windswept houses that desperately clung onto the shoreline. Geta was supremely confident in the abilities of his men and fully expected the village would pose little threat, despite its size. His men had had some easy target practice and their blood was up.

Geta knew the island had several names. One was the Bright Island. Whoever first suggested this depiction must have been blind and deaf, as Geta thought Tanneton a bleak, uninviting place. As he rode away from the farm the thatch was heavily ablaze. A pall of black smoke issued from it, carrying the smell of burning meat. Let them know death is coming, he thought.

Geta grinned as he remembered the island's other name. In the next few hours he and his soldiers would ensure the name was made appropriate — the Isle of the Dead.

# XXII

The sun was setting as Plautius walked around the camp on an inspection of its defences. Although bone-tired after the long day, he was nevertheless enjoying the brief respite, away from his officers and the multitude of decisions he was expected to make. Solitude was something Plautius rarely craved, but today he took it willingly, even if just for a short time.

Even in April, Rutupia was bleak and inhospitable. Jutting out into the sea as it did, it was subject to everything the local weather threw at it. A blustery chill wind that had started from the south-west after their landing had hardly added to its appeal. He wondered what the place would be like in the winter and sincerely hoped he was not here when the conditions closed in. He imagined the wind to be bitter and the rain sharp as arrowheads.

Plautius nodded at a shivering sentry who stood briskly to attention as he neared. The general let his cloak flap open despite the wind stripping the heat from his body, wanting the legionary to know they shared the same privations. The man smiled gratefully. When his back was turned Plautius could hear the sentry stamping his feet to warm himself up, the hobnailed sandals thudding into the hard surface.

Plautius found little fault with the camp. Not that he had expected to, but he was a man who liked to check details and it was a perfect excuse. The defences were strong, the men were well settled and morale was high now they were back on dry land and the crossing banished into the recesses of memory. A small band of horsemen had briefly tested them but they had been easily swatted away and since then the II$^{nd}$ had been allowed to build the rest of their camp unmolested. Beneficially, the attack made the legionaries more alert and keen eyes looked out into the dusk, hunting for any movement on the horizon.

Plautius turned to face out to sea. The angry eye of the sinking sun spread a livid scarlet haze across the horizon, like blood in water. He took it as a good omen and would say so to Narcissus when they ate later.

The general was pleased; the day really could not have gone any better. The force was safely banked, losses inconsequential and, albeit tiny, a piece of Rome was imposed on this barbarous terrain. Soon his task would be to spread his, and therefore Rome's, grip wider as the move inland began. Then blood would be spilt, as red as the sky above him.

## XXIII

The messenger waited outside, taking the opportunity of a brief rest and some sustenance with both hands. He waited for orders to take back across the country and whilst he did so listened to the recriminating argument that was underway.

"Why did we not plan for this?" Caradoc raged. He had not felt an anger of this measure for many years, but directed it more at himself than anyone else for ignoring his instincts and instead accepting the counsel of others.

"Yours was not the final decision," Kynthelig said soothingly, attempting, unsuccessfully, to placate Caradoc.

"That is irrelevant. I could have argued more strongly, kept some of my own men there. Anything!" Deep in his heart Caradoc had known the Romans were still a threat and that they should have prepared accordingly. Thanks to him, the Britons had left themselves exposed and could yet pay a heavy price for their failure to look ahead.

"Based on the information we had at the time and the circumstances we were in, it was the right decision to make," Kynthelig said, defending Togodumnus.

"But that does not make our position now any better does it?" Caradoc said, shaking his head. He squeezed the bridge of his nose as a dull throb at his temples threatened to spread and engulf his forehead. "The army has to be rebuilt, which will take time, more than we have to defend Cantium, which is as good as lost. Weland is on his own for the moment."

"Maybe he can hold the Romans."

"Maybe," Caradoc agreed, but it did not sound entirely convincing, even to his own ears.

"What do you suggest?" Kynthelig did not feel any better than Caradoc. It was not so long ago that he had been celebrating the success of his plans and now they looked as if they could be smashed into a million pieces.

"Let me think."

Caradoc paced up and down, deep in thought. He wished his father were here; he would know what to do straight away. But he could not think like that, he told himself. Cunobelin was dead and it was just Togodumnus and himself now.

The first thing to do, he knew, was rebuild the army. That would take time but they could plan in parallel. Caradoc called for messengers to be sent out to the tribal leaders — the Atrebates, Durotriges, Dumnonii, Dobunni and the rest. He needed men and he needed them quickly.

Then Caradoc called Weland's man back in. The messenger's mouth was still full of food, which he tried hard to swallow, coughing with the effort.

"Tell Weland he is to stand at Durovernon. Hold the Romans at all costs."

The messenger ran from the room, shouting for his horse, then galloped away.

For now it all depended upon Weland. If the Cantii were to fail, perhaps Britain would fall with him.

# XXIV

The smell of hot wine wafted around the lofty interior of the tent, mingling with the smell of burning lamp oil, producing a heady concoction. It was already warm and musty inside — the flaps were tied down whilst Plautius met with his senior officers. Outside, a pair of legionaries stood guard at the entrance. The select group sat around a large table, maps and plans spread out on it although their contents were well known to all.

"Proceed," Plautius requested. He waved the alcohol away and the servant moved onto the next officer.

Didius Gallus placed his goblet on the table. "The initial reconnaissance of the area has shown no immediate threats," the heavyset Cavalry Prefect rumbled. "The searches have been by small cavalry groups of five men. They have been told to avoid any settlements, which have been small farms at best, and simply to gather intelligence."

If Plautius were asked to guess which part of the army Gallus served in, his last choice would have been the cavalry. Such a large man had no place mounted and he assumed Gallus would not fit comfortably onto any conventionally-sized horse. However, he was certainly capable and his plain face shone with confidence.

"So far the Britons have not reacted again to our being here, since the brief skirmish after the landing," Vespasian said.

"We should assume that a response from them is just a question of time," Plautius warned. "There can be no relaxing of our guard." He looked at each of his senior officers in turn to ensure the message was received with nods of reassurance.

"The subjugation of Tanneton is almost complete," Geta said, his tone clipped and his speech rapid. He had arrived from the island that morning by boat, specifically for the briefing. "Resistance was minimal, as expected. A few people escaped by boat but they are inconsequential. The rest of the population are under control."

"I thought you said the task was mostly completed, Geta. Is Tanneton fully under our command or not?" challenged Curius, the Classis Britannica Prefect, languidly. He turned to look meaningfully at Plautius, an eyebrow raised in question and a smirk stitched on his face. Plautius knew there was history between the two but so far had been unable to determine exactly what it consisted of. Neither man would speak of it.

"It is good to see a few years on water have not taken the edge off your pompous attitude, Virginius," Geta sneered.

"How dare you!" Curius spat leaping to his feet, bristling at the use of the nickname he had tried very hard to leave behind him, a reminder of the distant past.

Geta laughed at the little man, Curis's faced now flushed a bright red hue that matched the colour of his receding hair, inflaming him even further.

"If you wish to challenge me, I will happily accept," Geta said. "In fact it would do you a favour. A few scars on that ugly face of yours may make it vaguely more attractive and perhaps get you a woman you would not have to pay for." He paused for a moment, apparently reconsidering. "Then again, you would need to pray for a miracle to survive with only scars."

Gallus sensed that his friend's short temper could soon cost him dearly and it was time to put a stop to his goading. He and Geta had been firm friends from childhood, and it had stretched into their adult lives. Wherever possible, and no matter how small the favour, the pair helped each other's career along, following a protracted tradition that stretched back generations between their two families.

Gallus planted his substantial bulk in front of Curius, whose Adam's apple bobbed nervously. He put out a hand and placed it in the middle of the smaller man's chest then, with minimal effort, shoved the diminutive prefect back into his seat. He landed hard, his feet lifting off the ground as he fell backwards, the chair almost toppling over.

"I suggest you apologise to Hosidius before this gets out of hand," Gallus advised.

"What?" Curius spluttered, trying to stand again, sweat prickling his brow. Gallus nonchalantly pushed him back into his seat.

"I will do no such thing. I have nothing to apologise for!" Curius gulped and looked wildly around the room, trying to find support in the others' faces but seeing little.

"Enough!" Plautius shouted, his tolerance finally stretched to breaking point. "We have more important aspects yet to discuss, far beyond your petty squabbles." He waited for Gallus to seat himself again. Curius opened his mouth, ready to protest his innocence, but wisely clamped his jaw shut when he saw the look on Plautius's face. He resorted instead to unconsciously fingering a large mole on his face that had several hairs protruding from it.

A tense silence fell, which Plautius eventually broke.

"Now, back to business. It is time to extend our control and move the plan to the next phase. First we need to direct what goes in and what comes out of the Uantsumu. The outpost at Rogulbio is well established and two hundred and fifty men are stationed there, so both ends of the channel are ours.

"Curius, order the warships out into the Uantsumu. Stop and board anything floating that moves."

"What do we do with them once we have stopped them?" Curius asked. Geta rolled his eyes in exasperation and sighed loudly. Curius glared at him.

"Judge whether the ship is a threat or not," Plautius said patiently. "If it is, sink it. It is your choice whether you take any prisoners or not. If you deem the vessel harmless, let it go about its business." Curius dutifully wrote down his orders in a neat, patient script.

"You only need board ships, Virginius. If it is a floating log, you can safely ignore it," Geta whispered from the side of his mouth.

"Shut up!" Curius said, making Plautius look at him. Geta looked surprised and shrugged at Gallus as if he had no understanding as to why Curius had spoken.

Plautius continued, ignoring the outburst. "As you know this morning I have ordered the third division to sail from Gesoriacum. Crispus assures me that the outer camp will be ready in time for their arrival." The tribune nodded vigorously in agreement. "Then, in two days time, we will advance towards Durovernon. It is a small town and lightly defended so should not pose too much difficulty for us. An early victory will be important for the men's morale. It will hopefully also damage that of the Britons.

"At the same time as the advance to Durovernon begins, a vexilation from the XX[th], supported by the Classis Britannica, will head the twelve miles south to take the port of Dubras. It will offer a superior base for the fleet to operate out of than Stanora, and the bulk of the ships will relocate there once the harbour is secure."

"Good," Geta mumbled, receiving another glare from Curius, which elicited a smirk from his tormentor.

Plautius ticked off the points he had covered. "Next..."

A sudden shouting in bad Latin interrupted the general. Despite the muffling effect of the thick hide material of the tent it was quite clear who was causing the commotion. Plautius swore under his breath and gave Narcissus a look of annoyance.

Outside he found Adminius ranting at a staff officer who stood between the fat man and his intended destination, and who was blithely ignoring the threats levelled at him. Two of Adminius's men were being forcibly restrained by several legionaries, their long swords lying a distance away.

Before Plautius could speak Adminius rounded on him. "This is an outrage!" he spat. "I tried to join your meeting but I was forcibly stopped by these, these...animals!" He waved a pudgy hand at the officer and the soldiers.

"Adminius insisted on joining you. His *companions* were armed so we stopped them entering as you ordered," the staff officer reported.

Adminius opened his mouth to argue but Plautius, white-faced, turned his back on him. He stepped towards Narcissus, dragging him to one side.

"This man is becoming more and more troublesome!" he hissed, his face close to the secretary's. "I advised you he would be impossible to handle and a liability to boot. He is supposed to be a guide, and no more, yet he acts like he *owns* the place. He is your man so please take him in hand or so help me *I* will."

Narcissus looked coolly at Plautius then lowered his eyes to the hand that gripped his arm. Plautius let go but did not retreat.

"Adminius is the emperor's man, not mine," Narcissus said, his voice icy. "I am merely here to observe and support the invasion process where necessary, as you well know. However believe me when I tell you that he will have his uses and you will see the benefit of these soon. But for now I will deal with him." He turned away.

"My lord Adminius, how good to see you. I trust you had a good night's sleep? No? Mine was awful too..." Narcissus took Adminius by the elbow and steered him away from Plautius's tent.

"This is not a good start, Geta," Plautius said, staring at the backs of the retreating pair. "I have a nasty feeling about that man."

"Which one?" Geta replied.

# XXV

Max was livid. First Adminius had made plain his distaste with the indignity of being located in the retentura, well away from the praetorium. His words were colourful and intermingled with numerous swear words — the Briton believed it was beneath him to be placed where he was.

If truth be told, Max was also unhappy. Most of the soldiers around him were boys, still unblooded in battle. They looked at him in awe, as if he was some walking relic, and for the first time in his career he felt old.

Max suspected it had been a double snub. Plautius was too polite to express his thoughts openly, but Max was astute enough to recognise the general would be unwilling to have a century in his party that was not entirely under his command. Max assumed it was a case of out of sight, out of mind.

After their one-sided argument Adminius had stamped off in a vile temper. Max was happy to see the back of him. It was like dealing with an overblown child and he was mightily sick of it. He had no experience of infants and certainly no desire to fill the gap in his knowledge.

However, the hour of respite Max gained led directly to his second, far more creative grilling. A red-faced legionary arrived panting at his tent with orders to immediately present himself at the general's quarters. Puzzled, Max did so, after leaving it a decent length of time. No point in seeming too enthusiastic, he thought.

Plautius then subjected Max to a furious tirade for allowing Adminius to wander off to the praetorium without an escort. Narcissus looked on with a disappointed look on his face. Worse still, Adminius had taken his own armed men with him. Max closed his eyes to mask the seething anger that coursed through his body.

Plautius then threatened to expel Max and ship him, and all of his men, back to Rome in dishonour. Only the fact that the Praetorians were in Britain to protect Narcissus was stopping him.

Max made his way back to his tent fuming at the ignominy of it all, the accusation of the irrelevance of the Praetorians ringing in his ears. He stopped in his tracks, causing a legionary to bump into him. He cut off an apology, retreating from the look of anger on the centurion's face, swung around and retraced his steps back to the praetorium.

Later Max and Anatolius shared an amphora of wine whilst Max repeated the events of his day.

"Plautius will learn he was wrong to underestimate us, and me," he said, taking a gulp of his wine. Finding the glass empty, he filled it up again, sloshing some onto the table in his pent-up irritation.

"How?" Anatolius had to ask, although he doubted he would like the answer.

"I demanded Plautius place us in the front line when we fight the Britons." Max took another drink whilst Anatolius choked on his own. "He said yes. I think he is pleased, hoping some ill might befall us. Then we are no longer a trouble to him," Max said bitterly.

"What about Narcissus?" Any port in a storm, thought Anatolius.

"There are enough soldiers to protect him a thousand times over. Plautius knows it and Narcissus does too. He just likes having his own personal bodyguard. Well, we are better than that. When we are in battle, then they will see how much we Praetorians can do on our own," Max said, raising his glass to buttress the promise.

"Why, Max?"

"It is a matter of honour, Anatolius. You should know that."

Anatolius grimaced but hid the look from Max. Honour meant nothing to him — it could get you killed — but it was everything to Max. On rare occasions, the desire for retribution and the maintenance of his principles overcame Max's usual calm calculation and led them down difficult paths. Anatolius fervently hoped this was not one of those times. Not that there was anything he could do about it.

Anatolius drained his wine. "Well, here's to death," he said and banged his goblet on the table.

They were going to war with the Britons.

## XXVI

Fionn watched the Roman legionaries moving about inside the recently-constructed outpost. It was an identical but much smaller copy of the camp at Rutupia, and so held far fewer soldiers —hundreds rather than thousands, he estimated. Comparatively speaking, it was a much target but nevertheless the defences were sturdy and the approach to it was a challenge. Assaulting it would not be *that* straightforward.

The outpost was located on the Rogulbio peninsula and faced across the northern end of the Uantsumu to Tanneton, where a single Roman warship roamed the watery expanse between the landmasses. The camp huddled on a low mound flanked to the south and east by marshland, with a vaguely drier approach between the sodden areas. Beyond the marsh were the margins of a dense forest. There was no human occupation to speak of within several miles of this elementally-challenged landscape and, shivering in the perennially blasting wind, Fionn could understand why.

After returning to Durovernon from Rutupia, Weland had proved inward and introspective, prompting Etain to voice several times how puzzled she was by his behaviour. But Fionn was utterly uninterested in the source of the Cantii chief's malaise and was instead resolute in harassing him to react aggressively to the Romans' presence.

Finally, in a burst of anger, Weland relented and agreed to allow Fionn to take some of his men to Rogulbio just to get rid of him. Bearach was included at Weland's behest so that at least there was one person he had a degree of trust in, but for his part Fionn was pleased Bearach had joined them.

But Weland refused point-blank refused to let Etain take part in the sortie, much to her evident disgust. Fionn smiled as he remembered some of the colourful descriptions, intermingled with choice swear words, she had levelled at her father. For a moment Weland had looked nonplussed, unsure how to respond without losing even more credibility in front of his men, who dared not laugh in case they were rounded upon and used as a pressure relief. After the unanswered tirade Etain withdrew in a stiff silence to her rooms and stayed there.

With Fionn were about fifty men of various capabilities. Most were on foot, a few on horseback. Some had bladed weapons, but many carried blunt farm implements or heavy sticks. Three carried slingshots and there were even a couple of bows besides the one Fionn carried. It was a motley band and one thing was clear — they were little threat to the outpost.

Fionn cursed himself for getting into such a position, wondering whether Weland had in fact engineered it that way. To go back now without even fighting, never mind any form of success, would be a disaster. Weland would think even less of Fionn, if that were remotely possible, and make his pursuit of Etain all the harder. Fionn took Bearach and Brennon to one side. They needed a plan.

"Sir, this is madness," Luburnius warned. The grey-haired veteran had not meant to speak so bluntly but the words slipped out. With mounting anxiety he watched the colour rise in the younger man's face. Fulvius's bottom lip pushed out in a pout that the most spoilt child would have been proud of, and his watery eyes blinked furiously. But Luburnius felt he had every right to be worried.

"How *dare* you question my authority," Fulvius said icily, bristling at the disrespect the grizzled centurion was showing him, the senior officer!

Fulvius's reputation as an arrogant man had preceded him and, unfortunately, was proving to be correct, and then some. He came from an old, illustrious family that had once been very wealthy and wielded considerable influence. But all that was long in the past. The family had fallen on hard times and plummeted from the upper echelons of Roman society.

But Fulvius saw himself as the source of his family regaining its power and prestige. He knew for certain he was destined to be one of Rome's high achievers; he had been told so by an old crone who had read the signs and he was desperate to believe her with all his heart.

So, like many others before him, Fulvius was using a period in the army as a stepping-stone on the way to prominence. But the weakness of the process was that it tended to deliver highly-ranked officers with little or no military knowledge into combat situations. Most tribunes took the sensible course of relying on their centurion's greater experience to get them through their brief military careers but Fulvius, of course, knew better and had absolutely no use for the older man. Why would he? Fulvius knew it all.

"In my opinion, sir, to patrol the woods is a course of action that could put us in significant danger. I think..."

"I am not asking you to think, I am demanding you *obey* me!" Fulvius shouted, finally losing his temper. "We will patrol those woods. There are no Britons within miles of here, but if there are, all the better. I will ensure they are slaughtered to a man!"

"Sir..."

"Enough!" He waved to the optio who warily crossed the parade ground to Fulvius, accompanied by two legionaries. "You, take Luburnius and put him under guard."

Fulvius turned back to Luburnius. "I will deal with you when I return. Fifty lashes should give you a healthy respect for your betters."

The open-mouthed optio looked uncertainly at Luburnius until the centurion unstrapped his gladius and pugio and placed them in the optio's hands. Fifty lashes was a probable death sentence, he knew.

The two legionaries led Luburnius away to be put under lock and key.

"Optio, what is your name?" Fulvius demanded.

"Ecimius, sir," he replied, still holding Luburnius's weapons and uncertain what to do with them.

"Assemble thirty men on the parade ground. We will leave on patrol in ten minutes."

"Yes, sir."

"At last, some respect," Fulvius muttered to himself. He was looking forward to seeing the disgraced Luburnius receive the lash. It was a fine way to keep warm.

A relieved Bearach had finally persuaded the distinctly reluctant Fionn of the benefits in returning to Durovernon. But just as Fionn was about to issue the order a horn sounded from within the camp. The trio turned to watch as a detachment of legionaries march out at a steady pace. The gates slammed shut behind them.

"Looks like they are heading this way," Brennon observed.

And they were. A smartly-dressed officer sat tight and erect on his horse followed by thirty legionaries in ranks three across. They were heading right through the middle of the marshy area and towards the trees.

The trio held a hurried discussion, all thought of returning to Durovernon banished.

Fulvius's armour had been buffed by his servants until it shone, then buffed again. He was immensely proud of the rich finery and at last the opportunity had arrived to wear it. How he wished his friends and enemies alike back in Rome could see him now. How they would sting with envy!

The patrol had been marching steadily for about fifteen minutes and so far had not encountered a soul. Fulvius was pleased that he had been proven correct, and he made a mental note to tell Luburnius so before the lashes were applied. Maybe an extra ten should be added for good measure, he thought.

The forest had been deathly quiet since they entered. A small alarm rang at the back of his mind but Fulvius pushed the nagging thought deeper into the recesses. It was probably the noise of his men that were driving the wildlife away. Yes, that was it. Placated, the alarm became muted.

Fulvius twisted in his saddle. Directly behind him marched the ranked legionaries, Ecimius bringing up the rear. They looked nervous and constantly cast their eyes around, trying to pierce the dark shadows. Fulvius sneered at their fear and turned away from them, too disgusted to look into their faces. Maybe Ecimius should be beaten after Luburnius, he considered.

And then the world went crazy.

Ecimius grunted. He looked down in amazement at the arrow sticking out of his side. He put his hand to the shaft and touched it. It was real and blood was on his hand when he pulled it away. His blood. Ecimius was amazed at how bright a red it was.

From the trees burst a multitude of wild warriors swinging sticks and swords and brandishing spears. Stones pelted the legionaries and within seconds several were down, hit in the face by whizzing missiles.

Fulvius was at a loss. His brain seized up and his mouth went dry as his men were massacred around him. Piece by piece the long-haired men were tearing his detachment apart, but before he could issue an order the tribune went rigid in his saddle. He opened his mouth to scream but could only gurgle as blood filled his mouth and throat. Fulvius looked down in horror at the spear that protruded from his gleaming armour. He toppled from his horse and fell hard on the floor, knocking what little breath was left out of him. As his world darkened Fulvius saw the bright future the crone had promised fading. He knew she had lied to him as the noises of his first, and last, battle receded to oblivion.

The surprise was so complete Fionn lost only a handful of men to a knot of legionaries with enough wits about them to react immediately to the attack, decimating the Britons, who were without armour and carried only feeble weapons. But the surprise and superior numbers soon counted. After five frantic minutes the entire Roman detachment was slaughtered.

Fionn allowed his victorious men to search the bodies, looking for anything of value. Weapons and armour were taken and corpses decapitated, all prized possessions. Fionn commandeered Fulvius's horse. It was a fine beast and a worthy reward.

Fulvius's head, tied to the saddle, briefly leaked blood onto the horse's legs.

Fionn led his men back to the edge of the woods. The outpost was still sealed up tight, legionaries tirelessly patrolling the ramparts. Fionn kicked Fulvius's horse forward. As soon as he emerged from the forest a horn bellowed a warning from inside the camp. He rode a few hundred yards into the open ground. Not so close to be in range of Roman weapons but near enough that they would have a good inkling of what was being left for them.

Fionn pushed the body off the horse. It landed on the ground with a soft thump. He sat for a moment watching the outpost. No one moved. Fionn wheeled his horse away and cantered back into the trees.

It was an hour before Luburnius would allow anyone through the gates. Soon after the horn sounded he was freed from the cell where he was being held and his gladius returned. The centurion ordered the men to watch the treeline closely but they had not seen any movement since the rider had disappeared back into its shadows. Luburnius's instincts told him the

Britons were gone and Fulvius was long overdue.

At last Luburnius himself rode out to where the corpse had been dumped, alert for any kind of attack. It was obvious straight away who lay at his feet. He felt sad that a life had been wasted, but he was certain where the fault lay.

"Pick it up," he ordered.

The torso was levered onto a horse by two legionaries. Whilst they escorted the grizzly package back to the outpost, Luburnius began constructing the report in his head to explain how his commanding officer had been killed and dumped like a slaughtered pig.

# XXVII

It was still dark when Plautius's servant roused him from a light and fitful sleep. The gentle shake of his shoulder was an unwelcome intrusion and it was all Plautius could do not to shout at the man.

He had slept badly and his body told him so as it struggled into sluggish activity. A nervous apprehension had twisted and churned in his gut throughout the night, as if he had eaten a heavy meal that he was digesting only with difficulty. Once alert, his mind stayed active, seeking the source of the worry — usually the smallest of things — and gnawing at his conscience like a rat attacking a piece of gristle.

Eventually he would open his eyes to stare into the darkness, rise with a heavy sigh to issue orders to an equally drawn-looking staff officer and crawl back into bed. Having pacified the gnawing he attempted to go back to sleep, only to find the tension winding up again before an hour was out.

It was not a lack of confidence in Plautius, far from it; he and his men were fairly bristling with self-belief. It was simply that Plautius was a meticulous planner; he could not help himself. He wanted to be sure everything was right, even though he knew that was impossible — the task was simply too big and there were too many people involved. Sometimes he wished he were more like Geta, more willing to take things as they came and deal with them accordingly. But with the start of the new day the march inland was upon them and it was too late for Plautius to do anything more. The intricacies had to be forced into the back of his mind.

The general sat up in bed and rubbed his hand over his face. He scratched at the day-old stubble on his chin, soon to be scraped off by his servant with a sharp blade, oil and hot water, then rolled out of bed. The space within the tent was warm from the blazing braziers stoked by the servant on his way out. A horn blew over the camp to rouse the legionaries who, knowing what the next day would bring, had slept as poorly as their general. The horn would later ring out three times -— to break camp, signalling that tents should be folded and baggage packed, to place the baggage on the mules and carts and finally to initiate the march —

but for now it simply awoke the camp and set it about its business.

As Plautius sat in the chair and the servant prepared the shaving blade (the general liked to be clean before he ate) he thought back over recent events. To his surprise the Britons had remained absent from the field, their only activity a bloody and apparently opportunistic attack on a patrol outside Rogulbio. The loss of any soldier was regrettable but, in the scheme of things, largely meaningless. A mere handful of legionaries had been killed and their slaying would have absolutely no effect on the outcome of today's action.

An entirely different matter was the need to keep morale high. This was particularly so at the beginning of a campaign and for the raw recruits who, like a father awaiting the birth of his first child, had absolutely no experience of what was to come and only fear to comfort them.

The action at Rogulbio had initially caused Plautius a lot of worry. The gossip spread across the camp like wildfire tearing through tinder dry brush, hot and fast. From his reading of the centurion's report the blame for the slaughter seemed to be laid squarely at the feet of an unproven officer who had failed to listen to his far more experienced but junior subordinate. If that were true — and Plautius knew it was easy to blame the dead as they had no voice to defend themselves — the loss of one green, arrogant officer was irrelevant as far as he was concerned.

But in this case the death of the officer — Fulvius, he recalled from Luburnius' report — actually proved to be a benefit. It transpired that Fulvius was deeply unpopular in the legions, even though he had only recently joined up. Astonishingly, the word coming back from the ranks via the centurions was that his death was being greeted with delight. That a few good soldiers had been lost with him were seen as an acceptable, albeit unfortunate, consequence. If anything, morale improved slightly — one less idiot to lead them into potential disaster was a good thing as far as the men were concerned.

Soldiers, Plautius thought, shaking his head, were strange and unpredictable animals. The servant lifted the blade away from Plautius' chin in a hurry, afraid of cutting him.

"Please, keep still, sir," he said apologetically and returned to his careful scraping.

In the days following the loss at Rogulbio, the third division arrived from Gaul, bringing more supplies and the balance of the invasion force — in particular the multitude of administrators and staff officers that the Roman army seemed unable to operate without. The new arrivals marched smartly into Crispus's freshly built and substantial camp. Quickly they spread out and bedded down, soon integrated with the advance party, the legions glad to be whole again.

The original camp at Rutupia had been dismantled, stripped of anything valuable and its defences slighted so it was of no use to an occupying enemy. The same happened at Tanneton. Only a garrison remained, inhabiting a much-reduced outpost to retain control over what was now, thanks to Geta, the almost entirely deserted island. Their sole task was to protect the southern entrance to the Uantsumu.

The already high risk of trading with the Britons increased to unacceptable levels for all but the most desperate of continental businessmen as Curius took Plautius's orders absolutely literally. As a result, Classis Britannica warships prowled at will along the three-mile length of the channel, looking for anything bigger than a stick which floated on the murky brown waters. Trade with the continent via the Uantsumu all but ceased as ships avoided the area. Instead, the gold flowed through other parts of the country and the poorer tribes welcomed the unexpected windfall with open arms.

But Plautius cared nothing for the short-term impacts on the economy. Today his mind was solely on Durovernon. He rose from the chair, his scraped skin tingling, and began to dress.

A pale yellow hue was creeping over the horizon when the scout returned from the field. He trotted into camp, dismounted from his mare and stretched to relieve the tension in his aching muscles. The young man wore no protective armour and just a gladius as a weapon, relying solely on speed and superb riding abilities to get him out of trouble.

He found Gallus in his tent and saluted smartly. The cavalry prefect was in the process of demolishing a huge breakfast, sampling a sea bird his servant had snared last night. So far he was not impressed. Geta sat by his side, attacking a considerably smaller but still substantial plate of food. He avoided the bird, which even his strong constitution baulked at.

"Well?" Gallus, his mouth full of food, prompted the scout.

"No enemy sighted, sir," the scout said, trying hard to ignore the press of his empty stomach. Even the bird looked tempting.

"What, no one at all?" Gallus glanced at Geta, his eyebrows raised.

"I did not see any armed men, sir, in the two days I have been in the field. The farms in the immediate area are deserted too."

"Anything else to report?"

"No, sir."

"Then you may go." The scout eagerly left the tent in an immediate search for food to settle his pangs of hunger.

Gallus sat back. Although he pushed his plate away his servant knew better than to withdraw it, as the big man could very easily, and sometimes literally, get a second wind.

"None of the scouts have reported any activity from the enemy," Gallus said, looking puzzled.

"It is certainly unusual," Geta agreed around a mouthful.

"What do you think?"

"They are so petrified of our might they have run away and left Britain to us!" Geta laughed.

Gallus responded with a half-hearted chuckle, not convinced and for once not appreciating his friend's need to see the joke in everything. "It is most puzzling."

"Let Plautius sort out what it means. That is his job."

"Good point," Gallus brightened. "Before I go to see him there is time for some more to eat!" He drew his plate back and snapped his fingers for it to be filled. "But no more of that bloody bird!" he warned. The servant swiftly reversed his path and wheeled the carcass away to be disposed of.

Plautius, with help, clambered onto his horse and settled into place with a little shuffling of his backside. Despite years of being in the saddle he felt far less comfortable trusting what he saw as an unpredictable, dumb animal with his welfare compared with a sturdy ship and its well-trained crew.

He made sure his cloak, the signature of his rank, cascaded properly over his shoulder and onto the back of the horse, and adjusted it slightly so it was just right. He nudged the horse forward and proceeded in a slow walk past the legionaries assembled in rows on the parade ground. They looked every piece the formidable force Plautius knew they were and he nodded to himself, satisfied.

"What a sight," Geta said from his own horse as he watched Plautius. "It is one I never tire of."

"Fabulous," Gallus agreed, rubbing his nicely crammed stomach.

The legionaries looked at their best now and fairly glimmered in the sunlight. But in the upcoming weeks of campaigning their clothes would be stained, armour dented, personal hygiene would become less important and gaps would appear in the ranks as some would fall in battle.

Equipment was recycled, sometimes willingly, sometimes not, until it was utterly useless. It could be inherited on retirement, passed from old to young or scavenged from the field on death. Personal preference or superstition also played a part in their selection. So the soldiers before Plautius were equipped in a mix of armour and weaponry. A small proportion of the items were brand-new but most were worn, the dents, nicks and scratches hammered out and the metal buffed to give the illusion of newness.

Some of the legionaries wore the latest armour — the ribbed cuirass — others had chain mail shirts. Their helmets varied in design too, some with wide cheek plates, other older types with narrower plates. Some helmets had grand plumes to mark seniority, but most were bare. Even the length and shape of the gladius varied, but this was not immediately obvious as their swords were sheathed.

Plautius completed his inspection and returned to the centre. He halted his horse, which snorted and shook its head. The general saluted his men, who seemed to stiffen even more and hold their chins that little bit higher, before he swung his horse about and ambled to the gate. He drew up alongside Vespasian to watch the men march out.

"Morning, sir," Vespasian said. "Did you sleep well?"

"Not particularly. I hate the night before a campaign starts." Unconsciously Plautius rubbed at his stomach in case the gnawing started up again. "How about you?"

"I sleep very little if truth be told. A couple of hours are usually all I need."

"Lucky you," Plautius grunted.

This morning, once dressed, Vespasian had followed his daily custom in the small hours. He took a silver cup, given to him by his grandmother, from his baggage and placed it on the table before filling it with wine. He lifted the cup to his mouth, paused for a moment to offer a prayer to her memory and then allowed the liquid to seep past his lips.

Today he broke slightly from tradition and offered a second appeal, for strength and for victory in the days ahead. Before leaving Germania, he had visited a shrine, a small building that was rarely used and had fallen somewhat into disrepair, becoming a little overgrown. Vespasian liked the place for its solitude — it was not an easy place to find — and its willingness to age gracefully. He was only able to spend a little time there but before leaving he left a prayer among the hundreds of others,who knows how many years old. Vespasian vowed that if he were to return from battle flushed with success a great reward would be sent the way of the gods. This morning he reminded the deities of his promise and asked that they meet their end of the bargain.

Plautius gave the signal that the march should begin. The musician drew in a great breath to fill his lungs to capacity, placed his lips to the mouthpiece and blew so hard his cheeks puffed out and his face went red.

"Move out!" Gallus barked as the note reverberated around the surrounding area.

A section of auxiliary light cavalry trotted out of the camp and, once free of its confines, spurred their horses into a gallop to take up a position at point half a mile ahead of the column, where they would remain as it stalked through enemy territory.

The first soldiers to march out of the camp, six abreast, were more auxiliaries. Lightly armed, they were specifically equipped to deal with enemy skirmishers and ambushes. Like the scouts they relied more on speed than equipment. The purpose of this initial section of the column was to actively seek out trouble by poking their noses into any cover which could conceivably conceal the Britons. If any traps were sprung then word would be sent to Plautius so the army could respond accordingly. If necessary, the advance guard would hold the enemy off until the main body could arrive and deploy.

The auxiliary were the workhorses of the Roman army. They were paid less, had fewer conditions of service and inferior equipment compared to their legionary counterparts. They were expendable fodder for the opening stages of a battle; the Roman senior officers took the view that it was better to see a foreigner and non-citizen die than a true Roman. So the upper echelons of command were not particularly interested in the auxiliaries, provided they followed the rules and fought well. In many ways, the auxiliaries more resembled in appearance the Britons they were about to wrestle with than their own comrades.

The auxiliaries, however, bore the criticism and prejudice stoically, because service in the Roman army brought a reward so great as to be worth everything the army and the enemy could throw at them — citizenship. If they survived twenty-five years of service they became members of the most powerful state in the world, a benefit they could pass on to future generations of their family.

And so the auxiliaries willingly pressed out deep into enemy territory whilst Gallus waited with his men, already citizens, ready to form on the right and left flanks of the column as it exited the defences. The regular cavalry would be a ranging form of protection that could move rapidly and at will to where they were needed should the column be attacked.

The true head of the column then stamped out of the camp, a mix of legionaries and heavy cavalry to deal with the enemy should the auxiliary horse, already a distant dust cloud, spring any traps.

Plautius let the head of the column pass then nudged his horse forward, out of the camp and, for him at least, into virgin enemy territory. Vespasian followed in his wake. He raised a calloused hand in response to Gallus's jaunty wave as they passed the cavalry prefect's position. Plautius's guard immediately fell in step behind the general. It comprised an ala of cavalry, another of pike men and the first cohort of the II[nd], the finest and most experienced fighters in the invasion force.

Behind the guard trotted the immunes, the men excused heavy

duties due to their skills. They accomplished whatever civil engineering task was needed to conquer the lands the Romans entered and carried the tools and instruments of their trade on their backs or over their shoulders, ready to deploy when needed.

Heavy cavalry accompanied the senior officer's baggage, behind which they themselves, rode accompanied by an infantry guard. Narcissus was pleased to be surrounded by grim-faced men bristling with armour and weapons as they exited the relative safety of the camp. The previous evening Plautius had suggested to him that perhaps he should stay behind in the camp, but the secretary was too proud to admit his fear, and with a resolve he hardly felt had told Plautius that he would ride with the column. Now he laughed to himself at his earlier worries, convinced that no barbarian could pierce his resolve.

Adminius rode beside Narcissus, wittily — in his own opinion — regaling Narcissus with tales and pointing out things of interest in the otherwise uninspiring landscape. In truth, Narcissus barely heard a word the flabby man was saying, but with a long honed political skill he nodded politely at the right times and feigned an interested expression. But his thoughts remained solidly elsewhere.

Narcissus watched as a centurion, marked out by a transverse crest on his helmet, raised a vine wood stick — his other badge of office — and smashed it down on the helmet of a legionary for some infraction. All along the column centurions patrolled, maintaining discipline and order in the ranks.

Much to the disgust of the infantry, Max rode slightly behind Narcissus, with Anatolius and the Praetorian century in his wake. However, Plautius would not stretch to allowing Adminius's own men, Britons themselves, to guard their master and so they were forced to march at the very rear of the column. Narcissus had expected Adminius to suffer an apoplectic fit at the insult but he barely argued, simply shrugged.

Buried well within the column, Martius carried the eagle proudly aloft. He was accompanied by the signifers with the standards of the four legions and an image of Claudius, so the soldiers would not forget who they were fighting for.

Despite all the men that had already exited the camp the largest section of the column was formed by the infantry. They marched behind the musicians, who would blow signals to convey orders on the battlefield. Along with the legionaries strode several auxiliary cohorts. Like the advance guard, their helmets were bronze and basic in their design to make them cheap. Rather than cuirasses they gained their protection from chain mail and carried oval and flat-faced clypeus shields, which gave a lot less shelter to the body than the scuta. They carried the long spatha sword instead of the gladius and the pilum was replaced by the hasta, best suited to thrusting. But the greatest cultural distinction was marked by the breeches they wore, scathingly referred to as feminalia by the legionaries.

Between the infantry and rearguard, which was made up of the rawest recruits, was the huge baggage train. To the soldiers this was the most vital part of the column, as it contained their worldly wealth, all they had fought so hard to gain. To give up the baggage would be a last and desperate measure in the most extreme of circumstances. Along with the soldiers' goods came the more mundane items: tents, construction equipment, food —

anything and everything needed to support the column. The mass of items was piled into carts, strenuously dragged along the track by oxen, or carried on the backs of uncomplaining mules.

The column snaked its way through the countryside to Durovernon. At standard marching pace it would take three hours for its head to reach the outskirts of the town, provided there were no distractions. The movement of so many men and animals was loud enough to be heard well before they came into sight. Hobnailed sandals stamped in time, pteruges jingled, weapons knocked against armour. Horses whinnied and carts creaked as oxen and mules strained to drag their heavy loads. The men muttered in muted conversation as their eyes scanned the horizon anxiously looking for trouble.

It took an hour and a half for the column to entirely exit the camp. It looked like an enormously long animal with protruding spines along its back. But the sound of marching feet, eerily in time, easily carried to Fionn where he hunkered down, telling him they were human after all. He noted the cavalry that ebbed and flowed with the column, knowing he must escape its attention if he was to get back to Durovernon with his intelligence. He turned his back on the camp and considered their route out of here.

"There are more of them," Brennon pointed to the camp and Fionn looked back again.

As the rearguard of the main column showed their backs to the camp another contingent of legionaries and horse cleared the gates. A vexillation of the IX$^{th}$, a cavalry ala and a cohort of Gaulish auxiliaries took a different route, heading almost due south from Rutupia once they had moved off the headland.

"Where are they heading for?" Fionn asked curiously.

"There is a small settlement a few miles south on the coast," Bearach said. "But Dubras makes more sense. It has a natural harbour. It is where I would go," he shrugged.

Unknown to Bearach he was absolutely right. Classis Britannica boats had already pushed off from shore and were heading around the coast to support the land-based operation. Any resistance would be squeezed between the vexillation and the fleet.

Weland was gambling everything on a stand outside Durovernon. No ambushes were set, because Weland believed any delay to the column would be insubstantial and a waste of precious men. Their arrival at Durovernon was inevitable. Just a few scouts were abroad gathering intelligence on the Romans.

"We must return to Durovernon," Fionn said. "Weland needs to know what he is facing."

Brennon grunted, suspecting what the Cantii leader's response would be but knowing it would not stop his friend speaking. The trio mounted and kicked their horses into a gallop, taking a wide loop to avoid Gallus's men.

## XXVIII

Verica was the first to enter the slighted Corinnion hill fort, trotting confidently through the open gates that were now merely seared wood and twisted metal. His companions were tired, dirty and hungry but the old Atrebatean chief felt elated.

It had taken much longer than planned to journey between the tribal capitals. Periodically Ahearn's group were forced to hide from unknown warrior factions, as everyone abroad had to be considered the enemy. Once they lost a whole day sheltering in some bleak woodland. A group of riders spotted them, changed direction and headed their way at full speed. The warriors searched for Ahearn and his men until they gave up as night fell. Verica gibbered in such fear that Ahearn found it hard to look him in the face now, such was his loathing at this outward display of cowardice.

Verica and his men were warmly welcomed and slept in relative comfort for the first time in what seemed like an age. But this proved to be a brief respite. The next day progress became mired in convoluted discussion. Ahearn endured meeting after meeting between Verica and the Dobunni chief, Cullen. Three days of endless talking felt like three weeks.

Cullen was a greasy haired weakling who, like some old hag bent over a cooking pot, continually wrung his hands and wailed about having to show allegiance to the Catuvellauni.

"It is easy for you," Cullen bleated. "You have friends and safety in Rome but what if Caradoc should discover my betrayal? Should I choose to side with you, of course.""" He added the last hurriedly, just in case his slip was seen as a commitment.

"We understand," Verica said soothingly.

"Do you? Do you really? It would be no quick death for me in battle, oh no. I would be killed, but very, very slowly. I have seen what Caradoc's men do to traitors. My whole family would be murdered before my eyes and the tribe decimated, the remnants scattered to the wind. The Dobunni would be scoured from the face of the earth to become a dim, tasteless memory."

"If you refuse to help then the Romans will do the same," Ahearn threatened.

This set Cullen off fussing and clucking again. He was caught in an impossible position and did not possess the mental ability to think his way out of it.

Verica glared at Ahearn. "Be quiet!" he hissed. "Do you want these negotiations to fall apart before they have even started?"

Ahearn shrugged as he got to his feet. "Have it your own way."

He stalked out, leaving the stifling heat of the roundhouse behind him. Ahearn could bear no more of the needless political wrangling. Given the choice, Ahearn suspected Cullen would happily sit out the next few weeks to see whether Roman or Briton emerged as the victor before flocking to their side, no doubt accompanied with some conciliatory excuses as to his inability to participate.

Cullen demonstrated his teetering loyalty perfectly the next day when a messenger arrived with a summons from Caradoc. The Dobunni chief was so scared about their being discovered, even in a town the size of Corinnion, that he had forced Verica and his men to ride out through the furthest gate and into the hills. After a chilly day in the woods they spent a damp night in the open without a fire to warm them.

Verica complained bitterly non-stop, saying he thought he could feel a cold coming on. The following morning Cullen called them back from their hiding place, but the reminder of Caradoc's presence had put some steel in his heart. Ahearn would have liked to ensure the steel was hard, sharp and driven there by his hand, but no such luck. Instead he went and got drunk.

Ahearn thought through the previous day's privations then tossed the huddle of furs to one side, rolled out of bed and stood up.

"What are you doing? It's freezing!" the woman complained, glaring.

"Shut up, you stupid cow," Ahearn said. He did not know her name and did not care either. He vaguely remembered meeting her, heavily under the influence of a particularly powerful ale.

She quailed at his burning look. Last night she had paid little attention to the huge warrior's birthmark and cruel expression in the dim light.

Instead she saw a powerful man that she could control with her looks as she had with every other warrior that had fallen into her grasp. But she regretted her mistake now, rolled herself back up into a foetal position in the furs and hoped to be forgotten about. She got her wish, for Ahearn had far bigger things to worry about.

It was late morning and he was sure the latest round of protracted discussions would be well under way. Verica would be displeased at his actions but Ahearn really could not care less. He growled in irritation and wondered why what had started so well with the Atrebates had ground its way to a halt so soon afterwards. Perhaps Verica's vaunted influence only stretched so far, he mused.

As he dressed, he made a decision on how to bring this circular debate about risk and reward to a radical conclusion. He tied his hair back so the scar would be seen by all then slid the two swords into their respective scabbards on either shoulder, muscled his way out of the roundhouse and stalked menacingly towards Cullen's hut. The guards, seeing him coming, fell away from the doorway and he went inside unmolested, a determined expression moulded on his features.

## XXIX

News of the foreign invasion had cut through Durovernon like a plague. Immediately, people began streaming out of the town and away from the source of the infection as quickly as their legs would carry them. The refugees carried what they could in their arms, on their own backs or, for the lucky few, on their pack animals. The departing multitude splashed their way through the ford and threaded up the far side of the shallow valley in a streaming procession heading for what they believed to be a safer haven — the disused Bicanbyrig fort, a two-mile trek through the Blahwōn woodland.

Anything that could remotely be regarded as a boat was loaded to the gunwales and rowed strenuously upstream. Downstream were the waiting arms of the Roman river boats, brought with the third division and now plying the marshy shallower waters almost as far as Durovernon. The only craft still moored to the jetties were those that were rotted through or so pitted with holes that they could not be repaired quickly enough for their sweating owners. They lay forlornly on the river bed, discarded and useless.

Durovernon, so recently in a shambolic chaos, was now eerily still, as if it had passed into the eye of a storm. Nobody stirred in the streets, no smoke seeped through the roundhouse roofs and no children played. The place was as still and silent as a tomb. Durovernon was left to the old, the sick or the simply uncaring.

A stray hound hobbled on its three legs, moving with practiced agility, and took the rare uninterrupted opportunity to investigate discarded containers in the pursuit of food, whilst jet-black crows cawed and picked over whatever remnants the hound and its compatriots missed.

Weland could have chosen to flee, retreating with the farmers and traders to Bicanbyrig, or even beyond to Ealdanbyri. He knew he would have been welcomed. But instead, no matter what Caradoc's orders were, he chose to stand his ground and defend Durovernon. He continued to turn over the decision over in his mind, querying whether it was the right thing to be doing. But he knew he must be seen to resist; his life would be worth nothing without at least a gesture.

So the black raven standard was rammed deep into the earth and the Cantii merged around it on what little high ground there was above Durovernon, leaving the town to its turmoil.

Weland, notified by a scout of the close proximity of the Roman column, was waiting impatiently for them to march into view, to be done with the whole spectacle. On his left were the men of Ealdanbyri, their position denoted by Brandan's standard, a long, curved sword. Brandan, one of the few Cantii princes that was here in response to Weland's summons, stood stony-faced with his men. He and Weland had hardly spoken since the westerner's arrival.

"We should be flying our own standard," Fionn mourned.

Fionn had adopted Epaticcus's eagle emblem. It was ironic, he thought, that the Romans have the same bird. He wondered whose side the raptor was on but guessed they would find out soon enough.

Fionn sat on the right flank with Brennon, their horses picketed close by. Both men huddled in furs against the cold on the exposed ridge and tried to ignore the light but persistent drizzle that had fallen steadily from the heavens for most of the morning.

"I would think your sword is sharp enough by now," Brennon said irritably as he watched Fionn scrape a stone along the blade for what seemed the thousandth time.

Fionn shrugged and carried on scraping. "Nothing wrong with a sharp sword."

"So where is that girl of yours?" Brennon asked, bored and needing some stimulation, even if it was just provoking Fionn. "She never seems to leave your side these days."

Fionn knew his friend too well and would not rise to the bait. "You are just jealous," he said nonchalantly and drew the stone across his sword in a particularly piercing scrape, which made Brennon cringe. But despite his nonchalance Fionn's heart surged at the thought. *His* girl.

A clever retort died on Brennon's lips as a carnyx blew a harsh note that grated on the ears. Along with thousands of other warriors, the pair sprang to their feet, scanning the horizon for whatever had created the alert.

"There," Fionn said pointing towards the east.

"Good, at last," Brennon said. "I am fed up of waiting." He touched two fingers to his lips and then pressed them to the blade of his axe, willing the god Esus to bless his blade for the coming battle.

Steadily the Romans came into view, an immense mass of men moving implacably towards Durovernon. At first it was hard to see any detail, the column just looked like a solid block gliding towards them stretching back into the distance. But as they neared Fionn could distinguish more easily between marching soldiers and trotting cavalry.

About a mile away from the ridge a horn sounded within the Roman ranks. Its note was very different in pitch to the carnyx and almost musical in its nature, but loud enough to carry easily to the Britons. The head of the Roman column jerked to a stop, as if at the sound of the horn some power had left the legionaries and they could no longer move forwards.

Then the horn sounded again, a series of notes this time, and the column began to break up as re-energised legionaries and cavalry steadily shuffled about in readiness for whatever they planned. One group moved forward and took up a defensive position whilst behind them a second team of men began to survey the area.

The appraisal was carried out quickly. Legionaries began to flow into an area marked out by flags and bent to their task, hacking into the earth with implements in much the same way Fionn had seen them do at Rutupia what seemed like an age ago.

"Should we attack, lord?" one of Weland's men asked him.

"No, there are too many of them," Weland replied. "We hold the stronger position, let them come to us."

"I think your men have made their own decision," Brandan called, pointing.

Even as Weland was speaking, and despite the odds against them, all along the British ranks warriors fell out of line and coursed down the slope towards their enemy. However, those of the Ealdanbyri held firm. The blue-painted warriors drew up within a stone's throw of the legionaries, where they screamed and shouted proudly of the enemies they had defeated, their strength, their valour. They insulted the Romans, questioned their parentage, called them cowards and bared their backsides.

The Romans were utterly impassive to the cacophony, to the point of disdain. They carried on building the camp as if there were no one opposing them, as if they were totally at home in the foreign land, treating it as if it were their own. This only provoked the warriors into an even greater fury and howls rang out from the Cantii. As a result, a small band of chariots and horsemen swept down the hill towards the Roman line, ignoring the orders to hold.

"Bloody fools!" cursed Weland.

The chariots were his most effective weapon; their mobility was one of his few advantages, and he would hate to lose even one of them. The carnyx blew, imploring the horsemen to come back, but they ignored the orders.

The legionaries were prepared. Quickly and efficiently they closed up into a tight square, the sharp points of their spears poking outwards. Against this any mounted attack would prove utterly ineffective. The chariots and riders raced impotently along the sides of the square, unable to find even the slightest of crevices to exploit. In frustration the charioteers cast spears and fired arrows into the square. Most thudded uselessly into upraised scuta but a few found their mark and legionaries fell. Their bleeding, screaming bodies were dragged backwards into the centre, and the gap immediately filled by another legionary from within. The formation stayed strong and impenetrable.

"Blow again," Weland ordered, and the carnyx wailed across the battlefield.

Reluctantly, the Britons at last heeded the carnyx and withdrew, more from a sense of futility than anything else. Once their attackers were well on the way back to the crest, the Romans returned to building their camp and the square became a line again. Steadily the ditches deepened and the banks grew, higher than the ones at Rutupia. Stakes were struck and lashed, the gates were built. Finally the Romans at the front, to jeers from the Britons, retreated behind their defences with the rest of the army and prepared to spend the night in relative comfort, warming themselves around flickering fires.

The man arrived in the middle of the moonlit night. It was cold but fresh and at last the rain had stopped. He rode as far as he could before the carpet of men impeded his progress. He looked around for somewhere to tie up his horse, a perennial sneer on his face as if he despised everyone and everything in the world. Finally settling on a shattered tree stump that appeared suitable, he dismounted with some difficulty, his sallow face, framed by lank hair, screwed up in pain. He panted for a few moments, letting the agony subside before he tied his horse up.

With a distinct limp he pushed his way through the outstretched forms of sleeping warriors, ignoring those he disturbed. His lips curled upwards, unsmilingly, at the curses that followed him to the crest of the hill. When he reached the peak he glanced up and down the line at the weakly fluttering standards, searching for the one he wanted, the one he had made the painful journey for. Finally he saw the black raven, though it was difficult to pick out in the darkness.

He pushed forward again until he finally reached Weland, who sat hunched over on the ground, a cloak about his shoulders, his eyes closed. The sneer widened. He roused the Cantii chief none too gently with his foot, ignoring the shooting pain up his leg as he did so. It was worth it.

Weland's eyes shot open, ready to berate whoever had stirred him, but he held his tongue as he recognised the man. He got to his feet, all signs of sleep banished immediately from his eyes. Instead they blazed in anger, his mouth twisted.

He grabbed the man by the arm. "What are you doing here?" he snarled, leading the still-sneering creature down the hill a ways.

"My lord wants an answer from you," the man said in a sibilant voice.

"As you can see, I have my hands rather full at the moment." Weland expansively indicated the small army.

"This little...*event* is hardly relevant in the grander scheme of things now, is it?"

"Why not stay and shed some blood with us? Then you will see whether it is irrelevant or not."

"Surely a warrior as great as you does not need a man with my lowly skills," the man mocked. "Even if so few have answered your call."

Weland glared, but it was effective as prodding a rock. No reaction.

"Are you with us, or not?" the man pressed, a nasty grin smeared across his lips. "Because this is the time to decide."

Weland stayed silent, eyes still locked on the other.

"I had a bet with my lord as to what you would do."

"It is a difficult choice."

"But which way will you blow? With or against, with or against?" The man made a swaying motion with his arm, like a tree bending this way and that in the wind.

Since the beginning it had been a game, a way of stretching the negotiations until he could decide who would benefit him most and what would be offered. Weland had chosen the path to follow many months ago, but he knew time was short now.

"Be sure to give Togodumnus my regards," Weland decided.

The man smirked. "You can give them to him yourself." Despite his demeanour, he was relieved. They needed Weland on their side.

He turned and limped back up to the crest, but paused before the peak and called back. "Have you summoned Andred to your cause?"

And then he was gone.

Weland stood for a few moments, then followed in the other's footsteps to the crest. He found his place, settled back down on the ground and pulled his furs around him.

"Who needs Andred," Weland muttered to himself.

He felt calm for the first time in weeks and quickly fell into a dreamless slumber. He had made his choice after all.

# XXX

"We will win a fine victory today for Rome," Narcissus predicted confidently.

"I do hope so," Adminius mumbled. The rain, after a brief respite during the night, had started again and it was dripping down the back of his neck.

Narcissus looked curiously at the Briton. Typically free and extravagant with his words, Adminius was today keeping his replies neat, short and clipped, to the point where he seemed withdrawn. A week ago Narcissus would have snatched the offer of relative silence from Adminius with both hands and gladly paid, with a hefty tip, whatever price was being asked in return. Now he found Adminius's stillness frankly disturbing.

"Do you feel ill, Adminius?" Concern showed on Narcissus's face.

"I did not sleep particularly well," Adminius lied. "And this rain... It never seems to end. I had forgotten how wet it can be here."

In truth he was scared witless of what the next few hours might deliver. Although night after night, for years, he had dreamed in ecstasy of exacting a just revenge from his brothers, now that he was actually about to face old allies, friends and foes in battle he chafed at the consequences that would befall him should the Romans lose. Throughout last night his worries festered, feeding on each other until, despite the Romans outnumbering the Britons more than three to one, he was convinced doom was just around the corner.

"Would you like Maximinius to explain our strategy?" Narcissus offered desperately — anything to break the mournful mood of his companion.

Adminius nodded; a distraction from his thoughts of impending disaster was welcome. Narcissus, mightily relieved, nudged his horse forward and searched for Max in the ranks. Adminius followed morosely behind.

Yesterday Narcissus had reluctantly agreed that the Praetorians could join the front line. At first he steadfastly refused but then, to his chagrin, Plautius reminded him of their conversation whilst sailing from Gaul: there were to be no passengers in this invasion. So, apparently on the general's orders, Max and his men were attached to a distinctly unwilling Geta, who scowled at being given the poisoned chalice.

"What does he want now?" Max frowned when he noticed Narcissus gesticulating at him. He tried to ignore the secretary, but his waving got more frantic, to the point where he could not hope to feign ignorance.

"Perhaps a foot rub?" Anatolius suggested. "Or a massage? Or..."

"Very funny," Max scowled, cutting Anatolius off before he really got into a sarcastic diatribe. "Do something useful for once. Get back into position and make sure the men are ready."

"Yes sir," Anatolius said, saluting jauntily. He raised his eyebrows to the signifer, who returned a guarded smile, then swaggered to the rear of the Praetorian century under Max's disapproving eye.

With a heavy, long-suffering sigh, Max clambered into the saddle and ambled over to the waiting pair as slowly as he could.

"Ah, Maximinius," Narcissus said in greeting, as if they were old friends. "I was telling Adminius something of our ways of doing battle but I am afraid my experience is rather limited. Could you fill in my gaps for our ally?"

Max kept his face blank, despite the irritation he felt inside. "It would be my pleasure," he said woodenly. Tutor to a freed slave and a barbarian. *How far I have risen in life*, he thought bitterly.

But to his surprise Adminius followed his words with a keen interest and he found himself responding in kind.

"The men have formed into three lines of cohorts, each cohort comprising six centuries," he explained, pointing out the groupings to an intent Adminius. Even Narcissus was paying attention.

"There are four cohorts in the first line, with three each in the middle and rear lines. The men are formed in close order, each with a space of exactly three feet either side of him. The next rank is six feet behind."

There were four ranks of soldiers per line, which spread the formation out quite widely. Shallow ranks spoke of the general's confidence in his soldiers.

"The legionaries are in the centre of the formation," Max continued, "with auxiliaries on the flanks to protect against encirclement and some cavalry alongside to give support during the advance. Most of the cavalry, though, is positioned to the rear."

Max did not add, cynically, that the cavalry would only be brought into play once the infantry had spilled their blood during the most gruelling fighting. He shared the view of most soldiers that the cavalry were mainly pomp and ceremony, all show and no substance.

"The men are arranged in line according to their strength and experience compared to that of the enemy. Typically the best and strongest men of the legion are placed on the flanks."

Max pointed out the tough first cohort in front of which they walked. They certainly looked a hard bunch, Narcissus thought, despite their being soaked to the skin.

"Each century has its own centurion and signifer, who stand at its front, and an optio who is positioned at the rear."

"Why?" Adminius asked.

"The centurion leads, the optio makes sure the men keep up," Max replied simply.

He pointed out the equipment the legionaries carried. The curved rectangular scuta shield was strapped to the left arm and in their right hand the soldiers held a short pilum spear. The stubby gladius, perfectly designed for stabbing whilst working at close quarters, was strapped on the right hip so it could be drawn easily without being encumbered by the shield. This left the pugio dagger strapped onto the left. However, for the officers, centurions and above, who did not carry shields, the location of the sword and dagger were reversed.

"Bluntly, they're cheap labour. Expendable," Max said. They had reached the auxiliaries.

Am I thought of in the same way? Adminius asked himself. Immediately he felt thankful that he had had the presence of mind to foment alternative plans. He dragged his attention back to Max, who was still speaking.

"...each auxiliary cohort has its own identity, its own cultural preference," Max said. "The Hamians are expert archers; the Batavians renowned horsemen and swimmers, highly skilled in river crossings. The Thracians, fierce fighters especially in rocky or hilly regions akin to their homeland, have often been employed as mercenaries. They carry the rhomphaia, a weapon combining sword, spear and poleaxe.

Quite fearsome when you see it swinging at your head."

Adminius struggled to picture the weapon and quickly gave up as Max continued.

"The auxilia also include the Alpini, from the great mountain range between Rome and Gaul, the Breuci, several Gallic tribes and the Gallaecians."

They continued their sauntering lesson past the auxilia, heading back to the knot of senior staff, at the centre of which was Plautius himself.

"Even where Plautius commands from is important," Max said. "If he is a long distance away, seeing how the entire battle is unfolding is more straightforward but this separation from the men means sending orders takes time, perhaps too long. Too close, and he risks being enveloped by the enemy and seeing the overall battle is almost impossible. Somewhere in between and he can observe much of what is happening but also encourage his men to fight well."

"Who are they?" Adminius asked, pointing to a large assembly of legionaries at the rear.

"The reserve," Max replied. "The entire XIV[th] Legion."

Plautius's army so outnumbered the Britons that the general did not feel compelled to commit all of his men in line. He disliked very large armies as they became unwieldy and slow to react, and preferred to control smaller groups of men through his legates.

Max fell silent, mid-sentence, as Plautius chose that moment to canter along the front line of the assembled men. When he reached its extremity he wheeled around and returned to the centre. The rain continued to lash down and rattled on the men's helmets and armour. To give his speech the general stood in his stirrups to raise himself as high as possible over the heads of the soldiers, even though most would be unable to hear what he said. He kept it brief and the legionaries, with encouragement from the centurions, broke into a cheer when he had finished. The general saluted his men and then spurred his horse to rejoin his staff officers.

"What did he say?" Adminius asked.

All Max had seen was Plautius's flapping mouth as the wind blew his words away. "That we must all be brave and prepare to die well for Rome and its glory," he guessed.

Adminius paled slightly.

Earlier, Plautius had assembled his senior officers in his tent for the consilium. During the briefing they ate breakfast together, attended by servants, seated around the table which had been swept clean of its maps and plans. The rain started, only lightly at first, as they ate.

Plautius popped a fig into his mouth and glanced around the group. Narcissus had separated himself slightly from the rest. A strange look of excitement and worry was on his face, his loss of the Praetorians seemingly forgotten. Plautius had refused entry to Adminius; perhaps this was what concerned him so. No matter, Plautius thought, and put thoughts of both to one side.

Gallus was tired and he squeezed the bridge of his nose. Too much drinking with his fellow officers was a mistake but it was too late to do something about it. Curius cast nervous looks around the tent, avoiding Geta's gaze completely. But Geta had seen it all before and it showed plainly on his face: he just wanted to meet the enemy, which was the best thing for all as far as he was concerned. In his experience all of this waiting around did no one any good. Vespasian looked dour, concentration pasted on his face as if he was trying to deal with a bout of constipation, rather than feeling any great concern for the future.

The two newly-arrived legates, Decrius of the IX[th] Hispana and Tadius of the XIV[th] Gemina legions, were in stark contrast. Decrius was upright and attentive, barely able to touch the food in front of him. He looked like a puppy wagging its tail furiously in front of his unresponsive master, uncertain what he would be asked to chase next but nevertheless ready to put all of his energy into it.

Impossibly young-looking, Decrius was immensely proud of his legion's history and desperate to add to its distinguished roll of honour. He was overawed by Geta's presence. He kept glancing at him but Geta seemed completely unaware of the younger man's trepidation. The previous year Geta had commanded the IX[th] in Mauretania. The rumours, which Decrius steadfastly believed, said he pursued a local warlord, Sabalus, into the desert.

The warlord laughed at the Romans' arrogance and stupidity. They were short of water and Sabalus, fully expecting them to succumb to a horrible death, awaited the opportunity to gather their bones as trophies. But Geta, right in the middle of the desert, performed a rain dance after which a deluge followed. The locals, superstitious to a man, threw down their weapons in capitulation. They could not hope to defeat a man that controlled even the elements.

Tadius, on the other hand, appeared bored rigid. In comparison to Decrius, he cared little for the XIV[th]. He looked like a large beached seal, pallid and grey with huge nostrils and puppy-dog eyes. His bulk, fat rather than muscle, was so squeezed into his narrow seat that he threatened to spill out of it at any moment. But it was not this lack of comfort that seemed to consume most of his attention, rather it was stuffing his face with food. Already he had devoured everything on his own plate, shovelling it in with barely a pause, and was starting on Decrius's too, scraping the young legate's food off his plate onto his own, after an irritated nod of permission from Decrius.

Accompanying the legates were their tribunes, six per legion. Plautius simply could not be bothered remembering their names. He paid scant attention to them because before long they would be gone, moved on from their temporary position and to the next career milestone, to be replaced by a new, wholesome crowd of blank faces.

Instead, it was the four primus pilus that Plautius gave his attention to. These 'first spears' were the most experienced, most highly-regarded officers, placed in command of the legion's first cohort after long and glittering careers. To serve at all in the cohort was an honour that had to be won, not given.

Plautius began to speak. He outlined his strategy, what he expected each of the officers to achieve. His words were quiet but firm. At the end he asked for questions, but there were none. Plautius dismissed his officers and they filed out of the tent to their duties. All of them would spread the general's words downwards through the ranks via their own consiliums.

Plautius looked down at his plate and saw that his own breakfast was barely touched. Tadius had not been so stupid as to ask for it. He knew in his heart that it was not because he had done all of the talking, though he hoped his men would think that. No, it was because the tension in his stomach had filled him up and left no room for anything else. Like an actor ready to tread the boards he was having an attack of the nerves. He rubbed at his gut, trying to push the feeling away, but he knew the only way to deal with the tension was to go on stage, to jump into the battle.

Plautius shoved the plate across the table and it clattered against the others, making his servant look up in surprise. He stood, took his gladius from where it hung from the back of a chair and strapped it to his waist. He swept his cloak over his shoulder and left the tent, ready for war.

Under Weland's stony gaze the Romans marched out of their camp and assembled themselves carefully into three lines. He watched officers moving up and down primping and preening the lines, straightening them sharp as a razor's edge. At last they seemed to be satisfied and, at the sound of a trumpet, the army advanced in a slow march to a point about a quarter of a mile away from Weland's position, where they halted. The legionaries remained absolutely silent throughout the whole process.

Brandan swore under his breath. "There are so many of them."

Weland shrugged. "We have faced overwhelming odds before and won," he said nonchalantly. "And we will do the same this time."

But Brandan knew that numbers won battles and the horde facing their five thousand men was huge — at least twice their number — and that there were half as many soldiers again assembled in reserve in a block well behind the main battle line. Brandan could never be called a coward but he did not share Weland's tenuous grip on reality.

With the Romans in such close proximity, many British warriors repeated the previous day's ritual of challenging their enemy to hand-to-hand combat well in front of their own line. Fionn watched Hueil's antics as he gesticulated at the Romans, even more red-faced than usual.

"Pointless," he said. "They will not react any differently today than yesterday."

He was proven correct. Despite the insults and taunts the provocation fell on deaf ears, not one Roman muscle was moved, and Hueil returned to his position, standing behind Fionn in the front line, panting from his wasted exertions.

"Feel better now?" Brennon asked.

"Piss off," Hueil snarled. Brennon laughed, annoying Hueil even more.

"Grow up, children," Etain chided the pair.

Against Weland's insistence, Etain was going to fight the Romans. She had turned her back on her father as he raged, and walked away, leaving him staring impotently after her. It was a habit she was developing that Weland was fast tiring of. Bearach was sent scuttling after her to see if he could fare any better, but to no effect.

Etain, once she was with Fionn, applied a complicated swirling pattern of blue paint made from woad to his face. He returned the favour, marking her face, arms and legs, dipping brush into pot many times. Now she stood with him, armed with a short but brutal sword, a helmet planted on her head and wearing a chain mail corset of fine, silver links. Nemausus felt the puckered scar on his forehead as he openly looked Etain up and down.

"The markings make you look even more beautiful," Fionn said to Etain.

Brennon rolled his eyes at Bearach, who looked too worried to care, but Etain glowed with the compliment and kissed Fionn full on the lips.

"I did not feel Andred's presence last night," Fionn said.

"I know what you mean," Brennon nodded. "The horde seems unusually calm."

Andred, the goddess of war evoked on the eve of battle, felt strangely absent from the battlefield. The rage was barely upon the warriors, even on the cusp of battle.

"If you are going to fight then at least move out of the front line," Bearach implored Etain, uncaring of Andred and her presence, or lack of.

"I *will* fight and I *will* stay here," Etain replied.

Bearach opened his mouth but clamped it shut as a group of archers trotted past them.

"It has started. Etain, please!" Bearach looked to Fionn for support.

"Come, Etain, let us do as he suggests," said Fionn. "He will just whine all day otherwise." He started to push his way through warriors who had their full attention on the events unfolding on the battlefield. After a volcanic glare Etain reluctantly followed, as did the others.

By now the archers had dashed to a position well forward of the Britons. They knelt to steady their aim, placing a bundle of arrows on the floor in front of them. At a barked order they indiscriminately fired a cloud of arrows high into the air towards the Roman centre.

"Shields!" Geta roared as the shafts arced in a deceptively lazy flight towards his line.

An arrow could easily penetrate even a cuirass at this distance and in close order the legionaries had insufficient space to dodge the missiles, so had to use other means to absorb the impact.

At Geta's order the legionaries crouched down and covered as much of themselves as they could with their scuta. Max did not have a shield himself and stood stock still, trusting himself to fate, the Gods and, of course, his own two eyes.

The crouched men listened to the zip of the arrows as they whistled down, smacking harmlessly into the curved wood of their shields. Later the shafts would be snapped off and discarded but for now the assault had to be borne. Despite the scuta sharp screams of pain exploded from points along the line as arrows embedded themselves into those too large or too careless to properly cover themselves.

Max watched a white-faced soldier in front of him vainly tug at an arrow fletched with grey feathers that had bitten deep into his shoulder, his mouth open in agony. Once the barrage stopped then the man could be dragged out of the line and sent to the rear to be patched up by the medics, but until then he would have to bear it. With a mental shrug Max turned his face back to the sky and the arrows.

"Rain," he said to himself as the drops hit his face. "I hate it when it rains."

Gallus waited on the wing, deep within the ranks where he loved to be — in the thick of battle. It was one of the many things he and Geta had in common. He watched Plautius despatch a messenger, a white feather attached to the spear he held vertically, signifying that he was carrying an order. The messenger dashed past him to the Aquitani cavalry cohort situated beyond his own men on the right flank. Gallus cursed, wishing the command had been sent to him.

The Aquitani horsemen grinned at the messenger's words and drew their weapons. Cavalry carried the spatha, much longer than the gladius and so giving sufficient reach to slash and cut at the enemy as they rode past at speed. There were some that preferred to use spears and javelins to skewer men on the run, reserving the sword for later, and these men hefted their weapons of choice in readiness.

Gallus watched jealously as the auxiliary tribune proudly led his men out. He nudged his horse forward, slowly at first, then broke into a canter and, once the distance was down to a few hundred yards, kicked into a gallop.

The kneeling archers looked up at the thunder of hooves and an accompanying warning blast on a carnyx. The Aquitani were approaching at gathering speed and the archers panicked. They turned and ran, leaving their arrows on the ground behind them to be trampled underfoot. But they had not the luxury of time or speed to reach safety. The cavalry ripped into them, chopping left and right into faces and stabbing bodies in a gleeful melee as the cavalry went this way and that chasing down the next prey. A Briton screeched horribly, the keening noise easily reaching the British ranks, arching his back as a needle-sharp lance skewered him in the spine. The lancer tugged at his weapon as the man fell, using his speed to jerk the weapon free, as he did so already turning his head to hunt down the next man for the slaughter. The archers wore precious little armour and were slashed to ribbons in moments.

"Why were the archers sent so far forward?" Fionn asked.

Bearach shrugged. No one else had an answer. They watched their own horsemen being sent belatedly into the field to protect what was left of the archers.

The Aquitani wheeled away from the approaching cavalry, their job well and truly done, no need for any further combat. Only a handful of the archers, those more attentive to the danger, managed to scamper back to their line alive. There would be no more arrows homing into Roman ranks. The auxiliaries rode past Gallus grinning and laughing, holding their unsheathed weapons high and proud, shimmering bright red with British blood.

Weland responded with additional skirmishers, armed with spears and slingshots. The warriors scurried into the no-man's land between the two armies. Those with spears hefted them, testing the weight and the muscle power needed to reach the Romans, and then cast them aloft in a sporadic wave.

Again Roman shields were raised, no need for an order this time, but the heavier missiles stove through the protection on occasion, shattering bones and ripping into flesh. Nevertheless, the overall damage achieved by the barrage was tiny. A few of the Roman infantry stooped to pick up the spears and flung them back towards the Britons in retaliation.

But the British slingers were more effective. They darted forward in small groups, carrying a small, rounded stone suspended in a leather sling which they twirled once around the head and released with a flick of the wrist. The size of the stones and the significant speed they were thrown at made them almost impossible for the Romans to spot and avoid. The missiles rattled into the ranked legionaries who crouched behind their shields, the sound like a sudden storm of heavy hailstones. A legionary stumbled and fell as a pellet glanced off his helmet leaving a deep gouge in it. The soldier stayed where he was, concussed despite the bronze helmet.

Plautius ordered the Hamian archers to break up the British skirmishers and another messenger skittered along his lines. Unlike the Britons, the Hamians were kept behind the main line, well protected from attack. However they could not see their targets and so fired wave upon wave of arrows into the air unsighted, seeking a barrage effect, rather than accuracy. A number of British skirmishers went down, pierced with arrows, and the attack broke up as the Britons lost their taste for fighting in front of their lines, afraid the Aquitani may advance again.

"Time to force the action," Plautius said, unwilling to let the Britons advance towards him and keen to put an end to the ineffective skirmishing. He was pleased. His men had stood silently and taken the punishment from the Britons. But so far the biggest danger, the chariots, remained uncommitted.

At a command from Plautius the cornicen player attached to the senior staff blew his silver horn. A loud blast issued from the bell that rested on his shoulder. Immediately, three tubas were sounded, the deep rumbling tone they generated easily carrying across the legionary ranks. Each cohort possessed their own tuba players in the ranks, two to a cohort, and they took up the message, passing it along the line.

Attack!

"At *last*," Geta mumbled under his breath with considerable feeling. "Forward!" he shouted to his men. "Gut the bastards!"

Max led his century towards the Britons. All along the first line other centurions did the same and a cavalry ala on either flank moved forward with the infantry. For the time being the rearward two lines remained motionless until their turn came, and the centurions yelled to remind the men of this. They did not want the uncommitted legionaries coursing into the fight in their excitement before they were needed, disrupting the attack.

The Britons ranted and roared at the approaching Romans, carnyx snarled and warriors banged their weapons against shields. The clamour was deafening. Then a section of the Britons started to run, whirling swords over their heads, shouting, cursing and screaming.

Other than the jingle of their equipment the Roman soldiers

remained completely silent. The legionaries walked steadily and confidently forward, their line hardly wavering, closing the gap on the Britons whilst apparently unaffected by the cacophony. Geta stayed close behind the advancing line, the exhilaration of the sights and sounds of the imminent battle coursing through him. He grinned as an optio pushed several men in the back with his hastile staff, forcing the laggards back into a neat formation. There were always those that were afraid of a fight.

"Keep your formation! Keep your formation!" Geta reminded them.

Within what seemed mere moments the two lines were only thirty feet apart. The Britons were running at full speed, mouths open and roaring. Geta could see their wild eyes and rotten teeth, and imagined their stinking breath rushing out to poison the air.

"Throw pila!" Geta shouted.

The legionaries raised their spears, muscles bunched as they swung them back over their shoulders and then unwound to deliver the spears en masse into the British ranks. Then, with a terrible roaring of their own, the legionaries drew their gladii and burst into a sprint, trumpets blaring even before the spears were plunging into the Britons, in an instantaneous shift from silence to deafening cries.

The pila, constructed from a wooden shaft and tipped with a three-foot long iron spike, turned the sky into a black cloud of death that rained down on the Britons. Those warriors that held shields crouched and raised them above their heads but they were flat and smaller than those of the legionaries and offered far less protection. But it was better than having none. Those without had nowhere to run to avoid the swarm, pressed in by others around them. Many were struck, screaming hideously as the blunt metal gouged into torsos and limbs. The British advance shuddered to a halt under the barrage and still the Romans were running and screaming their battle cries.

Fionn flung his shield to one side. Where two spears dug into it the tips piercing the wood were bent out of shape. No matter how hard he had tugged at them they would not come out. He picked up a spear from the ground that had missed flesh and armour, but even that was misshapen and completely useless. He tossed it away to join his shield. Fionn scanned the immediate area and saw a warrior with a pilum through his neck and shoulder, a surprising lack of blood issuing from the wound. The man's pristine shield lay next to him. Fionn picked it up — it was no use to its previous owner now.

"Here, take this one," he said, handing Etain the shield. Fortunately, she was unscathed.

"Is everyone all right?" Fionn asked.

"Fine," Brennon replied. He pressed his fingers to his axe blade again, invoking a blessing from Esus.

"It will take more than a scabrous Roman to kill me," Nemausus said.

Hueil simply grunted.

"Where is Bearach?" Fionn said.

"He went back to father before the attack began. He gave up trying to persuade me." Etain smiled and Fionn bathed in the glow.

In the mere seconds since the spears had been cast the legionaries closed ranks, brought their shields together in a wall to form a wedge-shaped mass of men with a centurion at the point, and drove hard into the front rank of Britons. The sound of the two armies clashing was like a peal of thunder that could be heard for miles around.

As they struck, the legionaries rammed their shields into the bodies and faces of their taller enemies, the heavy metal boss smashing bones and splitting skin where it came in contact with flesh. Then with a sharp stab they thrust gladii into the chest, stomach or crotch of their opponent. The warriors behind where the enemies met recoiled from this unexpected tactic, which cut through the Britons like a wickedly sharp knife into tender meat. Resembling a smaller fighter getting inside the longer reach of his adversary, the Romans used the advantage of the gladius and shield whilst giving the Britons no room to slash, swing or stab their swords or spears. It was devastating.

In a few short moments the Romans gouged their way deep into the British lines in several places. Weland responded quickly and fresh men were sent towards the trouble spots.

Fionn and his companions hurried forward to meet the Romans. It was a much easier journey than when they had moved to the rear not long ago. Along the line, warriors and legionaries were locked in private battles of life and death. A legionary saw the newcomers, stepped forward and jammed his shield into Brennon's face before he could react, breaking his nose. Blood gushed and quickly covered the lower part of his face in a crimson mask. But Brennon barely felt the blow and swung his axe in retaliation, cutting through armour and into the man's shoulder. The legionary sagged and Brennon withdrew his axe from the gaping wound it had cleaved, jerking it out before the blade stuck.

Fionn found a gap in the line and ran towards it. Spotting a legionary he skidded to a halt, almost falling over on the grass and mud. It was the first time he had seen a Roman up close. He quickly took in the helmet, tight-fitting armour and the large red and gold shield, from behind which the legionary reached to stab a Briton in the chest.

Even as the warrior fell Fionn swung his sword at the legionary. His opponent raised his shield sharply and Fionn's sword bounced off it, leaving a dent in the brass edging. Fionn swung again and again, both times hitting the shield with a harmless clatter. Then the legionary moved forward with short, quick steps, over the writhing man he had so recently stabbed, through whose fingers a stream of blood flowed from a stomach wound. The bright red blood mingled and spread through the brown of a muddy puddle. With a snarl the legionary stamped on the bleeding man, who yelled as a heavy hobnailed boot shattered his shinbone, and whipped his gladius forward in a lunge.

Fionn leapt backwards out of range but the gladius continued to prod and stab as the legionary worked from behind his shield, pressing his advantage. That Fionn did not have a shield of his own was a distinct shortcoming.

The legionary smiled nastily, spat something in a guttural language and darted forward again, sensing it was just a matter of time before he got his man. But the smile died on the legionary's lips. He tried to twist but instead keeled over, grabbing at his side. Brennon left the spear in the legionary and spat on the body.

"Thanks," Fionn said, catching his breath.

Brennon shrugged, as if it were nothing. "Take his shield. You are dead without one."

Fionn bent down to pick up the strangely shaped scuta. He examined it briefly then took a grip on the iron handle in its centre behind the boss. The scuta gave marvellous protection and he raised it to his shoulder. With a roar he ran into the Romans, towards Etain, holding the shield as he had seen the infantry do.

The legionary tussling with Etain paused for a moment, puzzled to see a scuta bearing down on him. The hesitation cost him dearly as Etain stepped inside his dipping gladius and opened his throat in a gout of blood that sprayed his cuirass. The Roman gurgled as he grabbed at his bleeding neck, trying vainly to stop the flow. He dropped to his knees, mouth open in a silent scream and Brennon removed his head with a swing of his axe. The torso flopped forward, already forgotten as the trio stepped over him.

Fionn, Brennon and Etain fought side by side for what seemed like an hour but was in reality only minutes. They hacked, cut and stabbed at any enemy that dared come near them. Aching muscles were ignored as adrenalin coursed through their bodies, the blood singing in their ears. Such was the press of sweating, swearing, bleeding bodies, who knew where Hueil and Nemausus were? Gradually the knot of Britons within which they fought began to regain some of the lost ground and the Romans began, imperceptibly at first, to fall backwards under the onslaught.

Geta shouted encouragement to his men as they fought and died for him. He was oblivious to a cut on his leg from a deflected spear thrust from which the blood flowed freely. His mind sang with the beauty of the battle and the wound was nothing in comparison.

Keen to get nearer to the action he pushed his horse forward. It almost cost him his life. A Briton hefted a spear and was about to throw it when Max stabbed him in the chest. But then, without warning, Geta's horse staggered and one leg collapsed under it, tipping him forwards. Geta rolled off badly and lay winded, staring up at the grey sky. Spots of rain landed on his face until a Briton with a bloody knife stood over him. The blade looked wicked. Only seconds before it had hamstrung Geta's bay, which thrashed on the floor, whinnying. Nemausus just stood looking at Geta. He was soaked to the skin and looked grimly at his next victim. Geta stared back, taking in the puckered scar on his forehead, an old wound that had gaped until it healed.

Nemausus motioned to Geta to stand up, which he did warily, making himself look slow whilst he appraised his opponent. Once upright Nemausus waved Geta forward, gesturing him to fight.

"Come on," he urged. "Come to die on my blade, you bastard."

Perhaps the Briton believed he was soft, Geta thought, just an officer, fat, old and overfed. Well, he would learn otherwise. He cautiously drew his gladius. The man with the scar grinned to show blackened teeth.

Geta circled slowly, Nemausus matching his moves but in the opposite direction. All sounds of the fighting around him drowned out to a background hum as he focused on the man between him and existence. Nemausus abruptly darted forward, catching Geta unawares. His knife flicked out, as quick as the tongue of a snake, and nicked Geta's arm, drawing blood. Nemausus flitted in again, easily avoiding the bigger man's desperately slashing sword.

As he stepped backwards, Geta saw blood on his sword arm. Two cuts in almost as many seconds. He would have to end this, and quickly, otherwise the Briton, far faster in his movements, would bleed him slowly to death. Nemausus started forward again, laughing with pleasure at the sport he was having. But instead of stepping backwards, away from the knife, Geta rushed forwards and crashed into his opponent, who grunted as all the wind was driven from his slight body by the far heavier, armoured man. Geta stabbed upwards and took the knifeman in the stomach.

Nemausus hissed and stood on tiptoes as if trying to draw himself away from the blade but Geta pushed harder and twisted, cutting organs and bringing a shuddering death, grimacing as he did so. He pushed Nemausus backwards and the corpse slid off Geta's gladius, just a small and insignificant huddle of flesh on the floor.

The sounds of battle came roaring back into Geta's ears as he panted deeply. That had been too close. He looked about him, instantly taking in the localised status of the battle. It was not good. Although Geta could see legionaries hacking their way through further down the line, here on the flank there was strong resistance and the

Britons were managing to regain some ground.

But Plautius must have read his thoughts for at that point the second line was committed. Geta turned at the sound as the soldiers came running and screaming into the attack.

They crashed into the Britons. The extra weight of the reinforcements enlarged gaps in the line where they existed and pressurised the points where the British were strongest. Fionn found himself outnumbered as fresh legionaries joined the battle. Those that had formed the front line stepped back to allow the newcomers in. The wounded withdrew for treatment whilst those that could still fight stayed in place.

Brennon swung his axe about him in a wide, scything circle, keeping three Romans at bay. He caught the shield of one with a crushing blow, splitting it down the middle. The big man kicked at the legionary, throwing him to the floor, his cuirass dented. But then more flooded into the attack and the trio were pressed backward, retreating one step at a time.

It was in the press that Etain became separated from Fionn.

"Fionn! Brennon!" she screamed as two legionaries mercilessly pressed into attack. One crouched behind his scuta to jab cautiously at Etain. Using her own shield she easily blocked his probing. But the taller of the two, a plume on his helmet and an ugly expression on his face, stepped in as Etain defended herself against the other. He slid his gladius into her exposed leg in almost slow motion, enjoying the incision. She screamed as the blade penetrated and collapsed to one knee, blood coursing out from the gaping wound.

Etain raised her shield as the tall man swung down. The strength of his blow forced her shield aside and shattered her arm. Fionn, alerted by her cries, struggled to reach Etain but there were too many fighting men in between. He called to Brennon for help and slowly, too slowly, they cut their way through, the legionaries falling back from their rage.

But the Roman slashed his sword down again, easily bypassing Etain's weapon held in hopeless defence, cutting into her neck directly in the gap between helmet and mail shirt. She fell back without a sound. The soldier looked up at Fionn's blood curdling shout. Their eyes locked. Fionn seared every part of Max's face into his memory as the rain ran down his face, mingling with his tears.

As Fionn stood gaping at Max the sound of the carnyx came, blasting the retreat. Immediately the ragged British line began to move slowly backwards, keeping their swords and shields up, unwilling to turn their backs on the Romans, in a full scale but cautious withdrawal from the field. The legionaries, tired from the brief hand-to-hand fighting, mimicked the Britons and also slowly withdrew, opening up a gap between the two lines, in which Fionn stood helplessly.

"Come on!" Brennon urged, pulling at Fionn, who was unable to move. "She is dead! You cannot do anything for her. We must go, Fionn. Now!"

Fionn's attention was still firmly fixed on Max, who smirked as he backed away. He started to walk towards Etain's body, a vague hope in his heart that she might still be clinging to life, but paused as he heard what had spooked Brennon — the unmistakable tattoo of hooves on turf. He looked beyond Max, past the retreating legionarie,s and saw Roman cavalry breaking from a trot as their path began to clear. Their long swords, glinting dully, were pointed out in front of them, straight at their exposed enemy.

Fionn stood his ground, a surging mass of grief, anger and impotence. He was ready to die but he would take every Roman with him that he could. A British warrior was running with all his might in a hopeless escape attempt as a cavalry rider bore down on him. The rider swung his spatha as he leisurely passed the warrior, opening up a deep slash in his face from his hairline, across an eye and into his mouth. The warrior buckled to the ground and lay unmoving. The rider slowed his horse and cast around for another target.

"Here!" Fionn shouted, drawing the rider's attention.

The rider grinned as he spurred his mount, brandishing a sword that looked as if it had been dipped in blood. Fionn moved side on to the direction of the horse, planted his feet and raised his own sword.

But as the cavalry rider neared, his attention focused on Fionn, Brennon stepped out of nowhere and with a tremendous swing he sunk his axe deep into the horse's neck. The beast reared up, whinnying in pain and collapsed on top of its thrown rider. The Roman screamed as his leg twisted underneath him and the bones shattered with the weight of the impact. He raised his hands, unable to move as the still twitching horse pinned him down, babbling as Brennon strode forward with his axe raised. Ignoring his pleas Brennon hacked once at the man, the sound like a blade smacking into soft wood, adding the Roman's blood to that already smeared on his weapon.

Brennon turned to Fionn, who still held his sword raised, ready to repulse the Roman cavalry. "She would not want you to throw your life away, Fionn. Etain would want you to live," he said gently.

After a moment Fionn nodded, looking again at her still form.

"We will get out of this and take revenge for Etain," Brennon promised.

"The Roman is a dead man," Fionn said. The pair clasped hands, fixing the pact.

There was no time for further talk as the cavalry continued their pursuit of fleeing Britons in an effort to wipe out the opposition.

Another horseman was bearing down on them, a taut grimace on his bearded face. Fionn unlimbered his bow and dropped to one knee. Calmly he drew an arrow, nocked it, took aim and let fly in one swift movement. The arrow smacked soundlessly into the rider's throat and he flew off the back of the horse as if kicked by a mule. The horse carried on past them at full speed, as if unaware of his owner's demise.

Steadily the pair retreated, bow and axe at the ready. Their heads turned constantly, seeking out the next possible source of danger. If a rider approached then Fionn would draw and fire subconsciously, the action entirely automatic as his brain homed in on other targets.

The pair were halfway back to Durovernon and four cavalry lay dead in their wake but the remaining distance looked insurmountable as Romans coursed this way and that, mopping up pockets of resistance. If the cavalry were to ride at them in a concerted attack then they could not hope to resist.

"Here comes another," Brennon said, pointing towards Durovernon. Now they were trapped, with Romans to their rear.

Fionn turned and raised his bow but held his fire. The man rode with a familiar, uncomfortable gait, making heavy weather of the gallop. In tow behind him was another, riderless horse.

"What is the matter? Kill him!" Brennon said in alarm, scanning the landscape. He had not heard the familiar rush of bowstring and arrow.

"It is Bearach," Fionn said.

Brennon turned in disbelief to see the young Cantii prince lolloping ever closer.

Bearach skidded to a halt. "Get on!" he yelled, pulling forward the horse he had been towing.

Without wasting precious moments speaking, Fionn slung his bow and quiver over his shoulder and climbed up. Brennon looped the cord attached to the handle of his axe over his arm and joined Fionn in the saddle. The horse sagged momentarily under the unexpected weight of the two men but then ,with an effort, straightened its back.

A shout came from behind them. Fionn looked over his shoulder and saw two cavalrymen pointing their way, gaining the attention of others.

"Let us get out of here," he urged.

Fionn kicked the horse in the haunches and it leapt forward as if bitten, despite the excess weight. Although the horse moved slower than they would have liked under its burden the gap was too wide for the pursuing Romans to close quickly enough and soon they were down the hill and away from the carnage of the battlefield. The Roman cavalry pulled up and let the trio go, wary of being caught too far ahead of their position.

Bearach took them on a detour past Durovernon through the Blahwōn towards Bicanbyrig. Fionn rolled unconsciously with the horse, oblivious of the rain that plastered his face. His mind was fixed on the Roman who had killed Etain.

Max's features were burned into his consciousness and he swore to Etain and all the gods that Max would die.

## XXXI

The Romans scoured the battlefield, scavenging the bodies of the British dead like carrion birds, arguing over the choicest morsels. Warfare and death generated booty for the survivors, and Max, stuck in this godforsaken country, was determined to capitalise on it. His Praetorians operated under a standing order that any loot they found had to be declared. Max and Anatolius would take a percentage for themselves and, of course, anything they found would not be shared in return. The legionaries grumbles were wisely kept to themselves and woe betide anyone who ignored the orders.

Anatolius was searching the breeches of a young man barely into his teens. Wispy hair on his chin had been cultivated in a vain attempt to grow a beard and he smelled vaguely of fish. Anatolius jumped in surprise as the Briton regained consciousness and moaned in pain. But the optio recovered his composure quickly and unsheathed his pugio dagger. He looked into the young man's eyes as he slid the razor sharp blade into his heart. The

Briton sucked in his last breath and his eyes rolled upwards. No prisoners were to be taken. Anatolius wiped the blood from the blade on the boy's tunic and resumed his search. His fingers felt money but he grumbled when he opened his fist — all he had found were a few measly copper coins.

"I did you a favour killing you so quickly," he said to the boy and gave the corpse a kick.

"Find anything?" Max asked from a few feet away.

"Nothing much," Anatolius shook his head in frustration. "Pathetic really."

"Or, maybe not," Max replied blithely.

None too gently the Praetorian tore a fine gold torc from round the neck of the woman, the one he had killed. He turned the ornament over in his hands admiring the patient handiwork that had gone into its creation. Like the torc, the deceased was a thing of beauty, even in death, even with her golden hair matted with blood and her mail mud spattered.

But as beautiful as she was the girl was still the enemy. She had tried to kill him and that could not go unpunished. Max thought about the tall warrior who had screamed at him as he had stabbed the girl. Her lover perhaps, husband or a close relative? He shrugged mentally. It was irrelevant. He knew neither of them would have shown any compassion if roles were reversed so he felt no remorse over her death. He bent down and searched the rest of her clothes.

Max looked up at approaching hoof beats and saw Geta coming towards him across the battlefield.

"Anatolius," Max warned as he stood up and secreted the torc within his uniform.

"A good day for us," Geta said as he drew up. He had seen Max hide something but chose to ignore it. Geta had been around long enough to know that looting the dead was a part of war but he preferred it kept out of sight. He was glad Max had been discrete.

"Yes, sir," Max agreed. "We lost relatively few men."

The hillside was littered with the bodies of the Britons, from the archers closest to where the Roman line had been assembled to the infantry strewn along the crest, killed in the hand-to-hand combat. Most of the Roman casualties were concentrated on the Briton's right wing where the stiffest fighting had been.

Already the Roman dead had been carried away for burial. But the Britons would suffer a different fate; they would be left to rot where they had fallen, the stench filling the air for miles around, a message to others who dared stand against the might of Rome.

Geta looked at the body lying at Max's feet. "For a barbarian she is a beauty."

Max shrugged. "She fought against us, she died."

"I wanted to thank you for helping me," Geta said. Max looked puzzled. "I saw you kill the barbarian with the spear."

Max shrugged again. "It was nothing."

"Nevertheless, I shall remember it and one day, if I can, I will repay the service you did me."

Max was pleased, but kept a straight face. Patronage from such an influential man was always welcome and could be of distinct value if used properly.

Geta prepared to move on. "Plautius and Narcissus are already in Durovernon. We have been ordered to join them so if you would accompany me..." He saw the scowl on Max's face, although it was quickly covered up.

"Yes, sir."

Reluctantly, Max walked to his horse, tied to a tree nearby, and climbed into the saddle. It was a pity to leave the field with pickings still available but he consoled himself with the knowledge that Anatolius and his legionaries would continue to fill their pockets, and therefore his, in his absence.

"Is that idiot Adminius with Plautius?" he asked Geta

"If Narcissus is present you can be sure Adminius will be too, and he would not be pleased if he heard you saying that."

"Despite it being a fact?"

Geta laughed. "I agree with you Max, but speaking it out loud is another matter entirely. Be careful with what you say and who you say it to," he warned.

Max had come to hate the very sight of Adminius and believed him to be the primary reason he had been dragged to Britain. Anatolius refused to be in the same room as Adminius, claiming the strong likelihood of violence towards a senior person as a reason to excuse himself, more often than not leaving Max on his own with the odious man.

"Can I be honest, sir?"

"Of course. For the moment we are alone, are we not?"

"I cannot bear to be anywhere near Adminius and he is causing morale issues with my men. They are just as likely to kill him as the enemy," he said, thinking of Anatolius.

"Then you will be glad to know that Plautius is ending our association with Adminius. He is to be installed as the client king ruling over Cantium on behalf of Rome."

"But I understood he was our guide through British territory?" Max was puzzled.

"Do you not think we will have plenty of Britons flocking to help us now? They will have knowledge that is more recent than Adminius has. The official line is that we need someone 'trustworthy' here who understands the people. But, in truth, Plautius hates him almost as much as you do. It is strange though," Geta looked perplexed for a moment, "but I actually find him quite entertaining."

"You would not if you spent any more than five minutes alone with him."

"Perhaps, perhaps. However, to rid yourself of Adminius you have one last job to do."

"I do not like the sound of that," Max said, his eyes narrowing.

Geta grinned wolfishly. "Before we can advance we need to ensure that what is left behind us is secure. So Plautius plans to pause in Durovernon for a week. The supply base at Stanora will be scaled back and instead a new position at Durovernon will be constructed and used to feed the invasion force."

"So where do I come into this?"

"Plautius wants you to keep Adminius under wraps. Ensure he does not cause us any trouble, Max."

"Easier said than done," Max said ruefully.

"Exactly, and that is why you were chosen for the job."

"Do I get a choice in this?"

"What do you think?" Geta laughed again at Max's sour look.

By now they had ridden into the heart of the town which, remarkably considering the nearby carnage, was untouched. The defeat of the Britons appeared so rapid and complete that there had been no time to pause and set Durovernon ablaze. A few Britons remained, the old or the sick. Those foolish enough to try and protect their homes and land had been swiftly and comprehensively dealt with and their corpses lay in the street.

Their horses ambled through the open gates of the ditched enclosure in the heart of the town. Max tied his horse up and entered the largest roundhouse after Geta, grimacing at the severed heads which were mounted around the doorway.

"*Barbarians*," he spat.

They walked straight into the middle of an argument.

"...*not* living in this hovel again!" Adminius ranted. "You cannot cast me aside like this after all the effort I have put in to get you here!"

Plautius looked primed to explode but paused as Geta and Max entered, letting out the huge breath he had taken in prior to subjecting Adminius to a verbal tirade. Narcissus used the hiatus to take the puce-faced fat man to one side and attempt to calm him down. Max watched Adminius waving his arms wildly as Narcissus made soothing motions in response. Max was pretty sure Adminius had little intention of doing as Plautius wanted. He wondered which of the gods he had upset to get stuck with Adminius.

## XXXII

The shattered Cantii army regrouped at the long-abandoned Bicanbyrig hill fort, leaving the spoils of Durovernon to the victorious Romans. Once Cantium had been governed from here but it had been sacked years before by the previous Roman invaders and was now only a sad shell, a perfect repository in which the silent, defeated Britons huddled. A smattering of lookouts was posted around the fort and its environs but as yet no enemy approached.

Fionn led the tired horse up the incline to the gateway and into the fort. The once heavy western gate, guarding the entrance through the single bank and ditch, had rotted and fallen away long ago. The eastern gate, however, was being shored up by Brandan and his men, and next they would turn their attention to the other. The defence was not perfect but it was a distinct improvement to being in the open.

The interior of the hill fort, particularly the old cattle enclosure, was overgrown and the earth bank had given way in places. Rusty implements and tools were enveloped by weeds and treading carefully was essential. The Ealdanbyri fort had been restored recently and Fionn wondered if Weland regretted not doing the same with Bicanbyrig.

Fionn's men waited inside the gates for Fionn. One of them was missing.

"Where is Nemausus?" Fionn asked

"Dead," Hueil replied. He was the only one who looked sad at Nemausus's passing, his angry frown replaced temporarily with grief.

Before Fionn could ask more details Weland strode over and enveloped his son in a bear hug.

"I am glad you survived your misguided mission," Weland said. He turned baleful eyes on Fionn. "I see you succeeded in saving his miserable life, but where is Etain?"

"Etain is dead, father," Bearach said, after pausing for a heartbeat. Fionn had told him the terrible news on the way to the fort.

Weland's face turned ashen. "How?"

Bearach looked at Fionn for an answer, and, although not ready to relive the experience, he explained what had happened.

"Her blood is on your hands!" Weland shouted when Fionn finished, distraught at losing his beloved daughter.

Weland lurched at Fionn, who stood, unmoving. The Cantii chief landed a crunching blow on Fionn's chin, sending him spinning to the floor where he lay, knowing he deserved the punch and much, much more. Bearach and Brennon leapt in and held Weland back,.

"Let go of me!" Weland shouted, and shook off Bearach's restraint. He spat on the floor by Fionn's feet.

"Maybe you are right," Fionn admitted. "Maybe it was my fault. She trusted me and I let her down."

Too tired to spar with Weland, he allowed Brennon to pull him limply to his feet, then stalked out of the fort, seeking the solitude of the surrounding forest. He wandered aimlessly for what seemed like hours. He sat on a bank and removed his weapons. Only one arrow, fletched with his customary black feather, was left in the quiver. He had not realised how low his stock had become. Fionn drew out his knife and, after asking permission of Nemetona to take some limbs, began to cut.

Later, his quiver full again, and his mind distracted for long enough, Fionn retraced his steps to Bicanbyrig in the gloom. He walked through the western gate and sought out Brennon.

"Feeling better now?" Brennon asked.

"No."

"Eat this." Brennon pushed some cold food into Fionn's hands. There could be no fire to warm the meal in case of alerting the Romans to their presence.

"Not hungry," he said limply, pushing the plate away.

Before Brennon could reply Fionn turned his back on his friend, stretched out on the hard ground and tried to sleep. Unconsciousness immediately claimed him and he dreamt of a grinning Roman officer and his sword dipped in Etain's blood.

It was pitch black. Fionn struggled to see what had woken him. A hand pressed across his mouth.

"Shhh," someone whispered in his ear, then the hand was removed.

"What is going on?" Fionn said, alarmed.

"Come with me."

Fionn recognised Brennon's voice. He picked up his bow and quiver and slunk after Brennon, stepping cautiously over sleeping forms. Brennon led him out of the eastern gate.

"Now can you tell me what this is about?" Fionn asked.

"We are going to get Etain," Brennon said. He pointed in front of them and there stood Bearach with three horses. "We are not going to let her rot or you consume yourself with guilt."

"It was Etain's choice to fight the Romans. Believe me, I know there was nothing any of us could do to stop her. Her course in life and her death were decided long ago by the gods. It is not your fault my sister died," Bearach said.

"Thank you," Fionn replied gratefully, the heavy weight on his heart lifting slightly.

"Now, get on your horse and come with us," Brennon told him. "No arguments."

The trio led their horses away from the fort before mounting up and picking their way steadily through the Blahwōn.

"Look at us," Bearach said, laughing. "The genii cucullati!" He meant the mythical hooded spirits that moved in threes carrying swords and spears.

They skirted wide around Durovernon and came at the battlefield from the south. Despite their caution there were no Romans abroad and they reached the site without incident, making their way on foot and leading the horses.

"Babdah is abroad," Brennon said quietly in case he brought them to his attention, "feeding on the corpses and souls of the dead."

And so it seemed. There was a stench of death in the air and something could be heard but not seen in the darkness, nuzzling the bodies with sickeningly audible sounds.

The self-named genii moved cautiously over the battlefield, eyes scanning the darkness for the equally black raven, hoping Etain's body was not being desecrated by the merciless god.

"Over here," Fionn indicated. He crouched down beside Etain's body. He breathed a sigh of relief — she was still whole — before smoothing her blonde hair away from her face before lifting her, as light as a feather, and carrying her back down the ridge.

Dawn was nearing by the time a tear was opened up in the earth, deep enough so not even Babdah could reach her corpse. Fionn stood in the pit and stretched his arms upwards to take Etain's body from Bearach. He held her for a moment then bent double to place her at its base. Squatting, he placed his own torc around Etain's neck, the lack of the heavy weight around his neck a constant reminder of his role in her death. After a moment Fionn kissed her cold lips and then clambered out of the pit, Brennon and Bearach pulling on an arm each.

One by one they threw a handful of spring flowers and wild herbs on and around her body, the fragrant smell wafting upwards to drive away the stiff odour of death. Then the genii began to replace the soil, which landed in great clods on her body. Bearach stifled a sob as Etain's unflinching face was smothered with earth.

When it was done the trio stood for a minute, each with his own thoughts before they turned away and left Etain to her rest.

# XXXIII

Caradoc paced the floor as his advisers and commanders sat silently, devouring breakfast. He had eaten little himself recently and looked unlikely to change his habit today.

A steady stream of messengers had ebbed and flowed between Caradoc in Calleva and the rest of the key points in the Catuvellauni empire, like pieces of flotsam and jetsam on the tide — dirty, bedraggled and tired from spending far too much time in the saddle. Only a few days ago a communication from Weland bluntly outlined the massive size of the Roman force he faced alone. If the Romans were to be defeated, every man, whether young or old, strong or weak, would be needed.

The process of raising the levy had not gone well. Despite all the assurances given only weeks before in Durovernon, the reaction from the tribes had at best been mixed and not particularly swift. The tribes that originally stayed away, the Dumnonni and the Durotriges, continued to do so. But this morning some good news at last arrived as Amon promised a contingent of his Atrebates, albeit small, from the south.

But it was the Dobunni that were giving Caradoc the greatest anxiety. Whether their potentially significant army would join or not was finely balanced. Cullen had listen politely to a multitude of messengers but sent them away without a clear answer. Caradoc was out of schemes to persuade them to join him.

Caradoc paused in his pacing as another mud-spattered messenger was ushered into the room.

"My lord," the messenger said. "I apologise for interrupting but I bring a report from Weland."

"Come on, spit it out," Caradoc demanded as the worried messenger chewed his bottom lip.

"The Cantii have been defeated and Durovernon is lost."

Caradoc looked at the messenger, his jaw clenched. The young man glanced away in embarrassment, unable to hold Caradoc's eye for long.

"We expected it would happen," Kynthelig reminded Caradoc, impervious to the glare he received in reply. The messenger remained in the middle of the room. He looked uncomfortable with all eyes on him.

"Well, is there more?" Caradoc demanded, wondering what could possibly cap the previous unwelcome revelation.

"Regrettably, yes. There was someone with the Romans that Weland thought you should be aware of."

Caradoc shrugged, "Who?"

"Your brother, Adminius."

An even deeper hush fell on the group, if that were possible. Caradoc had not heard anything of Adminius since his flight four years ago. He had hoped his older brother was dead, but unfortunately it appeared that he was back, well and truly alive.

"How does Weland know this?" Caradoc asked carefully.

"Adminius was seen riding into Durovernon by retreating Cantii warriors."

"Could they be wrong?"

The messenger shook his head. "I saw him myself. His presence is irrefutable, lord."

After a long pause Caradoc said, "Where is Weland now?"

"At Bicanbyrig. We are holed up in the old fort as best we can and await your orders."

Caradoc snorted. "And what of the Romans?"

"So far they have not moved beyond Durovernon. They were building a large camp outside the town when I left."

"Consolidating their position."

"It makes sense," one of Caradoc's men commented.

"Then we may have a little time before they move forward," Caradoc deliberated.

He was silent for a few minutes, deep in thought. Then he held a low discussion with his men, drawing diagrams in the dirt with a stick.

"We have to hold the Romans at the Meduuuæian. It is a natural barrier which we can defend, given enough men. If we can bottle the Romans up and stop their progress we have a chance of mustering the other tribes to push them out of the country. If we fail, Camulodunon and our empire will follow Cantium."

He paused again, thinking it over. "Perhaps it can work." Decided, he gave out the orders and messengers flooded out of Calleva again.

Kynthelig went cold at the prospect. The Catuvellauni were by far the strongest tribe in Britain. If they were defeated it was just a question of time before the rest followed, and with

that the druids would soon be extinct.
He would be a thing of the past.

# XXXIV

Max spent a languid two days in Durovernon, hating every waking minute. The boredom of babysitting Adminius drove him mad with frustration and the flaccid man was making sure he squeezed every drop of attention he could out of Max.

But the Praetorian came up with a plan, a way of benefiting from his enforced hard labour, and so managed to evade Adminius for half an hour and track Anatolius down. The pair sat in seclusion, throwing stones into the sluggish brown waters of the Stur.

"I thought you said the idiot was going to make us rich," Anatolius said, mildly reproachful and adopting his recently developed habit of refusing to refer to Adminius in anything other than derogatory terms. "So far I feel distinctly poorer."

"Stop exaggerating, Anatolius. We did not do badly from the battlefield."

"There is little wealth here, Max. We were lucky."

Max shook his head. "You make your own luck, you know that. And speaking of opportunities, Adminius is up to something. I can smell it on him,"

"Why should I care?"

"Plautius has dismissed Adminius from his plans but I do not think Adminius has the same outlook. Maybe there could be something in it for us if we play the game correctly."

"What game is he playing?" Anatolius grinned as a stone narrowly missed a bird that had been happily floating with the current. It flew away with an angry squawk.

Max shrugged. "There is the problem - I do not know. We need to get closer to Adminius. We need to gain his trust."

"We or you?" Anatolius eyed Max carefully, his arm half raised to throw another stone.

"*We*, Anatolius. I need you to play your part in this venture."

"Wonderful, more of my life wasted on that bastard." Anatolius flung the stone wildly in his pique. It crashed into the bushes on the far bank.

"You can hardly complain. Every time I turn around you have found some excuse to disappear."

"What can I say? It is a talent that I have," Anatolius said, receiving a sour look from Max.

"I am serious."

"So what do you suggest?" Anatolius asked heavily. If Max had decided to get closer to Adminius there was nothing he could do about it, he thought. Best to swim with the tide or face being swamped.

"A charm offensive," Max said. "Starting now. Adminius loves being the centre of attention and any form of flattery goes down well. We should take him hunting."

"Hunting? I cannot see that idiot being interested in bouncing after a boar."

Max shook his head. "It is the opportunity for favour it presents, not the sport."

"Maybe I can 'accidentally' kill him. We could blame the boar," Anatolius mused, brightening momentarily until he saw Max's stiff expression. "It was just a joke!" he promised.

"I am not doing it," Adminius said flatly, folding his arms and pushing out his bottom lip like an overweight adolescent.

Max looked to Narcissus for support. The secretary was puzzled by Max's suggestion but if it kept Adminius quiet for a time, who was he to argue?

"It is a popular pastime with Roman nobility," Narcissus remarked.

Adminius's reaction was electric. "What a fantastic idea, Max. Hunting! Why have you not suggested it before? I will have my horse brought immediately."

Narcissus raised an exasperated eyebrow at Max as Adminius waddled off, hollering for his retinue.

The hunting party, much smaller than Adminius would have liked, ambled out of Durovernon more than two hours later. He had spent the intervening time ensuring he was properly dressed for the event. The four auxiliary cavalry, two at the front and rear of the party, were consequently thoroughly irritated by the time they departed.

Max and Narcissus flanked Adminius as, yet again, Anatolius found some plausible excuse to slip away. Much to his own disgust, Max nodded ingratiatingly at everything the fat man said, no matter how inane or pointless. The short ride into the Blahwōn seemed to take forever. By the time they arrived at a suitable location Max's jaw ached from biting back sarcastic remarks.

Relieved at the distraction, he watched as a servant climbed down from his horse and retrieved the hawk from its cage. The bird hopped onto his outstretched arm at a word and hulked there broodingly. At a nod from Narcissus, the slave removed the hood masking the bird's eyes. Immediately, it leapt up into the sky and began to circle for prey, never straying out of sight.

Initially, Adminius was fascinated with the hawk. That it returned to its handler without question he found amazing, joking that he wished people could be trained in the same way. But after seeing the hawk twice return, bringing a rabbit and a vole, his euphoria had staled. Before long, Adminius made it plain that he was bored stiff and wanted some other amusement to spend his valuable leisure time on. Narcissus made a valiant, but ultimately fruitless, effort to keep him interested and so the party shifted into the forest to hunt boar, having spent barely half an hour with the hawk. With a squawk of derision, the bird was unceremoniously returned to its cage.

"How do you find the weather in Britain, Max?" Narcissus asked. He rode on for a few paces then realised he was enquiring of someone who was no longer there.

"I said, Max, what do you think of the weather in Britain?" He turned and saw the Praetorian sitting with his head cocked to one side, listening intently. "What is the matter?"

Max raised a finger to his lips for silence and continued to listen. Adminius looked unimpressed and was about to say so until Max moved forward again and came alongside the pair.

"There are enemies in the woods," he whispered. Adminius looked around with a dubious expression. He had not heard a sound, so nobody could possibly be there. "We need to leave now. If we move any further into the trees we will be an easy target." Max cautioned.

"I know this area well, and the people in it. We will not be attacked," Adminius swaggered confidently.

"I am sure you are correct, my lord, but at this present moment you are with Romans who are hardly in favour here."

Adminius was unable to think of a clever rejoinder to dispute this. "All right," he agreed. "We will return home."

He was actually glad to be able ride back to Durovernon and rest his aching backside, utterly bored with the whole venture and wishing he had never agreed to the stupid suggestion in the first place. In fact, he decided, whatever Max proposed in the future he would pointedly refuse to do, just for the hell of it.

Max turned the small party around. "Be on your guard," he warned the auxiliaries.

But, no sooner had he given the counsel, an auxiliary at the rear threw his hands to his face with a cry and sagged off his horse. At the same time, a knot of Britons burst from the trees behind them. Hollering and screaming battle cries, the warriors ran at full tilt, spears and swords raised. Sling stones stabbed around the hunting party and two spears slapped into the turf nearby, making Narcissus's horse skitter.

"Move!" Max shouted, grabbing Adminius's reins. He kicked his own horse into a gallop and bent low over its neck. As one the party dashed from the clearing, leaving behind them the Britons and the auxiliary splayed out on the ground.

After five minutes of furious riding Max slowed. The auxiliaries scanned the trees nervously. Adminius had a shocked expression on his face and Narcissus looked relieved.

"How can I ever repay you?" Adminius panted heavily.

"I just did my duty, my lord," Max replied with a shrug. "It was nothing so you owe me nothing."

As they rode back to Durovernon, Adminius continually praised Max, who accepted the platitudes with good grace, whilst Narcissus looked on thoughtfully.

Max left Adminius in Durovernon and rode back to the camp in high spirits. He dismounted, lashed his horse to a post for his servants to feed, water and groom and entered his tent. There he found Anatolius waiting for him, feet up on the table. Max swiped them off.

"Was I convincing?" Anatolius asked.

"Well, you certainly made Adminius believe he was under attack," Max said, pouring himself a drink and sitting down. "I almost fell for it too," he laughed.

"I always knew I was in the wrong profession."

"What about the auxiliary?"

Anatolius shrugged. "Dead when we reached him. Unfortunate but it could not be helped."

"No, I suppose not. It will be interesting to see what happens next."

Max refilled their goblets to drink a toast to their success, but before they could raise them a soft clapping sound erupted behind them.

"Bravo, gentlemen," Adminius said, patting his hands together lightly. He entered the tent without being asked. "May I join you? A drink of wine would be most welcome after all that hard work."

Max, his mind working frantically but his gut chilled with worry, poured Adminius a drink and handed it to him. Adminius dragged up a chair and flopped into it. He languidly placed one foot after the other onto the table and raised his eyebrows at Max who stayed silent.

"Anatolius is it not? You were quite good, quite good indeed. I think you have Narcissus almost convinced but you forget that I have lived with these people most of my life and cannot be so easily fooled. However, I am glad that you think I am so stupid!"

Max shrugged, caught red-handed. "So what are you going to do?" he demanded stiffly.

"Do? If you mean 'am I going to talk to Plautius' that rather depends upon you two." Adminius finished his drink and held out his goblet for more. Max's and Anatolius's wine sat on the table untouched.

Adminius lifted his feet off the table and leant forward, resting his elbows on it. "I cannot afford to be left here whilst Plautius ploughs through Britain to Camulodunon. There is much to be gained from this campaign but it will not come if I am beached in Durovernon. I spent too long as an underling to my younger brothers and I intend to take for myself what I should have had years ago. That is why I am here. That is why, for the moment at least, I have no intention of going to Plautius about the pair of you.

"But first, perhaps you should explain why you went to all the effort of your little charade. Then we will see what we can do for each other."

Max grinned and lifted up the decanter for Adminius. Perhaps it was going to turn out even better than he had hoped after all.

# XXXV

"Unbelievable," Bearach said.

"You sound impressed," Fionn admonished.

"The Romans have invaded my home town. Why would I be impressed with that?"

"You two bicker so much you should consider marrying each other," Brennon suggested.

Bearach sighed. Yet again what was supposed to be a serious point had been turned into a joke. "What I *mean* is it is unbelievable how quickly this has all happened."

Fionn had spent relatively little time in Durovernon and, other than Etain and Bearach, had no meaningful connection to the place. But he had to agree with his new friend. In only a matter of days the Britons had been swept out of the leading settlement in Cantium and left homeless in their own land. The deadening feeling in his heart from Etain's loss was steadily being augmented by a smouldering anger.

The trio had earlier left Bicanbyrig to gather information on the Roman positions. They were unable to approach the town itself as there were simply too many of the enemy abroad for that. Small groups of cavalry and of foot soldiers patrolled the immediate environs but, so far, the enemy had refrained from pressing too deeply into the dense Blahwōn, content to consolidate their position around Durovernon.

Instead, the genii, as Bearach now insisted on calling them, negotiated their way east by using little known paths and tracks that were concealed, overgrown and sometimes difficult to negotiate and which, well off the beaten path, were highly unlikely to be known to the Romans.

The genii huddled deep in tree cover. As well as the large camp on the outskirts of Durovernon, a smaller garrison outpost, like the one at Rogulbio, was in mid-construction. The stronghold occupied a strategic position on high ground, with commanding views over the Stur.

"Not much will get past that without them knowing about it," Bearach observed.

Long baggage trains snaked up to Durovernon, presumably from the direction of Rutupia, carrying vast quantities of materials and supplies.

The mule trains returned to the coast empty, suggesting that the centre of operations was being shifted. They knew already that Roman galleys and river craft negotiated along the nearby rivers. The Romans had a vice-like grip on the immediate area that the small force holed up in Bicanbyrig could not hope to break.

"I cannot see him," Fionn said.

Brennon and Bearach kept quiet, not wanting to provoke an outburst. By 'him' they knew Fionn meant the Roman officer that had killed Etain.

"We had better get back," Brennon suggested, avoiding the subject. "We have learnt as much as we can from here."

Fionn sighed, deeply disappointed that Max had not been found. "I guess you are right."

The trio moved back cautiously from the tree line and recovered their horses, battling past the thick undergrowth that clutched and clawed at their clothes and skin. After a brief journey they entered the sagging gates of Bicanbyrig. As they tied their horses up, a tired, dusty man on an equally weary mare entered the fort. He slid off the back of his mount and stretched his back, which clicked audibly.

"Iden!" Fionn said, striding happily over to the new arrival, a friend from Calleva, and embracing him warmly. "It is good to see you."

"And you, Fionn." Iden rubbed a grubby hand over his drawn face, stifling a yawn. "I see your lazy, good for nothing friend is still alive." Iden stabbed a finger at Brennon, who grinned back at him and gesticulated crudely.

"What are you doing here?"

"I bring a message to you from Caradoc. But first I need to speak to Weland. Where can I find him?" Iden asked, looking around.

Fionn pointed towards the bank where Weland had developed the habit of spending his days, the dappled sun playing on his face. Following the retreat to Bicanbyrig, Weland had withdrawn from those around him, almost to the point of being catatonic. He ate little and spoke less. Bearach worried himself half to death trying to understand the problem but was no nearer a solution, and Weland was not going to provide one.

Fionn, though, was pleased with Weland's mental absence; he didn't miss the habitual sarcastic comments. However, he did not share his opinions with Bearach, knowing they would upset him, and friends were of prime importance.

"Before you speak to Weland we need to find Brandan," Fionn said.

The task of keeping the Cantii in one piece had fallen to Brandan. With great reluctance he had delayed returning to Ealdanbyri with his departing men. Iden looked curious but agreed to wait until Brandan was found, and so stood waiting beside a disinterested Weland whose eyes were fixed firmly on the canopy.

"I bring orders from Caradoc," Iden said. He was unsure whom to address so looked at them both in turn. "You are to fall back to Durobrivis at the Meduuuæian crossing to join the army that is being gathered there to repulse the Romans."

Iden then went into greater detail regarding Caradoc's interim plans but, disturbingly, Weland just continued to stare blankly, seeming not to hear a word.

"Tell Caradoc we will do as he asks," Brandan said when Iden had finished. Iden looked uncertain, needing Weland's participation but, at a pointed look from Brandan, he nodded and turned to go.

"What is wrong with Weland?" Iden asked as he and Fionn walked back to retrieve his horse.

"I wish we knew. Will you tell Caradoc?"

"I have to," Iden said grimly.

"You said you had a message from my cousin."

"Caradoc wants you to join him at Bredegare as soon as you can rather than falling back to Durobrivis."

"Tell him I will be there. How is Caradoc faring?"

"He has the weight of the Britons on his shoulders but he carries it well."

"Why do you not stay the night? You look shattered."

"I would love to," Iden said wearily. The prospect of getting back into the saddle did not fill him with joy. "But I must get back to Caradoc. Time is short and we need every minute of it if we are to beat the Romans."

They embraced and then Iden climbed stiffly onto his horse and rode out of the fort. Fionn watched his friend until he was lost in the gathering gloom of the enveloping trees.

When Fionn returned, Brandan was in the process of organising the Cantii. The remaining warriors would start the walk to Durobrivis at first light.

The women, children, wounded and infirm would travel with them before separating to head to the safer haven of Ealdanbyri. There was much to do in a short space of time and everyone who was able to, helped where they could.

Weland proved to be the exception. He preserved his place on the bank, seemingly oblivious to the activity exploding around him, but inside his mind worked furiously.

## XXXVI

Max picked his way along the camp road through the periodic patches of light that spilled out from braziers that flickered in the breeze. His head was still whirling from his discussion with Adminius. The opportunities were spectacular, more than he could ever have dreamed of. But his task was not so simple; he must ensure Plautius reinstated Adminius as part of the invasion force. Much easier said than done, Max mused.

Eventually, he found Geta in his tent in deep conversation with Gallus. Max stood just outside the entranceway in Geta's eye line but did not interrupt. Instead he took the opportunity to clear his head and set his thoughts straight.

Finally Geta looked up. "Yes, Max. What is it?"

Max poked his head inside the tent. "Sorry to intrude, sir, but could I speak with you?"

"I will leave you two lovebirds alone," Gallus said, draining his wine and banging the goblet down on the table.

"Watch him," he advised Max. "He is in a foul mood today!" They could hear the prefect's continued laughter disappear into the night.

"Wine, Max?" Geta asked, pouring himself some and putting his sandaled feet up onto a stool. The evening was unusually warm and the breeze blowing into the tent was welcome.

"No, thank you." Max already felt drunk, and not from the effects of alcohol.

"So, what brings you here at this hour?" Geta repeated.

"I would like you to repay the favour I did you on the battlefield."

Geta sat forward in surprise. "So soon? What is it you want?"

"I would like Adminius to travel with the column when we depart."

"What?" Geta spluttered. Max thought he was going to explode but he pressed on whilst his superior officer was off balance.

"I think he can be of more help to us with the conquest than sitting here in Durovernon. Besides, with his local knowledge he may be able to persuade some of the tribal leaders to come over to us from the Britons."

"But only days ago you were telling me how much you hated him!"

"That has not changed, sir, I still do. But is this not about what is best for the army, not the individual?"

"What is really behind that grand statement, Max?"

"Nothing, sir," Max said, his expression as blank as if he were on parade and being inspected by a pedantic superior officer.

"By the gods, you do not ask for much do you, Max? Plautius wants to be rid of Adminius and I am not sure there is much I can do about it."

"He is more likely to listen to you than to me, sir. And there is Narcissus. Will he not he be keen to keep Adminius by his side?"

Geta pursed his lips. "That is true," he said thoughtfully. "Virginius owes me a favour and perhaps Gallus can help too." Geta made his mind up. If it were not for the Praetorian, he would be a corpse. "Leave it with me Max, I will see what I can do."

Dismissed, Max stood to leave. "Thank you, sir. Goodnight."

"'Night, Max." Geta returned to his wine and thought how to approach Plautius, still half-wondering why Max had changed his mind so abruptly.

## XXXVII

Adminius steered his reluctant horse off the Pilgrims Way, a major thoroughfare that Bicanbyrig had originally been erected to control. The horse picked its way slowly along a narrow, almost invisible path. The man cursed as a thin branch lashed across his face, wondering, yet again, what the hell he was doing here.

Before long, he arrived at the small clearing where they had agreed to meet. He climbed off his horse, tied it loosely to a branch and then moved into the centre of the dell. The night was moonless but at least it was warmer now summer was fast approaching. Above his head a blanket of stars twinkled in the inky sky but he took no notice of them. Instead, his eyes constantly roamed the tree line, waiting for a movement within it to signal that the other, the one he was here for, had arrived.

He waited, and waited, well beyond the time agreed. A lack of punctuality was one of the things he despised. It was as if the other was declaring that their time was more valuable than anyone else's.

He bent down to rub at his right leg, which tended to stiffen and become painful if he was in the same position for too long. Recently, he had spent a lot of time in the saddle and he was fed up of it. He limped around the clearing, trying to generate some circulation to ease the pain.

At least the throbbing distracted him from his nervousness. He was a long way from the safety of the camp and he disliked this cloak and dagger stuff. Scheming and politics, yes, but not meetings in the darkness. But he had no choice, it had to be done.

He stopped still and turned at the sound of a twig snapping loudly behind him.

"I am glad you decided to make it," he sneered.

"And how pleasant to see you again, too," the newcomer said, stepping into the clearing. "I had expected you to see me some time ago but I got bored waiting in the end."

Adminius looked indignant. "How long have you been here?" he asked.

"Long enough to check whether you were alone," the man replied. "And to know that you were not."

Adminius looked at the man sharply, a tic of fear jumping at his cheek. He hoped Anatolius was all right. Explaining to Max that his optio was dead would be a stiff discussion.

"You need not worry," the man said languidly. "Your companion is alive. However I expressly told you that our...relationship should remain between us, private, so to speak. So by rights both of you should be dead. But, as I am in an excellent mood tonight, I merely gave your soldier a headache he will remember for some time to come."

In his nervousness at the turn of events and his loss of control, Adminius sprang for his weapon but the overweight man had never been much at swordplay and, to compound the matter, was woefully out of practice. Before he could even draw the blade from its scabbard he felt the prick of steel at his throat. He swallowed, then laughed, raising his palm from his sword's hilt.

"You will not kill me," he said confidently.

"And why not?" the man asked indolently, transferring the sword from throat to stomach. "A wound to the belly takes a long time to die from," he mused. "It is very painful and I have seen men much, *much* stronger than you beg for a quick release."

"You need me to get to the Romans. I am far more connected to them than you are. How would you expect to get your reward on your own?" Adminius asked.

The man's sword flicked back up to Adminius' face and hovered there, glinting dully.

"But you could still take a message to them with only one eye."

Adminius swallowed hard and despite himself took a step backwards. He tripped over a fallen tree trunk and sprawled on his backside.

The man laughed and rasped his sword back into its scabbard. "You are correct. I do need you - for the moment." His voice hardened. "But do not try to play me again. If we make an arrangement, stick to it to the letter or next time I may not be so pliable."

Adminius climbed to his feet, brushed himself down and tried to gather his dignity. He pulled his cloak around him.

"The battle at Durovernon was harder than I expected," Adminius said. "I thought for a while that you had reconsidered whose side you were on."

"I thought it important to demonstrate some resistance as the real coup is yet to come. But I did consider my options for a while," he admitted.

"You made the right choice," Adminius said.

"You had better hope so."

"What information do you have for me?" Adminius said, cutting straight to the point of their meeting and tired of the threats.

"Caradoc's plans," he said with a grin, which Adminius returned tenfold. "Are you interested?"

Adminius nodded fervently and for the next ten minutes he listened intently to all Weland had to tell him.

# XXXVIII

Plautius spent a week in Durovernon securing what would become his rear position when the next stage of the advance began. The general chafed at the time spent doing so but, although maintaining the momentum against the Britons was important, it was critical to ensure he could not be outflanked, his supply chain cut off and escape route closed.

The main supply base had at last been relocated to Durovernon The logistics of shifting the multitude of provisions and equipment had taken longer than planned, a source of distinct embarrassment to the staff officers. The garrison to oversee the Stur and northern section of the Dūn was complete and populated with a cohort of men. Directly as a result of Adminius's help, the leaders of several smaller Cantii tribal factions had attended an audience with Plautius and subsequently sworn fealty to Rome. That Adminius helped at all was a great surprise to the general, particularly in the light of his recent decision to leave the Briton out of his future plans, one that Narcissus had argued against several times since.

Those future plans now needed to be fully fleshed out, turned from intentions into actions. So Plautius called a strategy meeting in his tent. A detailed map of the immediate area was spread out on the table, some of the gaps filled in by the scouts in recent days in a neat script. Chairs were pushed back against the walls and the senior staff pored over the document, talking through the options to reach Camulodunon, of which there were several.

"Durobrivis has good harbour facilities," Adminius suggested.

"They could be reached by the Classis Britannica?" Plautius asked. "The river looks wide enough on the map."

"Yes, easily. Even your biggest ships could manage to berth."

Plautius thought for a moment. "So you are suggesting we use Durobrivis as the next supply base to support the push through to Camulodunon."

Adminius nodded.

"It looks feasible," Geta agreed. "But the width of the Meduuuæian presents its own challenges."

"There are several bridges along the river," Adminius offered. "Most are quite small but one here," he pointed to the map, "is wide enough for several horses to easily pass side by side, and it is not well known."

"What is your opinion, Crispus?" Plautius asked.

"It is not perfect, but provided we can get enough men over to secure the far side of the river our engineers should be able to build a pontoon bridge to speed the crossing." Crispus nodded to himself. "Yes. Yes, it could work."

"So we need to get from here," Geta stabbed at Durovernon's location on the map, "to here,." He stabbed again, this time at the smudge of Durobrivis.

"What are our options, Adminius?" Plautius asked, surprising himself that he did so.

"We have three routes available to us." Adminius ran a finger along a ridge of hills that ran roughly east to west, humility in his voice. "There are routes either side of the Dūn or along the flat land towards the coast."

To the south of the Dūn was Lugus's river, the Ligan, which eventually flowed into the Meduuuæian and Stur rivers. To the north was the flat land Adminius had indicated.

"Advancing along the southern lip of the Dūn looks unwise," Plautius observed. "We would be cut off from all of our forces on the other side and unable to signal each other effectively."

"I agree," Geta said. "We would be too far away from the Classis Britannica and we would invite an attack on Durobrivis. The garrison is not large enough to do anything other than discourage."

"It is a longer route, too," Adminius said. "At least ten miles more than any other."

"So the supply chain would be more stretched," Crispus said, to nods from all around the map table. Nobody liked long supply chains; there was a greater risk of them being broken.

Plautius fell silent as his senior officers continued to talk over the options with Adminius. He dropped out of the conversation, listening to it subliminally as he thought the alternatives through himself. Every now and again he would fire a question at the group, someone would reply and then they would return to the map.

Plautius interrupted them after several minutes of consideration. "This is what I suggest..."

An hour later, following further refinements, the plan was cast in stone.

Plautius's officers filed out of his tent, tired after a long day.

"Could I have a word, sir?" Geta asked.

"Of course, what is it?" Plautius said, although he looked like all he wanted was some time to himself.

"I would like Narcissus to stay too, if possible."

Narcissus managed to look surprised at the request and nodded in agreement. The three retook their seats. Plautius waited for Geta to speak his mind as he picked absently at some stale food.

"I know I speak out of turn, sir, but I believe we would benefit from Adminius's help during the advance," Geta finally said.

The general was stunned. Of all the things his second-in-command could have raised this was the least expected.

"What makes you say that?" Plautius asked curiously.

Narcissus bided his time, his eyes flicking between the two men.

"I have watched the two of you," Geta replied. "Adminius seems willing to help now but you do not always willingly accept it. In fact you often reject it out of hand. It is my duty to say that you may be discarding something of value to us."

Plautius thought for a moment, wondering whether to be annoyed or not. "Such as?"

"He brought the Cantii chieftains into line very quickly. Perhaps he could do the same with the Catuvellauni when they are defeated, and possibly with the other tribes too."

"As a mere observer it is strictly not my place to interfere but I must say I agree with Geta on this," Narcissus interjected.

Plautius felt that he was being manoeuvred but was unable to understand why. Yet it was true that Adminius seemed to accept his place now. Maybe he was being unreasonable. Plautius was tired and could not be bothered arguing over such a minor matter.

"Perhaps you are right. Tell Adminius he can come with us," he said to Narcissus.

"That was very well done," Narcissus said to Geta after they had left the tent.

"Your support made all the difference," Geta replied.

Narcissus laughed. "Perhaps you should consider a career as a senator in the future!" he said and walked away, still chuckling to himself.

Geta was pleased. It was a debt repaid and he went to search for Max to tell him so.

## XXXIX

The first rays of sunlight were splitting the darkness when the Romans at last marched out of the Durovernon camp. The IX$^{th}$ and the XIV$^{th}$, led by Decrius and Tadius respectively, began their advance along the track that bisected the low-lying, open land, broken only by the occasional belt of trees, between the Dūn and the Sualua rivers. The XIV$^{th}$ were carrying the siege weapons, ballistae and onager, which had landed with the third division. At the rear followed Vespasian's II$^{nd}$, within which Plautius marched.

The senior staff had finally decided that the advance would follow the shortest route to Durobrivis, twenty-five miles as the crow flies, because the simpler logistics and contact with the Classis Britannica made it tactically the best choice. But Geta bluntly pointed out that dominating the low ground between the Dūn and the Tamessa meant the higher land on their left flank was a significant problem, as the Britons could descend on the legions from this superior position and cut them to bloody ribbons.

In appreciation of this insight, Geta was charged with leading the XX$^{th}$, a cavalry regiment and three auxiliary cohorts along this northern escarpment to protect Plautius's flank. The escarpment also gave Geta the advantage of having several options to strike at the Meduuuæian, should the need arise.

"I do not like the look of those woodlands," Amatius, the XX$^{th}$'s primus pilus said with a grimace. An old war wound prickled, as it often did when he felt there was danger around the corner.

"Nor do I," Geta agreed. He looked towards the dark smudge of trees as the legionaries marched in order at their backs, his eyes narrowed as if trying to look through the trunks to any danger beyond.

Had the pair turned around they would have taken in an excellent view of the land below towards the Hoe marshes, the Sualua river, the low hills of Scepeig and beyond to the Tamessa. The three legions they were charged with protecting were starting to cut through the countryside in a snaking line, as black as a coal seam.

"Before long we will be in the trees ourselves," Geta said, pointing forward to the looming Blahwōn forest. "Send the Aquitani forward. If there are Britons in there, let us flush them out."

The foliage closed around Geta as he led the XX[th] along the narrow pathway into the fringes of the Blahwōn. The canopy was high and dense, the branches and leaves had grown so interlinked over many generations that it blocked out much of the sunlight. Had he not known better, Geta would have thought dusk was approaching, so dim was the visibility. The air was still and smelt musty. The noise of their march was deadened by the carpet of vegetation that had fallen on the path.

The Aquitani had returned from the forest and reported nothing untoward, but despite this Geta turned his head this way and that. He felt his hackles rising. Something was not right and his instincts started to scream at him.

"There is no noise," Amatius said, eyes wide in the half-light.

Geta cocked his head and listened. Amatius was right. No sound issued from the canopy.

"Be on your guard!" Geta shouted to his men.

No sooner were the words were out of his mouth than his horse started as men burst screaming from the undergrowth and descended on both sides of the Roman column a few hundred yards to his rear. Within two paces of emerging, the Britons launched spears and javelins into the Roman ranks. Half-hidden at the path's fringes, slingers and archers added to the barrage. The legionaries immediately halted and spun ninety degrees to face their attackers as the wave of projectiles thudded into shields, armour and flesh.

Then, as quickly as they had appeared, the Britons melted back into the forest, the bombardment lasting but minutes yet leaving behind tens of legionaries dead or wounded. It looked as if a localised storm had blasted its way through several segments of the column, leaving the rest untouched.

"Send a century of Gauls in after the bastards!" Geta ordered, his eyes blazing as he surveyed the carnage.

Moments later the auxiliaries burst into the forest, following the lines of broken and flattened undergrowth left by the Britons. Immediately, the vegetation closed in around them, the trail disappeared and the column was lost to view. The Gauls slowed to a walk, slashing their swords to cut back branches and climbers, their initial rush dissipated in the constricted and unfamiliar space.

There was neither sight nor sound of the Britons but the sweating auxiliaries kept pressing forward until they were baulked by an unfamiliar sight. Branches had been interwoven across a line of trees, creating a sturdy barrier which reared up before them. The centurion, heaving in great gulps of stale air, stared at it. He had never seen its like before and was uncertain what to make of it.

"What..." he started to say, but never completed the question as an arrow fired from behind the barrier caught him in the mouth. With a strangled gargle he fell back, clutching at the shaft that protruded from the back of his neck.

Britons emerged from behind the barrier and surrounded the Gauls. The auxiliaries grouped together, forming a ragged circle to defend themselves. The optio, instantly promoted with the death of his centurion, tried to lead the century away but every available route led to an enemy's poised weapon. With a roar, the Britons attacked. Desperately the legionaries defended themselves, every man for himself, but one by one they were cut down, unable to manoeuvre in the space into which they had been squeezed.

From the path, Geta heard the bloody commotion, the screams and shouts of the wounded and dying and the celebrations of the victors. As the sounds of the battle died two auxiliaries, helmetless, weaponless and bloody from a hundred scratches, scrambled from the forest. Geta stared at them, open-mouthed.

"We were attacked!" panted one of the men, his eyes wide with terror. "They came from nowhere!"

"Where are the rest?" Geta asked, not quite believing what he saw.

"Dead, I would think," the other said, rubbing his hand over his face and looking relieved not to be sharing their fate.

"Put them on report for deserting their comrades," Geta said to Amatius, his voice black with anger. "We will deal with them later."

The Gauls protested their innocence as they were dragged away, but Geta ignored their pleas.

"Shall I order more men into the forest, sir?" Amatius asked.

"No, that is what they will want," he said. Looking along the column he could see his men were petrified of the unknown enemy that could be only feet from them. "Keep them moving, double speed."

The column, its dead and wounded dealt with, began to march again. This time there was no lull in attention, no idle banter along the rows as every eye warily scanned the forest for the slightest of movement. There were alerts as men saw shadows flickering through the undergrowth, and the column halted, only to march on time and again as each sighting proved a false alarm. The Romans, unsure whether the silhouettes were men or forest spirits, prayed to their gods for deliverance from the trees.

A nerve-racking quarter of an hour later the Britons flooded in again, bursting from the forest, screaming at the tops of their lungs. The Romans, the tactic no longer a complete surprise, quickly raised shields and, rather than waiting for the onslaught, charged straight at the Britons. The ambushers were chased back into the tree line but the Romans still suffered dead and wounded. This time, however, no one followed the Britons into the fringes and the column marched on.

Geta ground his teeth together. He stood with the setting sun bathing his face, frustrated with the lack of progress the column had made during the punishing day. Again and again the Britons attacked, on each occasion melting away to be lost in the forest. Although the only significant damage to the column occurred in the first sortie, the Britons had considerably slowed Geta's progress and it was this that provoked his ire.

He knew Plautius would not be pleased but he sent a messenger with his report nonetheless. It would be at least another day before they reached the crossroads at Bredegare, and the general should plan accordingly.

## XL

Verica was suffering with one almighty hangover.

The euphoria of finally reaching an agreement with the Dobunni after many, many days of negotiation had got to the old man, who drank far more than he intended at the hastily organised celebration. All night he was regaled by Cullen and his men and Verica felt the years fall away as past victories flooded back into his memory. Then, at an outrageously late hour, a stunningly beautiful and very young girl with wide eyes and alabaster skin took him to bed and treated him to an unforgettable experience. It had certainly been a night to remember.

Now Corinnion had been left far behind, as had the Dobunni guard that accompanied them briefly, withdrawing when they felt they had adequately discharged their duty. The subsequent half a day of travel failed to clear Verica's head. He sat slumped on his horse, happy for it and his companions to lead the way. His bones ached, he was tired and his head pounded, making him feel every one of his years.

Verica was long past the age of twenty and his body told him in no uncertain terms not to act like a callow youth again. He swore to himself that it was the last time he would do so.

He looked up as he felt a presence at his side, wincing as a sharp pain shot across his forehead with the effort. Ahearn had settled his horse into a shambling pace alongside him. Verica raised his eyebrows in surprise. It was rare for the stern warrior to condescend to speak to him.

"You did well, old man," Ahearn said, with what sounded to Verica like gratitude in his voice.

"Thank you," Verica nodded weakly.

"It is funny, but I am actually a little sad."

Verica did not understand and he betrayed the puzzlement. "Why? Our venture has been a great success."

"It has. Absolutely it has," Ahearn said reassuringly.

"So why be sad?" Verica brightened. "Instead you should rejoice!"

"You misunderstand me, old man. I am sad that your use has come to an end but I am sure I will get over it with the passage of a little time."

Verica shrugged. "I have done what I needed to. Now I want to see Caradoc and Togodumnus defeated by the Romans. If it is the last thing that I do, I will die a happy man."

"Look at me," Ahearn said softly.

Verica brought his bloodshot eyes to bear on Ahearn's pupils, as deep and as black as a lake.

"*I* am the last thing you will ever see," Ahearn said.

Before Verica could respond to these baffling words he felt a sharp pain in his side and everything went dazzlingly bright. Suddenly he understood Ahearn with utter clarity. With a sigh, he slid from his horse.

But Ahearn was wrong. The last thing Verica saw before the light faded and his vision darkened was his first wife smiling and beckoning to him. He returned the smile and gladly walked towards her as a final breath left his body.

"I feel better already!" Ahearn said, laughing deeply. With the death of Verica, what had been Narcissus's plan now belonged to Adminius.

Ahearn's men looked uncertain what to do next. "Leave him there for the animals."

Ahearn kicked the haunches of his horse and left the rest to follow. Destiny beckoned on the shores of the Meduuuæian.

# XLI

The sound of hoof beats, deadened by the soft ground and last year's rotted leaves, grew nearer as someone traversed the Blahwōn. Moments later, a Roman scout galloped out into the clearing. So focused was he on his mission that he never knew what killed him. The rider arched as three arrows burrowed their way through his mail armour, one piercing his heart. He stayed on the horse for a few paces before toppling off to the side, a bemused expression on his face. The horse carried on galloping and soon all sound of it had been lost. The scout's body was dragged away and thrown into the undergrowth, leaving a smear of blood on the grass as the only sign that he had existed at all.

Caradoc's force was split in two. A third hid on the flanks of the track and the rest in the undergrowth on the periphery of a large open space where the Blahwōn made a brief stop. Behind them were the dark spaces of the trees where they again took ownership of the land.

While they waited, the brief violence forgotten, a horse hitched to a chariot patiently cropped the stiff blades of poor grass that were starting to propagate in the late spring sunshine. Another snorted and shook its head. Its owner moved to quiet it, stroking its nose. Fionn listened intently, straining his ears for any man-made sounds.

Caradoc raised his hand at a birdcall from within the forest, the signal that the Roman arrival was imminent. Silently men drew swords and hefted spears. Fionn nocked an arrow and partially drew the bowstring back, feeling its tension and that inside himself as he fervently hoped the Roman officer who had killed Etain would step into range.

And then they came. A cohort of auxiliaries, a vanguard for the main column, trod warily into the clearing. Caradoc let them pass through; they would be dealt with later. Five minutes passed before the unsuspecting Geta led the column into the sudden sunlight.

Caradoc dropped his hand sharply in a cutting motion. With the howling carnyx, the Britons tore out of the undergrowth. To the appalled Romans it looked as if their attackers had appeared out of nowhere and were everywhere. Projectiles thumped into the ranks of legionaries, like a swarm of angry bees but inflicting a far greater sting. Most of the soldiers were sharp enough to raise their shields to protect themselves but those who were not were cut down and crashed to the earth wounded or dead. Chariots cut across the clearing, two men in each riding the jolts of the rough terrain. The warrior steering leant over, peering intently forward and feeling the horse through the reins, the other simply concentrating on hefting spears into the Roman ranks whilst maintaining his balance.

The Roman bodies quickly piled up under the onslaught and began to impede the marching column. It broke from its neat formation as the legionaries took it upon themselves to move around the obstruction and away from danger, despite the efforts of the screaming centurions. The soldiers still cocooned within the forest stayed there, refusing to move into the clearing. This created a bottleneck and a perfect target for the British warriors hidden along the pathway, who reared up and crashed down on the stationary line in a wave of fury. The attack severed the column as those at the back reversed into the Blahwōn and those at the front were forced into the clearing, despite the dangers it held.

Fionn shot arrow upon arrow into the Romans, indiscriminately at first. He took careful aim as every hit meant another, albeit small, payback for Etain. After a few minutes he slowed his rate of fire, looking for any of the enemy who looked senior -—cut off the head of a snake and the rest of the animal dies with it. Nearby, Brennon and Bearach fought, the genii near inseparable since Durovernon.

A bareheaded Roman, surrounded by a melee of legionaries, was carrying one of their pompous golden bird standards. Fionn took careful aim, held his breath and buried an arrow into the aquilifer, grinning as the Roman banner fell with the man. There was a flurry of activity from the ranks as the legionaries pressed protectively around their precious eagle, and within moments it was held aloft by a soldier, just a man from the ranks, who soon shared the fate of the aquilifer. Again the standard crashed to the floor but seconds later it flew aloft. Fionn laughed out loud with the joy of the battle and took aim at the latest bearer of the impotent bird.

Geta stayed lucky. As the Britons attacked, his horse uncharacteristically reared up in fright. An arrow, otherwise destined for Geta, smacked into his horse's neck and it slumped writhing to the ground. Geta rolled off, a slashing hoof narrowly missing him. For a moment he looked sadly as his favourite horse thrashed in agony. Another one gone, he mused, but then his attention snapped back to the pulsing battle. It was only a horse, after all.

Spilled around Geta's dying mount were a tumble of legionaries laid low by British projectiles and yet more were raining into their ranks, which looked bedraggled and uncertain with its leader down and aquilifer dead. Martius lay a few feet away, sightless eyes looking up to the sky, but at least the precious bird still flew over the heads of the legionaries.

Geta turned and looked at where the path joined the clearing. A trickle of legionaries was exiting the forest and so his group in the clearing was effectively cut off with no sign of reinforcements to bolster them. Despite their weaker numbers, the enemy had used the lie of the land supremely to their advantage and Geta knew he would have to act smartly to recover the situation.

He looked for anyone on a horse. There, thirty feet away on the edge of the battle. Geta ran over to the mounted officer, ignoring the zip of sling stones, and grabbed at his leg. The man turned with his sword raised to cut down, his face twisted in rage, but then held his blade when he recognised who it was.

"Get the column moving again, we need more men here! Now!" Geta shouted.

"Yes, sir!" The man scuttled off to the woods, keeping low on the back of the horse as arrows flashed past him, miraculously none touching him.

The carnyx rumbled angrily again, sending the British foot soldiers into a full-paced screaming dash at the Romans, whirling swords around their heads as they came.

"To me! To me!" Geta shouted. He grabbed the standard from a legionary and held it aloft, waving it back and forth like a signal.

The legionaries suddenly galvanised around their leader and the eagle. To lose the standard would bring eternal shame on the XX[th] and no man wanted that. With little time to do otherwise, they assembled in a haphazard formation around Geta, shields raised as the first of the Britons crashed into their ranks in an imitation of Roman tactics.

A collective grunt erupted from the front row of both armies as they clashed. The Britons laid about themselves with mighty swings of sword and axe, imperceptibly pushing back the Romans into a tighter group. The British flanks started to envelop the Romans, forcing some of the legionaries at the extremities to turn. Now they fought on two fronts, their strength divided, and this further weakened the line.

Geta kept shouting encouragement to his men but he saw them begin to waver as chariots advanced again into the battle, despatching more men to join the conflict just where they were needed.

Then the sound of a trumpet came from Geta's rear. With a roar of their own, fresh legionaries burst from the forest and dashed across the clearing to join their comrades, filling the front rank and the flanks. Geta's small band grew in numbers and confidence and fought renewed. Now it was the turn of the Romans to press on.

As the Roman ranks continued to strengthen, a carnyx blew and instantly the Britons broke off and began to retreat, moving stealthily backwards a few paces then turning and running. The chariots galloped away into the forest. Within moments the clearing was empty except for the blood-smeared, panting Romans.

"Hold, hold!" Geta shouted. The last thing he wanted was his men, with their blood up, in a hot-headed pursuit of the Britons, only to be caught again in unfamiliar terrain. The Romans needed to regroup and lick their wounds. Geta thrust the eagle into a legionary's hands and went to search for Amatius.

Caradoc moved between his men, congratulating some, offering words of support or condolence to others. Medics treated the wounded and howls of pain cut through the camp. Kynthelig offered some words of comfort to those who only had a short time left.

"We did well today," Caradoc said to Fionn as he joined him at a fire, soaking up the heat. They had withdrawn a few miles away from the

Romans and were well off the beaten track way. The sun was low in the sky and Caradoc did not expect to be discovered. He had a hot meal at last and tucked into it with gusto.

"Yes, we held them up well. For a few minutes I thought we were going to win."

"We gained a day, that was the win. Tomorrow morning we fall back to the Meduuuæian. Then we can end this."

But an intense disappointment burned within Fionn. No matter how many of the Romans he had killed today the Roman officer was not among them. He fervently hoped they would meet at the river.

There was still a settling of scores to be had.

# XLII

"I understand there are rumours swirling through the men," Gallus said, waving at a servant for more food, his voluminous plate starting to empty too much for his liking.

"Rumours, what rumours?" Narcissus asked, a tinge of concern in his voice. He put down the meat he was chewing on but no one immediately answered. Narcissus glanced meaningfully around the assembled men, all of whom, except for Plautius, who glared at Gallus, concentrated on their plates rather than meet the secretary's eye.

Eventually Vespasian spoke, puncturing the tense silence that enveloped the table. "That the Britons defeated us in battle."

"And did they?" Narcissus looked appalled. If it were true, the news would not play well back in Rome.

"Of course not!" Plautius insisted, his brow deeply furrowed in anger. "The Britons retreated as soon as Geta was able to respond to the trap."

He was irritated at the wasted time, and even more so that Narcissus the politician was picking over it. The decision was a simple military one. Without Geta able to provide protection on his flank the legions were far too vulnerable to risk marching further across the open ground ahead of them. So Plautius had ordered the legions to remain in camp whilst he waited for Geta to finish patching up the damage inflicted by the British ambush.

"So why the rumours?" Narcissus pressed, wanting desperately to be convinced but needing to leave no stone unturned.

Plautius shrugged. "You know how soldiers are. They feed on rumour and supposition. It is merely a minor setback. No more, no less."

"They are a black lot at the best of times!" Gallus laughed.

"Despite my best efforts not to, I fear I am starting to learn the ways of the legions," Narcissus said wryly, throwing a bone over his shoulder to emphasise the point and hide his relief. "How long before we march again?"

"First light, when Geta assures me he will be ready," Plautius said.

"He is cautious for such an outwardly confident man."

"Better vigilant than dead," Gallus said and belched loudly, to Narcissus's distaste.

Togodumnus watched the Roman camp from afar and wondered when they would make their move. The passage to Cantium had been difficult and error-strewn. The need to cross several rivers, still angry, swollen and fast flowing from the recent rains, caused problems, delays and deaths.

The journey had started badly when horses and men had been swept away crossing a raging torrent, the victims of a broken line. But Togodumnus and his warriors persevered and were rewarded by surmounting their final barrier, the Meduuuæian, this morning. Togodumnus then moderated his speed and advanced cautiously until the scouts reported the nearby Roman presence. To be ambushed himself was the last thing Togodumnus wanted.

The Catuvellauni king knew there was no way he could assault the camp in any meaningful fashion. His men would simply dash themselves uselessly against the walls, taking heavy casualties and achieving little, if anything, in the process. Neither could

Togodumnus afford to take on three legions on in a full frontal battle on the plain. A plan was needed.

All the Britons required was another day, a little more time to get into place. Maybe just a few hours would be enough...

# XLIII

Caradoc cursed as the warriors trailed over the bridge (a generous description in his opinion) at a slow crawl. Togodumnus had ordered all the other crossings over the Meduuuæian destroyed, leaving this, the smallest and the weakest, until last. The congestion was caused by the narrow link itself, just a few planks of aged and rickety wood in width, crudely lashed together with fraying rope. Usually it was used for moving a few scruffy grazing animals at a time from one side of the waterway to the other. Caradoc hoped the frighteningly pathetic-looking bridge was up to the task. So far it had proved to be, much to his surprise.

Delay was added as the horses proved nervous of the water that swirled darkly just beneath their hooves and of the flexing of the bridge, so they had to be hooded and led slowly over. Although this was painfully slow their loss could not be afforded.

Caradoc felt a wariness about the men that passed him by; not panic, but a sense that there were wolves nearby ready to pounce but no one quite knew where or when. Certainly not a single man wanted to be caught on the wrong side of the river, to be devoured when the Romans finally arrived.

Togodumnus's better knowledge of the environment, the shock of his attack and full speed pelt towards the river had given him some breathing space, but it was pitifully small. His real advantage was the ability of his men to quickly negotiate their way through the marshy areas that bordered the Meduuuæian. The route through was deceptive and potentially treacherous to the inexperienced. Soft ground lay where it looked firm, ready to trap and break a horse's leg, yet the safer territory was often unexpectedly hidden under inches of murky, fetid water.

So Geta's men were forced to slow their pursuit and pick their way through the devious narrows, too impatient to wait for a knowledgeable guide to direct them, even though they would probably have made better time overall. Caradoc watched the legionaries making their way steadily through the myriad of trails which converged onto the single narrow route to the bridge. All too soon he knew they would be pressing the Britons at the Meduuuæian shores.

"We need more time to get everyone over the bridge," Caradoc decided. He turned to Brandan. "Send some men forward to hold the Romans."

Brandan nodded. "Twenty should do it," he said. "And I will lead them."

"You know the bridge will be cut behind you," Caradoc warned.

"Just make sure you get everyone over. We will take as many of them with us as we can."

Brandan selected the men he wanted, the fierce and the brave, those strongest with the sword and spear and willing to die with them in hand. Despite their choice being a virtual death sentence, none refused to join him.

The small force moved off to meet the seemingly insurmountable odds that faced them. First they had to thrust their way past the Britons and, where necessary, Brandan used the flat of his sword to encourage the ranks to part. He planned to meet the Romans where the marshy paths merged together, edged by sluggish knee-deep water and whispering reeds. Here the Romans' superior numbers would count for little, as only a few could face his men at a time. To get to the bridge the Romans would first have to cut their way through the twenty-one Britons. Brandan intended to keep his promise that he and his men would die hard.

They reached the juncture well before the enemy, who were still apprehensively picking their way through the quagmire. Brandan assembled his men with their backs towards the Meduuuæian and placed himself squarely in the front row. He held his spear out horizontally in front of him and his shield up high. For the moment swords were sheathed — the Romans would be kept back by the long reach of the sharp spikes. Not a word was spoken as they waited. Just a light, twittering bird song reached Brandan's ears but he knew the peace would soon be shattered.

The Romans, a mixture of regular troops and auxiliaries, stopped when they saw the lines of fierce warriors facing them, a bristle of spears extended forwards like the spines of a cornered animal, its defences up, the tips held rock steady. They were uncertain how to proceed.

An officer, marked by a plume on his helmet, pushed his way through to the front. He surveyed the human barrier and then issued orders in a language Brandan did not understand.

"Hold firm!" Brandan shouted to his men. "Remember — not a single Roman bastard gets by whilst even one of us lives!"

The Britons howled their acceptance of Brandan's challenge.

The officer led his men, crouching behind their shields, in a rush towards the Britons' spears. He was the first to die, an easy target without a shield. He screamed as he was impaled upon the wicked points by the press of his men. The Romans retreated, leaving four of their dead behind on the pathway. Again and again they surged forward but each time they were forced back by the frightening accuracy of the spears that jabbed into exposed faces or limbs.

There was a temporary respite as the Romans withdrew to reconsider their tactics. Brandan began to see a faint glimmer of hope. Perhaps they could hold them off long enough and survive to swim the river. With a glance over his shoulder he saw the Britons were still crossing and a substantial knot remained on this side of the river. Not yet, he thought, it is too soon.

He turned back to his enemy to see a huge auxiliary, all bulging muscles and aggression, step through the amassed Romans. He had a helmet that looked far too small jammed tightly onto his head. His face was shrouded with a thick black beard the same colour as his pig-like eyes. Although noone had spoken he laughed at an unknown joke, a rumble like rolling thunder issuing from deep within his chest.

He lifted his clypeus shield, which covered just a small patch of his massive body, put his head down and ran like a bull, not rapidly but with a lot of momentum. He crashed into Brandan's tensed ranks, knocking the men aside as if they were rag dolls holding sticks. Several Britons were thrown into the marshy water and had to drag themselves out. Desperately, the warriors tried to close the gaping breach in the front rank but the Romans, with an exultant roar, followed in the track of the bull and were at last past the vicious points.

"Swords!" Brandan shouted.

As one, the Britons drew their weapons and bitter hand-to-hand fighting erupted as the Romans set about the men that had made them pay so dearly. The bull auxiliary battled with a handful of Britons in the middle of the group. He held them off with wild swings of his spatha but in his charge a spear had penetrated his armour to cut a deep and fatal wound. Slowly he was bleeding to death and with it his strength ebbed until his opponents, like a wolf pack sensing a weakening foe, pressed home and hacked him to death.

Brandan swung his sword in slashing arcs which kept the Romans too far back for their gladii to be brought to bear — he had learned the hard lesson at Durovernon. A legionary he was tussling with cried out as Brandan's blade caught him in the neck.

But the Romans had the impetus now and pushed steadily forward as, in tandem, the Britons retreated step by step towards the Meduuuæian. Now Brandan knew it was simply a war of attrition. Hack, stab, kill. Hack, stab, kill. On and on.

The warrior beside Brandan sucked in a sharp breath, his mouth an O, as a legionary stabbed his gladius upwards into the man's crotch, twisted it and yanked it out. The man fell into the marsh with a splash and lay face down in an expanding pool of muddy blood. Another Briton stepped in to take his place but Brandan had lost a few more feet of Cantium to the advancing enemy.

He could see his men were beginning to tire whilst the Romans had a seemingly unending body of fresh men to draw upon as more flooded down the path and pressed into the fight. He could feel the fatigue himself. As well as the advantage of numbers the Romans' training in close quarters fighting and their superior equipment was beginning to tell as one after another Brandan's warriors fell to the harsh cut of the gladius.

Brandan's arm and back muscles screamed and his lungs were on fire as he dragged in gulps of stale air when he could. But he kept shouting his war cry and hacked at them again and again. He stole another quick glance over his shoulder. There were still Britons on his side of the river, but far fewer now. Hope was still with him.

This momentary break in concentration ultimately cost Brandan his life. He grunted as a sword grazed off his chest. The chain mail he was wearing protected him from most of the blow but he heard the crack of something breaking. Brandan hacked back at the legionary, grinning as his sword cut into the man's head. The strength of his blow cut through his skull and into the grey brain matter beneath, which squirted along his sword. But a sharp pain shot across his chest with the effort and he hissed in pain.

He felt a weapon glance off his shoulder and then another. There were too many blows raining down on him now. A numbness spread through his shoulder and he began to have increasing difficulty in swinging his sword effectively. Another legionary stepped forward and the pair locked blades. He could feel the man's breath wash over his face. With a jeer Brandan shoved the soldier back and whilst his opponent was off balance he battered the man's shield out of the way and slashed at him. The legionary fell back with a cry as Brandan's blade cut across his chest, paring flesh from bone.

There were now only a handful of his men left filling the width of the path, with no one behind to step in and fill the gaps when men fell. Brandan knew it would be just minutes before they were all cut down. He could hear someone screaming with frustration, anger and rage, and he realised it was him.

He felt more cuts as steel seemed to swing in from all directions. Blood streamed down his right arm. He grunted as a legionary smashed a shield boss into his wounded chest. Brandan stabbed at the soldier but with less force now as his strength began to flee.

The Romans, sensing victory, pressed forward en masse. Brandan felt the sharp gladii cut into him again and again. He collapsed backwards onto his slain men, still screaming his battle cry, Babdah sitting on his shoulder ready to feed on him. But Brandan exulted in the knowledge that he had died well and would pass onto the next life with honour. The last thing he saw before his world went black was the grinning face of a Roman soldier with his sword raised to plunge down into his heart.

Caradoc watched Brandan's men die one by one, even as he hurried the final few warriors over the river and to safety. He was the last to cross the rickety bridge and only did so when two men started to hack into the wooden construction with their axes, chips flying in all directions with the ferocity of their activity. As the lashings were cut the shattered planks fell into the river and floated away. Bit by bit the warriors retreated across the link, steadily undoing its ancient construction. In a few minutes the bridge was destroyed.

Caradoc sighed with relief. Although he had lost some good men, they had saved many more in the process. The Romans, however, had Cantium.

Geta reached the bridge as the last plank fell into the water. He swore then wiped the blood from his sword. A Briton waved his axe jauntily at him from across the river. Geta snarled and gesticulated rudely but the Briton simply laughed and turned away.

The Romans were stuck on the wrong side of the waterway. But they had a captive.

# XLIV

The mingled smell of burning wood, cooking food and body odour filled the air as the massed British warriors settled down a short distance inland from the Meduuuæian.

"Did we do enough?" Togodumnus asked as he picked his way through groupings of men. He looked pale and drawn to Caradoc, a shadow of his usual self.

"We seem to have, yes," Caradoc replied, to Togodumnus's visible relief. "A messenger has just reached us from the Dobunni. Their army is only a matter of miles away now. They are the last."

Togodumnus winced as he stumbled on something on the ground.

"Are you all right?" Caradoc asked, with concern in his voice. He put out a supporting hand, which Togodumnus angrily shook off.

"Sorry," Togodumnus apologised. "I am just tired. It is nothing. I was injured in the attack but fortunately only lightly. My mail saved me from any real damage." He quickly changed the subject. "How many do the Dobunni number?"

"Cullen is bringing 17,000 warriors with him." Caradoc said, shelving any concern about his brother.

"Not many," Togodumnus said sullenly.

"Every man counts. Amon's Atrebates arrived yesterday with a further 10,000 men."

"I am surprised he came, and with so many."

"Most of us are. But thousands of Cantii have defected. Even with Weland's men they number only 13,000, far less than I would have anticipated. Clearly they believe we cannot succeed."

"What about the Durotrogies?"

Caradoc shook his head. "No, they ignored all of our advances."

"Even yours?"

Caradoc nodded. Togodumnus looked depressed, he had hoped for a last-minute change of heart from the fierce hill fort-dwelling tribe. Not only their numbers but their aggression would have been invaluable. But they were an introverted faction, not given to considering the world beyond their borders.

"It was a serious mistake not to have kept the army together at Durovernon," Togodumnus admitted with the benefit of hindsight.

Caradoc nodded. "I have told myself the same thing. However, what is done is done. We cannot afford to dwell on it now. We have to look to tomorrow."

"You are probably right." Togodumnus did some arithmetic in his head. "With Urien's Atrebates, and the Dobunni when they arrive, our army will be around 150,000 men. How many do the Romans number?"

"Less, a lot less. Maybe 50,000."

"Good, numbers win battles." Togodumnus brightened. "How is the mood of the men?"

"Confident! Can you not feel the buzz?"

The assembled warriors were in an electric mood. They laughed and joked with each other, positive that they could beat anybody they faced — that was if the Romans dared to navigate the Meduuuæian, of course. There were those who were desperate for the Romans to cross so they could have their revenge. But there were others that wanted to see the river god

Tamessa rear up and swallow their enemy whole.

"Tell me what happened," Caradoc said.

"I would prefer to sit whilst I do. It has been a long day."

"Fine," Caradoc pointed to a space on the ground.

Once he was settled Togodumnus stared into the middle distance as he thought back to the assault.

"I attacked the Romans as they left their camp. We were on horseback for speed. Part of their column had exited but most of it was still within the walls. We descended from the Dūn and cut into their men, but they reacted quickly with their cavalry. The chariots inflicted some damage but before we knew it foot soldiers were flooding out of the camp. It was like watching ants defending their nest when threatened. They were everywhere, and so fast!

"We had to retreat much sooner than I wanted and so we did not cause them a significant delay, but we also only lost few men. At first the Romans did not follow, but then some cavalry attacked from the Dūn. We barely managed to escape them."

"It matters not," Caradoc said. "The army is almost assembled and the Romans cannot quickly cross the river."

Caradoc knew the high tide of the Tamessa also meant they could not retreat if they wished; they were trapped between the two waterways. That left an escape to the west — but fifteen miles away the Derventio barred their course. The thought of being pursued all that distance and then attempting a river crossing under pressure made Caradoc go cold. Therefore the escape route to the Tamessa, a single narrow pathway to the north of them, was vital. But he kept the thought to himself. Nothing could be done about it, and his brother looked under enough pressure as it was.

Later, when Togodumnus was alone, he gingerly opened his cloak. He had to peel the cloth away from his chain mail, as the blood had dried and matted, fusing the two together. Then the mail had to be removed. Togodumnus sucked in a sharp breath as the wound reopened. Once the gash was exposed he cleaned himself up and applied a dressing. It hurt when he moved too quickly but Togodumnus hoped it would not be long before he was much improved. He had a battle to lead.

The legions funnelled onto the plain east of the Meduuuæian. They needed to be organised effectively, and so Plautius pushed the XX[th] back away from the river and placed Vespasian's II[nd] on the left of his position. The XIV[th] he kept in the centre, facing the Britons and the IX[th] moved to higher ground in the west. The riverboats of the Classis Britannica were being brought downstream but were not yet fully committed.

The two massive bodies of men faced each other across the ribbon of water that stretched from the sea to its source seventy miles inland. Plautius considered his next moves.

Ahearn pushed his way through the Britons, ignoring the muted protests. He was intent on finding Weland. He wore a huge helmet which covered most of his face except his mouth and his eyes, which blazed, causing men who saw them to step quickly out of his way. Those that did not were simply pushed to one side. The helmet, made of highly polished bronze, shone brightly. It was shaped to look like a snarling beast.

Cullen was about to lead the Dobunni onto the field and Ahearn needed to know where the tribes were positioned, and quickly. He spotted Weland at last and redoubled his efforts.

Adminius struggled to speak in much more than a monosyllabic tone. He attempted to make himself look calm and collected on the outside but inside he seethed with an energy which was bursting to be released. He felt as if his skin was stretching with the effort of retaining the pressure, and it was all he could do not to shriek it out. It was the closest he had been to his hated brothers for four years and the long-awaited revenge he had so carefully engineered was almost complete. His past fears of defeat and failure were long consigned to memory.

"We are agreed?" he asked through gritted teeth.

"Of course." Max looked offended that he needed to be asked of the bargain again. "Stay with my Praetorians. Find a reason to be away from Narcissus."

Adminius snorted. "That will not be hard." Narcissus seemed unable to bear the sight of him these days.

"Then what?"

"We cross and we find your brother, the king."

"And kill him." Adminius smiled a wicked grin.

## XLV

Brandan hissed as someone grabbed a handful of hair and yanked his head up. The vision out of his one good eye was bleary at best. The other had been taken by a sword cut, the gore still on his face and the shattered socket weeping bloody pus. He had no idea where he was, but the enclosure stank of rank body odour. It was absolutely silent. He shivered and realised he was naked. With great effort he eventually focused on a grey-haired man with a set, square jaw, who glared at him a few inches away.

"Where am I?" Brandan groaned.

"What is he saying?" Plautius asked Adminius, who translated.

"I can assure you that this is not the afterlife," Plautius grinned. "Not yet anyway."

Plautius released Brandan's hair. His head sagged momentarily before, with a struggle, he proudly raised it and stared defiantly at the general. Then Brandan turned and spat at Adminius. The fat man dodged the spittle, stepped forward and punched Brandan in the face. The pain in his cheek seared as the blow started the blood flowing again.

"Is that all you have?" Brandan laughed through broken lips when the worst of the pain had subsided. He spat blood onto the floor. "Pathetic."

Adminius raised his fist again but Plautius held him back. "He will suffer enough shortly. But for the moment we need him able to speak."

"I want information about your friend's plans," Plautius told Brandan through Adminius. "And you are going to tell me."

"You Romans! You think you're better than everyone else. You think that you can come to our lands and take whatever you want!"

"Yes, we do," Plautius answered quietly with a half smile. "And you will help us to do it."

Brandan swore. Plautius did not speak barbarian but he could interpret. As the general expected, he needed plan B. Plautius waved forward a little ferret of a man. Maro was short and hunched over. His face was pointed and he had large, protruding, rotting teeth. His breath stank. In his delicate hands he held a wickedly sharp knife which he had been using to pick imaginary dirt from underneath long fingernails. He was a disgusting individual, but Plautius did not require Maro for his table manners or etiquette.

"Go to work," Plautius said.

"With pleasure," the ferret said and stepped towards Brandan with an evil grin.

Brandan had experienced pain before, but never like this. The first cut of the knife was a sickening jolt. His mind lost control over his body as a hot flush coursed through him and stars appeared in front of his eyes. Brandan fought to retain consciousness and shook uncontrollably. His breathing became sharp and shallow and he felt like vomiting. He knew he would have collapsed were he not tied to the chair.

Maro grinned at the British warrior's response. He particularly liked it when the colour had drained from his face, as if all of his blood were leaking out of the single cut. But Maro knew that was not possible, not yet anyway. He enjoyed Brandan's desperation for a few moments before he picked up a bucket of cold water and doused him with it. With the soaking, Brandan's reactions returned to normal. It was like day and night. Although the pain of the cut was still present the other symptoms had miraculously vanished.

The ferret grinned again as he stepped forward with his bloodied knife. Behind him Adminius, still needed to translate, looked just as pale as the prisoner.

Maro had worked steadily on Brandan, attacking the most sensitive areas after because time was regrettably limited. Brandan was slumped forward unconscious in the chair, only held upright by the bindings. Fresh blood dripped from the myriad of nicks, cuts and slashes all over his body. A testicle had been thrown carelessly into a corner. The iron aroma of blood mingled with that of urine, vomit and sweat. But Maro was used to the smells of his job andthey barely registered with him anymore.

"Do you think he has told us all he knows?" Plautius said, utterly unemotional at the sight of Brandan's carcass. Adminius had already gladly left the enclosure, his job done.

"Oh yes. I am certain of it," the ferret said with a sharp, toothy grin.

"Good, well done. Now kill him," Plautius ordered and left the tent, he had better things to spend his time on.

Maro drew out his knife to use it on Brandan for the last time. He twisted the blade, watching light glint off it. It was an object of such contrasts, he thought. On one hand it was a beautifully fashioned item of distinction. But on the other it was dreadful, as it could be used to inflict pain, maim and, ultimately, kill. It all depended upon who held the knife, Maro thought, and snickered to himself at his ironic little joke.

He sighed. It was such a pity that blood would have to be cleaned off the knife again.

## XLVI

The ballista was assembled and ready. It closely resembled a crossbow, albeit one that was sixteen feet long. The huge projectile weapon was mounted on a tripod so that it could be angled to deliver missiles where desired. The three legs rested on a rare piece of solid ground overlooking the Meduuuæian.

The soldier operating it winched the hemp skeins, drawing the bow arms back. He then locked the arms, now under a high tension, in place with a ratchet, lugged a heavy rock from a pile next to the ballista and placed it in the sling, grunting with the effort. When he was happy with the trajectory of the ballista he tugged the trigger rope sharply to release the bow. With a sharp smack it lobbed the rock in a shallow arc into the mass of Britons assembled on the other side of the river.

There were other siege engines along the riverbank starting their work, placed above the high waterline — nine further ballistae and ten onagers, the legion's full complement. The onager, a much simpler weapon than the ballistae, comprised a single catapult arm. Soon smaller ballistae type weapons, called scorpions, which shot bolts with enough accuracy to pick off individuals, would be employed. Plautius's first aim was simple — mass bombardment to cause maximum terror.

Two engines hurled burning pitch over the watery gap. Others despatched single large rocks and the rest threw a collection of smaller, but still deadly stones. The weapons kicked and bucked as they were wound up tightly and then released, firing their missiles over the river in a variety of trajectories, so that there was no pattern to the assault.

The Britons had never seen anything like the strange contraptions that were being steadily assembled. They stood watching the activities of the Romans with curiosity and amusement — until the rocks started smashing into them, pulverising flesh and bone into an unrecognisable gore. The pitch burnt the grass where it landed, starting small localised fires. When it landed on skin it ate its way through to the bone. Chaos reigned in the centre as the Britons tried to escape the barrage.

Bassus led the eight Batavi cohorts east around the bend in the river. The Meduuuæian ran in a roughly south-west to north-east direction but beyond the Roman position the river traced a lazy U-shape and it was towards this that Bassus headed. The Batavi hugged the drier land, keeping away from the marshy margins. They trekked as far as they could until the quagmire opened so extensively that Bassus could take them no further. Besides a few stubby trees and reed beds the area was flat, wet and boggy.

He peered over the Meduuuæian, rubbing his long nose — a childhood habit that sometimes reappeared. Gregarious and upbeat in even the worst of circumstances, he nodded happily to himself. Although the river was at its widest here the water was sluggish and it looked as if the riverbed dropped away on a shallow incline — easy to get in and out of. The barrier would not prove to be any significant challenge to his men; they had swum much more difficult waterways under the eyes of the enemy.

What was most important was that there were no Britons in sight. The bend was indeed shielding them as Adminius had suggested it would. Bassus thought he could hear the faint thump of the siege engines firing. Bassus signalled to his men that they would negotiate the river here.

"Aim for the broken tree," Bassus told them, pointing to the far shore, where a trunk had been split in half by a bolt of lightning. Its dead branches dipped in the water as if testing the listless current as it drifted by.

The Batavi began to prepare themselves for the crossing with the minimum of fuss, as Bassus had expected they would. Their equipment was already strapped to the horses, leaving the men unencumbered and able to cross quickly.

The men stripped off their clothes; better to put dry clothes onto wet bodies than have them soaked through. Bassus rolled up his breeches and stuffed them into a pack. He knew the legionaries scathingly referred to these as feminalia, but he cared not. After only six more years of service he would receive the prize coveted by all auxiliaries — Roman citizenship. Then he would be their equal.

Bassus stepped into the murky river. Mud swirled around his ankles as he moved. The water was icy cold; it was too early in the year for it to have warmed up at all. He sucked in his breath as he waded further in and more sensitive areas were submerged. Although he had crossed unknown multitudes of waterways he never got fully used to their frigid kiss.

The Batavians and their horses entered the water in a broad procession and struck out strongly across the Meduuuæian, fighting against the sideways push of the current. A single cohort remained on the bank, bows ready, in case the enemy appeared and they needed to be held off. Even so, whilst he swam, Bassus kept a close watch for anyone on the banks; if they were caught in the water they were defenceless and could be massacred in short order.

Several nerve-racking minutes later Bassus stepped shivering out of the water. There had been no alarm, no spears splitting the air and no reception committee waiting to hack them to pieces. No one had been lost on the crossing and no kit damaged. It really could not have gone any better. Bassus signalled for the remaining cohort to cross, their role as protectors transferred to those on the far bank.

The Batavi quietly assembled themselves and slid their apparel from the horses. Clypeus shields, spatha swords and bow and arrows were strapped to their bodies over damp clothes. Brass helmets adorned with hair were donned, prayers murmured, thanks given. Their luck had held and the Britons were completely unaware of their presence. The Batavi were ready to go to war.

# XLVI

Caradoc was alerted by a shout. One of his men mounted on a horse was gesturing frantically to the north.

"What the hell is it?" Caradoc demanded.

"Enemy soldiers heading towards the Tamessa!"

"How many?" Togodumnus asked.

The young warrior spluttered, looking flustered. "I do not know. Thousands?"

"Slow down. Tell me everything," Caradoc commanded. The man took a deep breath and explained what had been seen, where they were heading and how far away they were.

Caradoc swore. "They are trying to cut us off from the Tamessa."

"Send out the chariots," Togodumnus ordered.

"Is that wise?" Caradoc asked Togodumnus quietly.

"What choice do we have? We cannot get the infantry in place quickly enough. They have a head start."

Caradoc was unhappy about stripping the army of its most flexible arm but Togodumnus was king, not he.

Although it was only a matter of minutes it felt like it took far too long for the mounted men to get organised and Caradoc constantly shouted and cajoled them to move faster. But, finally, Caradoc led the mass of horses and chariots in a torrent towards the enemy.

Bassus heard the thundering of thousands of pairs of hooves. The auxiliaries had managed to move about half a mile inland, picking their way through the marshy areas and onto drier land where they could move faster, before they had been spotted. They were caught in front of a low-lying hill up which Bassus was prepared to retreat, if necessary. He had known a response from the Britons was just a matter of time and that when it arrived the attack would come hard and fast.

"Form up!" he shouted to his men, the plan already agreed on the riverbank. Now it just needed to be implemented.

The Batavi drew themselves into rows. The first two were archers, those at the front kneeling, those behind standing. The cavalry assembled behind the archers and were to be held back.

Horse against horse was rarely decisive, Bassus knew.

It was the chariots that concerned Bassus the most. He had seen the speed and ferocity of their attack in the Blahwōn, his first and only experience of the archaic vehicles which had long since fallen out of use on the continent. Somehow they had to be nullified. Here they came, rumbling and bouncing behind energetic steeds.

"Aim for the horses! Not the men, the horses!" he shouted as he walked along the rank. "Wait until you can smell their stinking breath and then kill their horses!"

Bassus hoped it would be enough; otherwise their incursion would be short-lived.

The Britons laughed as they saw the Batavi — a pitifully small group just asking to be slaughtered. With swords and spears in hand the Britons spurred their horses on, smelling an easy victory, each wanting to be in amongst the enemy as soon as possible to cut, slash and stab before returning to the camp in glorious victory.

There was a deceptive whistling sound as the arrows were launched into the air, like a gentle wind through trees.

The shafts, fired on a low trajectory, smacked into the horses, chariots and sometimes men. Caradoc's horse reared in shock and pain, squealing at the arrow buried in its chest. All around him arrows were cascading down and men were being thrown to the ground. It was a scene of utter confusion.

Caradoc crouched behind the twitching body of his horse as the arrows continued to rain down. He watched a horse race past, heading in the direction they had come from, dragging behind it an empty chariot with only one wheel. The axle cut a gouge in the ground but barely impeded the animal's panicked headlong dash.

The hail of arrows stopped as quickly as it had begun. Strewn around the immediate area were the dead and the dying, mostly horses, killed in their hundreds. Those that had not been hit had skidded to a halt and reversed their direction, putting as much distance between themselves and the Batavi as possible.

"Fall back," Caradoc shouted to the unhorsed men. "Fall back!"

Slowly his warriors poked their heads out from where they were hiding, expecting the arrows to start again, but no death was shot their way during the tentative venture. A few at first, then in droves, the unhorsed warriors ran back the way they had come.

Caradoc was stunned. His chariot force had been almost entirely decimated and nothing had been achieved to stop the Romans cutting them off from the Tamessa.

Bassus, on the other hand, was extremely pleased. In a few short moments he had carved up the Briton's attack. Not one chariot had managed to get anywhere near his lines and none of his men had come even remotely close to being hurt. He had ordered the barrage stopped to conserve arrows, assuming the Britons would try again and every arrow would be needed.

"Move out!" he shouted.

The Batavi slung their bows, formed into ranks and struck north to continue with their mission, leaving behind the dead and the dying.

Togodumnus anxiously scanned the waterline, monitoring the increased activity on the far bank. Roman barges were milling along the Meduuuæian, keeping to the furthest shore. A few arrows were shot at the boats by impetuous warriors, the shafts burying themselves in the gunwales, but the damage was insignificant and the Romans arrogantly carried on about their business as if the Britons were not there.

Even worse, a large body of soldiers were massing directly opposite his position, although at least the pulverising siege engines had fallen quiet. The sound of horns carried easily across the expanse, directing the manoeuvres of the legionaries.

Togodumnus eyed them warily and then issued frantic orders. His centre started to form into ranks, drawing in the Catuvellauni and Trinovantes from the extremities of his army as they readied themselves to repulse the impending crossing.

Togodumnus touched his crown and prepared to make Cunobelin proud.

## XLVIII

The man with the feather-tipped spear raced unnoticed along the shores of the Meduuuæian. He paid no attention to the sights and sounds around him, intent only on reaching the II[nd] with his orders.

When he did so he stayed on horseback, breathing heavily from his exertions. Vespasian listened closely to his wheezing words and once Plautius's instructions had been given, the messenger scurried off to his next port of call -—Geta and the XX[th].

"We cross," Vespasian said grimly when asked what they were to do next.

The knot of Classis Britannica riverboats bobbed gently on the Meduuuæian. They lurched as the legionaries stepped aboard, equipment was loaded or horses led on. Then, once full, the boats were rowed to the other side. The crossing time was short, as the river was narrow here, but the boats themselves were relatively small and the transportation of the legion was not fast. Yet slowly but surely, the II[nd] were moved piecemeal across the waterway. Vespasian waited nervously for the transition to be completed, expecting discovery at any time, but at last the entire legion, including auxiliaries and horse, was across, and all without the Britons noticing.

"Good luck!" Curius called softly as the Classis Britannica boats melted back downstream. Vespasian waved in response and turned to head inland.

The centurions ran through the ranks and, under Vespasian's orders, shaped the legion into two lines of five cohorts. Each line was staggered to place three cohorts, with a break between, in front, with two more cohorts just behind them, closing the gaps in support. Each line was the shape of a triangle with the top cut off.

Vastly outnumbered, Vespasian knew he had to make the II$^{nd}$ look as imposing as possible. He sacrificed some of the speed a narrow formation imparted and instead spread the lines wider so the soldiers of each cohort were arranged three ranks deep.

Once ready the II$^{nd}$ advanced towards the Britons, steadily and silently. There was to be no skirmishing. Vespasian wanted to hit the Britons hard and fast. He held his breath, expecting to be noticed at any moment, but the British heads were turned to the XIV[th] across the Meduuuæian and the II[nd] managed to get within half a mile before the Catuvellauni eventually spotted them.

A cry of alarm rang out from the British ranks, taken up immediately by a carnyx ,which blared balefully. A sea of faces turned towards the II[nd] and a wave of noise rippled outwards as the warriors added their shouts of alarm to that of the carnyx.

The centurions kept the legionaries moving forward at the same quick pace, whilst frantically the Britons tried to form themselves into a makeshift defensive line. Within minutes the II[nd] had narrowed the fissure between the two armies to just a few hundred yards.

With a blast from the horns Vespasian unleashed the first line. They sprang forward, a huge roar released from their tense lungs. For the moment Vespasian held his second line and cavalry alae in reserve, wary of the sizeable numbers he faced and the possibility of being outflanked.

The assailants were led by the veterans of the first cohort on the right, who ran ahead of the rest of the line in their eagerness to fight, but not far behind them were the fifth cohort on the left flank, and the third in the middle. The Roman line crashed into the massed ranks of the Catuvellauni and the legionaries hacked and stabbed as the Britons desperately defended themselves.

The front ranks of the supporting second and fourth cohorts were armed with pila. No spears had been used in the initial charge, so as to retain them for use at this instant. As the two armies collided, the legionaries hurled their spears as hard as they could, grunting with the effort. The pila flew over the heads of their comrades to impale themselves in the mass of tightly-bunched Britons. Finally, the cohort of Gauls stationed to the rear, equipped with bows, fired at will to join the pila pouring down onto the enemy.

Hundreds of Britons were struck by the projectiles. Many died, as most of the men were too poor to afford protective armour. The relentless pressure from the legionaries as they hacked and stabbed pushed the already panicked Britons backwards. The combatants behind them, shocked from the assault from the sky and hearing the screams and anguish from the men in the front line, turned and ran. Within moments, it was a full-scale rout.

The next wave of disastrous news hit Togodumnus like a sucker punch to the gut, emptying all of the breath from his lungs in a sudden rush. The blare of the carnyx made him look over to the west sharply, but he was too far away and with too many men in between to see anything meaningful.

Then the clash of armour and weapons reverberated over the Britons. Screams of the wounded, shouts of the battle-crazed and the moans of the dying carried easily to Togodumnus. Now it was clear, they faced attack on a second front.

Caradoc had returned from the failed assault on the Batavians on a borrowed horse and was rounding up more men, cavalry and infantry, to wrest back the initiative and their lifeline from the Batavi.

"We have been attacked," reported a bloodied messenger, one arm hanging limply. "The Romans came from the west and fell on us before we had time to form up. The Catuvellauni broke and retreated."

Togodumnus swore. "I will have to respond to this threat myself."

The sound of a ballista firing came from the opposite bank. Instinctively everyone ducked. Caradoc, though, stood tall. Togodumnus was puzzled. The weapons had not been fired for some time and just the one sounded, the rest remaining silent. He watched the missile twist and turn slowly as it crossed the waterway and landed nearby with a soggy crunch.

"You might want to see this," Fionn shouted, beckoning Togodumnus over.

"What is it?" Togodumnus saw a pale round lump lying on the grass. Fionn rolled the object over with his foot. A single wide, glassy eye stared up at him.

"Brandan," Fionn replied. "Or at least his head."

A murmur of distaste ran through the horde, like a ripple when a stone is thrown into a lake.

"Urien," Togodumnus turned to the Atrebatean. "Hold the centre. If the Romans cross, push them back at all costs." Although the XIV[th] had not yet navigated the Meduuuæian, Togodumnus was sure they would. It was just a matter of time.

Urien nodded. "You have my word, my king."

Togodumnus turned away, calling for his comitatus. He mounted and spurred forward to deal with Vespasian. The yellow sun was beginning its downward drift towards the horizon. Togodumnus had to ensure the Britons could hold out for the rest of the day. Privately, he wondered whether they could.

Ahearn tried not to laugh out loud. The sight of Brandan's head lying in the grass and its effect on the Catuvellauni was, he thought, absolutely priceless.

He watched as Togodumnus mounted and choked off a snort as he cantered past. Not long, he thought, patting the soft lump under his mail. Not long before we meet.

# XLIX

Vespasian struggled to prevent his front line from pursuing the fleeing Britons when they broke. The horns repeatedly called for the press forward to halt. The older and wiser heads on the veterans of the first cohort were the first to stop. Soon the remaining legionaries followed suit, unwilling to be caught out in the open on their own. Finally they obeyed the horns and pulled back. Despite orders not to, the withdrawing Romans paused to loot a few of the dead, despite orders not to do so, but finally they sprinted back to their lines as British cavalry appeared.

Now the II$^{nd}$ held its position, waiting for the promised support from Geta to maintain the bridgehead won so surprisingly easily. Those soldiers not on watch took the time to rest and eat. Bloodied weapons were cleaned, the rage of battle now cooled. Vespasian, seated and taking a drink, pondered how the Britons would respond.

Curius's Classis Britannica boats had been busy since they had transported Vespasian over the Meduuuæian. But then so had Geta. The immunes of the

XX[th] and XIV[th] collaborated to construct a pontoon bridge, the parts ferried to where needed by the Classis Britannica. Even so, it would still be several hours before the work was complete.

"Vespasian will need more support," Geta said. "I shall take two cohorts to defend the bridgehead in case the Britons attack."

"Yes, sir," Amatius replied. He was pretty certain it was just an excuse for Geta to put himself closer to the enemy but the primus pilus knew better than to voice a contradictory opinion.

"Virginius! Doing some proper work at last! I bet you have managed to avoid breaking into a sweat," Geta bawled.

Curius flushed, furious to hear his nickname used in front of his subordinates. He stepped off the boat, making it rock in his urgency to bridge the gap with Geta.

"Gallus is not here to protect you now," he hissed, standing nose-to-nose with the larger man, his Adam's apple bobbing up and down.

"And neither is Plautius. We can deal with our unfinished business any time you like, Virginius." Geta rested a palm on the pommel of his gladius, pleased to see the red hue on Curius's face rise another notch.

"Excuse me. May I be permitted to interrupt?"

Geta whirled around, angry that his sport had ground to a halt just as it was beginning to get interesting. A response from Curius died on his lips and gratefully he pounced on the opportunity to stalk back to the river.

"What is it, Max?" Geta snapped, watching Curius retreat with a twinge of regret.

"Sorry, sir, have I caused a problem?" Max chewed his lip.

"No, Max, just an old wound I keep trying to cauterise," he grinned, the argument forgotten already. "I am sure there will be another occasion to do so. Something to look forward to. Now, what do you want after you so rudely interrupted me?"

"Your help, sir."

"What, again? What is it with you Praetorians?"

Max ignored the barb. "Plautius is ignoring my century. If he has his way I will sit out the entire battle on the wrong bank whilst everyone else fights for Rome."

"Upset you will miss out?" Geta asked wryly.

"Looking after that fat bastard, Adminius, has driven me into new realms of boredom. I just want to fight, that is all."

"You just want the chance for some plunder is probably more like it."

Max shrugged. "That is an additional benefit, yes."

"I like your honesty!" Geta laughed, slapping Max on the shoulder. "I am sure we can squeeze a few more men into our boats."

"Thank you, sir."

"But you will owe me a favour in return."

"Of course." Max said lightly and waved his men forward, hoping it would all be worth it.

Adminius, wearing a tight-fitting uniform, filed onto the boat in the midst of the Praetorians. He kept well away from Geta, as the helmet barely disguised his face. Adminius had almost given himself away when Max insulted him but a firm restraining grip from Anatolius, who fully expected Adminius's peeved reaction, stayed him. Adminius had snatched his arm away from the lesser man but swallowed the slur like a bitter tasting draft that was difficult, but necessary, to take.

The boat pushed off. Adminius stared at the shoreline, watching it, and destiny, inch closer with each pull of the oars.

## XL

Caradoc, for the second time that day, pounded north on horseback. He ignored the litter of chariots decimated by the Batavi. They were gone, forgotten. He estimated that the enemy were unlikely to have progressed beyond Gad's Hill, a second low-lying rise beyond where the disastrous encounter with the Batavi had taken place. So he split his force in three. The first two groups entirely comprised horsemen. One was to ride around the far side of the rise to cut off the Batavi; the other would loom up on the auxiliaries themselves in order to hold them. The third part of the force was foot soldiers and followed at a more sedate pace in Caradoc's wake. They would be used to grind the enemy into the dust once trapped.

Caradoc craned forward, straining his eyes. Then he saw them. His luck was good for once today and he thanked the gods. The Batavi had not reached Gad's Hill just yet.

Bassus's mood changed from pleasure to concern.

"Horses!" one of his men had called, pointing to a group of Britons riding well off their flank and beyond them. Bassus stopped the Batavi in their tracks and tried to determine the enemy's intentions.

"There are more," Bassus said. To his rear another group of horsemen were cantering slowly towards them.

"Bows at the ready!" Bassus shouted.

But the horsemen halted.

"They are scared of us," one of his men laughed.

"Maybe. Or maybe we are being held, ready to be squeezed when they want to."

Bassus looked about him. The river was to the right of his men. They had passed one hill but another was nearby. Heavily wooded, it afforded much better protection than the open land they were currently in. The cohorts only had so many arrows and their numbers were insignificant compared to the nearby British army.

"Double time to the hill!" Bassus ordered and the Batavi jogged forward again in a race to make the slopes before they were cut down. Their objective would have to wait for the time being.

Caradoc stopped his horse a few hundred yards away from the base of the mount, just out of arrow range. The gradient was fairly steep and covered by a mass of trees. Somewhere in amongst the foliage he knew the Batavi were secreted.

"They are not going anywhere," Caradoc said.

"We would be mad to go in after them," Fionn said.

"Agreed. We shall bottle them up and leave them there."

Caradoc spurred his horse back to the advancing foot soldiers and gave orders for groups of men to be stationed around the hill. Then he, Fionn's genii and the majority of the cavalry rode back to their army. One threat was neutralised, at least.

Togodumnus rode around the extremities of the Catuvellauni, the banner displaying Cunobelin's hound fluttering behind him. He placed himself at the front of his own lines facing the Romans, who had withdrawn a little, leaving the bodies of the British dead to be picked over by the carrion that flocked to feed in the no-man's land between the two armies. They stood at attention, a rippling line of shields that stretched into the distance, the setting sun glinting off their helmets and weapons.

A carnyx blew at Togodumnus's signal. The blast was taken up and repeated along the line. With a roar the Britons surged forward, stepping over the bodies of their brothers to reach the enemy.

The horns in the Roman ranks responded, unleashing the legionaries. The gap between the two armies closed rapidly and when they met there was a clash like thunder that rolled over the river.

The Britons fought with a fury, embarrassed at having been driven to retreat by such a comparatively small number of Romans, who themselves defended desperately under the onslaught. Vespasian had committed almost all of the troops under his command in an effort to avoid being enveloped by the far larger British army. Only the cavalry alae was held back,

Along the line men fought private battles, slashing and stabbing at their immediate opponent. But the aggression with which they struggled was energy sapping and after a quarter of an hour the two armies stepped back from each other, like sparring partners catching their breath.

Again the Britons were sent forward by the carnyx and the battle resumed. Repeatedly, the two armies clashed and withdrew, only to clash again, until the sun dipped below the horizon and it became increasingly difficult to focus on who was fighting who. The carnyx signalled a retreat and the Britons fell back.

The Romans had advanced no further.

## LI

The man, barely a shadow, slipped into the inky black Meduuuæian, ignoring its cold embrace. He was small, les than five feet tall, but his arms and chest bulged with muscles. He swam upstream with the current, his movements quiet and controlled, totally at ease with his environment. He made swift progress, the pressure at his back from the flowing water helping, and before long he reached his target.

He pulled himself up the bank, avoiding the reeds that would rustle at his touch. On this windless night, the noise would alert the legionaries to his presence. Slowly the man snaked his way forward, inch by inch. He spent fifteen minutes on the river bank making sure he saw all that was of significance before crawling back the way he had come and dropping into the river with barely a ripple.

The return journey was harder against the current and soon his muscles began to ache, despite their strength. He paused once to let a Roman river craft drift by and his muscles welcomed the rest. They did not see him, a small, insignificant hump in the black watery expanse. Soon there were hands grabbing at him, hauling him out of the Meduuuæian, then wrapping a cloak around his shoulders and taking him to where the leaders sat.

"We should retreat whilst we can," Urien suggested. "I do not like the sound of the Roman position."

"Weakling," Weland spat.

Urien sprang to his feet, sword already drawn. Caradoc stepped in between the pair. "Enough!"

Weland shook off Caradoc's restraining grip off, glared at him and sat down again.

"This is where we stop them. If we retreat now, we lose," Weland said, steel in his voice. "Our army is strong, far greater than theirs. Confidence is high. Only a few warriors have left the battlefield, the cowards. I hope I speak for us all when I say I have no desire to feel the yoke of the Romans about my neck. We have to stand here, no matter what the cost."

"The bridgehead is the key," Caradoc said, looking at the damp patch where the man had stood only minutes before, dripping river water onto the ground. "We must crush it, stop others crossing easily, otherwise all is lost."

"Agreed," Togodumnus said.

The leaders talked well into the night, working out their strategy. As a final act before they dispersed back to their tribes with a part of the plan, Kynthelig called upon the Goddess Andred to bring victory in the morning. This would be the druid's only task during the ensuing battle, which he was hardly suited to fighting. Each warrior present swore to sacrifice those enemies that survived to the Goddess of Victory. The rite complete the men returned to their beds to sleep out the final few hours of darkness.

All except one.

The sentry drew his sword, hackles raised by an unexpected sound in the blackness of the night.

"Put your weapon away," Weland said, stepping closer to the squinting guard so he could be recognised.

"Sorry," the sentry said, sheathing his sword, glad it was not Babdah roaming the battlefield. "Unable to sleep?"

"No," Weland replied with a weary sigh. "I am getting old and I dislike wasting the time I have left lying in bed."

"Not even with a warm woman?" the sentry laughed.

As they spoke Weland slowly closed the gap with the sentry then, when within reaching distance, he lunged forward and grabbed him around the neck, forcing his hand over the man's mouth. Weland plunged a knife into the man's side, gripping him tighter as he wrestled against the restraint. Weland dug the knife in further and twisted, tearing at vital organs. After a few moments the sentry stopped struggling. Weland dropped his body to the floor, breathing deeply with the exertion. A few years ago it had been child's play to kill like this. He grabbed the corpse by his clothes at the shoulder and dragged him away to hide the evidence.

"Late yet again," Ahearn observed. He had removed his helmet to let his livid skin cool in the night air.

Weland shrugged. "I had to deal with a problem. I was seen."

"I told you before, you are getting too old."

Weland ignored the comment. Despite himself he grimaced with distaste at the Romans standing beside Ahearn. Then he realised the one in the ill-fitting uniform was Adminius.

"You have put on weight," Weland said to Adminius. "It suits you."

Before Adminius could reply Cullen and Amon stepped out of the shadows and completed the group of conspirators.

"Why is he here?" Amon spat, pointing a stubby finger at Max.

"He is with me," Adminius said. "We need his help."

"We or you?" Weland said.

"What is the difference?" Adminius shrugged. "Do we not have the same aims?"

"I do not like it," Amon said.

"It will be daylight soon," Adminius snapped. "Shall we conclude our business or bicker until the sun comes up? The Roman stays."

"We are exposed here," Cullen said. He looked nervous. "Just tell me what I need to do so I can leave."

The group fell into discussion, with Max on the periphery, unable to contribute.

"So, on the signal, we act," Ahearn said five minutes later. The others nodded. "You must be ready, when the time is right."

"We will be," Weland promised.

"Amon, Cullen?" Adminius asked.

"Yes, yes!" Cullen hissed. "Are we finished?" His eyes had not stopped scanning the shadows since they had met.

"Just be ready," Ahearn warned.

Cullen hurried away with a sharp nod of his head and hastily the group split up to make their way back separately to their respective camps.

"Why do we not take this to Geta?" Max asked as they picked their way over the broken ground to the Roman line.

Adminius sighed. "I have explained this before," he said, sounding weary, as if Max was unable to learn the simplest of lessons. "We need the Romans to fight as if they suspect nothing. Our deed must occur at the right time. Afterwards, when all has gone to plan, then I will explain our part to Plautius himself. His reward will be all the greater when he realises quite what we have achieved on his behalf. Now do you understand?"

Adminius took Max's grunted reply for assent but the Praetorian remained unconvinced. They walked the rest of the way in silence, Max's head full of conflicting thoughts.

There was no sleep for the men of the Classis Britannica either. Work on the pontoon bridge stopped when darkness fell, but with quiet dips of oars into the water, the boats ferried back and forth, transporting more men of the XX[th] to join their commander. The legionaries filed into the camp and lay down immediately to get as much sleep as they could before the sun rose again.

Geta and Vespasian followed in one of the last boats to cross. Geta yawned. It had been a very long day and tomorrow, — no, today, he corrected himself — promised to be the same. He dangled his fingers idly in the river as the boat was rowed across the Meduuuæian. It had been a lengthy meeting with Plautius but they were ready.

Andred roamed wraith-like between the sleeping British warriors. She touched them lightly one by one. She called upon the powers to infuse them with battle strength, hate and rage sufficient to overcome the heathen warriors. For, when the sun rose, she would feast on Roman souls.

## LII

Togodumnus rode to the front of the British ranks. He turned his back on the Romans and looked along the sea of faces. Although the light was dim every British eye was fixed on their king. A chill breeze had risen, blowing with it the salty tang of the sea from the nearby coast. The sun was climbing over the horizon, trying to push its way through jet black, angry looking clouds. A peal of thunder rolled in the distance, confirming a storm was coming.

"My brave warriors!" Togodumnus shouted, hearing the portent. "Today we face our greatest challenge for a hundred years. There are invaders in our lands, poised to destroy our way of life, enslave our children and rape our women. Even the gods above feel our pain and offer their strength!"

Another roll of thunder cut across his speech, inflaming the already fervent warriors.

"But today we fight here to drive them back where they came from and I swear to you, whilst there is breath in my body, no Roman will go further into our lands than where I stand now!

Today this ends! Today we drive the bastards from our shores!"

There was an enormous roar from the assembled Britons. Andred had weaved her magic well. The Britons were suffused with a rage the like of which many had never felt before and they chafed to tear into the Romans. Weapons were brandished and insults hurled at the enemy who stood, impassively, a quarter of a mile away. Fionn glanced at Bearach and Brennon, seeing in their eyes that the same energy coursed through their veins. But Fionn possessed an extra tinge to his — revenge.

Togodumnus spurred his horse towards the left flank, where a 20,000-strong force of Catuvellauni warriors stood, charged with a special task that the king himself would lead. The responsibility of the remaining army fell to Caradoc who, with Fionn's genii, was stationed with the Catuvellauni and Trinovantes in the centre. Cullen's Dobunni were sandwiched between Togodumnus and Urien on Caradoc's left and on the right flank were Weland and his men. Amon's Atrebates were held back in reserve in case the XIV[th], still assembled on the far bank, chose to cross. The 135,000-strong British army faced the Roman might of almost two legions, with auxiliaries and cavalry in support.

At a signal from Caradoc the Britons marched forwards until the fissure with the Romans closed to just a few hundred yards. They came to a halt. The enemies stared balefully into each other's eyes whilst they waited for the signal to kill.

The siege weapons opened the exchange, thumping heavy stones over the river to plummet into the British masses, pressed so close together they could do nothing to avoid them. Rocks pulverised men into pieces of raw meat but their numbers were so great the ballistae made barely a dent. Yet still the weapons fired in an energetic attempt to redress the balance.

At last Caradoc let the straining Britons off the leash with a long, wailing blast on the carnyx. The crazed warriors tore towards the II[nd] like a pack of their own hunting dogs, brutal, bloodthirsty and ready to rip out Roman throats. The noise of the cascade of men was deafening. Within moments Roman horns responded and the legionaries began their own headlong, screaming rush of death. When the two armies clashed they generated a thunderous sound to rival that from the heavens as bitter hand-to-hand fighting erupted.

Togodumnus and his men fell upon the XX[th], who were charged with holding the bridgehead. The legionaries took the onrush crouched behind their raised shields but so great was the press that their line was forced backwards several steps. The Britons swung their swords over their heads, cleaving at shields, helmets and flesh. Spears and arrows soared over both armies to run through limbs and torsos.

After only a few minutes of fighting, Geta saw that his men were slowly but surely retreating under the British onslaught, such was its fury. With the river and marshland at their backs and reinforcements only trickling over by boat the situation looked treacherous.

"Follow me, Amatius. We are needed," he said to the primus pilus, who looked wary but nevertheless waved forward the reserve as ordered. Once at the front line the newly-committed force, fresh and flushed with energy, cut a bloody swathe through the Britons. Geta swung his cavalry sword about him, scything any warrior that dared to come within its reach, his horse smashing dying men into oblivion with its flailing hooves.

Immediately, at the sight of its commander's actions, the wavering XX[th] rallied and the legion standard, a bear, was lifted strongly. Piece by piece the Romans began to regain some of the lost ground.

But Geta, consumed by his boyish enthusiasm, pushed forward a little too hard. With Amatius at his side they tore open a small bridgehead of their own, an abscess in the British line. As Geta tugged his sword out of a warrior's chest and looked for his next victim he realised the precarious position he was in, almost cut off from his own forces. With a cry Amatius was dragged from his horse and died under a hail of stabbing swords. Then the Britons turned their attention to Geta. He tried to retreat but was hemmed in by the press of bodies all around him.

Geta swung his sword with deadly accuracy, adrenaline and the burning desire to survive strengthening his arm, but still the enemy kept pushing towards him. As one man fell to his spatha another would willingly spring into the gap. For all of his training and experience Geta knew he could not defeat the crushingly overwhelming numbers on his own.

Geta severed a man's hand and stabbed at another but finally he was pulled off his rearing horse and fell to the floor with a jarring crash, all the breath knocked out of him, his spatha tumbling a few feet away and out of reach of his scrabbling fingers. A heavy foot pressed down on his arm and a bearded face grinned at him, sword raised.

So, this is where I am to perish, Geta thought.

But at that moment of Geta's death a carnyx blew and the warriors stayed their weapons. He lay on the ground, wondering how he was still alive and what the hell was going on. He managed to work his arm free and grabbed his spatha from the dirt, stood up and retreated to his own line, thanking the gods profusely.

A few hundred yards away a huge warrior, head and shoulders above the rest, yanked off his helmet, hurled it to the ground and roared. The livid disfigurement on his face blazed like the rising sun. On the end of a spear, Ahearn unfurled the banner that he had carried since being driven from British shores four years ago and shouted his blood curdling battle cry as it fluttered in the wind.

The Dobunni, to a man, turned and started to hack at the Catuvellauni, the anger of the years in which they had lost out to their richer neighbours pouring forth. Geta and every other Roman was forgotten about as the tribes turned and fought one another. The legionaries watched the incredible turn of events, astonished, unsure who was friend and who was foe but glad it was not they doing the dying.

Ahearn handed the banner to Cullen who waved it aloft to the celebratory cries of a carnyx, then pushed his way through the struggling men, carving aside the few opponents that dared stand in his way.

Togodumnus, just minutes before in the ascendancy, sat on his horse momentarily stunned into inaction by the shocking developments. He stared in bewilderment, blinking at the banner, its yellow shooting-star emblem something he thought he would never see again.

"Hello, brother."

Togodumnus dragged his eyes away from the standard and downwards into the face of the speaker. He felt as if everything was moving incredibly slowly, as if he were drunk on heady, strong wine. With a jolt he recognised Adminius. He looked older and stouter but the same cruel sneer he remembered from childhood was etched on his brother's features.

Togodumnus tried to back his horse away but he was trapped by his men, who fought desperately for survival. Then Ahearn was beside him. Togodumnus, galvanised at last, swung his sword down but with a grin the massive warrior easily parried the stroke, Togodumnus hampered by his wound. It was like hitting a piece of rock and the king's sword snapped with the impact.

Ahearn laughed and reached out a huge arm. He grasped Togodumnus by his mail shirt, tugged him off his horse and held him in suspension above the ground, feet dangling. Togodumnus felt Ahearn's hot breath on his face as he bellowed with laughter again, a sound hollow and empty of any humour.

Ahearn showed Togodumnus his sword, the sunlight glinting off it, then with agonising slowness thrust it upwards, the blade tearing into the king's stomach and reaching towards his heart. Ahearn watched Togodumnus twitch and jerk on the point of his weapon, then threw him onto the ground like a discarded child's toy. The King of the Catuvellauni lay staring up into the cloud-ridden sky as blood gushed from the rent and through his fingers.

Adminius, the terrible smile still on his face, knelt down and looked into Togodumnus's eyes as he died.

"See you in hell, brother," he said as he removed the circlet of gold from Togodumnus's head.

The legionary drove his left foot forward, keeping the scutum across his body. Fionn waited until the soldier peered tentatively around the rim, looking for an opportunity to jab, then ran his sword through the roof of the man's mouth before jerking the blade out again, covered in gore. The man looked shocked, the pierced brain barely able to register the blow, before he fell backwards into his own line.

Fionn stepped over the body and into the gap the legionary had left. Immediately blows rained down on him from the soldiers on either side as they tried to close the tear in their line. Brennon and Bearach followed in his wake, axe and spear probing.

A Roman raised his shield to protect himself from the vicious cut of Brennon's heavy axe, but he changed the direction of the blade mid-flight and instead cut at the man's legs cleaving with ease through the brass greaves the legionary wore on his shins for protection. He fell to the ground with a blood-curdling scream, both legs severed. Fionn stabbed down and the wailing cut off abruptly.

Fionn placed his foot on the legionary's body and dragged the sword out of his chest, the blade audibly scraping against the corpse's ribs. It was nicked badly and the edge was beginning to dull. He paused as a carnyx sounded on the left flank again and again. A responding call came from the right and a roar issued from within the British ranks.

Warrior turned on warrior as the Cantii attacked the Catuvellauni and Trinovantes. Instinctively Fionn defended himself as the man who had only moments before been fighting at his side turned away from his Roman opponent and swung his sword at Fionn instead. The need for self-preservation instinctively kicked in and Fionn cut the warrior down before he realised what he was doing.

Two Cantii ran at Caradoc, eager for the prestige killing the prince would bring. But the toothless grin froze on one warrior's face as an axe cut through his helmet. The other arched backwards as Bearach's spear severed his spine.

"We have been betrayed!" Caradoc said, fending off another attack. The Cantii seemed to be all around them.

"It is your banner!" Fionn said. "It is drawing them to you like moths to a flame."

"Leave us, lord! We will carry on fighting whilst you escape!" one of his men shouted, bleeding profusely from a deep cut on his leg.

But with Romans to their rear and warriors attacking them on all sides Caradoc could see no way through.

"It looks like we die here!" he shouted and stepped back into battle.

## LIII

Caradoc prepared himself for death. Most of his comitatus had been killed, their corpses strewn around the standard displaying Cunobelin's hound. The wounded had been decapitated where they lay. The Cantii were not taking any prisoners, but for the moment they had halted in their grisly task.

"You have no way out. Why do you not give up, Caradoc?" Weland called from where his men had withdrawn to, just a short distance away. He waved his hand expansively across the Cantii that surrounded the few remaining Catuvellauni. "I am sure the Romans will look after you well in their capital."

"I will not be displayed like some animal in a cage!" Caradoc spat. "I would rather die."

"I can oblige you with that request," Weland laughed, then turned serious. "Bearach, come and join me. Do not waste your life here."

Bearach looked pale. His father's betrayal had come as a complete shock.

"I cannot," Bearach said. "You are a traitor and I will not be part of it."

Weland shook his head. "I am not surprised, you always were weak. Like your mother, the bitch."

"Etain would have hated you for this."

"She would gladly have joined me, as would you if you were half the man she was!" Weland drew in a deep breath to calm a temper that was threatening to erupt. He forced himself to smile again and turned his attention back to Caradoc.

"If you will not surrender, fight me for your life," he offered.

"I will fight you," Bearach mumbled before Caradoc could reply.

"What did you say, boy?"

"I will fight you!" Bearach roared and ran forward.

Weland, taken momentarily aback, had to scuttle out of the way of Bearach's thrusting spear. "So be it," he said, fending off the attack.

The two, father and son, circled each other warily, Weland held in check by the longer reach of the spear which constantly prodded towards his eyes and chest. He casually dealt with the blows on his shield. Bearach lunged forward again but appeared to stumble. With a grin Weland stepped inside the reach of the spear to kill his son.

But suddenly Bearach straightened and whipped the shaft of his spear into Weland's face, catching him with a solid blow to the temple. His father crumpled to the floor, stars in front of his eyes.

Bearach threw his spear aside, stooped and gathered up a bloodied gladius. He stood over Weland, whose breathing was laboured and shallow, blood spilling down his face. Bearach grasped the hilt tightly in both hands, raised the blade over his head and plunged it into Weland's heart so hard the weapon lodged in the ground beneath. Weland jerked and lay still, mouth wide open in death. Bearach walked away leaving the hilt of the gladius pointing skyward.

A great moan passed through the Cantii but before they could react, Urien, with hundreds of horsemen, smashed through their ranks. The Cantii warriors were cast aside like leaves blown in a gale, unable to resist the greater force.

"Get on!" Urien urged as horses were dragged for Caradoc and the others to clamber onto.

Adminius twitched, eager to start the hunt for his remaining brother. He sat on his horse in preparation, staring north to where he imagined Caradoc to be whilst the Romans debated how to proceed. The bridgehead was complete, the last pontoon boat in place, and the rest of the XX[th] was about to cross. But all Adminius cared about was finding Caradoc. He twirled Togodumnus's crown, the circlet of gold, in his fingers.

Finally Geta gave the order. Adminius spurred his horse forward, following in Max's wake, eager to write the final chapter in Caradoc's miserable life.

## LIV

"Amon attacked our rear," Urien confirmed over the sound of hoof beats, the Cantii left well behind in their wake. "They caught us by surprise and we lost many men in the first few minutes of fighting. But Amon underestimated us. I killed the bastard myself."

"Do you have any news of Togodumnus?" Caradoc asked.

Urien paused, unsure how to deliver the news. "Togodumnus is dead, by Adminius's hand," he said grimly. "You will now be king."

Caradoc's head spun as he tried to take it all in, but there was little time to do so.

"Look!" Fionn shouted, pointing to the Meduuuæian.

The XIV[th] was crossing the river at the point where Amon was supposed to have been holding them back, their way now clear. The first of the legionaries were stepping onto rafts and river craft, with many more waiting on the bank but they would not traverse quickly enough to cause Caradoc and his men any delay. They spurred their horses on, past the hills where only yesterday Caradoc had fought the Batavi, of which there were now no sign. There were pockets of retreating men all around them, some on horseback, some walking.

After a hard ride the party arrived at the marshland that bordered the Tamessa, their mounts covered with sweat and foaming at the mouth. Like the Meduuuæian, the margins could be treacherous to those inexperienced in its ways. It was at its most dangerous at low tide, when the area was a mass of pools and bogs and, confusingly, looked wider than when the water was at its height. It could only be safely navigated at specific points, which were not immediately obvious to those unfamiliar with the river. Fionn hoped this would buy them some time. Lines of men were crossing the Tamessa and, once on the other bank, turning west towards the Derventio.

But as Caradoc began to ford the Tamessa himself, a horn sounded. Fionn twisted in his saddle — there, less than a mile behind them, was a knot of Roman cavalry. He assumed they were an advance party and would be severely delayed picking their way through the morass that was the Tamessa margin.

But the Romans, rather than approaching cautiously spurred their horses into a gallop, apparently confident of their path.

"I will leave some men on the bank to hold them up," Urien said, ordering a contingent of his men to return across the river.

When they were only half way over the Tamessa, Fionn heard the clash of weapons. He looked back. The Atrebates were dying hard, despite being quickly overwhelmed by the Romans' greater numbers.

"Adminius," Caradoc said grimly. His brother's star banner flew in the Roman ranks and explained the speed they had made.

With the Atrebatean rearguard wiped out the Romans and their traitorous British partners forded the river, horses splashing through the water as they were urged on.

Caradoc was the first out of the Tamessa, closely followed by Urien, the genii, then Urien's men and the remnants of Caradoc's comitatus. They filed along the narrow path, only wide enough to allow two horses side by side, their progress impeded as a result. Once through the marshy margins the landscape opened up again and they made greater speed. But Caradoc suddenly wrenched back on his reins, dragging his horse to a halt.

"What are you doing?" Fionn shouted, following suit. Urien looked back, swore and shouted for his men to stop.

"I will not run from them," Caradoc said. He turned his horse to face the Romans, who first slowed their pursuit at the sight of the waiting British cavalry, then stopped a short distance away.

"Are you with me?" Caradoc asked.

"We are, my king," Urien said, eyeing Adminius's banner. "We shall feed the bastards to the crows!"

The Britons spurred their horses. Seconds later the Romans imitated them. With thundering hooves the horsemen closed the gap and met with a clash of swords, all except Caradoc. He swung this way and that trying to engage but the Romans veered away as he neared.

"They have left you for me," Adminius screeched. "You will die by my hand only!"

"Then fight me, you bastard!" Caradoc shouted at his brother. He climbed off his horse and drew his sword. Adminius smirked and motioned forward the massive hulk of Ahearn.

"I do not care who I have to fight first, Adminius, before I kill you!" Caradoc snarled.

He swung at Ahearn who, despite his size, moved more swiftly than Caradoc anticipated and met the strike with ease. Caradoc darted sideways to avoid the swing of Ahearn's second sword, taking a heavy blow on his shield that hammered him to one knee. Adminius sat and watched the furious battle with a hum of pleasure, certain that Caradoc was going to die.

The genii hewed their way through the Romans. Already Fionn's shield had slices hacked out of it and the length of his sword was covered in blood. He slipped on the guts of a legionary and Bearach stepped in to save his life, thrusting his spear into the face of the Roman who darted forward to take advantage of Fionn's mistake.

Fionn recovered as another legionary came at him. He parried a stroke and then stabbed the man, who sagged onto his shoulder, his eyes bulging in disbelief. He moaned something incomprehensible as he died.

Then Fionn pulled up short, hate swelled within.

"He is here," Fionn said, disbelieving, stopping in his tracks.

"Who?" Bearach asked, fending off a legionary.

"The bastard that killed Etain!"

In a rage Fionn started to cut his way through Romans to get to his adversary, leaving Brennon and Bearach behind him. Those unfortunate enough to be in Fionn's way vainly tried to defend themselves against his sword but died of its venomous bite. Suddenly a space opened in front of him into which Fionn's anger spilled. He shouted again for Max and this time he heard. He turned, grinned and beckoned Fionn forward.

"Stay out of the way," Max said to Anatolius. "This one is mine."

Fionn discarded both bow and shield. He pulled off his chain mail and threw his helmet onto the ground, not caring where they landed. Max followed suit, untying his armour and letting it slip off his body. He retained only his gladius in hand.

"You will pay for what you did," Fionn promised.

Max did not bother to waste breath on a reply and instead lunged at

Fionn. However, he instantly checked his forward movement as Fionn swung his longer, curved sword in an arc that almost took Max's head off. Max stepped under Fionn's swing and stabbed at his stomach, but Fionn jerked out of the way and punched the Praetorian, hitting him in the cheek with the pommel of his sword. Max reeled away as blood gushed from his mouth. He spat a gout of crimson onto the floor and touched his hand to the gash where Fionn had connected.

"I have been punched by children harder than that," he sneered.

Fionn swung his sword again and again, Max giving up ground in the process. His gladius, strongly made, resisted the blows but the Roman felt the pressure of Fionn's attack as his muscles strained to respond quickly enough. He was beginning to tire and knew he could not keep up with the younger man for much longer. But he was an experienced and dirty fighter, having learnt the hard way on the back streets of Rome as a boy, and with age he had become as wily as a fox, too. He would have to fall back on these old skills if he were to survive.

Max briefly regained the advantage with several vicious jabs of his gladius.

He took two quick steps forward, then grabbed Fionn in a bear hug and plunged his pugio into Fionn's left shoulder. Fionn shouted in pain and shock, throwing a hand up to grab at the weapon buried to the hilt. Max charged in for the killing blow. In desperation, Fionn parried time after time as Max pressed his advantage, forcing Fionn towards the marshy margins of the Tamessa.

Fionn felt as if time slowed down to a crawl. All around him he could see other fraught battles, soldier against soldier in private tests of strength where to lose meant paying the highest price. A Roman screamed as he was unmercifully hacked down by two Britons to join the bodies that littered the area, some floating face down in the sluggish black waters. He saw a Briton on his front in the mud. A legionary stood above him, grabbed his hair to expose the warrior's neck, and then sliced his windpipe with his dagger.

Max closed in on Fionn, moving as if wading through the Tamessa, deliberate and purposeful, his face twisted with anger and hate. Blood streamed down Fionn's left side from the shoulder wound. It would be so easy to give up now, he knew, and for a moment he almost did, ready to accept the older man's blade, knowing the pain would only be brief.

But then he remembered Etain and the promise he had made at her graveside with the genii. His attention snapped back to Max. He forced the pain from his shoulder out of his mind and rained blows back on a shocked Max. The Praetorian made another grab for Fionn and they locked together, holding each other's wrists, snarling in an animal desperation. Max kicked at Fionn, who took the blows on his shins then smashed his forehead into the Roman's face. Max's nose exploded with the impact and he reeled away. He could not see anything, his vision was blurred and his head pounded. He could feel blood coursing from his nose and over his lips. The Praetorian was unarmed, having dropped his gladius with the blow. Through watery eyes Max searched frantically for his sword but failed to see it.

Fionn hissed in pain as he was finally able to pull the dagger from his shoulder. He watched Max stumbling around and thought of Etain. Fionn could feel Etain standing beside him and he thanked her for giving him the strength needed. Then Fionn gathered himself and plunged the pugio into Max's stomach and tore upwards. The Roman curled over as if enveloping the steel. His mouth opened in an agony of disbelief but no sound came out.

"This is for Etain," Fionn whispered into Max's ear and then pushed him backwards, leaving the dagger embedded in his body.

Max's fingers curled around the hilt and he fell back into the water, where he floated face upwards, his mouth still open in a cry of agony. Fionn felt a weight lift as some of the guilt of Etain's death left his soul. He would never be entirely free, but he breathed a sigh of release nevertheless.

Then his present circumstances came shooting into focus. After a quick glance around, he saw Caradoc desperately fending off Ahearn. He stooped, gathered his bow and arrows from beneath a Roman corpse, hastily nocked an arrow and let fly.

The arrow pierced Ahearn's massive neck, an ugly bulge protruding from the left hand side as the shaft pierced the mass of sinew and muscle. He put his hand up to his neck to confirm what his brain was telling him, felt the shaft and snapped it off. He looked blankly at it, vaguely seeing the black feathers. Caradoc seized his opportunity and sliced at Ahearn's throat. The sword tip opened a gaping wound and air rattled out of the gash as Ahearn gasped. He dropped his sword and grabbed at his throat with one hand to stop the blood flowing.

Caradoc swung at the back of Ahearn's knee, severing the sinew. Ahearn collapsed and he rolled onto his back. The scarred warrior watched with wide, disbelieving eyes as Caradoc walked slowly towards him. Ahearn tried to speak, but no words would come. Caradoc raised his sword in both hands and chopped the blade down and through what remained of his neck. Ahearn's head rolled away down the shallow bank.

Caradoc drew in great gulps of sweet air. Then he remembered Adminius and he swung around, frantically searching for him. The star banner had been discarded and was ground into the mud a few feet away, the bright yellow stained a dirty brown. Then Caradoc spotted him. Adminius was fleeing on a horse and was already well over the Tamessa, heading back to safety on the far bank, where the Batavi were assembling.

"Adminius!" Caradoc raged. His brother cast a fearful look over his shoulder and urged his mount onwards.

Caradoc shouted for a horse to be brought.

"He is gone," Fionn said. "You will not catch him now. To go after him will only mean your death."

"I do not care. I want him dead!"

"And if you follow Togodumnus to the next life, my king, what happens to your army, your country and your family?"

"Fionn is right," Urien counselled. He slid his sword into its scabbard. "We should regroup at Camulodunon. This war is not over yet. The Romans can still be beaten."

Caradoc watched Adminius's horse scramble up the bank to be enveloped by the Batavi. He felt his blood cool as the wiser part of his character took charge. There would be another day, he promised himself.

"My family need to be taken from Calleva and protected," he said, recent events immediately consigned to history and looking to the future. Caradoc remembered Kynthelig's words and his promise.

"I will do it," Fionn offered.

"And I," Brennon and Bearach said together and looked at Fionn for approval. He nodded to them both, a grin on his face. Fionn seemed to have acquired some followers and he was surprised to find he liked the idea. The genii had a new purpose, to protect a future saint.

Anatolius reached down and grabbed Max. The centurion was as pale as a corpse, his hand still clasped around the pugio blade embedded in his torso as he floated sluggishly like a waterlogged tree trunk.

Perhaps he was too late and Max was already dead, Anatolius thought. He certainly looked it.

Anatolius struggled to drag the dead weight out of the water and onto the bank, his heels slipping several times on the slick grass. But at last Max was fully out of the river. Just then he heard the thunder of hoof beats and hunkered down behind a thin partition of reeds, his hand on the hilt of his gladius. A band of British warriors rode by, bent low over their horse's necks, intent only on escape. Anatolius heaved a sigh of relief when they were gone.

The optio bent down and put his ear to his superior officer's mouth, the bloodless lips still parted in the rictus of pain, the teeth in a clenched grimace. After several long moments, just as Anatolius was about to give up, he heard the faint whisper of a breath, the merest tickle on his skin.

Max lived. Just.

# Epilogue

Kynthelig whipped his horse mercilessly, leaving the battlefield of Durobrivis far behind. He was stunned how events had conspired against him: Togodumnus a carcass and Caradoc in retreat. All his plans were laid to waste by Weland's betrayal, his death scant consolation.

Should he have seen disaster coming? Kynthelig started to berate himself but then pushed the recriminations to one side; there would be time for that later. First the Druid Council needed to know, for they must line up in support behind Caradoc and bring the other tribes along with them.

The tears of frustration and despair in defeat dried on his face and his hair was wild in the wind. He had a mission and he rode to Mona to initiate it.

# Historical Note

There is only one record of the Roman invasion of Britain in 43 AD, written by the historian Cassius Dio some one hundred and fifty years after the event. It is, at best, fragmentary, and over the intervening years many authors have written many books and documents interpreting the paragraphs that have survived almost two millennia of turbulent history.

In writing this book I have sifted through some of the multitude of works available on the Britons and Romans. In all of these publications at least some use of archaeological data and interpretation has been utilised to flesh out the vague events Dio outlines. Of course, the conclusions drawn vary and adapt over the years as more data is gathered and also depend to a degree on the perspective of those committing pen to paper.

So I had to make a number of judgements, which some scholars are bound to disagree with. Such is the life of a writer of historical fiction. There are differences of opinion about the location of the landings and the battle sites. However, I chose Rutupia, now called Richborough, these days a landlocked ruin of a fourth-century AD Roman fort. The idea appealed to me most and appeared to be a better fit with the archaeological and historical evidence than the alternative site of Fishbourne.

I live on The Isle of Thanet (and I have to say I disagree with Geta's conclusion that it is a bleak place) and have been to Richborough several times to walk through the remains of the triumphal four-way arch through which the Romans of later years would enter the country via Watling Street ,which begins on the edge of the camp. The arch, when it existed, was probably over 85 feet high and faced with white marble transported from Italy. It must have been an impressive sight.

Likewise, there is continued debate as to the site of the river battle which Dio refers to. The Medway is one of several proposed. Its proximity to Richborough makes it another plausible selection for the purposes of this story.

The relationship between the Catuvellauni and their neighbours, the Trinovantes, is unclear and the two tribes are often referred to jointly. Barry Cunliffe does so in his excellent tome

*Iron Age Britain* and I for one am certainly not qualified to argue with him. So, for the purposes of this story I assumed the two tribes were closely interlinked and hence the rare mentions of the latter tribe.

Many of the characters such as Cunobelin, Epaticcus, Togodumnus, Adminius and Caradoc (Caratacus to the Romans) did exist and, to varying degrees, resisted the Romans. Caradoc went on to fight the invaders for more than a decade and was the inspiration for continued resistance against the Roman yoke for others, most notably Boudica. Perhaps there should be a statue to Caradoc, rather than his more famous disciple.

Almost the entire book is based in the tribal territory of Cantium which covers much of modern Kent. The presence of the Cantii tribe still persists in the modern name for Durovernon — Canterbury.

There are a bewildering number of books that the student can read on Roman and the Iron Age Britons. For information on the Roman army any of the books written by Dr. Adrian Goldsworthy make excellent reading but for this book his *The Complete*

*Roman Army and The Roman Army at War 100BC – 200AD* was of relevance.

Graham Webster's books on the Roman army are also excellent. Webster has also written a series of books on events in Roman Britain, including *Rome Against Caratacus* which, although starting five years after the events in this book, is nevertheless worth tracking down.

Barry Cunliffe is the recognised expert on Iron Age Britain and makes essential reading. All his publications are well researched and authoritative. Creighton's *Coins and Power in Late Iron Age Britain* proved the inspiration for Togodumnus's ascension ceremony. R.D. Van Arsdell provides an in-depth analysis of coins and the relationships between the respective tribes, which, in conjunction with Cunliffe, sheds some light on this murky subject.

The location of the invasion and subsequent events are covered in a military fashion by John Peddie in his book *Conquest: The Roman Invasion of Britain*. This can be contrasted with John Manley's book of a similar title that proposes the alternative landing site of Fishbourne. Graham Webster has also published a book on the same subject and gives valuable information.

Julius Caesar wrote a number of books on his own campaigns. Some information on Britain, albeit scant, is included in his Gallic War series.

Last, but certainly not least, is Guy de la Bedoyere. He has written many excellent books on life in Roman Britain, some of which have been used as a source for this story.

To the hard work of all these authors I express my gratitude and any errors in the construction of this book are purely my own.

# Also by Keith Nixon

**The Fix**

Murder. Theft. Sociopaths. And Margate. Just another day in banking then...

It's pre-crash 2007 and financial investment banker Josh Dedman's life is unravelling fast. He's fired after £20 million goes missing from the bank. His long-time girlfriend cheats on him, then dumps him. His only friends are a Russian tramp who claims to be ex-KGB and a really irritating bloke he's just met on the train. His waking hours are a nightmare and his dreams are haunted by a mystery blonde. And to cap it all, he lives in Margate.

Just when Josh thinks things can't get any worse his sociopathic boss — Hershey Valentine — winds up murdered and he finds himself the number one suspect. As the net closes in Josh discovers that no one is quite what they seem, including him, and that sometimes help comes from the most unlikely sources...

Part fiction, part lies (well, it is about banking) and excruciatingly funny, **THE FIX** pulls no punches when revealing the naked truth of a man living a life he loathes. This is a crime fiction novel with a difference...

**The Konstantin Novellas**

1. **Dream Land**

**DREAM LAND, Konstantin's first 48 hours in Margate. Neither will be the same again.**

From the author of best-selling **THE FIX**, comes an introduction to Konstantin Boryakov, the enigmatic tramp who claims to be ex-KGB and in hiding. A man with a dark past and a darker future.

Konstantin has just arrived in the UK, Margate to be specific, having escaped persecution by the authorities in his own country. The second he steps out of a car he gets into trouble, targeted by local villain Dave the Rave. But Dave chose the wrong man to pick a fight with...

2. **Plastic Fantastic**

From the author of best-selling **THE FIX**, comes another chapter in Konstantin Boryakov's life, the enigmatic tramp who claims to be ex-KGB and in hiding. A man with a dark past and a darker future.

Fidelity Brown has a problem. She owes a local up and coming hard man cash, lots of it. Cash she doesn't have because her night job – a dildo wielding, rubber clad dominatrix going by the name of Plastic Fantastic – isn't paying enough yet.

But Fidelity thinks she knows someone who can help her...

All Konstantin Boryakov wants is to be left alone. Cast out by the organisation that had nurtured and trained him Konstantin is a man without purpose, that is until Fidelity comes knocking on his door.

Cue double dealing, kidnap and revenge as Konstantin rises again.